HECATE'S MOON

Also by CAROL ANNE DOBSON

~STORKS IN A BLUE SKY~

~FREEDOM~

HECATE'S MOON

Carol Anne Dobson

Appledrane

APPLEDRANE

Published by Appledrane 2015

ISBN   978-0-9558324-4-4
The characters in this book are the product of the author's imagination and have no relation to any living person.
Printed by CPI Antony Rowe, Eastbourne.
Illustration by LOKE.

Appledrane
Torquay, Devon. TQ1 1NA

To XAVIER and ALICIA

Strasbourg 1793

1

The king rat lurched and slithered over the muddy bank of the River Ill. It was not just one rat, but five, whose tails were fused together to create a pitiful monstrosity of a creature. Newly born, its only immediate prospect was death, and a gawping crowd had gathered to jeer and pelt stones. Armand watched his fellow citizens with distaste, not least because most wore a bunch of tricoloured flowers above their heart. He picked up a broken branch and prodded the rats into the dirty water. Hardly able to move on land, the current liberated them and they were quickly carried downstream and disappeared from view.

The crowd turned on him, their enjoyment of the spectacle destroyed, and he hastily took to his heels and ran towards the Rohan Palace, whose classical columns were swathed in red, white and blue banners, and whose doorway was enlivened by a pig's head with a crown on it, placed on a stake in a flower pot. A stone hit him in the back, shouts of 'traitor' could be heard, and he sprinted down the narrow Rue Rohan, across the cobbles of the Place du Chateau and into the square in front of the cathedral. Breathless, he glanced back to see if he had been pursued, and smiled to only see market stalls and the usual bustle of people going about their business. He kept his back to the cathedral wall, pulled out his knife from its scabbard and ran his finger over the sharpness of its blade, before pulling his black felt hat over his forehead and settling down to await his servants.

It was hot in the square and he wished he had chosen a less public place to meet his men. The sun reflected off the windows of the medieval, half-timbered houses lining the Place de la Cathédrale, dazzling him, and through the noisy mayhem of the marketplace with its squealing pigs and a crowing cockerel, came the distant sound of Rouget de Lisle's marching song for the Army of the Rhine, and the heavy tread of booted feet. He shifted uneasily and looked up at the giant metal Phrygian cap covering the spire of the cathedral.

"The world's gone mad," he muttered. "Rats joined together, and a spire saved from being destroyed by putting a bonnet on it."

The stall keeper selling Kugelhopf brioches on the nearby steps, glanced curiously in his direction, before unpinning the tricolour cockade from his hat and offering it to him.

"Here you are, citizen. I think you need this more than I do."

He reluctantly took it. He grimaced and attached it to the brim of his hat, as the music became louder.

"Thank you," he said gratefully to the man, suddenly recognising his benefactor as the son of a former gardener from the chateau.

At that moment, the square was invaded by blue-uniformed revolutionaries marching noisily in from the Rue des Hallebardes and singing the Marseillaise at the tops of their voices. Fishmongers from inside the cathedral rushed down the steps, pike and carp hidden in their clothes in an attempt to hide their produce from the hungry soldiers. Armand cursed himself for his foolish choice of meeting place; the next minute, a clatter of hooves on cobbles heralded his servants who thundered towards the cathedral, scattering people before them. A cry went up, "It's the Duke de Delacroix's men! Kill them!"

He ran towards his horse and leapt into the saddle. He threw his hat and the cockade onto the ground, and galloped into the Rue des Veaux, and along the narrow streets of Strasbourg towards the North Gate. He and his men rode in a tight group as they approached the city's entrance, and forced their way past the barricade. Musket shots echoed around them, and they escaped onto the plain beyond. They continued riding northwards, passing through whole villages deserted of inhabitants, where even the hinges on doors and windows had been confiscated, leaving the furniture-less houses open to the elements. In the surrounding fields ploughs lay idle and dying crops and animals littered the land.

Finally, late in the day, they reached the chateau. It was hot and still. The weeds growing in the courtyard drooped in the heat, the ruined side wing bearing witness to the ferocity of an early assault, not long after the fall of the Bastille and the sacking of the Strasbourg town hall. Several thousand peasants had marched on the building, quickly looting all the registers and title deeds from the charter room in the side wing. It had been set on fire, a May tree had been planted in the middle of the lawns, and all the feudal emblems hung on its boughs, before the peasants had moved on to destroy the Abbey of Murbach. There had been no further attacks, partly, perhaps, because the Delacroix family was related to the Marquis de Lafayette, a hero of both the American and French Revolutions. Now, however, he had been declared a traitor by the Assembly and was a prisoner of the Austrians; protection from his influence had disappeared and everyone at the chateau, from the lowliest kitchen maid to Jean-Luc, Duke de Delacroix, knew that the end was imminent. He and his family spent much of their time in their hunting lodge on the other side of the Rhine, where the sharp blade of the guillotine did not reach, but he had briefly returned to oversee the dismantling of his laboratory equipment and the crating of his plant specimens, which were being transported to his small estate in North Devon in England.

Jean-Luc ran down the flight of steps leading from the front door of the chateau, and stood waiting to greet his son, as the horsemen careered across the courtyard, coming to a halt in clouds of dust.

Armand dismounted and embraced his father.

"The news is not good from Strasbourg. I found the Comtesse de Haguenau, who is in her mansion by the Ill. Her husband has escaped to Berlin and she has divorced him in the hope of keeping their property. However, there are so many divorced noblewomen now that the authorities are suspicious and starting to execute them, and she is considering abandoning the house to save herself. I gave her the jewellery and the money for the Catholic rebellion in the Vendée, and she will entrust it tonight to a priest who comes from Cholet. She has given me a list of émigrés in England who are planning to mount an expedition to help the Chouans, north of the Loire, and she hopes you

3

will aid them when you reach Devon. The other aristocrats in Strasbourg have been guillotined, or have fled, as well as many of the townspeople."

"This revolution is destroying our country and bringing war to our people. You did well, my son. I am proud of your courage today," said Jean-Luc, putting his arm round Armand's shoulders as they walked into the chateau. "Your mother and I have nearly finished and will leave before nightfall."

"It is best to go now," said Armand. "It is a tinder keg in Strasbourg. Soldiers are everywhere, the dungeons are overflowing, and the guillotine is being taken from village to village. We no longer have sufficient men for our defence. Most of the servants have deserted us to join the Army of the Rhine."

"Yes," agreed his father sadly. "However, my work is important. I must take everything. Lavoisier has been guillotined and I want to continue his studies. It may be a long time before we can come back."

He strode towards his laboratory, where, through the open door, Armand could see his mother, Antoinette, rummaging through papers, discarding some and packing others in boxes. Her long hair was loosely piled on her head, and the sun's rays caught it, emphasising its whiteness. Jean-Luc placed his arm about her waist and they stood happily talking together, as though oblivious to their dangerous situation.

Armand wandered disconsolately through the rooms and out into the garden where dandelions and daisies were resplendent in the flower beds. Storks were flying across the brilliant blue of the sky, or standing on one leg by the stagnant lake whose fountain had long since failed to function; their ramshackle nests clinging untidily to the chimneys, adding to the pervasive air of decay. The heat was oppressive, baking earth and plants, and a far-off rumble of thunder sounded near the mountains of the Vosges. A murmur, as though from angry bees, irritated the air, and thunder boomed more loudly now. A wind gusted suddenly, quivering the leaves and bending the trees. Raindrops scuffed the dusty ground and thunder reverberated again, but this time it was accompanied by an alien cacophony of shouting and the monotonous beat of drums. Armand ran to the front of the chateau where men heavily armed with staves and pistols were already rampaging across the courtyard. He rushed inside and found his father

4

wearing a sword and holding two pistols, trying to marshal the few servants left in the house to bar the main door and guard the lower windows.

"There's too many!" shouted Armand. "We have to flee."

"You must hurry!" said Jean-Luc. "Your sister has gone with Heinrich. The horses are ready at the stables. Take your mother!"

"I am not going," cried Antoinette. "I will stay with you. Your fate will be mine."

"No," shouted Jean-Luc. "No!"

At that moment, the stout front door was splintered by an uprooted elm tree used as a battering ram.

"Go!" shouted Jean-Luc again and violently pushed Antoinette towards the back of the house.

The door gave way and men in ragged combinations of red, white and blue clothing poured through the breach. Shots rang out and Antoinette fell forward onto the mosaic floor, her blood patterning the tiles. Jean-Luc howled in anguish and dropped both his pistols to sweep her up in his arms. Her head lolled back and it was obvious she was dead. More shots rang out and he staggered, mortally hit in the chest and head. Blood poured from his mouth and he sank to the ground, dropping Antoinette and falling onto her in a final, deathly embrace. Armand took one last, horrified glance at his parents, then ran for his life through the corridors. He jumped through an open window in the ballroom and fled along the path to the stables, where the groom was already holding his horse. For the second time that day, he leapt onto the saddle and galloped frantically away, followed by a screaming horde of angry men and the crackling of muskets. Lightning tore the heavens, thunder pealed, and rain drenched him, as he escaped towards the Rhine. He momentarily caught sight of his sister, Antoinette, the name-sake of her mother, in the distance, before the deluge and his tears obscured her from view.

Devon 1794

2

Armand, Duke de Delacroix, reined in his horse and thirstily gulped brandy from the silver flask he took out of his pocket. Its fieriness made him feel almost human again, waves of warmth exploding across his body and down the stiffness of his arms and legs. His mind, however, remained stubbornly devoid of feeling. The sadness and anger which had ravaged him, had departed, and, instead, he had become detached from what had happened and from his present situation. He waited until his servants caught him up on the horses he had bought in Plymouth, before continuing to canter northwards, following the ancient ridgeway across the hills, rather than the deep Devon lanes meandering near to the River Taw. Every so often he stared towards the black uplands of Exmoor, a blur on the horizon, and tried to close his mind to the memory of tickling trout with his father, lying next to an eddying pool of the Lyn.
Finally his journey brought him to the track leading to his estate on the outskirts of Ilfracombe. He passed the first cottages with their thatched roofs and cob walls, and began to be aware of shouting and the fragrance of burning wood. He turned a corner and found himself caught up in a gang of people spilling out into the lane from a

hawthorn-enclosed garden. Men and women were shrieking abuse at an elderly woman standing in the doorway of her cottage.

"What have you done with Bess Mudge? Where is she? Witch! Witch! Burn in Hell! Hang her!"

The shouting echoed into the trees, frightening two magpies which rose screeching into the air. The tidy garden was being destroyed. People were uprooting plants and slashing bushes, and a man was using his greatcoat to fan the flames erupting from a shed stacked with twigs. A bat escaped from the smoking roof, quickly followed by several others, emitting high-pitched squeaks as they zigzagged backwards and forwards. Panic seized some of the women and they ran for safety towards the lane, screaming and clutching their mob caps firmly to their heads.

The old woman was holding a wriggling frog in her hands and turned sideways to the cob wall to try and protect it.

"Leave David alone!" she exclaimed angrily. "Leave my beloved alone!"

A concerted howl of anger rose up from the crowd.

"So it is possessed of a spirit! It is your familiar!" shrieked a woman, whose frilled bonnet encased a pink, plump face with a short snout of a nose, giving her the appearance of a pig in fancy dress.

He reined in his horse to look curiously at what was happening. His men's horses clattered to a halt behind him, and the collective rage of the witch-baiting mob died to a silence as they regarded the newcomers suspiciously. Seconds passed while the two disparate groups eyed each other. The sun caught the braid on Armand's coat and it shone brightly gold against the purple velvet. His men were not dressed in livery, but in Alsatian clothing. They were wearing long trousers, their coats were of black, brown or blue bombazine, some had red waistcoats with many buttons, and they all wore black, felt hats. Each man possessed at least one pistol, often two, as well as a variety of knives, daggers and swords.

The townspeople, by contrast, were dressed poorly, some in drab rags and without shoes, and several had the round woollen Monmouth hats of sailors. Their weapons consisted of staves, pitchforks and one cutlass, and it was very evident they could not prevail against the weaponry of the Alsatians. One of the horses neighed and pawed nervously at the earth and broke the moment of calm.

7

"Dirty vurriners!" muttered the man with the greatcoat.

"She is a witch. Let's leave her," called out Dietrich to Armand. "Look at the plants!" And he flung out his arm to indicate the wolfsbane, with its brilliant blue monk's cowl flower, the neat rows of nettle, the pink poppies of opium, the downy green leaves of mullein and the delicate flowers of deadly nightshade. They always have a hawthorn hedge," he added, as though to clinch the matter.

Armand crossed himself as he saw the extensive herbal pharmacopeia growing before him. He and his men stared suspiciously at the elderly woman who had now grabbed a besom broom in one hand and resembled even more the embodiment of a witch as she jabbed it in the face of her nearest aggressor. Her black dress was bejewelled with amber beads on its sleeves and hem, her grey hair was secured on her head with a comb fashioned from jet, making her an unexpectedly exotic sight in the depths of the North Devon countryside.

"Witchcraft does not exist," he said without conviction. "It is illegal to burn witches any more in France since the Revolution and it has been illegal to hang them here in England for even longer."

He remembered the fury of his father when he found out Dietrich had been involved in the annual Easter cat burning and his face hardened. "Superstition is wrong. We must keep to our true Catholic faith."

His words rang hollow in the bright sunlight, his face betraying his indecision as to whether to intervene in a situation where the sympathies of his men clearly lay with the rioters. His hand touched his pistol. Then he hesitated as a black crow flew straight above the crowd and alighted on a rafter of the cottage, whereupon relief seemed to flood across the old woman's face and she smiled.

"You will regret this day," she said calmly. "You will regret threatening an old woman who has never harmed you."

She turned her head and spoke to someone behind her, who emerged from the shadow of the room. A young woman, dressed in a plum-coloured riding habit, a wide-brimmed hat of the same hue perched on luxuriant black curls, stood facing the crowd. In one hand was a riding crop and, in the other, a silver dagger which glinted in the late rays of the sun. She appeared nervous, but defiant.

"Esther would never hurt anyone and has nothing to do with Bess Mudge's disappearance. You should be ashamed to accuse her. She helps your wives give birth and aids you with potions when you're ill.

You yourself came here last week, Lemuel Draper, when you cut your leg with an axe. How dare you turn on her like this?" she said, addressing the man with the greatcoat, who looked at her sullenly.

Armand urged his horse forward through the press of people, his indecision suddenly resolved. He dismounted on reaching the young woman and drew his sword.

"Armand de Delacroix at your service, madam," he declared to her, ignoring the alleged witch.

The young woman looked as coldly at him as at the crowd. Her eyes were so dark, they seemed almost black, and a single strand of green malachite beads around her neck, emphasised the olive of her skin.

"Thank you, sir, for your support, but I think enough violence has already taken place here today and we have no need of strangers to intervene on our behalf."

Armand's surprise at his rejection showed in his face as he regarded the two women, armed only with a dagger and a broom, facing a belligerent mob.

She softened her tone. "It is very kind of you, but I believe my guardian, Mr McAlpine, is even now on his way to put paid to this madness. He is a Magistrate and I am sure will have many of these good people taken to the Bridewell in Exeter, where they will have plenty of time to think about the consequences of their behaviour."

"That crow's making me afeared!" suddenly called out a fat woman in a blood-stained apron.

"Yess, it be looking at us," called out another. Other people started muttering about crows, and he glanced at the bird which, as far as he could tell, looked very like every other crow he had ever seen.

The crowd was now strangely subdued and shifting restlessly. The fight appeared to have left them, like the air from a pig's bladder when kicked too hard by boys. He and his men were ignored, and had to stand aside as buckets of water were rapidly ferried from the nearby stream to extinguish the blaze. People were disappearing from the garden, and the warbling of blackbirds and thrushes replaced the previous shouting.

"May I know your name?" he asked quickly, as the young woman retreated back into the cottage.

"Isabella," she said reluctantly, after a moment's hesitation, then turned on her heel and went inside.

9

The old woman's pale brown eyes stared hard at Armand.

"Welcome home, Seigneur. When you've recovered from your journey, come and visit me and I will help you recover from your pain."

"I have no wound," he replied.

"Your wound is not visible," she said.

He angrily crossed himself, before remounting and galloping out of the garden, trampling the only belladonna plant still standing.

"She knew I was coming," he muttered. "She's been talking to the servants at Wildercombe House."

He continued to ride at breakneck speed up the lane to the lichen-encrusted pillars, surmounted by stone birds, guarding the entrance to the estate. He paused momentarily, before continuing at a slower pace along a beech-lined avenue, until he reached the grey stone manor house, its slate roof graced with tall, rectangular chimneys. Candle light glimmered in several of the rooms, the brass-embossed door opened, and a bevy of servants poured down the front steps to greet their new master.

3

Bess's vomit-splattered apron reeked in the confines of the small cabin. The erratic pitching of the ship had ceased. The wind no longer gusted so strongly and the frenzied clucking and bleating of hens, sheep and goats from the nearby poop deck, had become a less terrified whimper.

Her nausea had likewise retreated, although she still sat, frozen by fear. Her wrists were raw from the rope which had bound her, her mouth was swollen from the choking gag tied violently around her head, just as she had finished milking Daisy in the barn. The sailor had bundled her over his shoulder and she had kicked and pushed him away with all her might. His tarred canvas coat was rough against her cheek and the dagger strapped to the small of his back jabbed into her face. He and his two accomplices had run rapidly through the moonless night, up one of the hills of the Torrs and down the steep cliff on the other side towards the sea. Pebbles on the beach crunched underfoot. Waves crashed onto the shingle. She was thrown into a gig, and the men rowed hastily across the cove to a ship which was almost as dark as the night itself, with only one lantern flickering on the prow.

She stood up gingerly from the low couch and held onto the table to keep her balance. She glanced at the salt beef and bread on a platter which a sailor had brought to her earlier, but did not eat it, and, instead, sipped the ale thirstily from a pewter tankard.

The man had ignored her pleas to be freed. He had left the cabin as quickly as he had arrived, turning the key in the lock, and leaving behind a rank smell of rum and tobacco. She had stared at him with incomprehension as he spoke to her in a broad Scottish accent. He noticed her puzzlement, and annoyance clouded his face.

"Do ye no ken English, lass?" he shouted, and gestured to her to eat the food. He put his finger to his mouth to indicate she should be quiet, and made a cutting movement across his throat.

She walked unsteadily as the ship rolled, and reached out to an ornately decorated frame of a mullioned window. She hung on to it and peered through glass trickling with runnels of water from spray, each time the ship plunged downwards. A coast loomed large. A barren coast of high cliffs and sandy coves, with an occasional, stunted tree. Granite cottages clustered on a steep hillside, and a stream splayed out brown sediment into a grey sea.

"Tis Cornwall," she muttered. "We've left Devon behind. Dear God, please help me."

The cornflower blue of her eyes dimmed with tears, she covered her face with her hands and sobbed.

The long, lonely day was interspersed by distant sounds of men swearing and shouting; the rigging creaked and the ship shuddered as it raced westwards. Late in the evening, the setting sun burnished the sky and sea a deep yellow, and a rich, warm light flooded the cabin. She ate a few morsels of the stale bread and beef and looked out of the window again. The timbers of the ship began to heave and groan, and the vessel swung towards the land.

"What's happening now?" she exclaimed, clinging on to the window frame and pressing her face against the dirty glass. "Perhaps they're going to put me ashore. They know they've made a terrible mistake."

The ship glided under the lee of huge cliffs, and came gradually to a halt, accompanied by the rattling of an anchor into the depths. The darkening sky blurred the landscape, but the indistinct shape of a tall chimney on a narrow building was visible on the hillside. There were no trees or bushes, only moorland singed with black where it had been burnt. People on horseback were descending a winding path leading from the tin mine to the beach below, and a long boat from the ship was being rowed towards them.

The men dismounted on the shingle and roughly hauled a man from his horse. He stumbled, losing his balance. Another man kicked him, pulled him to his feet and forced him into the water, where he was thrown into the boat.

"His hands are tied," she muttered. "He's been snatched from somewhere, like me. He's a prisoner." And she stared at the unfortunate wretch, now sitting hunched in the stern.

They quickly neared the ship and she saw he was dark-haired, in a black coat and breeches, his white shirt stained dark-red with blood. Then the boat reached the side and disappeared from her line of vision. She scurried to the door and pressed her ear to the wood to try and hear what was happening. Boots tramped above her, and there was shouting, followed by the noise of men in the corridor outside her cabin.

"In wi' ye," she heard. The adjacent door banged shut; footsteps sounded in the corridor and gradually faded away. There was silence, followed by groans of pain.

She knocked on the thin wall and called out loudly, "I'm imprisoned in the next cabin. My name's Bess Mudge. I'm from Ilfracombe. Who are you?"

"I am Jacob Goldstein," a low voice replied in English, but with a strong foreign accent.

"Why have you been captured?" she asked.

"I'm a diamond cutter, from Antwerp, but I work for a merchant in London. He was going to send his son to buy a priceless diamond from Lord Falkener, who lives near Exeter. His son fell ill with smallpox, and so he sent me instead." His voice faltered, and it was some minutes before he was able to speak again. "It was all a trick. There was no diamond and they kidnapped me instead of his son."

"I'm just a poor milk maid," she said. "Why would anyone want to abduct me. It must be a mistake, like you."

Jacob Goldstein did not reply. Anchor chains clanked, the water slapped noisily against the hull, and Bess fell onto the floor as the ship lurched forwards.

4

Armand woke to brilliant sunshine dappling through the branches of the horse chestnut tree outside his window. Patterns of light were dancing across the wallpaper, illuminating dust motes in their rays. The day was already warm. He could hear servants talking nearby and the raucous call of a seagull. His body ached from so many hours in the saddle and he stiffly abandoned the four-poster bed and stood, in his shirt, barefoot, on the threadbare carpet, absorbing the strangeness of being back at Wildercombe House, alone, without his parents and sister.

It was bittersweet to walk to the window and look out at the garden. It was now his garden, his lake, his wood. His parents were dead. Their last minutes on this Earth seared his mind, and he clenched his fists in hatred of the men who had killed them, and the revolution which had caused them to be killed.

His eyes were without tears, and he stared unseeingly at the lawns and trees in front of him.

"I will avenge you," he said. "You will not have died in vain."

A soft knock on the door was followed by a fresh-faced young valet entering the room, timidly fumbling with a long robe. Armand threw it over his shirt, then descended the creaking wooden stairs to the dining room, where a footman in a new blue livery was clumsily placing dishes piled high with beef steak, eggs and rashers of bacon on the table.

He sat down and bowed his head in prayer. He murmured the words, and when he had finished, waited a moment before eating. He gazed at the portrait of his mother in the hall, which was visible through the open door, and ate slowly, drinking claret from a crystal glass. He had barely finished his meal when the clip-clop of a horse came from the drive, and a subsequent knocking at the front door announced a visitor. The footman, Ben, glanced out of the window and announced loudly, "It be Mr McAlpine of Crow House come to call."

"Crow House?" he queried. "That's an odd name."

"It be really called Dunscombe Manor, but all the volks round y'ere call it Crow House," replied Ben.

"Please have him shown to the library," he ordered. "Tell him I will see him shortly."

He returned to his bedchamber and quickly dressed in a more formal attire of breeches, stockings, waistcoat and coat; the valet arranging his dark hair into its usual queue. Then he went downstairs again to meet the owner of Crow House.

He was a narrow-shouldered man of average height. His sandy eyebrows, pale eyelashes and freckle-blotched face, where the veneer of white cosmetic powder had rubbed off, suggested that his hair was probably ginger. However, whatever Nature had bestowed was concealed by a tightly curled, grey wig which reached almost to his waist. His green velvet coat, Paisley silk waistcoat and fawn breeches, were well-tailored, and clung to his thin frame; and he had not chosen to sit on an oak chair, but was pacing backwards and forwards, giving an impression of restrained energy. He bowed courteously and introduced himself as Raphael McAlpine.

"I believe, your Grace, you helped my ward and Esther Cerfbeer yesterday and I am here to thank you for your assistance. I arrived soon after you left, and although most of the miscreants had vanished, I ken the names of the ring leaders and I can tell you they will be severely punished in my capacity as Magistrate." His voice was nasal with a pronounced Scottish accent.

"I did very little, I can assure you," replied Armand. "The situation resolved itself."

"My ward is forbidden to ride anywhere other than my estate. She disobeyed my instructions and will be confined to the house in future." His tone was ice-cold, his eyes the grey of slate. "Esther Cerfbeer is sometimes of help to me. She is very skilled in herbs and potions and has a knowledge of plants which far exceeds that of anyone living here in this outpost of civilisation. She is, of course, not a witch. She is of the Jewish faith, and as I expect you are already aware, the fear and hostility which some people extend to supposed witches, is also shown to Jews. They are still not equal in law in your homeland of Alsace, even though the Revolution has given them this right."

He stopped speaking, walked to the window and looked towards the wood. A faint smell, not of perfume, but of incense, emanated from his clothing, and Armand glanced curiously at him as he turned and continued to speak. "We can discuss France at a later date. I am here on another matter. May I enquire as to whether you intend to reside permanently in North Devon, or are you just making a visit?"

"I have had to flee Alsace," replied Armand grimly. "My parents have been killed, my chateau has been confiscated, and I intend to live at Wildercombe House for the immediate future."

"I believe you also have a plantation in the United States of America?" remarked Raphael McAlpine.

"Yes, my sister, Antoinette, has gone to Virginia to oversee the land there."

"Well, in that case, I would like to make a proposal to you. Your estate is very small, but it could be useful to me, and I would be interested in making you an offer for it."

"An offer?" queried Armand.

"Aye. If you tell me what you consider its value to be, I will attempt to match it." He lowered his gaze for a moment to Armand's hands, which were bare of any ring.

"My estate is definitely not for sale, at the moment," Armand declared dismissively. "However, I intend to return to Alsace, once the Revolution comes to an end, and it is possible I might wish to sell it then."

Raphael McAlpine openly laughed, the white powder round his mouth cracking slightly. "It is not going to come to an end in the manner you wish, my dear sir. The United States of America and France are showing us the way forward. Nobles are a dying breed these days. It is men of commerce, like me, who are taking over the world."

Fury made the blood pound in Armand's head; he touched the sword at his side and moved threateningly towards his visitor.

"Get out of my house!" he exclaimed. "Your words offend me, sir!"

Raphael McAlpine's features remained immobile, but he hastily stepped backwards, his hand gripping his silver cane more tightly.

"Calm yourself. I have come as a friend, not as an enemy. Perhaps we can speak of your estate another day. In the meantime, I would like to invite you to dinner. I often hold meetings for the local gentry and we discuss science and politics. I am holding a soirée next Thursday at five o'clock, if you would care to join us."

"Thank you," Armand replied curtly, attempting to control his temper. "I will consider it."

He looked at Raphael McAlpine for a moment, his face still flushed with anger, but his words were polite. "I wonder if I might have the pleasure of calling on your ward, Miss Isabella?"

"She is already spoken for, your Grace," Raphael McAlpine said sourly. He bowed low and took his leave.

Armand waited until the hoof beats of his visitor's horse had faded away. He realised the man's sharp gaze had noticed his lack of a family signet ring, which had remained on his father's hand.

"I must have one made," he muttered. Then he strode, still in annoyance, across the flag stones of the hall, down the steps and into the gardens. The day was hot and a haze was shimmering over the lake, distorting the reflections of sycamores and oaks. The whiskered head of a catfish surfaced, before disappearing into the depths, leaving ever-widening concentric ripples to disturb a moorhen family. He watched dragonflies with gossamer wings darting erratically, and a tiny frog, croaking tunelessly, crouching on exposed tree roots dangling stiffly into the water.

He restlessly paced the moss-bound paths laid out between unkempt box trees and lawns of long grass, and roamed round the rose arbour, its few blooms besieged by bees. He made his way to the vegetable garden at the back of the house, where he contemplated the groundsel-choked ground, before entering the glittering, glass edifice of the greenhouse. A sweet scent of soil, fruit and flowers greeted him; he pushed past a thicket of giant ferns extending almost to the roof, and touched a peach on a gnarled bough twining up through an espalier. More peaches hung from a tree against a wooden trellis, and, as he reached out to pick one, his foot knocked against a hard object half-hidden among the foliage. He rummaged in the leaves and uncovered a metal chain, with wide, circular bands at regular intervals along its length. He picked it up and examined it.

"What is this for?" he muttered. "Surely it is not for gardening?"

He stared at it in growing disbelief. "They are manacles for convicts. What are they doing in my greenhouse?"

He threw down the chain with disgust, jumped the fire burning in a sunken pit in the floor, and left behind the tropical humidity of the greenhouse for the bright sunshine outside.

5

Isabella stood in her nightgown peering through a gap in the damask-curtained window of her bedchamber. Downstairs, a clock chimed, making the two wolf- hounds, Cain and Abel, howl in response. The sun had risen but the shadowy outline of the night moon was still a round disc of shadows in an amber sky, streaked by honey-gold cirrus clouds. Black flapping wings momentarily obscured the scene and a crow alighted on the ivy-covered window sill.

She pulled the curtain to see better and was rewarded with the vision of two servants shouldering the huge body of Mrs McAlpine from the mounting platform to her horse. The animal quivered as the full weight of its rider came down heavily onto the side saddle. It flared its nostrils, neighed in distress and tried to bolt, but was held firmly by the chief groom. Mr McAlpine was already mounted, and she touched her cheek where he had angrily punched her the previous night.

"How dare you disobey me!" he had shouted, his face almost purple, a sign that his customary bad temper had escalated to a fury. He had raised his hand to hit her again, as she flinched back against her chair, but he was stopped by Mrs McAlpine.

"Don't mark her dear. She'll be damaged goods!" she shrieked, in her high-pitched voice, which issued strangely from her gargantuan physique.

He had restrained himself with difficulty, and she had been sent to her bedchamber until further notice.

The McAlpines were both dressed for the hunt; Raphael McAlpine's red coat, black hat and fawn breeches were complemented by his wife's emerald green riding habit and statuesque hat, ornamented with lace and an imitation bird. Stirrup cups of brandy were downed greedily.

"Tally Ho!" he shouted, and the horses and riders moved off in a stately fashion across the cobbles.

She abandoned the window and, without the aid of a maid, dressed rapidly in a cream muslin dress, leaving off her usual stays and bulky petticoats. She went to a corner of the room, where she prised up a broken section of floor board and removed a wooden box from its hiding place. She opened it and rummaged through her treasures. A shell bracelet had been a gift from her first suitor, Daniel Stribling. His family owned a fishing boat and he used to hawk mackerel, crabs and lobsters round the large houses in Ilfracombe, trundling his wares by donkey and cart. He had collected the tropical conch shells from Barricane Beach at Woolacombe, and had threaded them on a silver string. He came to Dunscombe Manor on Fridays and would sweet-talk her, his smiling face and chestnut hair always a cheerful sight. One day, Mr McAlpine had caught him as he was slipping his arm round her waist. He had been furious and had sent her back into the house, where he had beaten her almost senseless with his cane.

Daniel Stribling never came to Dunscombe Manor again, and a few weeks later his body was found, his eyes gouged out, at Crewkerne Cave in Ilfracombe.

Mrs McAlpine had been pleased to tell Isabella the news. "Good riddance to a bad lot," she had remarked, smiling.

Isabella placed the bracelet on her wrist, and took out of the box the sketch she had made of her second suitor, Thomas Kemp, a shy young man from Lee, who was in the Devonshires. This time it had been a more serious affair. She had been careful to conceal her acquaintance with him even from the servants. They had only managed to meet a few times, but Thomas had proposed, and she had accepted. They had set a date to elope and go to Exeter to be married, and she had prepared her clothes and placed them in a cotton bundle. She had waited many hours for him by the gate at the end of the garden, but he did not come, and she had to creep back to her bedchamber in the dark, trying to restrain her sobs. The next day, his body had been found in the River Wilder, near the beach. His heart had been cut out, as well as his eyes.

The McAlpines had never mentioned him directly, but Mrs McAlpine had spent many weeks muttering, "You bring a curse, my dear. You bring a curse."

She looked sadly at the drawing before taking out the sketches of the other girls who had once lived with her at Dunscombe Manor.

"Why don't you write?" she enquired of Harriet. "We were so close. We loved each other. Why does marriage mean that I never hear from you again?"

She stored the drawings away in the box, which she replaced under the floorboards, and glanced uneasily at the small, framed painting of Captain James Petrie, her fiancé, on the dressing table. Mrs McAlpine had thrust it at her, and had said,

"Mr McAlpine has arranged a decent marriage for you, just as he has done for the rest. It is more than you deserve, you ungrateful wretch. He took you in and has given you a good home. He has fed and provided for you all your life and it is time to repay him."

"How am I repaying him?" she had asked. "Is James Petrie giving a dowry?"

Mrs McAlpine had slapped her. "You impudent girl. You will soon be gone."

She looked unhappily at the pleasant features of her intended. "I don't know you, sir. I don't know how you will treat me. Will you beat me, as I have been beaten here?"

She frowned and went down to the kitchen where Mrs Gubb poured her a dish of tea, and provided her with a plate of laver, bacon, mushrooms and bread.

"Do you know where they have gone?" she enquired.

"They be stag hunting at Heddon on Exmoor," Mrs Gubb replied. "They won't be here afore dimpsie. You be safe til then."

She stood up, gratefully thanking the cook.

"You take care, my lady, the master's in one of his foul moods today. Make sure you're back afore night."

She left the kitchen and escaped from the gloom of the ancient house into the brightness outside. Her step lightened, she skipped over the cobbles of the courtyard, and followed the white-dust path up the steep hill to Chambercombe, and down past Larkstone to the harbour.

The lantern on St Nicholas's Chapel was reflecting the early morning sun as the sea flooded past the quay and over the mud. The Strand was cluttered with mooring ropes and anchors, and the incoming tide rippled under the herring boats. The building yard in the cove at one side of the harbour, was busy with men hammering on the skeleton of a ship, and three women dock workers were carrying large bags of salt on their heads across the sand.

She walked up Fore Street and made her way towards the outskirts of Ilfracombe, until she came to the track leading to Esther Cerfbeer's cottage. She wandered along the high-banked Devon lane, in shadow from the sun, until she reached Esther's garden. The gate was partly open, and she stood, for a moment, contemplating the ravaged plants. The alders in the hawthorn hedge had been slashed; the pale heart of the wood had turned red, as though the trees were bleeding, and she solemnly placed her hand on this reminder of the Crucifixion.

She picked her way between the broken twigs and stems and approached the cottage door. A singed bat abruptly fell from a charred branch of a stunted elder tree and she jumped in horror.

"The wood of the tree used as the cross of Jesus," she muttered.

Another bat lay dead amongst the nettles, and a host of butterflies, the embodiment of dead souls, were fluttering, fragile in the sunlight, over the trampled opium poppies.

"Esther," she called in panic at the three symbols of death. "Esther. Where are you?"

Only the fluting trill of a chaffinch answered her. She ran to the door and pushed it open.

"Esther," she called again.

The room was neat, in contrast to the garden. A three-legged cooking pot hung over an unlit fire. Dried mullein sticks, to burn as light tapers, were propped by the wall, and the fragrance of burnt elder blossom and bark hung heavy in the air.

22

She rushed to the back of the house and into the little barn. Mordecai, the donkey, was not in his stall, and a crescendo of bells ringing out from the Parish Church suddenly disturbed the quiet.

"It's a wedding," she said out loud in relief. "It is Saturday. It is Esther's Sabbath. She is at a house in Barnstaple for a religious assembly."

A quick movement at the entrance to the barn made her look towards it. A reddish-brown fox stood in the sunlight, his yellow-gold eyes with their vertically-slit pupils watching her, as though she was a prey he was stalking. She clapped her hands and moved forward and he bounded away into the vegetable patch. He delicately sniffed at a vervain plant, glanced back at her, then trotted into the hawthorn hedge, his tail a flash of white.

She stood pensively for a moment, before reaching down and picking the vervain. She crushed its dark leaves and lilac-coloured flowers in her hand and returned to the cottage. She hurried out of the room and into the garden, where she sprinkled the fragments over the dead bats, the splintered branches and uprooted plants.

"You staunched the wounds of Christ on Mount Calvary. You will defend Esther against the evil that was here," she murmured.

She shut the door and ran out of the garden and into the lane, towards the pillars of Wildercombe House. She stopped and looked briefly at the empty drive, before rushing past the stone birds and along the dusty track to the hillside.

She slowed her steps as she reached the wood. Its hushed quiet deadened the sounds of the outside world, and she followed the stony path winding upwards through the deciduous trees. Ferns were damp with moisture, and rivulets of water trickled down the earthen banks. A circle of red and white-spotted, fly agaric toadstools was vivid in the gloom, and a fairy trail of bright green grass was being enjoyed by an adder basking in the warmth of a slender ray of sun, escaped from the leaves above.

She crept warily, on the far side of the path, past the snake, and peered through silver-white branches of holly at Wildercombe House in the valley. She looked unhappily at the wide-open windows and the smoke curling from the chimneys, before continuing upwards, until she reached the grass beyond the trees at the summit of the hill. She regarded the waves rolling diagonally across the bay, crashing onto the silver crescent of the beach far below, and then walked nimbly down the narrow cliff path to the dry sand beyond the high-water mark. A sea breeze caught her long black hair, and she gazed round at the deserted cove. For a moment, she glanced in the direction of Wildercombe House

"No, you are not for me," she murmured, remembering the interest in his eyes. "Two men who loved me have already died. I carry a curse, as Mrs McAlpine says. I cannot risk a third. I will marry Captain James Petrie, as my guardian wants, and whatever will be my fate, at least I will be free of Dunscombe Manor."

She took off her shoes and stockings and wandered to the sea, where even in the shallows, the current pulled strongly against her feet. Water washed over her legs and the muslin dress was soon clinging wetly to her body.

6

Armand looked at the manager of his land.

"Mrs Widdicombe, the housekeeper, is your wife, I believe," he remarked.

"Yess, yer Grace," replied the red-jowled man, holding an ancient tricorn hat in his hand.

"I've been examining the accounts and it is apparent that the whole estate is only growing enough food for Wildercombe House. My chateau in Alsace has been confiscated and it is important that my farm here produces crops and livestock to sell."

"It be difficult," said Ezekiel Widdicombe, shifting uneasily on his feet. "The zoil is poor. It be good fer nought."

"I will visit the estate with you tomorrow and see for myself. I am not acquainted with farming practices in England, although I know about cultivating grapes and making wine."

Ezekiel Widdicombe snorted loudly and wiped his face with a dirty red handkerchief.

"Do you know anything about convict manacles that I have found?" Armand asked.

"No, yer Grace," he replied, glancing through the window in the direction of the vegetable garden. "You need to ask Samuel Crang fer aut to do with there."

"I didn't say where I found them," said Armand suspiciously. "What makes you think they were in the garden?"

The man scowled, his eyes almost lost in the thick, fleshy folds of his face.

Armand shrugged. "That will be all today. I will see you tomorrow."

Ezekiel Widdicombe knuckled his head, and lumbered from the room.

"Do you know why there are convict chains in the greenhouse?" he asked Ben, the young footman.

"No, your Grace. I was just taken on the day afore you came. I worked on my uncle's pilchard boat, but it sank off Clovelly in a storm. I was the only soul saved."

"I am sorry to hear that."

He looked at the tall young man for a moment. "I would like you to accompany me when I visit the estate tomorrow. Fresh eyes might be useful. Can you ride?"

"I've ridden a donkey," he volunteered.

"Well, good enough," said Armand. He rifled again through the papers on his desk, grimaced, and strolled out through the house and into the garden. The sun was hot and he rambled past the rose arbour and across to the magic wood, as his mother, Antoinette, had always called it.

The leafy coolness was a respite from the summer heat, and he stood in the shadow of an oak, loosening his cravat and looking around him. Shimmering shades of green and blue were marking the boundary between trees and sky; shafts of sunlight were being scavenged by the ground, briefly capturing the iridescence of a dragonfly and the ghost-white of fungi parasitically jewelling a fallen tree, and, for a moment, he felt himself at peace, before sadness gnawed at him once more. He glanced briefly in the direction of Esther Cerfbeer's cottage, and saw again the face of the young woman who had haunted his dreams.

"Sorcery," he muttered.

He set off up the path and was suddenly startled by yellow-gold eyes scrutinising him from behind a bush. A fox turned tail, vanishing into the undergrowth, and he crossed himself, before continuing to stride up the hillside.

He reached the summit of the wooded hill and blinked as he emerged into the bright sunlight. He sat down on a rocky knoll and gazed at the sea, which was azure blue as far as the horizon. A ship in full sail was tacking slowly towards Bristol. It was struggling against a shifting wind; a sudden gust from the north made it keel dangerously and a stinking odour disturbed the salt tang of the air.

"A slave ship?" he muttered.

The wind veered south-westerly, the sails billowed out, the vessel raced forwards, and the stench faded. He looked with interest at the ship, before glancing at the beach where a small, black-haired figure was walking alone at the edge of the tumbling breakers. He stood up in surprise and watched as the skirt of her dress floated around her as she wandered in the bubbling surf.

"What are you doing in the sea? You don't seem very confined to the house, milady. It might not be your wish, or that of your guardian, but fate seems to have brought you to me," he muttered.

He saw that the sea was rapidly advancing, cutting off any other route to return to the headland, except that of the cliff path, and he frowned as he saw the speed and ferocity with which the breakers were racing onto the beach.

. . . .

Oblivious to her audience, Isabella waded slowly, making her way towards the reefs by the cliffs at the far end of the cove. She left the water and scrambled over the slippery rocks to a deep pool. She plunged her hand into it, turning stones to see crabs scuttle away, and blennies dart in fright to hide under sea anemones. Waves were careering into the bay and she abandoned the pool and clambered back towards the sand, hurrying from the incoming tide.

Birds screeched angrily above her and she glanced at the cliff face. A buzzard was attacking a mottled-brown, baby seagull, but was being beaten back by a gang of seagulls and crows, which were harassing and pecking it, before rising up again and circling aggressively overhead.

She tilted her head back to see the birds, forgetting her precarious situation. The next minute, she lost her balance and fell headlong into a chasm. A wave roared onto her and she was swept ferociously along. The churning water pushed her downwards, and she bumped along the floor of the small ravine, unable to come to the surface and thrown against the rocks. The wave retreated, and she was left floundering and gasping for air. She attempted to stand, and hauled herself to her feet. She swayed, the approaching thunder of another breaker already nearly upon her. She was unable to escape and clung to a rock in an attempt to remain upright. The wave broke over her, its force sweeping her onto the ground, where she bumped along the sand again, until it ebbed back, leaving her stranded once more. The tattered remains of her muslin dress were streaked red with blood from the cuts and grazes on her body and she struggled to sit up, pressing her face against slimy tendrils of bladderwrack, as the next wave roared down, flinging her violently against the rocks, and forcing her against the sandy bed.

Suddenly, there was someone else in the water. Strong arms grabbed her and held her upright, and she gulped desperately for air. The wave retreated and the man picked her up and climbed out of the chasm and onto the rocks. He threw her over his shoulder and ran across the uneven reefs towards the sand above the high water mark. A wave caught him several times more, but the sea was now shallow, and he splashed rapidly along until he unceremoniously dumped her onto the shingle. He sat next to her, gasping for breath almost as much as she was, his clothes sodden. He reached into a pocket and took out a silver flask.

"Here. Drink the brandy," he said, putting his arm behind her back to help her sit up. He held the flask to her lips and she choked at the fiery liquid. She flapped her hand to indicate she did not want any more, but he continued to pour it down her throat, until he finally placed her back onto the sand where she sat like a stranded fish amongst the bleached cuttlefish bones and piles of seaweed, tipsily looking up at the sun and the large body of her rescuer.

His face swam into focus and she saw Armand de Delacroix. He stared grimly at her and she shivered.

7

He glanced down at her bare legs and feet, ribboned with cuts from which blood was trickling onto the sand. His gaze slowly travelled upwards, and she clasped her hands in embarrassment to her muslin dress, which hung in tatters.

He sat next to her, his clothes dripping with water, his hair escaped from its queue and hanging over his shoulders, and watched her as she slowly revived.

"Have you broken any bones?" he asked.

"No, I haven't. I am just bruised and cut," she murmured weakly. "Thank you for rescuing me. I am very sorry to have trespassed on your land."

"This coast is dangerous. You should not be here alone and you should not be in the sea. I know ladies sometimes swim, but I hardly think they enter waves like this in their normal clothes and without any servants present."

"It was an accident," she said. "I was looking at the birds and I fell."

"That's not true," he replied bluntly. "You were in the water before you went over to the rocks."

A silence fell between them and he continued to watch her. The waves crashed onto the nearby shingle, and seagulls screamed on the cliffs.

She delicately brushed the sand from her face and gathered her hair into a coil at the nape of her neck. She looked regretfully at the torn muslin of her dress, and draped its folds over her bare, bloodied feet. She huddled on the sand, clutching her knees, as though she was somehow trying to make herself smaller and less visible.

She glanced at him, her eyes dark in her pale face. Her hair broke free again and her body trembled as she hunched herself even more closely to the ground.

"I must go," she murmured, her voice breaking with exhaustion.

He said nothing. He took his flask and raised it to his mouth and drank, then stretched out his hand and offered it to her.

She shook her head. "Once more, thank you. I would be very obliged if you would say nothing to my guardian."

The words fell between them, sounding oddly stilted, as they sat together on the beach, both battered and bruised, in torn and wet clothing.

"Yes, I know. You are forbidden to leave the house," he remarked. "I recently had the pleasure of meeting Mr McAlpine."

She glanced questioningly at him, and he thought he saw a terror coming into her eyes at the mention of her guardian's name.

"He will beat me," she murmured. "I have disobeyed him."

"Don't worry. I will say nothing, although I don't know how you will explain your injuries and your clothing. It will be our secret and, in return, I would like to see you again."

"I cannot," she said. "I cannot go against his wishes. They died...." Her voice trailed away.

"Who died?" he asked.

She shook her head. "It does not matter." She breathed deeply and regained her poise.

"I am already betrothed to Captain James Petrie. I cannot make any such promise."

He shrugged his shoulders in annoyance and stared crossly at her.

"Who is Captain Petrie, may I ask? He is happy for his future wife to wander in the sea?"

"He lives in the United States of America, in somewhere called Virginia."

"And how do you know him?" he questioned.

"I do not know him," she confessed. "Mr McAlpine has arranged the marriage for me."

"When will you meet?"

"I cannot say, but we are to be married quite soon," she said, her own doubt reflected in her anxious tone. She looked at the seaweed. "I am an orphan. It is very kind of Mr McAlpine to have brought me up at his own expense and to have arranged a marriage. I am the only one left now. There were nine girls whom he brought into his house, and they also did not see their husbands until the marriage day."

"Where are your parents?"

"I have no idea. I have only known Dunscombe Manor. Mr McAlpine has always refused to tell me." She agitatedly rubbed the grazed skin on her wrist and suddenly cried out in anguish. "My bracelet! It has gone. The sea has snatched it."

"Was it expensive?" he asked.

"No, it was a bracelet of shells, but it was very dear to me."

"Well, I think I can manage to obtain a shell bracelet for you, even in my present financial state," he replied and smiled at her.

"I must go now. Thank you again for saving me," she said, not replying to his words, and very gingerly stood up. She swayed and flinched in pain and he jumped to his feet, took off his coat and wrapped it round her shoulders, covering the ragged dress. Then he picked her up in his arms and walked steadily across the beach.

"No. Please stop this," she said, and struggled against him.

He took no notice, and, after a few minutes, she fell silent as he laboured up the steep hillside, gripping her tightly. He stopped at the knoll he had sat on earlier and put her down, wiping his sweating forehead with his sleeve.

"You're heavier than you look," he remarked conversationally. "Although I must say in my defence that I have already done battle with the sea, and my strength is not quite at its best."

"Thank you again for rescuing me. You must leave me now and I will make my own way home. I do not want my guardian to know," she said.

He looked at her, gazing at her face for a moment, then he shrugged. "What you want and what you can do, appear to be two different things. You obviously cannot walk very far. We will return to Wildercombe House and a carriage will take you into Ilfracombe."

"No, I beg you. Let me go to Esther's cottage and I will find some clothes there. The Widdicombes often visit Dunscombe Manor. I do not want to be seen by them," she pleaded.

"Is that right? They often call on Mr McAlpine?"

"Yes," she said.

He frowned for a moment, before giving an elaborate bow and offering her his arm. "May I have the pleasure of escorting you down the hill, madam?"

He saw her look at the strands of green seaweed and a piece of bladderwrack caught in the front of his silk shirt. She glanced at her bare feet and torn dress, her eyes moist with tears, and bit her lip.

"Thank you," she murmured. She held onto his arm and they proceeded slowly down through the wood, until they came to the edge of the trees. She let go of him and collapsed onto the ground, next to a rowan tree.

He looked uncertainly at her. "Are you alright?"

"Yes," she replied, catching her breath. "Yes, I will be fine."

"Wait here and I will bring a horse and some clothing," he said, and immediately rushed off through the bracken. He jumped the stream, strode past the stone birds and along the drive to Wildercombe House.

The twilight closed clammily around her; a dew drop fell delicately from the bell of a foxglove onto a bed of moss. She stood up carefully, using the rowan as a support, and limped to the brook trickling between rushes and flag irises. The coat hung heavily on her shoulders and she ran her fingers over the buttons and buried her face in the tobacco-smelling fabric. She parted the irises and waded into the cold stream, splashing her legs and dress and cleansing them of blood. The water ran faintly pink around her; she cupped her hands in it and washed her face. Then she regained the bank and sank onto the moss. She turned her face to the sun and drifted into sleep.

8

Armand cantered down the drive on his black stallion, leading a roan mare on a long, leather strap. A side saddle had been quickly thrown onto it by the groom, and he glanced back at it to check that the ancient buckles were holding fast. His mother's green cloak, which he had found in her dressing room, had been laid carefully across his saddle, and her silver cross which he had also found, was now in his pocket. He emerged from the shade of the beech trees into the sunlight, and looked anxiously towards the wood.

She was still there. She had moved from the rowan tree and was now sitting asleep on a bank of moss, his coat next to her. He quickly dismounted and saw her eyes open as he approached. Her skin was no longer bloodied, but her face was pale, and had an unearthly quality about it, which reminded him of the angels in religious paintings.

"I've brought you a cloak to cover your dress," he said, as he reached her.

She stood up. She was unsteady on her feet, and her gown hung in shreds. He gave her the cloak and she draped it over her shoulders. She pulled the hood over her hair and peered out at him, the whiteness of her face accentuated by the deep green of the velvet.

"Thank you. I can never repay you for your kindness today."

Her voice was soft and gentle and almost lost in the babble of water from the stream and the fluting birdsong.

"I have already told you I want to see you again. That will be your repayment."

He watched as she took fright at his words. Her eyes were startled and she flinched from him. He wanted to stretch out a hand and reassure and steady her, but managed to restrain himself. He wanted her. This ethereal, unknown woman had cast a spell on him. Her eyes had held him in their power at the cottage, and he felt a fear that she had ensnared him by supernatural means.

His desire, however, was real, and as he looked at her, he knew that she knew. She backed away. The hood of the cloak half-covered her face and he glanced at the familiar garment of his mother, now concealing a stranger's body, which he had already held in his arms. His eyes held hers.

"You have nothing to fear from me, as I have already shown you," he said.

She relaxed. She breathed more slowly and forced herself to speak.

"I am afraid to meet with you again, but I owe you my life. If that is what you want, I will obey your wishes." She glanced coldly at him.

"Let me escort you home," he said, picking up his coat from the ground and placing it on his saddle, annoyance and disappointment rising in him at her obvious reluctance.

He stood by the second horse and put his hands together. "Can you manage to mount? Put your foot here in my hand."

She gripped his sleeve, and placed her foot in the palm of his hand, her flesh briefly touching that of his. She swung herself up onto the side saddle, pulled on the reins, and moved away, whereupon he mounted his own horse and caught her up at the entrance to the lane.

"Ride in front. It is a long time since I was last in Ilfracombe," he told her.

She followed a circuitous route through the woods behind Esther's cottage, down the steep hillside and across the River Wilder. She avoided the large houses on the edge of town and climbed a winding track to the summit of a hill overlooking Ilfracombe and the sea. The summer heat was fierce. She threw back the cloak's hood and her black hair gleamed in the sun.

She sent her horse cantering towards a ruined lime kiln in the corner of the field, and then descended the lane which led to Chambercombe. High banks and overhanging trees darkened the path, whilst the arching foliage overhead was shot through with sun-stars, twinkling in the twilight. The noise of the horses' hooves was muffled by the earth and grass, and they quietly descended the hill. She stopped at a dilapidated oak door in a dry-stone wall, slid off her saddle and landed nimbly on the ground.

"You are an excellent horsewoman," he declared, as he also dismounted. "Perhaps we can ride together sometime?"

She looked at him questioningly and he shrugged his shoulders.

"You haven't forgotten your promise?" he enquired.

"No, I have not," she replied. "But it is not possible. I can only leave the house when the McAlpines are away."

"He's a Magistrate, I believe," he remarked with determination. "When does he go to court?"

"On Fridays," she said, after a pause.

"What about Mrs McAlpine?" he asked.

"She accompanies him to go shopping," she said.

"Well, there you are then. I will meet you at my beach next Friday about midday," he declared triumphantly.

She looked dubiously at him, and then at three crows perched on the wall. A fourth crow alighted next to them and she caught her hand to her mouth in a gesture of fear.

"No," she said suddenly. "No, I can't come."

"Sacré Bleu!" Pas encore les corbeaux!" he shouted, for the first time breaking into his native tongue. "What is wrong with the crows round here, may I ask?"

"They were once white," she remarked. "But they were evil and so they were changed into black."

"Rubbish!" he exclaimed. "Your head is filled with foolish thoughts you have probably been informed of by your friend, the so-called witch. In any case, I was not referring to their colour, but to why people seem afraid of them."

"It is not always wise to disregard old ideas," she murmured.

"It is not always wise to take advice from nonsense," he retorted.

35

She slowly took off the cloak and gave it to him. He stood in front of the door and folded his arms, and for a few seconds they stood in silence.

"Very well," she said, her face and voice expressing her displeasure. "Thank you once more for saving my life. I will see you next Friday on the beach."

He looked at her thoughtfully for a moment, and slowly took out the silver crucifix from his pocket.

"You will be happy to swear on this holy cross of my mother, then, that you will meet me."

She hesitated, and he knew that her words had been a lie, and that she would not be there to meet him. He stood, blocking her way, and she gave a sigh of exasperation.

"Very well. I swear on the cross that I will meet you. It is not in your interest that I should do so, and it is certainly not in mine, but it is true that I am in your debt, and I will do what you want." She stared at him, her eyes clouded by exhaustion and annoyance, and touched the crucifix as she spoke.

He stood back to let her pass; she brushed past him, pushed open the door and disappeared into the grounds of Dunscombe Manor.

He tied the horses to a tree and followed her. She could be seen hurrying past rows of tall, dark green plants of hemp and he watched until she vanished from view. He turned to leave, and, as he did so, his eye was taken by pink opium poppies growing by the wall. His gaze slowly travelled over the garden and he saw the same plants he had seen at Esther Cerfbeer's cottage, but grown on a far more extensive scale. Purple-flowering belladonna occupied three large beds, as did mullein, whilst nettles grew in ranks next to a grove of apple trees with bunches of mistletoe nestling in the crooks of their branches. The large, hairy leaves of a plant growing near to him smelled unpleasantly and he picked two of the brownish-yellow flowers with mauve centres, and put them in his pocket.

He glanced quickly round the garden and made his way to a greenhouse set back against the wall. He entered and was again met with an unpleasant odour, this time coming from several large thornapple bushes, nearly as tall as he was. Their handsome white flowers were only partly open, waiting for the evening moths, and he looked curiously at them for a moment, before turning his attention to plants with enormous, dark-green leaves which lay upon the ground, and which had white flowers, similar to a primrose. Above them, on a rack, hung dried roots shaped like naked men and women.

"Mandrake!" he exclaimed, in surprise. Men's voices suddenly sounded in the distance, and he hurriedly left the greenhouse and returned to the lane. He untied the horses and galloped back up the track, whistling the tune he had heard whilst waiting for his men at Strasbourg Cathedral.

9

The sun was high in the blue of a cloudless sky. A sky lark rose vertically into the air, warbling its song, and flew back to the ground, still singing. Water was quietly seeping through clumps of sphagnum moss and the cupped leaves of marsh pennywort in a ditch by the stone track. The riders came to a halt and sat on their horses, with the exception of Ben, at the back of the file, who tumbled off onto the ground.

Armand looked at the yellow fields of charlock, interspersed with a scattering of mustard, on either side of the path.

"Neeps," said Ezekiel Widdicombe, waving his red, calloused hand dismissively.

"Neeps?" questioned Armand. "What crop is this? I don't recognise it."

"Turnips," translated Ben from the Devon dialect, as he scrambled back onto his mount.

"I can't see any," said Armand, peering at the field.

Ezekiel dismounted clumsily from his grey mare and waded into the two-foot-high vegetation. He located several puny turnips, almost suffocated by their rampant neighbours.

"Neeps!" he announced triumphantly.

"But the field is growing something else," remonstrated Armand. "It's growing weeds."

Ezekiel Widdicombe pulled his tricorn hat further down onto his sweating forehead, trampled a few charlock plants, and remounted his horse in silence.

The riders set off again, the dust rising from the horses' hooves as they followed the track along the bottom of the coombe. Pink-flowering meadows succeeded the harsh yellow.

"Dashels," commented Ezekiel Widdicombe.

"Don't tell me. Let me guess the crop," said Armand to Ben. "Thistles. This is a field of thistles."

Ezekiel Widdicombe scowled. "Yess, dashels. The zoil yere be good-for-nothing," he muttered.

"I was only a child when I last came here," said Armand, "but I remember the estate as very fertile."

He looked at the clouds of butterflies attracted by the sweet-smelling muskiness of the thistle flowers, and glanced at a buzzard circling above the wooded hill opposite. He gazed blindly at the countryside for a few minutes, seeing his parents, before pulling on the reins of his horse and setting off at a trot along the path, quickly followed by Dietrich and Hans, leaving Ezekiel Widdicombe and Ben to follow in their wake.

They left behind the meadow of thistles and entered a common of furze and fern. He stopped his horse once more and stared at the land.

"My knowledge of farming is very limited," he said to his estate manager, "but surely ferns are poisonous to livestock."

"Yess, yer Grace, but animals know this and don't eat them," replied Ezekiel Widdicombe.

Armand looked disbelievingly at him and turned his attention to a dilapidated cottage, its windows stuffed with straw and hay, huddled at the edge of the common. Black forge cinders had been mixed with white mortar and smeared in stripes across the front of the building. Some had oozed out of the joints and spread haphazardly over the surface, the dirty nature of the façade not enhanced by a sagging thatch of reeds with a jagged hole next to the chimney.

"Does one of my tenants live there?" he asked, as a baby's cry sounded plaintively from the hovel.

"Yess, yer Grace," replied Ezekiel Widdicombe.

"It's not suitable as a habitation. It needs to be mended. Would you please have repairs done."

He glanced again at the cottage with displeasure and cantered on.

The open path became a lane, the summer heat disappearing into a cool twilight. The banks of the hedge were formed of mounds of earth, eight feet wide at the base, narrowing to six or seven feet at the top, and this was covered with oak, ash, birch and hazel, at least twenty feet high, so making the whole structure about thirty feet tall. At the same time, tree canopies intertwined, allowing very little light to penetrate.

He rode hesitantly forward, peering hard to see the path. Dietrich cursed behind him, as his horse stumbled, and they continued slowly in the gloom of the twisting and turning lane for over a mile. Armand whistled the Marseillaise, its notes rising and falling, and Dietrich could be heard swearing again, until, finally, the banks grew smaller, the leaves thinned, sunlight streamed down upon them, and they left the Devon lane and came out into open countryside.

Hens ran clucking backwards and forwards, narrowly missing the horses' hooves. Several were roosting in trees and one was perched on a wagon. The immediate ground was bare earth, but the rest of the enclosed field was growing wheat and was being harvested by a large gang of men and women. The men, their trousers tied at the ankles to stop mice and rats running up their legs, were using long-handled hooks to slash horizontally at the stalks, which some women were binding, whilst others raked up the loose straw.

Armand's face brightened to see the harvest, and Ezekiel Widdicombe's demeanour also became more cheerful as he noticed flagons of cider left over from the provisions brought to the field at midday. He picked up one and downed a vast quantity, before wiping his sweating face with the sleeve of his coat. As he did so, his skin above the wrist was exposed and a design of a black circle within which was a circular maze of lines surrounding another circle, was visible. Ben was standing next to him and his face paled. Ezekiel Widdicombe glared at him and muttered, "Keep yer mouth shut, boy, if ye want to make old bones."

Ben turned away and concentrated on mounting his horse, keeping his eyes averted from the estate manager.

Dietrich's mood also lifted as he chased a rabbit towards a warren of burrows near the hedgerow, and caught it, slitting its throat with his hunting knife. He hung it as a trophy from the saddle of his horse and said with satisfaction to Armand, "It's not wild boar, but never mind."

They set off again, two of the nearest labourers knuckling their heads as they noticed the new master of the estate. They passed two more enclosed wheat fields, which had not yet been harvested, and followed the stream along the bottom of the coombe before climbing upwards over a steep hillside of rough pasture, the horses picking their way delicately along the uneven, rocky path. On the other side of the valley, a coppice of oak and ash shimmered in the haze, and, in the distance, the sea was a pale stripe, merging into the darker blue of the sky. Dark red cows sat forlornly in the heat, twitching their cream tails to ward off flies, and in a bare corner of the same field, long, thin, white pigs were grunting and foraging.

"Red Rubies," called out Ezekiel Widdicombe. "Best cattle in England."

"Are they for milk?" enquired Armand.

"They be fer milk, fer meat and fer carrying," replied his manager.

They reached the summit and continued along the track towards Ilfracombe. Dried-up stream beds traversed the route, a cascade of white stones and yellowing plants tumbling downwards over the spiky grass to shale cliffs fringed at their base by silver shingle.

Grey-faced sheep, some horned, others hornless, roamed freely.

"Do they ever fall over the edge?" asked Armand.

"No," replied Ezekiel Widdicombe. "They be too stupid to back out of brimbles, but they never go over the cliff."

The path wound steeply down the hills of the Torrs and he pointed out a farm on the neighbouring hill.

"That be Samuel Mudge's land. 'Ee's the third owner on a contract of ninety-nine years, so when 'ee dies it all goes back to yer estate. It be a good bit of farm land there."

"What about his wife and family?" enquired Armand.

"They 'ave to go," said Ezekiel Widdicombe.

"So he owns the farm, but his family doesn't?"

"Yess," said his estate manager.

"That's a strange system," he remarked. "And is Samuel Mudge in good health?"

"No.'Is leg was crushed by a tree 'ee was cutting down, and 'ee's not expected to last the week," replied Ezekiel Widdicombe.

"I have no wish to evict his family in such circumstances," said Armand. "Can we call on him?"

"Yess, if 'ee wants," replied Ezekiel Widdicombe with obvious displeasure, and turned his horse towards the barton.

The trotting horses awoke a sheep dog sleeping on the farmhouse porch and it bounded up to them, yapping and nipping at their legs. A plump woman in a brown dress appeared at the half-door and stepped back, a look of fear on her face as she saw the estate manager.

"Oh, please sir, my husband's not dead. Please don't evict us yet. We've got nowhere to go," she pleaded piteously.

Armand swung down from his horse and the woman clenched her hand to her mouth as she saw his fine clothes.

"Yer Grace," she said, between sobs, and gave a curtsey.

"Don't worry. I'm not going to evict you. I am sorry to hear about your husband," he tried to reassure her.

"You're not going to make us leave," she said fearfully.

"No, I'm not," he repeated.

A young woman came out of the cottage and glanced timidly at the men and their horses. Her hair was so fair it was almost white, her eyes a brilliant blue.

Dietrich had been eyeing a wood pigeon cooing amongst the leaves of an ash tree, but on seeing the girl he abandoned his sport and leapt off his horse.

"I won't disturb you any further," said Armand. "Please tell your husband that whatever happens, you and your family can remain here for as long as you want. You have my word."

"Oh, thank you, your Grace," said Mrs Mudge.

Ezekiel Widdicombe's face was furious. "No," he spluttered.

"It is not for you to tell me what to do," snapped Armand in annoyance. He inclined his head towards Mrs Mudge and her daughter.

"Good day," he said, and turned his horse and trotted out of the farm yard. The others followed him, with the exception of Dietrich, who stood silently for a few seconds, as though reluctant to leave. He removed the rabbit from his saddle and handed it to Mrs Mudge.

She held the still-warm body in her hand. "Thank you," she said to the tall, well-built Alsatian, whose hair was nearly as blonde as that of her daughter.

He bowed his head to the two women, jumped onto his horse and cantered away.

"I've seen enough of the estate for today," said Armand to Ezekiel Widdicombe. "I will look at the farm buildings and the rest of the land another time. I expect you want to go and attend to the wheat harvest."

"Yess," said his estate manager dourly. He slapped the rump of his animal and headed off in the opposite direction of the wheat fields, down towards Ilfracombe.

10

Isabella opened the casement window and leaned out into the sunlight. Her face was thickly powdered, disguising the bruises she had received from the sea, and she laughed at her ghost-like reflection in the glass. She idly trailed her fingers along the sill and gazed down at the courtyard. The voice of Raphael McAlpine was coming from the library, whose window was also open in the heat, but the conversation itself was muted by the distance.

From her vantage point on the side wing, she stared at the main part of the house, her attention caught by the sun's rays diamond-sparkling the library window. She looked to the corner of the Norman manor, then back again.

"That's strange. The window's at the end of the library inside the room," she muttered. "But the outside wall goes far beyond. I've never noticed that before. What's there? "

She stared at the ivy foliage which had fallen off part of the sun-baked, crumbling masonry. The leaves were an unhealthy yellow, the woody stems veined the stonework, and a rectangular outline of a window was exposed beneath the creeper.

She looked at the house for a few minutes, before wandering downstairs and out into the summer sun. She scurried quickly past the library, where a man was now speaking in English, but with a markedly French accent.

"We will need at least twenty more donkeys. We will have to move it all very quickly this time."

She reached the corner of the house and was glancing curiously at the wall behind the ivy, when the McAlpine's small carriage, pulled by two horses, suddenly appeared, trundling along the path from the stables. It stopped by the front porch and she went to stand, half-hidden, in the shadow of an ancient yew, as Mrs McAlpine emerged from the front door in a buttercup-yellow satin dress which trailed behind her. She installed herself in the carriage with the muscular help of two servants, and was soon followed by her husband, in the company of a short, dark-haired man.

"You would be rid of an enemy of France and his land would be useful to me," Raphael McAlpine said, his words carrying clearly in the air.

They both climbed into the carriage and it clattered off across the courtyard, its iron-shod wheels striking the cobbles, before lurching through the main gate and onto the steep track beyond.

Isabella waited, stroking Cain, who had come to join her in the shade, until the carriage finally disappeared, hidden by the trees on the hillside. Then she returned to the porch and entered the hall. She glanced at the closed door to the servants' quarters and at the narrow, wooden stairs leading to the landing. There was no one to be seen and she slipped quietly into the library, where blue tobacco smoke wreathed the air and the linnet in its cage trilled a greeting. She walked rapidly to the far wall, which was partly covered by a tapestry hanging from the ceiling on a brass rod. Its thick brocade was embroidered by gold and silver thread, and depicted four paths meeting at a crossroads, a large dog sitting amongst blue flowers of wolfbane, below a yew tree, and a faint crescent moon glowing in a night sky.

She gazed at the tapestry and gently caressed a flower. Suddenly, from the kitchen, came the sound of a door opening and the scolding tones of Mrs Gubb. She stood motionless. The kitchen door grated shut and the cook's voice was cut off in mid-sentence.

She pulled back the tapestry, which slid easily along the brass rod, and discovered carved oak panelling. She knocked on it and was rewarded with a hollow noise, as though the wall was not solid. She ran her hands over the embossed surface, but nothing happened. She tried again, this time pushing and pulling a rounded knob, which appeared larger than the others. There was a click, a panel moved, and she found herself staring into a large chamber, smelling of a musty dankness, infused with a scent of incense and rye.

She gasped in surprise. She took a deep breath and stepped forward into the concealed room. Sunlight streamed into it from the library window, illuminating white walls and a floor patterned by a mosaic of a large circle, within which was a black maze bulging out in three places, and enclosing another, smaller circle, with a star-like design.

She gasped again as she saw an upturned crucifix on a table resembling an altar, next to two rows of metal receptacles holding black candles. She advanced timidly towards it. Her foot knocked against a bowl on the floor; a liquid splashed from it, and she gave a shriek as a cobweb brushed her face.

She breathed deeply and went further into the room. On her left was the opening of a corridor which descended into the ground, and just by it, in an alcove, was a shelf on where were two, tattered books. She moved closer and glanced at the ancient lettering on the vellum cover of the first book.

"Maleus Maleficarum," she murmured.

The title of the second book was in English, not Latin, but the writing was so spidery and faint, she had to stare at it for a long time to make it out.

"Book of Shadows," she finally muttered.

She took a few hesitant steps forward and peered into the foetid blackness of the tunnel. A rat scuttled past; she gave a muffled scream and fled from the chamber, back into the brightness of the library. She closed the panel, hastily rearranged the tapestry, and suddenly noticed her shoe was streaked with red.

"Blood!" she exclaimed. "There was blood in the bowl, not water!"

Tell-tale footprints marked the floor and she bent down and hurriedly wiped them with the hem of her dress. She straightened up, and as she did so, Reuben, the hunch-backed, elderly servant entered the room.

He looked at her, his hazel eyes shrewdly suspicious.

"Miss Isabella. I have not seen you in the library before." His tone lacked his usual good-naturedness and carried a note of suspicion.

"I heard the linnet sing and wanted to look at it. I know I'm not allowed in here. I won't come in again." She smiled sweetly at him and walked hurriedly out of the room and up the stairs to her bedchamber.

She sank onto her bed and clung to one of its wooden posts for support.

"You were right, Daniel. You always said an old smuggling tunnel linked Dunscombe Manor with Rapparee beach. I think I have found it," she murmured.

A giant beetle scurried across the counterpane towards her and she scooped it into a kerchief.

"Will you bring me luck, as people say?" she asked it. "Let me take you home."

She stood up and carefully carried it down the stairs and outside to the garden. She freed the insect by a beehive and was returning to the house just as the carriage came through the gate. It stopped at the front door, next to her, with Raphael McAlpine now the only occupant.

He descended its steps, and regarded her coldly. "May I remind you that I have a dinner party tonight and I expect your presence at the table. I want you there because I am going to announce your forthcoming marriage. You are, however, only to speak when spoken to by a guest."

"When will my wedding take place?" she asked.

"The date has not yet been set," he replied.

"And will Esther be allowed to accompany me to the United States of America?" she enquired boldly.

"You will certainly be accompanied. Have no fear of that." And he swept past her into the hall.

She stood, absentmindedly crumpling the kerchief in her hand, then slowly entered the house and climbed the stairs to her bedchamber, where she sat on the bed again and anxiously looked at the picture of her fiancé.

In the library, Reuben had just finished cleaning the spots of spilled blood from the floor of the secret chamber. He closed the panel and rearranged the tapestry into its correct position, with the moon visible, and not hidden in a fold of the brocade. His face was sombre as he heard the footsteps of Raphael McAlpine.

11

Captain James Bowen led the toast.

"Our beloved sovereign, King George. May he reign long and prosperously."

The assembled gathering dutifully raised their glasses, some more enthusiastically than others.

Isabella sat next to Guillaume Thibaud, the dark-haired man who had visited earlier, and who, at close quarters, appeared very shabbily dressed, his coat frayed at the cuffs, his shoes scuffed and worn. He frowned as the toast was announced.

"Which side are you on, Mr Tibby?" boomed Captain Bowen at him. "We are at war with France. Have you left that wretched country to save your skin, or are you here to spy on us for an invasion?"

Everyone fell silent. Guillaume Thibaud's eyes narrowed, but he answered strongly and confidently.

"I have escaped, to save my skin, as you put it, sir. I am a refugee. As to fears of an invasion, it will not happen. France is fighting so many European nations it cannot invade England."

"I hope General Kléber is of the same opinion," Captain Bowen snorted belligerently.

Isabella glanced curiously at her neighbour, remembering the words she had heard earlier in the day. He looked at her and the other guests and said with emotion. "You are very fortunate, mesdames and messieurs, to have food on your table, a warm bed at night, and not know Madame Guillotine, unlike my fellow countrymen."

He wiped his face with his napkin and turned his attention to the roasted goose skins on his plate.

"Our fair ladies must be protected from the evils of this new French Republic," said Lieutenant Hargreaves, dressed in the black uniform of the Customs and Excise, and he regarded Mrs McAlpine briefly, before letting his gaze linger on Isabella.

The late afternoon was sultry, and from nearby Exmoor came a clap of thunder. The sky outside was darkening with approaching storm clouds, and a crow flapped down and settled on the window sill.

"Why are there so many demmed crows here?" demanded Captain Bowen to Raphael McAlpine. "Do you know the townsfolk call this Crow House?"

"I engage in scientific pursuits, and I breed and collect crows to help me in my studies," he replied dismissively.

"That's an odd thing for a man to do," Captain Bowen exclaimed. "Is that your trade?"

"No, I am a merchant, as is Mr Samuel Butler here. His ship, the Louisiana, is currently moored off the coast." And he indicated the corpulent, red-faced man on his left. My scientific activities are for pleasure and I would be happy to take you all on a tour of my work room after dinner, if you wish."

"If you're going to show us crows breeding, I'd better drink plenty of your good wine and brandy to equip me for the experience," guffawed the Captain, his large bulk shaking.

His wife, Mrs Elizabeth Bowen, did not share his laughter, and she and her daughter, Georgiana, continued to fan themselves with dainty, lacquered, Chinese fans. Their frilled gowns revealed an expanse of white bosom, but the rest of their bodies were encased in padded underskirts and thick petticoats, caricaturing Nature's natural curves, and ensuring that they were almost suffocated in the August heat. Mrs McAlpine was similarly attired and her cheeks were a pale crimson, their underlying high colour somewhat concealed by a veneer of white. Her bouffant hair had also been white-powdered, and gold dust sprinkled over the whole confection. Mouse-skin eyebrows arched high above their normal position, and a heart-shaped beauty mark enhanced her chin, whose rolls of fat wobbled tremulously as she ate. Mr McAlpine sat next to her, his thin body wraith-like in comparison with the enormous girth of his wife, and he frequently cast admiring looks at his beloved, who rewarded him each time with a fluttering of her lashes.

"Are you suffering from the heat, Miss Isabella?" enquired Guillaume Thibaud.

"No, I enjoy it," she replied, and nervously fingered the malachite beads at her neck.

Samuel Butler suddenly stood up, swaying slightly on his feet. "A toast to President George Washington."

"A scoundrel!" shouted Captain Bowen. "A traitor! I will not give him a toast!"

"He is a patriot to the United States of America," cried Samuel Butler and raised his glass.

"I agree," remarked Guillaume Thibaud and quickly downed his glass of red wine, defiance in his eyes. Captain Bowen reared up, his fists clenched like a Cornish wrestler, and Georgiana squeaked like a mouse, and dropped her fan.

At that point, a clattering of hooves on the cobbles heralded the arrival of horsemen. Mrs and Mrs McAlpine glanced at each other with a satisfied air, and then at the empty chair by Samuel Butler.

. . . .

Outside in the courtyard Armand hastily dismounted and he and the crows on the window ledges stared at each other for a moment. Drops of rain fell from the overcast sky and wind quivered the swollen-trunked, dark green yew at the far end of the manor house. He glanced suspiciously at bushes growing by the wall, but only saw two innocuous lilac shrubs and an ash tree.

A hunch-backed old man held open the front door to him and he entered the darkness of the house, which smelled of roast meat and a faint hint of incense. The flames of two candles flickered in the draught of air, making shadows dance over the flagstones of a hall bare of furniture, and over a painting on the wall, partly obscured by the gloom. As he passed it, he involuntarily shuddered to see a three-headed woman with snakes writhing on her shoulders, and a cluster of blue flowers of wolfbane at her feet. He cursed softly in French and touched the cross in his pocket, before following the servant into the dining room.

He took a step back, just past the threshold, surprise catching him a second time, on being confronted by a large man dressed in the blue coat with white facings, and white breeches, of British naval uniform, whose bearing appeared aggressive. The elderly servant, however, ignored whatever was happening and tremulously announced, in a reedy voice, "His Grace, the Duke of Delacroix," whereupon the man calmed, bowed, and resumed his seat at the table.

"I am pleased you are able to join us, your Grace," said Raphael McAlpine. "May I present Captain and Mrs Bowen, their daughter Miss Georgiana, Mr Butler, Lieutenant Hargreaves, Mr Thibaud, who is a compatriot of yours, and, of course, my wife, Mrs McAlpine.

Armand's body stiffened with hostility as he regarded the white-powdered face and red-painted lips of Raphael McAlpine, and he attempted to suppress his annoyance at being in the house of a sympathiser to the Revolutionary cause and who, moreover, grew plants associated with the occult. He had not intended to come, but, at the last minute, had weakened at the thought of seeing Isabella, and at the fear she would not fulfil her promise to meet him on the beach. So, against his better judgement, he now found himself about to enjoy the hospitality of the McAlpines, and he bad-temperedly looked around at his fellow guests.

His spirits rose as he saw her. She was sitting quietly, in a cream dress, at the table, her eyes lowered. His distaste at being there faded away; he heard McAlpine's voice, as though from a distance, and recognised that her name had not been mentioned. Anger surged up in him; he gave an exaggerated bow in her direction, and was delighted to see her blush. A servant pulled out an ornate, gilt chair; he sat down heavily and immediately drank from the nearest glass of wine. His usual appetite had disappeared, and he drank a second glass, letting the wine's familiar warmth calm him and endeavouring to steal a glance at the beautiful woman who had enticed him into this unholy den.

51

"Captain Bowen was the master of the Queen Charlotte, Earl Howe's flagship at the battle of the Glorious First of June. It is a great honour to have you at my dining table, sir." Raphael McAlpine's nasal tones disturbed his thoughts.

"You British fought well. Your navy has my admiration," remarked Samuel Butler in a conciliatory tone.

"It was not really a victory," protested Guillaume Thibaud. "The grain convoy from America arrived safely in France to feed the starving population."

"The French fleet was mainly destroyed," responded Captain Bowen, his cheeks still beetroot-red.

"Are you a supporter of the Revolution?" Armand exclaimed to Guillaume Thibaud, his temper flaring up again. "Our people go in hunger because of it."

"I have been forced to leave France, but I feel pain for the suffering of my countrymen. People had no food when the king was in power, and that was one of the main reasons for the uprising," he replied.

"France needs to abandon its Revolution and stop the Terror. At least that villain, Robespierre, is dead." Armand retorted angrily.

"Yes, I agree with you there. Robespierre was a cruel and pitiless tyrant and I rejoice in his death."

"May those who executed Louis XVI die in Hell!" declared Armand.

Raphael McAlpine exchanged a glance with Guillaume Thibaud and the conversation turned to the excellence of the goose vell dish with its roasted skins, and the succulence of the squab pie.

The early evening sky blackened and servants scurried around the room, lighting more candles. Hail struck the windows, ricocheting from the cobbles, and Mrs McAlpine glittered eerily in the half-light, the gold dust from her head having found its way to her face and clothing. A curved seven-branched, silver candelabra adorned the middle of the dining table and Mrs Bowen exclaimed in admiration, "What a magnificent ornament. I should think it is very valuable."

"Yes, I believe it is," replied her host.

The hail rattled more fiercely against the panes and Raphael McAlpine remarked, "Not good for the wheat harvest. It will flatten it."

"Is that right?" said Armand.

"Have you crops to cut on your estate?" he asked.

"Yes, there are still two fields of wheat."

"I expect your Grace can easily bear the loss," he replied, a sly expression in his eyes. "But if you ever decide to sell, I hope you come to me first."

"I am not selling," said Armand brusquely, and, for the first time, his eye caught that of Isabella. She quickly looked away towards Georgiana, who was clutching at her tiny waist with one hand, and appeared to be gasping for air.

"Are you ill?" she enquired in alarm.

"No," Georgiana said, breathing heavily. "It will pass."

"My daughter has a delicate constitution and a very refined, English complexion," said Mrs Bowen, looking pointedly at Isabella's black hair and olive skin.

"Perhaps it is the food," remarked Armand, peering at the squab pie in the middle of the table, and went back to attacking a pheasant which had been intended for the whole party, but which he had commandeered onto his plate.

"Why have you an estate here in England, as well as in France?" enquired Mrs Bowen.

"My grandmother was English and the property comes from her side of the family," he replied.

"So you are not a penniless émigré," said Captain Bowen with interest. "And you are also a Duke. You will have the ladies flocking to you."

He shrugged his shoulders. "The estate is badly in need of improvement. However, I intend to take an interest in farming and make it profitable."

"Have you animals on the land?" asked Mrs Bowen.

"Yes, madam. There are pigs and sheep and red gems."

"Red gems?" she questioned, with even more interest on her face "You have precious stones on your estate?"

"I think he means Red Rubies," said Isabella, a hint of amusement in her voice. "The cattle are called Red Rubies."

Raphael McAlpine frowned at her intervention, but she ignored him and sat, quietly composed.

"Thank you, milady," said Armand, taking the opportunity to look directly at her. "I can see you are knowledgeable about farming."

"No, I am not at all," she replied.

"Well, you obviously know about Red Rubies," he said, and smiled at her.

She did not smile back, and touched the malachite beads, as though for reassurance.

"I am a former naval man myself," said Lieutenant Hargreaves, "and I'm now in charge of the Customs and Excise in North Devon, so I have very little experience of farming. However, if you want to find a market for your produce, the dockyard in Plymouth is the place to ask. Because of the war, the navy needs to provision the ships, and I expect the army also needs food."

"Thank you. I had not thought of that. I will make enquiries," Armand said.

"And very strangely," the Lieutenant continued, "I know, for a fact, that all the eggs bought by the dockyard come from North Devon, even although the route is not easy and the distance is great."

"My hens seem to spend much of their time up in trees," he replied. "I have no idea where they lay their eggs, but presumably they do."

"It is wonderful that you have decided to live here in Ilfracombe, your Grace," said Mrs Bowen. "Perhaps you would care to dine with us at the Castle."

"Yes," boomed Captain Bowen. "You would be delighted to be entertained by Georgiana on the spinet. She plays exquisitely."

"Thank you," said Armand. "It is a treat I will look forward to in the winter."

"Oh, before then, your Grace," he replied.

"Do you play the spinet at all, Miss Isabella?" said Lieutenant Downs.

"No, I am afraid not," she answered.

"What pursuits do you enjoy, milady?" asked Armand. "Do you like walking or even, perhaps, swimming in the sea as many ladies do?"

"No, I do not," she said firmly. "I spend most of my time at Dunscombe Manor."

He finished the pheasant and toyed with a slice of the squab pie, poking it with his fork. "What sort of bird is this?" he enquired.

"It is pigeon," replied his host.

"I thought perhaps it was crow," he muttered.

The meal drew to a close. The rain stopped and the sky lightened. A watery evening sun shone into the dining room, brightening the white panels of ceiling between the dark oak beams, and giving colour to a painting on the wall of ruined buildings in flames and ships being overwhelmed by enormous waves. The sun harshly revealed various aspects of the dining party; the white mask-like features of Mr and Mrs McAlpine and Mrs Bowen; a faint scar on Guillaume Thibaud's cheek; the grime around Samuel Butler's neck and underneath his finger nails; a louse running over the servant's wrist as he placed a dish on the table; and strands of bright red hair on Georgiana's head, where the cosmetic powder had worn off. The air was still. Then the brief lull in the storm ended. The wind roared down through the valley again, candle light replaced the sun, softening the faces of the guests. Lightning flashed towards the east, and thunder crashed overhead.

Raphael McAlpine rose to his feet. "Let us forget the tempest. It is an honour to welcome you all to my house and I would like to make an announcement. My ward, Isabella, has been betrothed to Captain James Petrie of Virginia and will shortly be married in a ceremony there."

"That is wonderful news," said Mrs Bowen to Isabella, with obvious pleasure and relief, her face in a rictus of a smile.

"Thank you," Isabella replied, flatly and without emotion.

"My congratulations also," said Lieutenant Hargreaves, disappointment in his voice.

Samuel Butler said nothing, his face impassive as he killed a fly on the table cloth with his bare hand, whilst Captain Bowen slapped Raphael McAlpine on the back. "Well done, man. You have married off all your wards. I have four daughters at home. You must tell me your secret."

"My sister, Antoinette, is in Virginia. When you go there, perhaps you would care to make her acquaintance," said Armand, raising his glass of brandy in Isabella's direction and downing it in one go. His words were polite, his face remained impassive, but the black despair he had experienced since the death of his parents was once more gnawing at him.

A loud knock at the front door interrupted the less-than-festive celebrations, and a servant escorted a short, swarthy man, his dark coat of the Customs and Excise, dripping wet, into the dining room.

"I am sorry to interrupt," he said, "but the talk at the taverns is of a smuggling run tonight at Heddon on Exmoor."

Lieutenant Hargreaves looked doubtfully at the rain beating against the windows.

"Well, they've picked a poor night for it," he said dourly. "Is the cutter ready at the harbour?"

"Yes, it is," replied the officer.

"Well, I must attend to the tax-dodging thieves, I suppose," he said reluctantly, and looked at Captain Bowen. "Perhaps I can call on Miss Georgiana?"

Mrs Bowen mumbled a response and her husband did not reply. Lieutenant Hargreaves bowed to the guests and made a second, very low, bow to Georgiana.

"I would like to see your scientific work another time," he remarked to Raphael McAlpine.

"Certainly, my dear sir. I understand that duty calls, and I hope you catch the scoundrels," his host replied.

Lieutenant Hargreaves left the room with his fellow Customs and Excise officer, the drumming rain obscuring the noise of their horses galloping away up the hill, and the dinner party resumed.

Armand saw Isabella sit very still on her chair, the hum of conversation flowing around her. She reached out to clasp the base of her wine glass, but her hand clumsily shook, red tears of wine resembling blood, trickled down onto the white, damask cloth, and she replaced the glass on the table and clenched her hands together.

She caught his eye and, in that moment, he realised her extreme distress. He looked at her, then turned quickly towards Raphael McAlpine. "You have a very fine brandy here."

"Yes, importing wine and spirits is one of my business pursuits," he replied.

"Not at Heddon, I hope," said Armand sarcastically.

"No, you can rest assured. The brandy you are drinking has never been smuggled in at Heddon, or anywhere near there. Now, if the ladies would like to retire to the drawing room, I would be pleased to give a guided tour of my work room."

12

The crows stared malevolently from their aviary constructed along one side of the room. The evening sky was temptingly in their sight, but they were constrained to perch on a branch denuded of leaves, and flap their wings desperately in a caged space too small to adequately fly.

"A crow prison in Crow House," remarked Armand.

"Your father understood the value of scientific study," Raphael McAlpine said in a critical tone. "His laboratory is very well equipped."

"You have visited it, have you?" he asked in surprise.

"Some time ago," his host replied vaguely. "We both shared the same interest in discovering the components of air. It is a great sadness that Antoine Lavoisier is no longer with us. However, Joseph Priestly and Humphrey Davey are not at risk of being guillotined like our fellow scientists across the channel, and they are making important discoveries."

"Lavoisier evidently blinked his eyes fifteen times after his head had been cut off," said Guillaume Thibaud. "He asked his assistant to record it. You have to admire his scientific spirit in the circumstances, even if he was a tax gatherer and deserved to die."

"He did not deserve to die. None of these victims deserved to die. You are an imposter, sir. You are no true friend of France," declared Armand bitterly.

"You are mistaken," said Guillaume Thibaud. "I believe that France had to change, which is what your relation Gilbert de Lafayette thinks. However, I do not agree with the excesses of the Revolution and the Terror which has accompanied it. I believe in a constitutional monarchy. I am more a friend of France than you are."

"Gentlemen. Please have your dispute somewhere other than my house," intervened Raphael McAlpine.

Armand glared at Guillaume Thibaud in anger and then glanced at the mandrake roots hanging on a cord at the end of the room and at vials of different herbs and mixtures in a row on a dresser.

"Do you grow these?" he asked Raphael McAlpine. "It is more like a witch's kitchen here than a scientific laboratory."

"Yes, I grow them. Esther Cerfbeer has advised me on their preparation and use and I have found her knowledge invaluable. It is only fools and ignorant people who do not understand the wisdom it has taken centuries to obtain."

"What do you do with the crows?" asked Captain Bowen.

"I breed them and I am also training them in a variety of ways, but my work is still in its early stages, so I am unable to show you," he replied, with an air of pride, a tic of his eyelid, however, making him blink repeatedly.

Armand looked around the room suspiciously. He stared at the cages and absentmindedly ran his hand over the ornate, horse's head clasp of one of the doors.

"They remind me of something," he remarked.

"Well, I think that is enough for today, gentlemen," said Raphael McAlpine abruptly. "Shall we return to the dining room for some serious toasting, now that the ladies are safely out of the way?" and he quickly shepherded everyone out of his work room and back down the stairs.

"The rain is less heavy, so I will forgo the toasting and take my leave," said Armand. "I only have my Alsatian men with me. We don't know the road and it is dark."

"There's a full moon tonight," his host said. "If the storm dies down you will be able to find your way easily."

"I thought that smugglers never chose a night with a full moon," he commented. "It is rather surprising that they have picked tonight."

"Perhaps they have not," said Raphael McAlpine. "Perhaps Lieutenant Hargreaves will discover he's on a wild goose chase."

Armand looked at him thoughtfully. "Why would that be?"

"Who is to say," he replied. "I am just a simple merchant from Dundee. I know nothing of evil goings-on in this wild county of Devon. I gather there even used to be cannibals who lived at Clovelly."

"Luckily Lieutenant Hargreaves has arrived to sort out this smuggling problem," said Captain Bowen. "He's got a fearsome reputation. He'll soon put paid to it. There are also these disappearances of young women which are concerning the authorities. There's evil afoot and it has to be rooted out."

"Hear, hear, sir! We must protect our ladies, as we said earlier," said Raphael McAlpine.

"It is not just one woman who has disappeared then?" questioned Armand. "There are others."

"Young girls can be headstrong and foolish and run away from home," replied Raphael McAlpine. "However, to talk of a different matter, it has been a pleasure to have you both at my table this evening and I would like to invite you to a different sort of soirée, which is of a more robust nature than our genteel affair tonight. I can promise you, sirs, you will not be disappointed."

"I'm off to join my ship shortly, so I'm afraid I will be unable to participate," replied Captain Bowen.

"Oh, is that so?" said Raphael McAlpine. "You will not be with us in the locality?"

"No," said the Captain. "I might be interested at another time, though."

"And what about you, your Grace? Would you like to join our revelry?" he enquired.

"No, thank you," replied Armand quickly. "Tonight has been a delight enough. Goodnight gentlemen. I will be interested to know what Lieutenant Hargreaves finds at Heddon."

He bowed to his host, whose eyelid had once more taken on a life of its own and was rapidly blinking and winking. He did not acknowledge Guillaume Thibaud at all and as he turned to go, beyond a door on the opposite side of the hall came the shrill tones of Mrs McAlpine.

"And I resemble Hecate so closely Mr McAlpine says we could be sisters."

Mrs Bowen's voice was dulcet in response.

"Really? I have never heard of such a lady."

"I would like to thank my hostess for the evening," requested Armand.

"Certainly," replied Raphael McAlpine, and flung open the door to reveal Mrs McAlpine, Mrs Bowen and Georgiana, seated by an unlit hearth, their conversation halting at the appearance of the men.

"Good night," said Armand, bowing low. "Thank you for the enchanting dinner. I have rarely tasted such delicacies. And Miss Isabella? I am grateful for her intervention about the Red Rubies."

"She has gone to her room, your Grace," declared Mrs McAlpine flintily.

He bowed again, and went out into the rain-drenched courtyard, where Hans and Dietrich were already mounted and waiting for him, having spent an enjoyable evening with the servants and the local cider. He stood on the cobbles and glanced through the downpour at an upstairs window where a candle flickered, its yellow glow illuminating the distinctive shape of Isabella. He gazed at her for a second. Then he swiftly mounted his horse and cantered through the courtyard entrance and up the narrow lane of the hill, which was sheltered from the storm by the trees. However, when he and his men reached the steep descent by the coast, the full force of the wind suddenly blasted at them, howling about their ears and driving the rain into their clothes and faces.

A man loomed out of the darkness, carrying a lantern. He was followed by others, some with lanterns, some pushing carts. People were running down towards the sea, and they were caught up in a moving stream of humanity flowing desperately over the rough ground.

"What's happening?" shouted Armand.

"A ship's being wrecked on the rocks at Rapparee," came the reply.

The wind shrieked, buffeting the hundreds of men and women now converging on the cove at the foot of the hill, and Armand stopped to survey the scene from the cliff edge.

"Look, there it is!" exclaimed Dietrich. "It's caught on that reef."

In the darkness was the outline of a three-masted ship wallowing in the heavy seas, its back broken by waves pounding it on to the rocks. Men were struggling to launch a boat, but the surf was so strong, it kept being flung back on to the shingle, battering the rescuers. One man lost his footing and was sucked into the surging water and only stopped from being carried away by the brave action of other rescuers who dashed into the waves, risking their lives as they grabbed him.

Armand and his men cautiously made their way down a rocky path to the beach, the wind lashing them, wailing eerily as they neared the sea. It was strangely reminiscent of human voices, and Hans shouted, "There are people on board, below decks. They are calling out."

The awful truth dawned on them. "There are hundreds in there!" Dietrich cried. "There are hundreds trapped!"

At that moment, the side of the ship broke in two, the masts snapped and crashed with the rigging onto the deck. Figures appeared in the breach and jumped into the surging sea. Some were swept below the surface, others were bobbing up and down like helpless corks in a maelstrom, dragged by the waves towards the shore.

Men ran into the breakers and tried to reach the drowning captives, and Armand, Hans and Dietrich also urged their horses forward into the swell. Armand was suddenly knocked off his saddle by a wave and half-fell into the water, but managed to pull himself up by the reins.

A figure surfaced directly in front of them, macabrely cart-wheeling like a jester, and making the horses whinny in fright. Dietrich reached out and grabbed a foot and hauled the body on to his horse. They struggled back through the waves to the beach and he let the corpse slump onto the shingle, where it lay motionless, blood and vomit trickling from the mouth.

"It's a woman. She's dead," he shouted.

Armand dismounted and covered her nakedness with his coat, just as the ship gave a ghastly groan, as though it was alive. It lurched off the rocks, the waters closing over it, and, in a few seconds, it had disappeared. The wind shrieked like a banshee, and the crowd on the beach fell silent. The woman was bundled onto a handcart and taken to the top of the beach, where she was joined by the bodies of two men, also naked, and also black.

Armand wetly clambered onto his horse and he, Hans and Dietrich slowly made their way back up the cliff, hampered by hordes of people rushing down.

13

Bess flinched as the sailor pushed her with his cutlass. He motioned towards the open door of the cabin.

"Oot, lassie, git oot wi ye!" he ordered.

She stumbled towards the corridor and struggled up the rickety galley steps towards the deck. She blinked as she came out into the sun and stood trembling, her clothes soiled, her white-blonde hair falling lankly onto her shoulders.

She looked curiously at her fellow prisoner who was standing by the rail of the ship. Jacob Goldstein was similarly dirty; his long black coat was torn, and his shirt was smeared with dried blood, as it had been on the day of his capture. He was tall and very thin and at least a head taller than any of the sailors. He looked back at her with hazel eyes, a faint glimmer of a smile crossing his gaunt, bearded face.

"We've talked a lot," he muttered. "It's a pleasure to actually see you, even under these terrible circumstances." He shuffled his feet and tried to reach out to touch her arm, but was prevented by the shackles on his wrists and ankles.

The ship was moored near to a white sandy beach, which curved between two rocky headlands. A granite cross dwarfed the low cliff on which it had been erected, but there were no houses, or any sign of human activity, except that of the religious monument.

Bess sighed as she surveyed the scene.

"Where are we?" she asked Jacob.

"I think we're in Brittany, in the west of France. It is famous for crosses like that," he replied, nodding his head towards it.

The ship had been becalmed since early morning. The sails were hanging limply from the masts, the air was still, and the sea was shimmering in the sun. A gig was drawn up on the beach, next to a stream, and sailors were filling the casks with water.

"It is good to breathe fresh air again," said Bess.

"Perhaps," agreed Jacob, glancing unhappily both at the cliffs and at the horizon. "I think we've been brought on deck for a purpose."

A man in the crow's nest suddenly shouted, "There!"

Bess and Jacob peered in the direction of his outstretched arm, but the sea appeared bare.

"There's no wind," she exclaimed. "There can't be any ship coming."

Jacob Goldstein said nothing, the expression on his face even more sombre than before.

"Be brave," he said quietly. "Be brave, my dear."

"What is it?" she asked in alarm. "What do you think is happening?"

Even as she spoke, a black speck was visible on the horizon. A black speck which was very rapidly becoming bigger.

"What's that?" she exclaimed. "What sort of ship is that? There's no wind. We are becalmed. How can it sail so fast?"

It's not sailing," muttered Jacob. "It's being rowed."

"Rowed!" exclaimed Bess. "It looks like a large boat. How can it be rowed?"

"I have seen one before, off the coast of Sardinia," said Jacob. "They are very fast."

He looked at her, his eyes moist with tears.

"I am worth nothing for ransom money," he continued. "I am only a diamond cutter."

"What do you mean? I am just a dairy maid. I am also worth nothing as a ransom," she exclaimed.

"You will survive," he said. "Be brave and you will survive. I think that for you there is no ransom. I think that you are wanted for

64

something else….." His voice trailed away as he gazed at her beautiful face with her blue eyes and very fair hair.

"What do you mean?" she exclaimed in fright.

"But for me there will only be slavery and the galleys," he continued. "And as I am a Jew, my fate will probably be even worse than that."

The sailors' eyes were on the approaching vessel and he quickly shuffled in his leg irons to the side of the ship. He threw himself into the turquoise sea with an almighty groan and sank straight down through the water, weighted by his chains. A sailor grabbed Bess to stop her doing the same, whilst two others jumped overboard into the clear water where his body could be seen on the sea bed. The sailors reached him and hauled him to the surface as he kicked and shouted to make them let go. Other sailors pulled him back onto the deck where he lay, choking and vomiting from the seawater he had swallowed.

Bess pushed and pummelled the sailor holding her, with her fists, trying to free herself to go and help Jacob; but the sailor swung her up by her wrists, like a marionette, and laughed in her face.

She stared hopelessly, tears pouring down her cheeks, at the fast-approaching vessel which had oars projecting from its sides, all beating the sea in unison. Maroon sails were unfurled from the masts, whose foremast raked forward, and on which hung an unfamiliar flag. Sailors were standing on the deck, wearing very brightly coloured clothes. Some wore turbans, and all had baggy trousers. A large man was standing alone on the prow, his clothes decorated with silver and gold, glittering in the sun. His beard was dyed red, his head was turbaned, and he was holding a curved scimitar.

14

The path was narrow and so steep that the high hedges did not prevent a view of Great and Little Hangman on the next part of the coast. At the bottom of the hill the land became a common of gorse and furze, traversed by a swollen stream tumbling down into a cove. The horses cantered across the sand, past a rocky headland, before splashing through a second stream spilling out over a wide shingle beach. Women were busily washing garments on steps leading down to the mud-brown water, and they all stopped to stare at the three horsemen.

"I should think the clothes are dirtier after being washed there than before," remarked Dietrich.

The tide was low, fishing boats lay marooned on their sides, and nets were hanging from poles to dry. A smell of fish tainted the air, and decaying parts of lobsters and crabs littered the sand above a high water line of broken branches, twigs and dried black seaweed. A fisherman mending a net raised a surly face to them.

"I am looking for Rose Cottage," said Armand. "Do you know where it is?"

The man scowled and pointed up the valley. "Pack of Cards," he grunted.

"Thank you," said Armand and gave him a coin.

The fisherman took it, spat on the ground, and went back to his net.

The cottages by the sea were built of sturdy grey cob, but as they proceeded along the straggling village, the dwellings appeared poor and mean; black smoke from lime kilns drifting low over crumbling walls and thatched roofs, which had often caved in. People watched them as they passed, and ragged urchins with bare feet ran alongside, occasionally throwing lumps of dried manure at the horses. Patches of ground were growing dark green hemp, and chickens, pigs and sheep roamed freely, scuttling under the horses' hooves, occasionally causing them to rear up.

"I think that is what the man was talking about," said Armand, as they reached a tall building, strangely resembling a house of cards. "That might be Rose Cottage next to it."

And he pointed to a cob-walled house, whose sides and thatched roof were resplendent with rose and jasmine. Cream honeysuckle flowers twined through the wood trellis of a porch; their scent, and that of the roses, mingling with the pungent odour of manure from the street. He dismounted, and as he walked up the garden path, Henriette, the Marquise de Landenberg, opened the cottage door. She smiled at him, the curls of her brown hair framing her pale face. Her simple green gown was high-waisted, a fichu of lace at its bosom, and a blue-eyed, fair-haired young boy in a blue shift dress, clung to her skirt, his thumb in his mouth.

She greeted Armand with a curtsey. "Please come into our home. It is not quite a chateau," she said, laughing, "but at least we have our heads and our children."

A knot of people had gathered at the corner of the street and were watching them sullenly. "Frenchies! Dirty Frenchies!" called out a plump woman, carrying a basket of mackerel, and wearing an apron, which had once been white, but was now nearer black than any other hue.

"I think she's washed that apron in the stream," said Dietrich. However, he kept his hands from his weapons, as did Hans, not wishing to provoke the crowd.

Henriette ignored the jeers and ushered Armand into a low-ceilinged, sparsely furnished room where her husband, Charles, Marquis de Landenberg, was sitting on a chair, his leg bandaged.

"Please excuse me," he said, struggling to his feet, "but I fell off a wall when I was building a pigsty."

"Really," said Armand. "You were building a pigsty?"

"Yes, bit of a surprise, I know. I have spent a life at the gaming table and drinking, and now I am growing vegetables and rearing animals." He grinned and ran his fingers through his dark hair.

His wife placed glasses on the wooden table and poured out wine.

"We have no servants," she said apologetically.

"I hope I am not causing trouble to you by coming here," replied Armand. "The villagers seem hostile."

"They are all afraid of an invasion," said Charles. "They see spies and French soldiers round every corner. However, most people have been very kind to us."

As he spoke, the door opened at the back of the house. Neat rows of cabbages and gnarled trunks of apple trees were revealed, as well as the stocky figure of Guillaume Thibaud, who walked in, carrying two eggs in his hands.

"We meet again," he remarked to Armand. "However, I believe I have the advantage, as I knew of your intended visit."

"Guillaume helps us," replied Henriette de Landenberg. "Without his advice we would have found it difficult, if not impossible. We only knew a life of luxury. We had no idea how ordinary people lived."

"I am surprised to see you here," said Armand to him. "Your words yesterday would suggest you are not on the side of the aristocracy or interested in any revolt."

"You are right on one point. I think an uprising in the Vendée is a foolish venture. The Chouans will also be defeated. If you join in you will just be throwing away your lives. I want an end to the bloodshed, an end to the Terror. Not to have more fighting. The ideals of the Revolution are very good, but they have been twisted by evil. However, I have no quarrel with decent people who have suffered as much as I have."

"You do not convince me you are not a spy," declared Armand. "I have some sympathy with the views of the Combe Martin inhabitants."

"I am not a spy," he replied forcefully, "and I resent what you say. I fought with your relation, Lafayette, at Brandy Wine in the American War of Independence and I share his views on the equality of man.

68

The situation is not just one colour as you portray it. There are many shades of views on the Revolution. You have to realise that the old way of life is ended. It was cruel and unfair. The question is, what is going to replace it?"

"You fought with Gilbert?" said Armand.

"Yes, much has happened since then and now. France is struggling to follow America's lead, and, I fear, has somewhat strayed from the true path."

"I agree with many of his views on equality," declared Armand. "But France needs a strong monarchy."

"There we must differ. I believe we should have a monarchy, but a constitutional one."

Henriette looked at Armand. "My ideas have changed since I left France, and although I am delighted to see you, I agree with Guillaume and do not want my husband to go to the Vendée, where he will perhaps be killed. I have seen so much suffering. My parents and sisters have all been executed. I just want to live a simple life, and watch my children grow up."

"Well said," declared Guillaume Thibaud. "I would like to stay longer and debate with you, but I must go now. I have some work to finish with Raphael McAlpine."

"What is your business with him?" asked Armand.

"I help him sometimes with his wine imports," he replied.

"Do you know that the Louisiana sank off Ilfracombe yesterday?" said Armand. I believe that was the name of Samuel Butler's ship."

"Yes, it was his ship," he agreed.

"He's a slaver," said Armand. "Hundreds of people died, imprisoned below decks. We were there on the beach when it happened."

"The United States has just passed the Slave Trade Act to ban American citizens from equipping ships for slave trafficking, and to prohibit the transport of slaves to foreign shores, so I think his business will now be very restricted," he replied.

"Might the law affect your plantation?" asked Charles.

"I have no idea about slaves on the estate," said Armand. "I have never been to Virginia, but I know that my father disagreed strongly with the practice."

"Thomas Jefferson thinks that all men are fair and equal. However, he still has slaves on his plantation at Monticello," declared Guillaume

Thibaud. "So I think you will find that your land is worked by slaves. Good day, sir. I am sure we will meet again."

Armand shrugged, and Guillaume Thibaud left, escorted out of the cottage and garden by Henriette.

"Just in case," she said. "The boys won't attack you with stones and horse dung if I am there. I give them apples."

"Why are you living in Combe Martin?" Armand asked Charles. "Would you not be better in London, or a large city, where there would be other émigrés?"

"No, it is much cheaper to live here. We managed to escape with some money and we use that, as well as grow crops and rear animals. There are actually a large number of French refugees here in Devon, so we sometimes meet. And there will be a gathering in Exeter on Friday in two weeks' time, at twelve o'clock, at Mol's Coffee House in the Cathedral Close. It is not a social occasion, it is to discuss the possibility of going to fight in France. I can't go because of my leg, but perhaps you might like to."

"Yes, I would," said Armand as he walked over to the back window and looked out at the garden.

"Be careful you don't step on Marie-Thérèse," warned Charles.

Armand glanced down, and saw with surprise, that at his feet, in a drawer lined with muslin, lay a new-born child.

"Edouard is my son and heir," said Charles, very proudly indicating the little boy. "Marie-Thérèse is our daughter. She is only two weeks' old."

Armand looked sadly at the tiny baby in its drawer, and at the bare, white walls of the cottage, adorned with a single crucifix.

"She is not yet baptised," said Charles. "There is no priest here."

"I have a chapel at Wildercombe House," he replied. "And I am trying to obtain a priest as it is no longer against the law to hold a Catholic service in England. I haven't yet managed to find one, but when I do, perhaps you would care to have a baptism there?"

"Thank you," said Charles gratefully, as Henriette returned with a strongly smelling mackerel, which she placed on the table.

"I thought it best to buy something from Mrs Venn," she declared, pulling a face. "Now let me show you our vegetable garden. We have also bought some strips of land at the end of the village and Charles has planted hemp, which evidently does well here, and we grow potatoes and cabbages."

She opened the back door and he followed her outside. A vine trailed up the cottage wall, almost to the bristle edges of the thatched roof. Black grapes hung in clusters and he gazed at them, suddenly recalling the heat of Alsace, the Vosges mountains, and storks flying across a blue sky.

"A vine in North Devon. I would have thought that impossible," he said, concentrating his thoughts on the present.

"Why?" said Henriette. "It is warmer here than Alsace in winter, although not so hot in the summer."

"Can I take a cutting?" he asked.

"Yes, of course."

He took out his knife and spliced a branch from the stem. "I will plant it in the greenhouse. I can see it has grown well, but I am not so sure about Ilfracombe. I believe Combe Martin is reputed to have a particularly good climate, even if it is on the edge of the moor, and has a lot of lime kilns which cause smoke."

He placed the cutting in his pocket and looked round the garden, which sloped down to a stream at the bottom of the valley; wizened apple trees were giving shade from the sun, rows of potatoes and cabbages were flourishing in the brown soil and chickens were scratching at the ground, as they ran in and out of a small shed.

"Charles has planted everything," said Henriette. "But he would not have known what to do without Guillaume. He told us to build a little house for the hens and since then they have laid many eggs."

"I am very fortunate to have an estate. However, it is hardly producing anything and if I cannot make it profitable I might be forced to sell. The plantation in Virginia is in the same financial position, and my sister, Antoinette, has sailed there to see what can be done."

"Why don't you ask Guillaume for advice?" she suggested.

"No," he said firmly. "No."

Seagulls screamed above the wooded hillside opposite. A cloud went across the sun and Henriette shuddered.

"Our lives have been overturned. Our parents have all been killed. Charles and I are so pleased to see you, even although it awakens old memories. Let us have another glass of wine and forget that we are in a foreign country, a long way from home and from our chateaux."

The faint cry of a baby sounded from inside the cottage and she smiled. "Come and let me introduce you to Marie-Thérèse."

15

The sea was flat; a limpid blue irregularly shaded by clouds and currents; a pallor at its edge, not of waves, but of transparent, gelatinous masses of moon jellyfish. The tide had ebbed, stranding hundreds on the beach, and Armand wandered along, occasionally using broken spars or struts from debris caught up in seaweed blackly contouring the sand, to nudge the dying creatures back into the water.

He was early. The sun was not yet high in the sky. He was dressed impeccably, a ruffled, white silk shirt and cravat, a purple coat braided with gold on the lapels and cuffs, and very polished leather boots.

One giant jellyfish had flipped over, exposing its underside, where four pink and blue horseshoe shapes were fringed by short tentacles; and he squatted down to scrutinise it more closely. A seagull joined him, but after tentative stabs with its beak, it retreated to smash a barnacle against a stone. Jellyfish lay everywhere, some caught in rock crevices, others fortunate to be trapped in pools. He continued across the beach, crossing the reefs at the far side of the cove, stopping to rummage in clumps of bladderwrack, infested by jumping sand hoppers, or to turn over stones and watch crabs scuttle away. He picked up cream conch shells, placing them in his pocket, and resumed his meanderings across the parallel lines of rocks.

The tide was unusually far out, exposing ancient tree stumps and a part of the cliff that was generally inaccessible. Towards its base, a cave gaped invitingly and he stepped inside, his booted feet sinking into soft wet sand. Water was trickling down one side into a pool where a single jellyfish floated; the air was chill and smelled of the sea. He wandered into the gloomy depths of the cavern, where beyond the high tide mark on the rock above him, the cave extended much further into the hillside.

He shinned up the flaking shale and reached a platform from which several tunnels spread out in different directions. He heaved himself on to the floor of this second chamber and looked curiously about him, noticing that the rock had been hewn out and pick marks were still evident in places. A piece of wood was jutting from a cranny and he pulled at it; it became dislodged and fell with a crash, covering him with stones and sand.

He ruefully brushed his coat with his hands before examining the barnacle-encrusted, rotting plank, which had the letters 'SAN' painted on one side. It disintegrated in his hands, the wood crumbling to the floor, leaving only a few shards held together by molluscs and seaweed. He blindly reached up into the crevice again and his hands closed around another wooden object. He pulled it free and caught a wooden doll as it tumbled from its hiding place. He glanced briefly at it, then thrust it in his pocket and started to clamber back down the rock. His boot slipped on a growth of slimy seaweed and he fell headlong onto the ground, tearing his coat. He picked himself up, grimacing as he looked at his clothes, which were now not in quite the same condition as earlier in the day. He retraced his footsteps through the lower part of the cavern, passed the solitary jellyfish, and emerged into the light of the outside air.

The sun was much higher in the sky. He cursed softly to himself and hurriedly returned over the reefs to the crescent of silver sand, where Isabella was already standing in the shade of a lilac tree, at the foot of the path. She looked severely at him as he approached; his spirits sank, and the smile on his face faded. She was dressed in the same plum-coloured riding habit she had worn on the day of the riot and her expression was not dissimilar to that she had shown him then.

"I am sorry I am late. It is unforgiveable of me. I was exploring a cave on the far side of the cove, where there was a hole, high up in the cliff, from which tunnels cut into the hillside, and I forgot the time."

"I can see you have been exploring," she remarked, repeating his word, and looking at his torn coat and dishevelled appearance.

"Perhaps Captain Petrie will be more to your taste," he said, shrugging his shoulders.

"Don't mock me, sir. You know I have no idea what he is like, or how he is dressed. He is being forced on me and I have to accept him. You are a Duke, and even although you have lost your chateau, you will marry someone of the same social standing as yourself. You will have your pick of marriageable ladies," she continued bluntly.

He stood close to her, enjoying the sensation of seeing the softness of her skin and her gleaming, long black hair. His world had shrunk to this small patch of shingle by the lilac tree and he looked at her face and smiled happily, uncaring about the anger in her eyes. He listened politely to her words and watched a butterfly flutter from a mauve bloom and settle on the sleeve of her jacket.

"Why are you trifling with me, a poor orphan who has no choice in the matter, and who is fortunate that her guardian has kindly found someone for her to marry?"

"I wanted to see you again," he replied.

"I am in your debt. You saved my life, and that is why I agreed to meet you today. However, I do not wish my reputation ruined, or I will never find a suitor. I will have to remain with the McAlpines, or perhaps even worse, will be thrown out onto the street." She looked at him angrily.

"My father loved my mother from the day he first saw her here in Ilfracombe. Her social status was not important to him." He was finding it difficult to speak; his voice was taut with emotion. "They were killed as we were about to leave our chateau near Strasbourg."

Her expression softened. "I don't know what it is to lose a parent you love. I have never known my father or mother or anything about them. I am sorry for your loss. It must be very hard for you."

"Yes," he said bitterly. Sadness suddenly overwhelmed him. For the first time since his flight from Alsace, he was unable to curb his grief. He sat down on the stony soil, put his head in his hands and sobbed.

He felt her kneel next to him and place her hand on his shoulder. His tears stopped, as quickly as they had started, and he looked at her with reddened eyes, smelling her rose perfume and seeing the delicate sweep of her lashes. She scrambled to her feet and he realised that, yet again, she had realised his desire.

He stood up slowly. "Please excuse me. I had no idea I would not only present myself in clothes that are dirty and torn, but that I would also make a fool of myself."

"You have not done so now. At least you knew your beloved parents. You saved my life and I will remain eternally grateful," her voice was low, reminding him of the softness of velvet.

"Will you walk with me?" he asked, fearing her response.

"I have met you here, which is what you made me promise. I think that is enough," she said.

"A life saved surely warrants more than just a few minutes," he declared in exasperation.

She looked at him sternly. "Yes, that is true. However, I must say again that I do not wish my reputation to be ruined. It was very wrong of you to insist on meeting me here alone and therefore I have a chaperone."

"Where is your chaperone?" he enquired, looking round at the empty beach.

She pointed to the grass at the top of the cliff where the black-robed figure of Esther Cerfbeer could be seen, sitting facing the sea.

"The witch. You've brought the witch," he said.

"Women and children have been burned to death for that accusation," she retorted. "Be careful what you say, even in these times. I don't want Esther hurt."

"Well, since etiquette is being somewhat observed, shall we go to the sea?" he asked cheerfully.

"Yes, I would like that," she replied, and immediately set off across the beach. He caught her up and they walked together, quickening their steps as they came to the swarm of jellyfish.

"What has happened? Why have they all been washed up like this?" she asked. "In the Bible there are plagues of locusts. Is it some sort of plague like that?"

"No, it's not a plague," he said. "Perhaps the storm has brought them in."

She stood for a moment, indecision on her face, then curiosity and compassion clearly overcame her wish to remain dignified, and she bent down, picked up a stick and tried to lever a jellyfish into the water. It slithered off the wood and she shrieked.

"At least it's not dead," she said, laughing.

"Be careful you don't touch the tentacles," he told her. "They might sting."

He used his booted foot to manoeuver a jellyfish back into the sea, where it pulsated strangely, floating off, at the mercy of the tide, its transparent bell-like body appearing oddly alien in its own natural habitat.

"Look at this," he said, upending another, and pointing out the colourful horseshoe markings.

"I've never seen these animals before," she remarked. "I've seen many strange creatures here, but never ones of jelly."

She stopped to investigate a rock pool and he showed her a flower with undulating tentacles. "It's a sea anemone. If you prod it, it closes up." He poked it with a pebble, whereupon it retracted itself and metamorphosed into a drab, brown blob.

"You are French, but you also speak English. Why is that?" she asked.

"My mother spoke English. So I speak French, Alsatian and English, which is lucky for my present situation."

"I only know English," she said.

He looked at her as she spoke, and, for the first time, realised that she might speak English, but her olive skin and black hair suggested she was of foreign descent.

"How did you get here?" he asked. "Did you walk? If so we can ride back together like we did the other day."

"I came on horseback and I can return alone," she said. "Mr and Mrs McAlpine have gone to London with Mr Butler because his ship has sunk. Many people drowned, I think. Mrs Gubb, the cook, has been telling me about it."

"Yes, that's right. I was at Rapparee cove with Hans and Dietrich. We came across it when we were returning from the dinner. It was a terrible sight."

"The McAlpines often go away and when they are, I do what I want. The servants never say anything as I grew up in the kitchen with them.

It is only in recent years that I have been given a bedchamber and treated as Mr McAlpine's ward," she remarked.

"And he has brought up other girls?" he queried. "It's surprising. It seems out-of-character."

"They were only at Dunscombe Manor for a short time, whereas I have lived there all my life. It was much better for me before he married Mrs McAlpine as he was rarely at home. Now I am often beaten because they say I am wicked and ill-behaved."

"How dare he! I detest the man," he exclaimed. "It is not just his political views, his crows and his plants for the occult. There is something which seems very unpleasant about him and his wife."

"I am here today secretly and against their wishes, as you know very well, so perhaps there is some truth in what they say," she replied regretfully."

The afternoon grew hazy. The sun retreated behind wisps of clouds and the sea began to flow rapidly into the cove, quivering the beached jellyfish and floating several.

"I must go. I had not intended to be here so long," she said.

He stuck his hands into his bulging pockets and retrieved the conch shells.

"These are for you. I found them earlier. I think they come from a far-off, hot country. I know it is not a shell bracelet, but I will do better next time."

"I am afraid there will not be a next time" she said firmly. "You know very well it is not suitable. Thank you for the shells and for the afternoon. I wish I could also give you a present, but I have nothing."

"I want to see you again," he told her. "I will see you again."

She looked at him, but did not reply. She glanced at his coat and pointed to a wooden arm which was sticking out.

"What is that?" she asked curiously.

He glanced down. "Oh, it's nothing. It was by a ship's plank that I found in the cave. It was near the second cave high up inside the rock. I had forgotten it. It's just a piece of rubbish." He removed the doll from his pocket and offered it to her.

She looked at it for a moment. Then, very slowly, she took it from him and gently caressed it, running her finger over its battered face and down the side of its one-legged body.

"Shall we go back to the jellyfish?" he asked.

"No!" she murmured. "No!" Her eyes glazed and her face paled.

"What's the matter?" he asked in alarm.

"Men," she muttered in distress. "There were men. They were shouting. And there were waves. And a woman in a silk dress. And the doll. My doll. It had a gold necklace and earrings....the sea was so cold, the sand was red..."

"Calm," he said, and placed his arm around her. "Calm."

"No!" she exclaimed, and moved sharply away from him. "I think the doll is mine."

"Well, it certainly is. It is rather a battered object, but if you want it, I am very happy to give it to you," he declared.

"No, I mean I think I've seen it before, a long time ago. I believe there was a storm. I was on a ship which was wrecked." She glanced wildly about her.

"You're probably just thinking of the Louisiana the other day. It was awful. It's preyed on your imagination."

"I have no idea," she replied, more calmly. "It seemed so real a few minutes ago, but now it's fading and I can't properly recall anything."

"I want to see you again," he said, not wishing to continue the conversation about the doll. "I don't care how many chaperones you bring. I want to see you." He grabbed her arm. "Do you understand? I am in earnest."

"I must do what the McAlpines want. I owe a debt to them and I think that Captain Petrie is giving them money for my marriage. And there is also something else," she muttered.

"Go on. Tell me," he said, as she hesitated.

"I have had two other suitors."

"So what? That does not matter to me?" He shrugged.

"They died. They were both killed," she said.

"Killed?" he queried.

"Yes. Daniel was found dead at Crewkerne Cave, and Thomas in the Wilder near the Strand at the harbour."

"You were unfortunate. Although it is perhaps fortunate for me," he replied.

"They were killed in a horrible way. They had cuts all over their bodies, and their eyes were removed," she said reprovingly, at his flippant tone.

"So the same person murdered them both," he remarked.

"Well, possibly. I had not thought of that," she said.

"And does anyone know who did it?" he asked.

"Mrs McAlpine says it's my fault. She says that I bring a curse," she murmured.

"Sacré Bleu!" he exclaimed, reverting to French. "Your head often seems filled with superstitious rubbish, ma belle. Their deaths might be connected to you somehow, but they have certainly not happened because you have a curse."

"And that is also one of the reasons why I do not want to see you. If two men have died on account of me, I cannot allow it to happen again," she said.

"You say that their eyes were removed?" he questioned.

"Yes," she said, blinking back her tears.

"That's very odd," he remarked. "Extremely bizarre. England often seems a very strange country to me."

He glanced towards the grass above the foot path. "Your chaperone has disappeared. I hope your curse hasn't afflicted her as well, and she's fallen off the cliff."

She looked anxiously at the cliff top for a moment, taking him seriously. Then she smiled, reassured. "No, there she is." And she indicated a grey-haired figure near the lilac tree. "I must go. Esther obviously wants me to leave. Otherwise she would have stayed where she was."

"You are very close to her, aren't you?" he suddenly guessed.

"Yes, she is like a mother to me. She has come to Dunscombe Manor for as long as I can remember, and given Mr McAlpine, whom she detests, some of her herbal secrets so she can be with me."

"Surely she is unhappy you will abandon her and go to Virginia with Captain Petrie?" he asked.

"She is intending to come with me and live in America," she said, and started to walk quickly across the sand.

"I want to see you again," he repeated, following her.

"No, I refuse, for your sake and mine. I have done what you asked and met you here today and that is the end of it, sir." She looked enigmatically at him and turned to greet Esther Cerfbeer.

"Good day, Seigneur," Esther remarked to Armand, as she came up to them. "I believe you are beginning to feel better."

He looked at her sourly, and, at that moment, men appeared above them on the cliff.

"Ezekiel Widdicombe," he exclaimed, recognising his estate manager. "What's he doing?"

"I heard voices from the wood. That is why I have come down to the beach to escort Isabella. You had better stay," she told Armand. "It is not in your interest that Mr Widdicombe knows about your meeting today.

"We must go quickly," she said to Isabella.

He opened his mouth to protest, unused to being told what to do, then closed it, and waited impatiently until Isabella and Esther had passed the two men descending the path. Disappointment and anger tore at him. He kept his eyes on Isabella until she disappeared from view and then he went to meet Ezekiel Widdicombe.

"What is your business down here?" he shouted.

Ezekiel Widdicombe knuckled his head, as did the labourer with him.

"Us be looking at yer land," he muttered.

"I expect you to be supervising the fields and the harvest, not wandering over a beach," he shouted again.

"Yess, zur," Ezekiel Widdicombe replied.

"Well, since you are here, you can be useful. You can collect the seaweed and pile it into heaps and take it back to the house on carts. It can be used for fertiliser on the fields, as in France."

"Us don't put seaweed on the land. Sea sand from Barnstaple sometimes, but not seaweed. Us grows vegetables, not fish."

"I don't think you grow very much at all," he declared. "Go on, get working."

They knuckled their heads again; he strode rapidly away from them and up the stony path on the cliff face.

Ezekiel Widdicombe looked with interest at Isabella and Esther who had now gained the grass just before the trees.

"The master will want to know about this. There's summat been going on 'ere. He won't want 'is plans ruined."

....

The fox accompanied Isabella and Esther down the hill, slinking through the trees and bushes. Esther hurried, refusing to speak until they had reached her garden.

Isabella showed her the doll. "It was in a cave by the headland. I think it's mine. When I saw it, I suddenly remembered a ship sinking and waves crashing over me. I was drowning and men were shouting and the beach was red with blood. And I was clinging on to a woman in a silk dress."

Esther looked at the doll and then at Isabella.

"It is better to concern yourself with your life now, not worry about the past. I understand you want to know about your origins, but it is a mistake to be too imaginative."

"I did not imagine it," said Isabella stubbornly. "Have there been shipwrecks near the Torrs?"

"Ships often founder near Ilfracombe, as they run to the harbour for shelter," replied Esther. "You know that the rocks and reefs are jagged and cruel. What has happened has happened. Whether these are true recollections or whether you are just thinking about the Louisiana is not important to how you act now."

"You don't believe me," cried Isabella.

"No, I am not saying that. I am just saying you must live in the present, not dwell on the past." Esther's expression was almost harsh and Isabella glanced at her in surprise and was silent.

"Now tell me about Armand de Delacroix," Esther said, her tone softening. "I knew his father and mother well. They were very kind and gave me my cottage. I used to live at Bischheim near Strasbourg, in Alsace. Jews were not allowed to live in the city, and my uncle is the first Jew to have done so. Jewish people were often attacked and I had to flee. I owe everything I have to Armand de Delacroix's parents and I want to help him."

"I told him I would not see him again," replied Isabella. "I also told him about Daniel and Thomas."

"That is wise. His attention to you has complicated matters, just as I thought you were about to escape McAlpine."

"I don't want him killed," said Isabella, as they reached the gate of the cottage garden, where McAlpine's favourite piebald mare was tethered to the hawthorn hedge. "And there's something else I must tell you. I found a secret chamber at Dunscombe Manor yesterday. It was at the end of the house and there was a tunnel which went towards the coast."

"A hidden room!" exclaimed Esther.

"Yes, and it is used to worship Hecate. There was an upside-down crucifix and a mosaic of Hecate's Wheel on the floor."

Esther paled. Her eyes narrowed in anger. "You must not go in there again. He has never involved you in his rituals and for that I am grateful. Perhaps even his depravity has its limits, although I do not think so. I do not know the reason. But, at this stage, when you have nearly escaped, you must not meddle in his affairs and annoy him." Her breathing became rapid and she spoke with difficulty.

"Can I get you the digitalis powder?" asked Isabella fearfully.

"No. It is nothing. Ride back now, so that the servants are not too suspicious."

Isabella untied the horse from the hedge. She embraced Esther, then mounted and cantered off down the lane, sitting astride the animal in spite of her dress, and carefully clutching the doll in one hand, along with the reins.

16

Jellyfish were smothering her, their soft bodies flopping over her face. They buzzed and droned, chasing her into waves which were crashing over her head, drowning her.

She woke up. Cain's paw was heavy on her face, Abel's head lay on her legs, a bee was bumbling desperately against the window and she was clinging to the doll. She moved the dogs onto another part of the counterpane and jumped out of bed to open the window.

"Fly away, little drumbledrone," she said, using the Devon name. "Fly away."

The bee obligingly did so, its wings beating invisibly, and disappeared into the trees. She perched the doll on the sill and looked into its one glass eye.

"What's your name? Have I really seen you before, or is it just my imagination playing tricks?"

She left off her stays and put on a white muslin dress to allow herself ease of movement for what she was intending. She pinned up her hair on her head and secured it with a comb. For a moment, the sensation of being carried across the beach by Armand, and the look in his eyes as he said he wanted to see her again, made her resolve towards him weaken. Then she pushed him out of her mind.

'No, he is not for you,' she told herself sternly.

After a substantial breakfast of laver, eggs, mushrooms and two dishes of tea, provided by Mrs Gubb in the kitchen, she set off to Ilfracombe. The intense August heat had finally abated, but the day was still warm; the banks below the hedgerows bright with celandines, red campion and the occasional foxglove.

She reached the seaward slope of the hill and gazed at the coast below. The sea was a dark blue and the windows of the lighthouse chapel of Saint Nicholas twinkled like a day-time star. An unpleasant smell of decomposing flesh drifted on the wind to her and she looked round to see its cause. A body of a sheep was huddled next to a stone wall, and as she came nearer, she saw it was dead and its eyes had been pecked out. Two crows were perched on a hawthorn bush and a third was on the grass next to the carcass. She glanced at them with distaste and hurried down the hill to Ilfracombe.

She walked past the harbour. The tide was out as far as Hillsborough, and ships and fishing boats lay on their sides in rows on the mud. Men and women were digging for worms, and dock workers were loading coal onto carts. She continued briskly up Fore Street towards the seven hills of the Torrs, avoiding the steaming heaps of manure on the road. At the parish church, masons were repairing the parapet of the tower and the noise of their hammers and chisels striking the stonework lent a discordant note to the fluting birdsong.

She did not stop at Esther's cottage, but hurried on, passing by the stone birds without looking towards Wildercombe House. She climbed the path through the wood and stood on the exposed headland beyond the trees, smiling with relief to see the deserted beach and an extremely low tide, as it had been the previous day.

She descended the cliff path and removed her shoes, stockings and garters, which she left under the lilac tree. Then she made her way, barefoot, over the sand and the reefs to the grey cliffs at the far headland. She rounded the corner of a large rock and immediately saw the arch of the cave. Brown fronds of seaweed were growing in a fissure above its entrance, revealing the height reached by the sea, and she glanced with trepidation towards the water lapping the sand a short distance away.

She shivered as she stepped out of the sunshine and into the wet bleakness of the cave, one side streaming with water from the hillside above, droplets pittering softly into a pool. The sand was cold beneath her feet and she advanced cautiously into the bowels of the cavern. A dead seagull entangled in scraps of fishing net was hanging from a rock, its wings gracefully stretched out, and a dark green crab scuttled sideways across the shingle, making her flinch nervously. A lost raven flew squawking from the vault of the cave; she dropped to her knees and screamed, the shrillness of her voice reverberating in the chamber. She hunched over in fear, and it was many minutes before she was able to creep further into the darkness. She peered upwards and saw the hole, high up above her, on an almost perpendicular cliff face, just as Armand had described.

She started to climb, her feet gripping the rock, her hands searching for nooks to cling to. She inched upwards, resisting the temptation to look at the ground, and finally hauled herself over the edge of a flat platform of rock, from which branched three tunnels. The uneven ledge was strewn with pebbles and remnants of wood and she looked upwards, in the half-light, from the debris to a trail of broken shale leading to a crevice on the cliff. She reached up, but was too short, and had to briefly climb once more until she was able to plunge her hand into the gap. She scrabbled at the loose stones inside, but there was nothing.

 She felt a rising sense of panic in the claustrophobic darkness and, for a moment, was again on a ship foundering in a storm. Her heart raced; she felt the cold sea close over her mouth and nose, drowning her. She pressed her face into the roughness of the rock and extended her hand further, dislodging a soft-bodied creature which wriggled away. Her fingers touched hard metal; she pulled it towards her and saw she was holding a tiny chain. It was dirty with grime, but a glint of yellow glimmered, and she scrambled back down the cliff, clutching it in one hand.

She held onto the edge of the platform and lowered herself over it, feeling with her foot for indentations in the rock, and carefully climbing downwards. Her foot slipped on the same patch of slimy seaweed which had caught Armand, and she tumbled downwards, sliding over the shale and landing awkwardly on the floor of the cave.

A roaring sounded in her ears, a mist descended in front of her eyes, she whimpered, and a terrifying blackness claimed her.

She regained consciousness to find the sea swirling over her face and body. She choked and spluttered as it entered her mouth, and raised her head up out of the water. The cold saltiness cut through her befuddled state and she tried to lift herself away from the fast-flowing tide. She clawed at the rock and managed to hoist herself further up. She looked towards the entrance and knew that her only hope lay in remaining out of the reach of the sea. She shuffled slightly higher on the cliff and clung desperately to it, trying not to faint, as she would then fall and drown.

17

Esther was sweeping the floor of her bedchamber, as David jumped round her feet, from time to time immersing himself in a basin of water. She flung a handful of rose petals onto the bed and went to the window, from where, a short time earlier, she had seen Isabella pass by.

She stood pensively for a few minutes. Then she went down to the garden and out into the lane.

"Where are you, Isabella?" she muttered, looking anxiously along the path. "Why didn't you come in to see me, as you always do? Have you gone to the beach or to Wildercombe House?"

She frowned and set off along the track, arriving at the stone birds on their lichen pillars.

"No. You would not have come here," she muttered, glancing at the tree-lined drive. "I fear you are trying to discover about the shipwreck and your family."

She turned away from the entrance and set off up through the wood, quickly reaching the cliff edge. She looked at the cove. Nothing moved, except the tide, which was starting to flow past the headland.

A flicker of alarm crossed her face and she hastily followed the path down the hillside. At the lilac tree she stopped as she saw the shoes and stockings.

"No," she shrieked. She ran frantically across the silver crescent of sand and clambered over the reefs, her hair coming loose, her shoes wet from the rock pools, until she arrived, gasping for breath, at the far side.

"Isabella!" she called. "Isabella!"

A seagull squawked in response, but there was no human reply. She waded into the sea, floundering up to her knees, the shingle shelving steeply under her feet. The water swirled deeply around her and she was unable to continue.

"Isabella!" she called again. "Isabella!"

This time, not even a seagull answered, and she rushed back across the reefs and sand and up the cliff path. She glanced briefly at the beach below, holding her hand to her chest, then hurried through the wood towards the lane. She ran out from the trees, her black dress and grey hair flying behind her, her feet hardly touching the ground, just as Armand and Dietrich came cantering out from the drive on their horses.

"Is the devil after you?" called out Dietrich. "Or are you after the devil?"

She grabbed the mane of Armand's horse. "Help me," she cried.

"What's the matter?" he asked.

"I think Isabella is in the cave by the headland, and the tide's coming in. I am afraid she's trapped," she said.

He looked at her for just a second; he dug his heels into his horse and galloped off into the wood, the stones scattering under his horse's hooves. Dietrich galloped after him and the two horses could be heard, racing up through the trees, whilst Esther collapsed onto the ground.

Armand and Dietrich rode furiously across the beach to the far end of the cove. The horses splashed through the water to the headland and reached the cave, whose entrance was already half-filled by the sea. Armand gave his reins to Dietrich, threw himself off his horse and waded waist-high into the cavern and through the flooding tide to the cliff at the back. He gazed desperately round him in the gloom, and suddenly caught sight of the white of Isabella's dress, whose skirt was floating in the black water. He waded towards her and saw that she was lying, almost submerged by the sea, clinging to a rock, her face streaming with blood.

He rushed to her and picked her up in his arms, staggering as the current caught him. Her head fell back limply against him and she mumbled a few, incomprehensible words. Water reached his shoulder and he held her higher, her head touching his jaw. Then, with unwieldy steps, he floundered towards the entrance, which now had only the crest of its arch still showing.

The sea finally claimed even that last remnant before he managed to reach it, and the cavern was completely plunged into darkness. He continued to push against the incoming tide, and when he finally felt the roughness of the rock wall, he breathed deeply, then fastened his mouth onto that of Isabella. He blindly stepped forward, the water closing over his head, and he plunged towards the invisible opening in the cliff.

The sea suddenly became filled with light, its turquoise-blue colour returned, and, just as his feet were swept from under him, Dietrich's hand closed onto his collar and hauled him into the freshness of the outside air.

He rested a moment, gulping for breath, exhausted, his head on the flank of Dietrich's horse, whilst Dietrich pulled Isabella up in front of him, where she sprawled in a faint across his saddle. He weakly slithered onto his own horse and together he and Dietrich urged the animals towards the beach.

18

The smokiness of mullein tapers filled the room. Isabella lay white-faced and motionless on the high feather bed. Her head was bleeding, the blood trickling to her chin and down her neck into her dress. Esther thoroughly cleaned the wound, applied a poultice of comfrey, and bandaged it with muslin cloth.

Armand stood at the window and watched the shadows lengthen by the trees. He looked again at Isabella. Her eyes were closed. There was no sign even that she was breathing, that she was alive, except that the bandage was quickly staining red. He stared at her, willing for her to show she had not joined his parents in the afterlife. He saw her tremble, with just a slight movement of her hand, and he made the sign of the cross.

Esther ignored him. It was as though he was not there, and she even bumped into him as she carried a dish to the table.

"I would like the doctor in Ilfracombe to come," he said.

"My skills are superior to his," she replied. "It is not necessary and it is also, perhaps, a danger. Very few people seem to survive his ministrations."

"Is that so?" he queried sarcastically.

"Yes," she replied.

He prowled round the room, looking unhappily at the frog on the edge of his bowl, and at Tabitha, the black cat, peacefully asleep on the floor.

"Don't worry," said Esther. "I will keep her in this world, although you will not be able to have her, in spite of your intentions."

He stared at her. "You presume too much, madam. I hardly know her. It was pure chance I was able to help."

"Yes, that is true," she said. "Her death would have meant nothing to you."

"That is not the case," he snapped. "You are too clever for your own good, old woman. You will come to a bad end. People are ignorant and superstitious enough without you, with your animals and herbs," and he glanced at a bowl of yellow liquid infusing with chopped parts of mandrake root on the table.

"It was given to men on the cross. It is an ancient and a powerful remedy, and now I will treat Isabella with it," she said, picking up the bowl. "You must leave. You can visit tomorrow," and she pushed him towards the door where he stood his ground, his large frame dwarfing her.

"Do you think she will recover?" he asked humbly.

"I will do my best," was her response.

He remained in the doorway. "I will pay for whatever is needed. My servants will bring chicken and fruits tomorrow. And candles, so that the air is not filled with smoke from the mullein. Can I give you anything else?"

"No. You have done enough. This is the second time you have saved her life and I am beholden to you. Good day, Seigneur."

She shepherded him down the boxed-in stairs to the room below, unlatched the cottage door and looked at him.

"The McAlpines will not return for at least two weeks, probably much longer. London is far away from North Devon. You are safe for the moment."

"You mean Isabella is safe," he corrected her.

"No, I mean you are safe," she repeated. "I do my best to protect Isabella. I cannot protect you."

"Well, you're not doing very well," he retorted. "She has nearly drowned twice! And you most certainly do not need to concern yourself on my behalf."

"There is evil here," she replied. "I understand a part of the puzzle, but not all."

"Good day, madam," he said, frowning at her words and at the three-legged cauldron by the hearth. "I will return tomorrow."

He left the cottage and walked through the dark garden. He glanced at the upstairs window and stood, quietly saying a prayer. He crossed himself, and walked slowly back along the lane, the funereal gloom of the night an echo of his own spirit.

....

Sirius, the Dog Star, sparkled in the night sky, and the white-brilliance of the moon cast a cold light over the ground; three mullein stalks and a black candle were burning next to a pewter dish containing a crescent of honey cake.

Tabitha sat on the step. An owl hooted in the elder tree, the fox lingered near his den by the hawthorn, and incense smoke from sandalwood, cypress and mint rose from a brass bowl into the air.

Esther gazed at the moon and quietly spoke her incantation.

"I am Alvilda, your faithful servant.

Hear me please, Hecate, divine Goddess.

As the candle burns,

so does the wound heal.

Let it melt like the beeswax,

let it vanish,

let her be whole again,

bless her with health once more."

She raised her arms to the moon and slowly let them fall. She quenched the mullein and watched the candle as it burned. It hissed and spluttered, its flame waving from side to side. She bowed to it. "Thank you."

It slowly guttered to a halt; she gathered up its stub and thrust it into the soil. Then she and Tabitha returned to their vigil at Isabella's bed.

19

Armand drank a glass of claret as he picked at a plate of eggs, ham and steak. The early morning air was sultry, the dawn chorus was serenading the sunrise, and the night was fading. He was dressed in his robe, his expression sombre as he glanced through the window in the direction of Esther's cottage.

"Do you know anything about shipwrecks on this part of the coast?" he asked Ben, pushing his plate away.

"There's often wrecks round here. It's always dangerous to enter Ilfracombe harbour in a storm. And from Hartland to Lynmouth, it's known as the graveyard."

"Have you heard of a shipwrecked boat whose name began with 'san'?" he asked.

"No. But most of my family are seafarers. One of my uncles has a herring boat and the other fishes for cod off Newfoundland every year. I'll see if they know."

"Have the servants at Dunscombe Manor been there long?" he asked.

"I don't think so. When Mr McAlpine married, he hired a lot of people for the house, but before that he only had a housekeeper. Local folk didn't go near the place. If Mr McAlpine found anyone trespassing, they would end up in the Bridewell, at Exeter. There used to be sailors there with cutlasses and knives, and a pack of wolfhounds, but that all changed when Mrs McAlpine came."

"What was the name of the housekeeper?"

"I'm not sure," he replied.

"Eliza Redmore," said Jonah, the other footman, who had been listening to the conversation. "I know it was Eliza Redmore, because she was a friend of my aunt."

"Where is she now?" he asked.

"She used to live at the Golden Rose Inn at Bideford. Her son is the innkeeper. But she is very old. She might be dead."

He flinched at the word 'dead', but recovered himself.

"Thank you," he said.

....

The dawn chorus had finished as he walked through Esther's garden, still littered with broken plants and bushes from the rioting; the burned shed a blackened shell, its scorched rafters on the ground. The sky was ominously dark, and grey cumulus clouds tinged with black, were racing inland from the coast. He knocked, and as he waited, he noticed a moon-shaped cake on a plate by the step. He knocked again, and suddenly hungry, picked up the cake and ate it.

Esther opened the door, wearing a bright purple gown, with beads of jet at the hem and sleeves.

"I believe a storm is coming," she said, glancing at the heavens.

"Is she alive?" he asked.

"Yes. Would you like to pay her a visit, Seigneur?"

"That is why I am here at this unearthly hour," he said sharply.

She looked at the empty pewter plate, smiled, and stood back to let him pass.

He followed her up the narrow staircase and entered the bedchamber, fragrant with the scent of sandalwood and roses. His heart leapt as he saw her. She was lying in bed, propped up by cushions, a bandage on her head spotted with blood. Her eyes were black and sunken in her white face, her hands limp on the coverlet, but she smiled wanly at him in recognition. "Thank you for saving me yet again," she murmured.

"Are you in pain?" he asked.

"My head hurts. But I am very happy to be here and it doesn't matter," she said.

"What were you doing?" he questioned. "Were you in the cave trying to discover more about the shipwreck you thought you remembered?"

"Yes. And I found the gold chain I told you about." Her voice was so soft he had to strain to hear.

"She is too weak to talk," intervened Esther. "She has to rest. You can sit here with her, but you must be quiet. I have just given her more of the mandrake potion, so she will shortly fall asleep."

He sat down on the chair next to the bed. The cat rubbed herself against his legs and the frog gave a long croak as it hopped onto the edge of its basin.

"They like you," said Esther. "They do not generally take to strangers."

"Well that is something we can be grateful for today then," he replied, as Esther stirred the bowl of mandrake liquid and placed it on a dresser, next to a curved seven-branched candelabra.

"It's unusual," he remarked. "It's similar to the one at Dunscombe Manor."

She looked at him, and, for a second, he thought he could see hatred in the depths of her eyes, before her expression became veiled.

"Yes. It is a menorah. It is Jewish and is sacred to me," she said, and then went out of the room and down the stairs.

He looked at Isabella, who lay like a rag doll, her vivacity extinguished. She tried to speak, but her voice trailed away. Her eyes closed, her breathing deepened and became more regular.

He covered her hand with his and felt the coldness of her skin. He gazed at her and gently stroked her face, his heart surging with joy and despair in equal measure. He sat very still and willed her to survive, and suddenly felt the presence of his parents. He glanced round, but they were not there. However, he spoke to them.

"I should have saved you. I should not have let you stay in the chateau. I knew it was dangerous. I had seen the revolutionary crowds in Strasbourg in the morning. You need not have died. It was my fault and I have lost you. Don't let me lose her as well."

He sat and waited. The sun rose higher in the sky and warmed the room. He watched her. From time to time, he caressed her face and touched her hair which had escaped the bandage. In the room below, Esther was noisily busy. Pots clattered and the besom broom was being vigorously used. He frowned as he heard it, and caught the eye of Tabitha.

"Have you been left to spy on me?" he asked.

She purred.

"Yes, I thought so," he replied.

A stork, made of material and stuffed with straw, was hanging from a hook on the wall. He picked it up and teased Tabitha with it. She pounced and attacked with her claws and he smiled. "I'll have to keep you from Dietrich. He is not your friend. He has not been caught in a spell, as I have."

At midday, Esther returned, carrying a tray on which were steaming bowls and a large cake. The smell tantalised him, but he declined.

"As you wish," she said. "Perhaps you don't like choucroute and kugelhopf? Are you afraid, perhaps, you will be turned into a frog?"

He laughed and took the tray from her. "I think I've already been caught by magic. I need something to set me free, not enslave me more."

This time it was her turn to laugh, and it surprised him to see her elderly, wrinkled face smile. He ate quickly and thanked her. "It seems a long time since I have eaten that. We are both a long way from home, I think."

Isabella suddenly moaned and shuddered, and Esther rearranged the counterpane over her and felt her forehead.

"I will give her more of the infusion. She needs sleep in order to heal. The wound is deep."

"She said she found the doll's necklace?" he questioned.

"Yes, but it was not with her. Perhaps she is mistaken. In any case, it is not important."

"I think it is very important to her," he commented.

She was silent. The bells of the parish church rang out in the distance, and a crow cawed loudly. A strengthening wind was banging the gate, the sky was now very dark and rain was beginning to fall.

"Sometimes it is best to forget the past," she said. "I speak from experience."

"You don't want her to discover her origins?" he queried.

"No, that's not so," she replied crossly. "You must go now. I need to treat her."

"You want her to marry a stranger who lives on the other side of the ocean. Is that your idea of happiness?" he asked, as he reluctantly stood up.

"It is what Raphael McAlpine wants and there can be terrible consequences if he does not get what he desires. She lives in his house and is vulnerable. You have just arrived in Ilfracombe and have no idea what goes on. You are an innocent here, just as she is." Her voice and her expression were severe.

She escorted him downstairs, and as he stood at the cottage door, he gestured at the garden.

"I will send a servant to clear the plants. You are busy with Isabella."

"No, I don't need help," she said fiercely. "Also, I do not want the Widdicombes to know that she is in my cottage. Please do not talk about any of this."

"Why is that?" he asked. "I would like to know more about them and Raphael McAlpine."

"We can speak of this another time," she said. "Please have trust in me. I helped bring you into this world. I have your interest at heart."

He regarded her with amazement. "You were at my birth?" he replied, disbelievingly.

"Yes, at the chateau, near Strasbourg. You have a birthmark in the shape of a circle, on your shoulder. When you were born you did not breathe straightaway and I had to hold you by your feet and slap your back."

He stared at her, lost for words.

"I will send Ben to help," he finally managed to say. "I want you to be able to look after Isabella. He will be sworn to secrecy, so don't worry. Good day, madam." He bowed very politely, and walked slowly away, avoiding trampling on the torn branches and roots.

20

The shackles on her ankles were chafing and Bess shifted her position on the cabin floor to try and ease the discomfort. She rose slowly to her feet, the chains clanking, and looked out of the narrow window next to her. Her spirits momentarily lifted to see the brilliant blue of the sea and a family of dolphins moving in formation, playfully jumping the waves. She smiled at the creatures and remained upright, clinging to the window for hours, escaping, in some sort of way, from the confines surrounding her and the ghastliness of her future. She clung to the window, and prayed, as she gazed out at the ocean.

"Dear God. Help me in my hour of need, and help Jacob too."

Jacob had been taken to the hold. He had been stripped of his clothes on the deck, and the sailors had jeered and beaten him, when they had discovered they had been given a circumcised Jew. Tears ran down her face at the memory, and at the utter humiliation and despair in his eyes. The stench from the open hatch had been nauseating and he had been pushed violently down into the foetid blackness, from which whimpering cries and groans could be heard.

She had expected the same treatment, and had clutched her dress to her in abject fear, but instead, she had been taken to the cabin and given a meal of black bread, vinegar, and olives.

The sailors were the physical embodiment of frightening childhood tales about Barbary pirates. They were dressed in outlandish garments; brightly coloured baggy trousers and blouse-like shirts, and several wore turbans. When they came to her cabin they often carried beads, which they continually touched. Curved scimitars and daggers hung at their waists, and their language sounded as fierce as their appearance.

The man with the red beard, she had first seen, was the leader, and had spoken a few words of English.

"Cabin. Much money paid," he had said.

She stared out to the horizon and suddenly caught her breath as she saw a white sail. Footsteps thudded on the deck above her and it was obvious that she was not the only person to have noticed the ship. Sailors were shouting and heavy objects were being rolled over the planks. Below her cabin came the noise of a heavy rattling of shutters, followed by a similar sound on the port side of the boat.

They were rapidly gaining on the other vessel, which, far from saving her, appeared to be attempting to race in the opposite direction. Every so often, its sails would dip below the horizon and it would disappear. Then a glimpse of white would be visible again, and, like a cat stalking a bird, slowly and patiently, the pirate ship came up to it.

Now she could see the sails billowing out, and the crow's nest, and people scurrying over its decks. She peered at the main mast to distinguish the flag, and had a moment of disappointment as she saw it was not the British Red Ensign. It had stars and stripes on it, which, for a moment, baffled her.

"It's the United States of America," she suddenly murmured. "It's not an enemy. Dear God. Save me."

The frigate was now so close, she could see the sailors. Its side had cannon protruding from port holes, but the pirate vessel was approaching fast from behind. Musket shots were fired from men drawn up in a line on the deck and, as the two ships came close together, the Moors swung on ropes and landed in their midst. They had scimitars in their hands and daggers between their teeth, and, in a matter of minutes, they had cut down most of the American sailors and she could not look at the carnage any more. She turned away from the sight of bleeding and badly injured men, and, as she did so, the hull of the pirate ship came up against that of the American, and her cabin was plunged into darkness.

She hobbled as quickly as she could, to the other end of the room, the shackles trailing after her, fearful that the wooden hull of the ship would cave in. The two vessels grated against each other; there were shouts and more musket fire, and the shuffling of many feet across the deck. The pirate ship relinquished its hold on the other vessel and sunlight bathed the cabin again. The air was tainted by the smell of gunpowder and she sat, huddled on the floor, grateful that she was still alive, and not drowned, chained within the womb of a ship which had sunk to the seabed.

Cannon boomed in succession, juddering the wooden planks, and she stumbled back to the window, and watched as the American frigate slowly foundered, split in half. Bodies were lying on the deck, their clothing stained red, and corpses floated in the water, alongside wooden chests and spars and other debris. The waters closed slowly over the mast, until, finally, only the flag, with its thirteen stars and stripes, was left stranded. That too, was devoured by the sea and only a bobbing table, chest and a black hat remained. She stood in shock, overwhelmed by what had happened.

Above her, there were shouts in English, the march of feet, and the drawing back of the hatch. The voices ceased, the hatch was slammed shut, and she knew that the Americans were now imprisoned in the stinking quarters of the hold.

21

The gurry butt had lurched against a boulder; its load of dung had overturned and spread thickly over the road. The high hedges prevented escape into the neighbouring fields, so travellers had to walk or ride through the foul waste.

A file of pack horses in front of Armand and Dietrich was pulling faggots of wood piled between willow crooks, and each contraption had to be dragged through the morass. A queue of horses, carts and people on foot was forming and Dietrich started to complain loudly about the slowness of the journey. Finally, it was their turn, and the two horses picked their way delicately through the quagmire of manure, before continuing on the stone track towards the town of Barnstaple.

The hedges diminished in size, revealing the surrounding countryside. Four oxen and two horses, with two men and a boy behind them, were ploughing a field, and Armand stopped to watch.

"The plough is hardly cutting into the ground at all," he remarked to Dietrich, whose face showed a complete lack of interest. "I wonder how my estate is ploughed. I will look into it."

A pack of hounds, followed by red-coated men on horses, erupted in full cry across the fields and Dietrich became more cheerful.

"Perhaps we could have a hunt like that," he suggested. "It would be good to eat boar."

"There's no wild boar round here," remarked Armand. "I think they're chasing a fox."

"There must be boar," said Dietrich. "Who would want to eat a fox?"

"That's true," he admitted. "You must be right."

From a hilltop came shrieks of laughter, as women stood winnowing wheat, throwing it up into the wind, whilst below them, in large square fields, stacks of wheat, thatched with reed, stood in rows.

"Arrish mows," said Armand, trying out his new-found knowledge of the Devon dialect.

The hedges disappeared, the land became flat, the road following the shore of an estuary. The tide was out, and men were standing on the river bed, shovelling sand into pannier bags on horses.

Armand quickened the pace of his horse from a canter to a gallop, and he and Dietrich soon came to the borough of Barnstaple. They crossed the river Taw by an ancient, arched bridge, and galloped steadily on towards Bideford, through countryside where the coppice fences were shorn by the wind, and heaps of lime and compost in the fields were almost as high as the roofs of houses. The whole landscape was punctuated by oak woods, the strength of the southwest wind evident by their bent trunks and branches.

They pressed on at a rapid pace, overtaking strings of pack horses carrying bags of lime. Some vehicles they passed were just sledges, whilst others were carts pulled by two horses, guided by reins. At one point, they encountered the rare sight of a carriage, which had halted by the side of the highway, overlooking the wide sweep of Bideford Bay. A table and chairs had been set up on the grassy verge and a man and woman were eating from porcelain crockery with silver cutlery which sparkled in the sunshine. Four soldiers in white and red uniform were waiting by their horses and drinking from tankards, and the group eyed the approaching riders with curiosity.

Armand swung down from his horse and introduced himself, bowing low.

"Pleased to make your acquaintance," said the bewigged man, rising to his feet, on hearing his name.

"I am Lord Fortescue, the Lord Lieutenant of Devon, and this is Lady Fortescue." He indicated the lady next to him, who was fashionably dressed in a lemon silk dress, her face shaded by a wide-brimmed hat, decorated with ribbons and artificial cherries.

"Would you take refreshment with us?" he enquired. "We always enjoy an outdoor meal."

"Thank you," said Armand. "I would be delighted."

Dietrich joined the soldiers, who offered him a tankard of ale, and Armand was given a chair and a large slice of cold tongue and ham pie.

"I believe you have an estate near Ilfracombe," remarked the Lord Lieutenant.

"Yes, that is correct," he replied. "Do you live nearby?"

"At Filleigh. I am on business for the king. There's more smugglers round here than wives who gossip. The revenue that is being lost is enormous. I am here to meet with the Customs and Excise to see what can be done."

"I believe there was a smuggling run at Heddon, the other day," said Armand. "I was at dinner with Lieutenant Hargreaves when he had to go and investigate."

"They were too late," exclaimed the Lord Lieutenant. "All they found was an empty brandy tub on the beach. The criminals had made off with their ill-gotten gains."

"So there actually was smuggling going on," remarked Armand.

The Lord Lieutenant threw his hands in the air. "I don't know. It is not the first time the cutter has arrived too late off Exmoor. I think they need to get the army in there and search all the houses from Lynmouth to Heddon. The moor is awash with thieves and vagabonds."

"What is your business, your Grace, in these parts?" enquired Lady Fortescue.

"I am going to Bideford, to see the market," he declared, after a moment's hesitation. "I have become a farmer and I need to sell my produce."

"Terrible times in France," said the Lord Lieutenant.

"Yes," he agreed. "Hopefully the Revolution will soon be overthrown, and I will be able to return to my homeland."

He stood up and thanked his hosts. Then he and Dietrich continued along the road and finally crossed the river on a similar arched bridge to that at Barnstaple.

The town of Bideford rambled over a steep hillside, the streets winding and narrow, the houses poorly built, most of timber, but some of brick and mud, the roofs covered with sagging thatch or badly arranged slates; whilst at every corner there were composts of earth, mud and ashes, as well as huge mounds of furze faggots piled against walls.

A market was being held at the corner of a wide street, lined with substantial houses, and Armand dismounted to look at the farm produce. He inspected the cattle and the sheep, and ran his hand through wheat packed in long, two bushel bags, before strolling round the Shambles.

"It's only selling mutton," he remarked to Dietrich, who had discovered a large salmon and was asking where it might be fished. He stopped to buy red and blue ribbons, as did Dietrich, and he asked the stallholder the way to the Golden Rose.

It overlooked the quay by the River Torridge, and was a white-walled building with a prosperous air about it. Its sign was newly painted and showed a ship with a large, gold rose painted on it, sailing through enormous waves. Trade was brisk; people were constantly coming in and out of its low, iron-studded door and Armand and Dietrich had to bow their heads in order to enter. A fug of tobacco smoke greeted them, dominated by a smell of brandy and rum, and sailors with Monmouth caps, wide trousers and tarry jackets, armed with a variety of daggers and cutlasses, were loudly drinking and smoking pipes. The buzz of conversation faltered as they made their way through the throng, a parrot in a cage cackling as they approached.

"Land astern! Walk the gang plank."

Armand kept his hand on his sword, Dietrich following close behind to protect his back, and they were met by a serving maid carrying two tankards of ale on a tray who blocked their path.

"Yess," she declared, eyeing the men flirtatiously.

"I am looking for Eliza Redmore," said Armand.

"What do you want an old body like her for?" she asked, flinging back her dark curls and pouting her lips.

The men around her stared malevolently at the strangers and there was quiet in the previously noisy tavern.

"I have something for her," replied Armand, and pulled out a coin from his pocket, which she regarded greedily.

"I wish to speak to her in private," he said, and produced another coin, which he gave to her, whereupon she held the heavy tray precariously in one hand and pocketed it deftly with the other.

"Come with me, my 'andsome," she said, giving the tankards to two men at a nearby table.

She led the way out of the room and up wooden stairs to a chamber whose open windows looked over the quay. An elderly woman was sitting in a chair, a shawl round her shoulders, a lace mobcap on her head.

"Two gentlemen to see you, Mrs Redmore," announced the serving maid.

"Thank you," said Armand to her. "You can leave us now."

"I will be downstairs if you want any more favours," she replied, and winked and flounced out of the room.

"Good day," he said politely to the old woman. "I am interested in finding out about the origins of Isabella, the ward of Raphael McAlpine at Dunscombe Manor. I will pay you for your information." And he showed her a coin.

The woman peered suspiciously at him with watery blue eyes. "And who might you be, sir?"

"That is not important," he replied.

"It is to me," she said sharply.

"You were the housekeeper, I believe. Were you there when she first came?" he asked.

Eliza Redmore looked him up and down and touched the sleeve of his coat with a bony finger. "Fine clothes," she muttered. "A vurriner in fine clothes."

"Was she in a shipwreck?" he continued, moving out of her reach.

Mrs Redmore sucked her teeth. "She was just a little thing, but she was wild, always climbing the trees or running away. I broke some of my best wooden spoons on her."

"Where did she come from?" he asked again in annoyance.

"The pixies brought her. One day she wasn't there, the next day, she was. It was the pixies." She looked at him slyly, her eyes close-set in her wrinkled face. She sucked her wooden teeth again and they fell out of her mouth and clattered onto the floor.

Dietrich cursed in Alsatian and moved to look out of the window, as the elderly woman reached down, and picked them up.

"Was there a shipwreck?" Armand asked.

"No. Not a shipwreck. Lots of shipwrecks," she muttered, and laughed, her open mouth revealing bare pink gums.

"Do you know Esther Cerfbeer?"

She shot a glance at him, as though in fear. "She won't put any spells on me?"

"Not if you tell the truth," he declared.

At that moment, the door was flung open and a thick-set, bearded man burst in. He was dressed in seafaring clothes, like those of the customers downstairs, but the cutlass stuck in his belt was curved and a gold chain decorated his chest.

"Who are you?" he bellowed at Armand. "What are you doing here?"

"He wants to know about Dunscombe Manor and Isabella and shipwrecks. He knows about the pixies," his mother answered.

The man glared belligerently, his eyes darting from Armand to Dietrich and back again. He pulled at his cutlass, but Armand and Dietrich had already reached for their swords and both held the tips of their blades to his throat as he slowly retreated to the wall.

"Throw it down," shouted Armand, and the innkeeper reluctantly let the cutlass drop onto the floor. Dietrich picked it up and threw it out of the window, narrowly missing a drunken sailor on the road outside singing the refrain, "Now you're safe ashore Jack, don't forget your old shipmate."

"You first," he shouted to Armand, who sheathed his sword and followed the cutlass out of the window. Dietrich then jumped, landing on top of the intoxicated singer who stopped in mid-sea shanty, with a strangulated, "Polly, Pol..." They quickly leapt to their feet, mounted their horses which had been tied to a post outside the tavern, and galloped off down the quayside accompanied by shouting and swearing from the Golden Rose.

22

I asked my uncle Matthew about ships which were wrecked whose name began with 'san', remarked Ben at breakfast the next morning, as he placed a plate of buttered toast on the dining table. "He said there had been a lot of shipwrecks at Brandy Cove, but that he had never heard of one whose name started with those letters."

"Where is Brandy Cove," asked Armand.

"It's near here. It's by the Torrs."

"So wreckage from ships might have been washed up on my beach," he said.

Ben did not reply and busied himself with rinsing a glass in a bowl of water behind a screen. He emerged and poured a generous helping of claret into it.

"Does everyone call it Brandy Cove?" enquired Armand.

"I don't know," said Ben, exchanging a glance with Jonah, his fellow footman.

"It's used for smuggling," Armand guessed. "I should think a lot of smuggling goes on near Ilfracombe."

"I don't know," repeated Ben, his face as red as the claret.

"Don't worry. I don't care about that. I'm only interested in shipwrecks," he told him.

Ben looked down uncomfortably at the floor. Armand stared at him for a minute and then slowly stood up, grimacing as he did so.

He left Wildercombe House and limped towards Esther's cottage. In the lane the long, hot summer had left the grass yellow and shrivelled, and blackberries were already forming on the brambles. Grasshoppers chirruped and jumped amongst dock leaves and nettles, and a dead frog lay flattened in a dusty rut of the track.

"I hope your name isn't David," he said.

The garden had been tidied; the broken vegetation piled in a compost heap, and the skeleton of the shed cleared of burnt wood. White-spotted, scarlet toadstools of fly agaric were growing by the hedge and a multitude of brown and cream mushrooms had sprung up beneath the rowan and alder trees.

He glanced at them uneasily and muttered in German, "Hexensessel. Witch's chairs."

Esther opened the cottage door and looked in surprise at him. "Have you been in a fight?"

"No, not really. I had to jump out of a window and I'm a bit bruised," he admitted.

"I was in Bideford. I went to the market."

"Bideford?" she queried. "That's a long way to go to a market. Why not Barnstaple?"

She stood in the doorway and looked searchingly at him. "Is there something you are not telling me?"

"I went to see Eliza Redmore, who used to be the housekeeper at Dunscombe Manor, to ask her about Isabella," he muttered.

She stared at him, clearly aghast, and did not speak for several seconds.

"You went to the Golden Lion? Did you meet John Redmore, her son?" she demanded.

"Yes, unfortunately. That is why I had to jump out of the window."

"Did you tell him who you are?" she questioned.

"No. We did not get that far in the conversation. Do you know John Redmore?"

"Yes. He used to be a captain on one of Raphael McAlpine's ships and he will soon hear that you have been asking about Isabella. Even if you did not give your name, you are very distinctive. Were you alone?"

"No. I was with Dietrich."

She threw up her hands in exasperation. "He wears Alsatian clothes and does not look like anyone round here."

"It is not important what Raphael McAlpine thinks," he said angrily.

"I told you not to meddle with things you don't understand. Isabella has survived all these years at Dunscombe Manor, and now McAlpine's going to finally let her leave. I asked many times if she could come and live with me, but he always refused. I was afraid he was intending to marry her himself, but he met Mrs McAlpine and his plans changed. Everything he does is for money and so I believe there is a great financial benefit to him for this marriage to go ahead. It is not a good idea to hinder Mr McAlpine in what he wants."

"I can't see why I shouldn't enquire about Isabella's origins," he replied defiantly. "And I have also found out that many ships were wrecked off this coast several years ago."

"Did you mention a shipwreck to John Redmore?" she asked, almost spitting out the words.

"No," he answered.

"Never mention it again," she cried, anger in her eyes. "You don't realise how you are placing Isabella at risk."

"I don't," he agreed. "Perhaps you can enlighten me."

"No, I am not saying another word on the subject. I will only tell you this. Do not meddle in events that do not concern you. You are putting both yourself and Isabella in danger."

"You speak in riddles, old woman," he said crossly.

"She is nearly free. I have feared for so long that she would be killed. She is like a daughter to me, and when she marries this Captain Petrie, whoever he is, I will go and live in America to be near her."

"Why should Raphael McAlpine kill her?" he said slowly.

"I have said too much," she replied. "I do not wish you to visit her today."

She shut the door and slammed the bolt on the inside, leaving him standing on the step. He banged furiously on the wood, before sitting down next to Tabitha.

He stroked her fur for a few minutes. Then he stood up, took the red and blue ribbons out of his pocket, placed them on a ledge in the porch and limped out of the garden.

He returned along the lane to Wildercombe House and went straight to the stables where the groom brought out his horse. He asked for Dietrich, but he was nowhere to be found, so he mounted and set off in the direction of Ilfracombe. He followed the Wilder to the marshland near the Strand, tethered his horse to a railing and walked to the shipbuilding yard in the cove by the harbour.

Carpenters were working inside the hull of an unfinished vessel; tar was bubbling in an iron pot over an open fire and a grey-haired man was overseeing the nailing of curved wooden struts.

"Did anyone survive the sinking of the Louisiana?" he asked.

"No, everyone died," the man replied. "They've all been buried at the top of the beach."

"Not in the churchyard?" he queried.

"No, they were heathen," said the man. "And even if any were Christian, the parish graveyard is too small."

"Have there been many shipwrecks round here?"

"Yes, a fair few," he replied.

"Have you heard of a ship whose name began with 'san', which was wrecked many years ago by the Torrs?"

The man reflected for a moment. "Yes, there was the….." he stopped in mid- sentence. His manner appeared to change and caution crept into his voice. "No, I don't think so," he muttered, and occupied himself again with the business of the nails.

Armand shrugged and walked to the cottages on the other side of the harbour. He passed by several young fishermen mending nets, until he came to an elderly man with a wooden leg, who was smoking a pipe. He stood for several minutes, breathing in the smell from the lobster pots on the quay and looking at the ships at anchor, before turning to his neighbour.

"Are you a fisherman?"

"I was in the navy," replied the man, "until I lost my leg fighting the Frenchies. Now I live at Saint Nicholas chapel, with my family of fourteen children, and light the lantern."

"Have you heard of a shipwrecked boat whose name began with 'san'? It was probably wrecked off the Torrs."

"Lots of shipwrecks off the Torrs. As well as near the harbour, like that one the other day at Rapparee. It's dangerous to come into Ilfracombe in a storm."

"So I am told," said Armand in irritation. "The last thing I think I will ever do is to try and sail into Ilfracombe harbour in a storm. I will drown out in the Bristol Channel instead."

He turned to go back to his horse, and just as he started walking away, the lantern-keeper said, "You were one of they vurriners who tried to rescue the poor souls at Rapparee, weren't you?"

"Yes, that's right."

He puffed on his pipe, his expression friendly. "The Santa Rosa was wrecked off the Torrs. Perhaps that's the ship you're after."

"The Santa Rosa. That sounds Spanish or Portuguese."

"I don't know where it came from. I only know where it ended up."

"Were there any survivors?"

"I shouldn't think so," he replied, raising his eyes to the sky. "There's not generally any. They're always buried on the beach."

"Like the Louisiana."

"Yes," the lantern keeper agreed.

"Thank you. You've been very helpful," said Armand, and gave him a coin.

The man knuckled his head, and he limped quickly back to his horse. He set off along Fore Street and up the hill towards the tall, round building of the Castle. Two little girls with red ringlets were scrambling with spinning tops and dolls on the ramparts, next to three cannon, and they shrieked with excitement as they saw him. "Mama, Mama. There's a visitor."

A servant showed him into a drawing room which looked over the steep hillside to the harbour and the Bristol Channel. It was clearly the residence of a seafaring man. A telescope was in the bay of the sash window, and paintings of ships in battle, adorned the walls. Trophies of voyages to far-off places were positioned on a marble mantelpiece, and the gruesome nature of some of the exhibits, which included a human skull, a Polynesian face mask with blue-ringed eyes, a dead rattlesnake and a tarantula, contrasted with the otherwise conservative décor of cream wallpaper and polished oak furniture.

He tapped on the spider's glass case, but it did not move, and he was on the point of investigating the snake, when Captain and Mrs Bowen entered the room, accompanied by Georgiana. Their welcome was warm, and he was content to sit down on a padded chair, rest his leg and be given a glass of brandy.

"I am leaving soon to join Earl Howe," said Captain Bowen. "So it is a pleasure to see you before I go."

"Would you like to hear Georgiana play the spinet?" asked her mother, and without waiting for an answer, installed her oldest daughter on the instrument's stool.

Georgiana melodiously sang a rendition of Robin Adair; the afternoon sun shining through the window, revealing the pallor of her skin and the unusual green of her eyes. He sank back against the softness of the chair, and tried to keep awake.

"You are injured, your Grace?" Mrs Bowen's voice sharply interrupted his drowsiness. "Have you had an accident?"

"Not really, it is nothing. My reason for coming here today is that I am interested in shipwrecks on this coast. Have you heard of the Santa Rosa, which, I believe, ran aground off the Torrs?"

"We've only been in Ilfracombe for five years," remarked Captain Bowen. "I'm afraid I don't recall the name, but I can find out for you."

"That would be very kind."

"I hear that you and your men helped at the sinking of the Louisiana the other day," remarked the Captain.

"We were passing after Raphael McAlpine's dinner, so went down to the beach, but were able to do nothing."

"That's a rum do at Dunscombe Manor with all those crows," remarked Captain Bowen.

"Well, I'm used to that sort of thing. My father was a scientist and always studied animals and plants, so I don't find it too strange."

"Did I hear you say at his house that you are not going to one of his meetings?"

"I don't intend to. I don't think Raphael McAlpine and I share the same views."

"I believe it's some sort of religious gathering. It sounds blasphemous to me," Captain Bowen declared.

The two little girls who had been playing in the garden, appeared in the doorway with a toy ship and a plaster doll. Their skin was as pale as Georgiana's, but their hair gleamed with a brilliant redness, only hinted at, in her case, by a few strands which had escaped the cosmetic powder.

"My mother's hair was that colour," he remarked, looking at them. "It was beautiful. But it turned white when my younger brother Robert died from measles. She also played the spinet very well. Perhaps Miss Georgiana would care to play another tune for me?"

"I would be happy to please you, your Grace," she said. "What would you like?"

"Well, I'm very taken with the new revolutionary tune in France. I know I shouldn't be, but it reminds me of Alsace and Strasbourg. If I whistle it, do you think you could play it?"

"I'll try," she said timidly.

He whistled the Marseillaise and she attempted to imitate it. A few false notes sounded and then the strains of Rouget de Lisle's marching song filled the room.

"It's a very pretty melody," said Mrs Bowen. "I've never heard it before."

"You say it's from the Revolution?" asked her husband. "If so, I don't think it should be played in my house."

"I heard it when I was last in Strasbourg. I suppose it should make me think of the terrible events occurring in France, but somehow it doesn't, and it's been in my mind ever since."

"We're at war now. I know that you're an émigré and also partly English, but there's much hostility towards the French in England. I noticed you came here alone without a retinue of servants. To be quite frank, that is not to be advised in the present situation. You need to be careful, your Grace," said Captain Bowen.

"Thank you for your concern. In fact, I gather there's been various attacks on men in Ilfracombe, and that they've had their eyes and parts of their bodies removed."

"Yes, there have been some strange goings-on here, and no one has discovered the cause. Young girls have suddenly gone missing, like poor Bess Mudge," said Mrs Bowen.

"I arrived the day of the riot at Esther's Cerfbeer's cottage, when she was being accused of her disappearance. I gather no one has any idea why these girls have vanished?"

"No, it's as though they've been spirited away. There have been two girls taken from Ilfracombe, one from Lynton and one from Combe Martin."

"I expect they've just eloped with someone," said her husband. "There's probably no mystery at all."

Armand drank more brandy and was persuaded to stay for dinner, and it was late in the afternoon before he eventually took his leave.

"Would you care to dine with us again next week, on Thursday?" asked Captain Bowen.

"Yes, I would like that very much. Thank you. Can you tell me where the doctor is? My ankle seems to be getting worse and I will go and see him before I return home."

"He lives at Wilderscot, near the Parish Church," said Mrs Bowen. "He has a good reputation in the town, both for medical matters and for butchery, as he owns a herd of cows and is proud of his abilities in that area also."

"Really," said Armand rather dubiously. "Perhaps I won't bother, although it is true he is on my route to Wildercombe House."

"He's very skilled," she said. "You won't regret seeing him."

The whole family escorted him out of the Castle and waited while he mounted his horse with difficulty. As he did so, his eye was caught by a small black cloud moving rapidly towards them. The sky was blue and cloudless, and he stared at it curiously. It came nearer and revealed a flock of crows flying closely together.

"Crows don't usually fly like that," he commented, as the birds alighted on the branches of an oak near the ramparts, cawing aggressively, before becoming quiet.

The youngest Bowen child, Ann, her necklace gleaming round her neck, ran across the grass, spinning her top. A large crow suddenly left the group and swooped threateningly towards her. Armand galloped across the lawn, quickly unsheathing his sword, and just as the bird reached her, he slashed at it, decapitating its head in mid-flight. It fell twitching to the ground and Captain Bowen kicked it with disgust into a hedge. The girls screamed in fright and Georgiana and Mrs Bowen gathered the children into their arms and ran back inside the castle with them.

Armand looked at the remaining birds still perched in the oak tree.

"I've never seen a crow attack anyone before. I think it was perhaps her necklace which it wanted. It was shining in the sun."

"I'll get my pistol and frighten them away," said Captain Bowen.

"Yes, that's probably a good idea. Good day sir, we will meet again next Thursday."

He cantered down the hill on his horse, following the street towards the Parish Church. He stopped at a white-walled house on the bank of the Wilder, and was greeted by Doctor Conibear, a small man, wearing a greasy brown wig, and with eyes the colour of honey.

Several hours later, many pounds lighter in his pocket, and much less blood in his body, he emerged onto the front porch, and held one of its pillars for support, as a servant brought his horse. His ankle and clothes smelled strongly of the mixture of toad skin and rabbit droppings, which had been smeared onto his skin, and he took out his silver flask and swigged a generous helping of brandy. The world spun round him, and he muttered, "A mistake, I think," before clumsily mounting his horse and continuing his homeward journey.

He looked blearily at the Torrs, where, on the nearest of the seven hills, harvesting was taking place at Samuel Mudge's barton. A gang of men was methodically moving forward in a row, scything the wheat, and two women were working behind them, gathering up the stalks. Snatches of their conversation carried through the air, even at that distance, and he heard, to his surprise, the deep tones of Dietrich's voice. He peered at the labourers, one of whom was very large and wearing an Alsatian black felt hat.

"Well, I'll be damned," he said, slurring his words. "That's why he couldn't be found."

He started to canter across the fields to the barton, then changed his mind and galloped up the lane towards Esther's cottage, to the other recipient of the blue and red ribbons from Bideford.

At her gate, he again took out his flask, but after much consideration, placed it back in his pocket. The round moon-eyes of an owl in the alder tree, stared unblinkingly at him in its round moon-face, and the sphere of the moon glowed in the rapidly darkening evening sky, its brightness eclipsed by the brilliance of Venus.

"Too many moons for my taste," he muttered. "Let's go and see the witch."

He rode his horse right up to the front of the cottage, and fell off, rather than dismounted. He kicked the front door heavily with his boot to force the latch, but it was unbolted and opened easily; he lost his balance and staggered into the downstairs room.

Esther was sitting at the table, which was covered with a white cloth on which were burning two candles in candlesticks, next to a plate of plaited bread. She was speaking aloud in Hebrew and continued to intone the rituals of her religion, "Baruch atah Adonai, Eloheinu Melech ha'olam." She raised her voice, "Hamotzi lechem min ha'aretz," while casting venomous looks at her unwanted visitor.

"You're not going to stop me with your spells," he shouted, and stumbled across the room and up the narrow staircase. She did not follow him, but stayed seated, as she recited the sacred words and performed the centuries' old rite.

Isabella was lying in bed, as he had last seen her. Her head was again bandaged, but without any stains of blood; her face was still very white. The Hebrew words resounded in the bedchamber; she moved slightly and seemed to listen and relax. He lumbered to the chair and sat down. He fell asleep and suddenly awoke to find Esther standing next to him.

"What are you doing here Seigneur? And what is that smell?" Her face was contorted in anger, her eyes were dark orbs piercing into his befuddled state and sobering him.

"I visited Dr Conibear. It is one of his special medications," he mumbled.

"Medications! He doesn't know the meaning of the word," she exclaimed. "The man's an imbecile, as are most of his patients. Go home and wash off anything he has rubbed on you, and don't come back until you are clean and not incapable with drink. I might owe a debt to your parents, but I will not allow you to interfere with my life and someone I hold very dear. Away with you!"

She glared furiously at him and he sheepishly stood up. He looked at Isabella, who continued to sleep, in spite of the noise, and then he looked at Esther.

"Do not tell me what to do, old woman," he said coldly. "Your practices are not Christian and you will bring trouble down onto yourself. I want her to be roused from this trance you have put her in."

"You have no understanding of anything," she shrieked. "However, it is almost time for her to be woken, and if you come back tomorrow, you will see the wisdom of what I say. Go now."

For a moment, his temper flared up, before he quietened and limped to the stairs.

"I will come back tomorrow and this time you will let me in, or I will break down your door and you can fear the consequences."

He stamped down the stairs, and slammed the front door as he left.

She waited until he and his horse had departed from her garden, before opening the window wide and scattering rose water round the chamber.

"Do not cross me, Armand François de Delacroix," she muttered. "Or you will regret it!

23

Isabella screamed out from her heavily drugged sleep. "Blood. A crucifix upside-down. It's too dark. I'm afraid. Let me go to her. A door... a red door, iron bands, a skull. I want her....." she sobbed, tears running down her cheeks."Shadows. Shadows, Shadows. Shadows. Maleus."

Esther wiped her forehead with a wet cloth and she opened her eyes and appeared to be drifting between reality and nightmare. She clung desperately to Esther. "No, I can't return there!"

Esther held a spoon to her mouth and she sipped the yellow liquid thirstily. Her eyes gazed unseeingly; she slumped against the bolster and fell back into sleep again.

"She's right. You must stop giving her the mandrake. It's killing her," said Armand angrily.

"Mandrake calms. It quietens. She would be far worse if it were not for that. Her head has been injured and it is making her see strange and terrible sights."

She wiped Isabella's forehead again. "She needs to be less fevered and then she won't remember so much."

"What do you mean 'remember'? She's not remembering. She's imagining," he said.

"No, I think she's recalling past events," she replied. "It is possible it is helping her to heal."

"I don't think so," he shouted. "You are completely mad, old woman, and you're harming her."

"No," snapped Esther, cold disdain in her eyes.

"You told me she would be a lot better today. Well, that doesn't appear to be the case. Is there any doctor other than Conibear round here?" he demanded.

"No," she said again. "You have to be patient."

He looked at her suspiciously. "What does she mean? An upside-down crucifix? What sort of blasphemy is that? How could she have seen such a thing?"

"Calm yourself. It's difficult enough caring for Isabella without having to concern myself with you," she exclaimed.

"Well, what do you know about an inverted crucifix?" he said, trying to curb his temper.

"She saw it when she found the secret chamber at Dunscombe Manor, the other day," she replied.

He was shocked into silence.

"So McAlpine's some sort of Devil-worshipper," he muttered. "I knew it was a house of wickedness. And she's found a secret chamber. I wonder what evil practices go on there? And what about the red door?"

"I don't know what that is. I've never heard of it before," Esther replied.

"And shadows and Maleus? What's that?" he asked.

"I am not sure. Isabella has not spoken of them, but I fear they may be books," she said.

"Books?" he queried.

"I will ask her when she is properly awake," she replied.

"You think she will recover then?" he asked meekly.

"Yes. Now go outside and chop some wood for me."

He stared at her.

"You need to do something. It is no use sitting here. You are in my way. And you are not helping. The other émigrés have discovered what work is, even if you haven't, as you own an estate. Go and get the axe from the shed and chop the branches that are next to it. It will do you good. Just don't injure yourself. I would not have the time to treat you."

He looked uncertainly at her.

"Go. Let me look after Isabella. If you don't want to help me by chopping wood for the fire, return home, and I will do it myself later."

He looked at Isabella who was now lying quietly asleep. Then he went downstairs to the garden, where he took off his coat and, for the first time in his life, chopped wood. He stacked the logs neatly when he had finished and sat down on the front step. He spat on his blistered hands and was rubbing them on his shirt when he suddenly caught the sound of Isabella speaking to Esther in the bedchamber. Her voice was normal. The delirium had obviously passed. He immediately jumped to his feet and ran back inside the cottage and up the stairs.

She was sitting up in bed, her face flushed, her eyes bright.

He smiled with pleasure. "Good day, madam. I can see you are feeling better and without the slightest help from the doctor. I hope you like your presents," and he indicated a varied assortment of objects on the table near the bed.

She looked at the bracelet of shells, the red and blue ribbons, the sugared plums, the ginger-bread man and the red roses in a Chinese vase.

"Are they all for me?" she said.

"Only if you promise never to visit my beach," he replied.

She reached out to touch the biscuit figure. "I think I can safely promise you that," she murmured. "I never want to go near the sea again."

"I made the bracelet. And I picked the roses. But the cook has made the sweetmeats," he told her.

"They are lovely. Thank you very much. Have I been asleep a long time?" she asked.

"Nearly a week," said Esther, "But you are much better now."

"I remember falling in the cave. What happened then? How did I get here?"

"I was pleased to be of service, yet again," he replied.

"You?" she said slowly.

"I owe my life to Dietrich many times over. I have lost count of how often he has saved me," he answered, shrugging his shoulders.

"That is different," she replied unhappily. "He is your servant, whereas you have no reason to help me."

"It is God's will," he said. "I was placed in a position to save you and I am delighted to have done so." He bowed low.

"I have nothing to give you. Nothing," she repeated and lay back weakly against the bolster.

He stood gazing at her and she blushed.

"That is very true," said Esther. "And as it was the will of God, the Seigneur will receive his reward in Heaven, not on Earth."

"We will see," he replied, glancing at her, and took a sugared plum and ate it.

"I found the doll's gold chain," Isabella said. "It proves I was there in a shipwreck, perhaps with my parents."

"You did not have it when I rescued you," he remarked.

"I know I found it," she said determinedly.

"It is more important to think of regaining your strength," said Esther. "You must forget all this for the moment."

She looked curiously at Isabella. "When you were fevered, you kept repeating the words, 'shadows' and 'maleus'. What did you mean?"

"They are part of the names of the books I saw in the secret room. They were on a shelf there. Why? Is it important?"

"Do you remember the whole titles?" asked Esther.

"I think one was called Book of Shadows and the other was Maleus something," she replied.

"Maleus Maleficarum?" Esther enquired.

"Yes, that is it," said Isabella. "Have you heard of them?"

"They are ancient books. 'Maleus Maleficarum' is Latin. It means 'Hammer of the Witches' and was used for centuries to detect witches. It is one of the most evil books ever written. 'Book of Shadows' is very different. It contains witchcraft secrets which have been handed down from one generation to the next."

"It is strange Raphael McAlpine has them," remarked Armand grimly.

"I have given him some of my knowledge of herbs, but I have always suspected he has an interest in the dark arts." A look of anxiety crossed her face. "I will go and prepare chicken broth now for Isabella to help her recovery," and she walked slowly out of the room, her shoulders stooped, her body frail.

"It pleases me greatly that you are better," he said, as the sound of Esther's footsteps receded.

Isabella looked enigmatically at him for a moment. Then she slowly closed her eyes and drifted off into sleep again.

He sat down on the chair and ate the last sugared plum, and when she was sleeping soundly, he bent and kissed her hair and her cheek.

"I intend my reward to come sooner than in Heaven," he said. Then he stood up and went downstairs.

He had eaten humble pie in order to remain on good terms with Esther. He had returned, clean and sweet-smelling, the day after his drunken visit, and had listened politely as she informed him of the benefits of finding a wealthy young lady to marry.

"A Dukedom is worth at least £25,000 in marriage," she had said. "It would save your estate, which appears to be in a precarious, financial position, without much hope of being improved."

"I am intending to make it profitable," he had declared.

She had merely thrown up her hands and looked heavenwards.

"Isabella is a penniless orphan, so her marriage prospects are very limited, but Raphael McAlpine has managed to find her a suitor."

He had held his tongue at that point and had just listened to her words.

"Captain Petrie lives in Virginia and I feel that is a very suitable place for Isabella to start a new life. I can accompany her there. The American Charter of Independence gives all men the right to be free and equal, so I would not be attacked because I am Jewish."

"Not all men," he remarked. "Evidently not black slaves."

She ignored him and continued. "I would be very sorry to leave Devon. I have found England a tolerant and peaceful country. There are many other Jews here, particularly from Germanic speaking countries and there has been a synagogue in Exeter since 1764."

"Perhaps Captain Petrie would not wish you to be there with his new wife?" he had queried.

"I am sure it can be arranged," she had replied.

"You believe Mr McAlpine to be a ruthless and dangerous man?" he had said. "A man who might kill Isabella?"

"I know him to be so," she replied.

He had kept his face impassive, and his temper in check, and watched her as she stirred a mixture of wolfbane and belladonna in a bowl.

"And you have never heard of the Santa Rosa?" he enquired.

123

"No," she said firmly.

"Well, I will forget about it then, in that case," he had declared.

She smiled at him. "Would you like a poultice of hemlock on your ankle?"

"No, thank you. It is, in fact, much better," he replied quickly.

"You can visit again," she had said. "I think we understand each other, even if we are perhaps not completely in agreement. Now I have work to do. You must go. I am sure there is somewhere on your estate which needs your attention."

"Yes," he agreed, and had taken his leave, waiting until he had reached the sanctuary of the lane to drink generously from the silver flask of brandy in his pocket.

24

Autumn chased away the heat of summer. The blackberries were ripe and juicy, deliciously perfuming the air. Late blooms of lilac flowers colourfully brightened every patch of waste ground and trailed over the fire-blackened shed. Wasps were gorging on fermented, fallen apples and making drunken flights across the garden.

"Devon people call them appledranes," said Isabella to Armand. "You can see why. And this is a chuggypig," she said, as a wood louse scuttled over the earth.

"Speaking of pigs, I need to finish inspecting my estate. I've only seen half of it, and that wasn't very satisfactory. My time has been taken up with rescuing a damsel in distress, and running round after a witch."

"You are getting on very well with Esther," remonstrated Isabella. "She likes you."

He shrugged. "What about the damsel in distress? Does she like me as well?"

"Perhaps. It might depend on how many presents he brings," she said, laughing.

"You are mercenary, my lady. It is not a quality I had associated with you," he replied severely.

She turned her attention to Tabitha who was playing with a piece of matted grass.

"She actually reminds me of Esther," he muttered. "She always wants her own way and has a strong personality I've never seen in a cat before. I've already advised her to stay away from Dietrich. He does not treat cats well at Easter."

"You accuse her of superstitious practices, but you and your men have more than she does," she said.

He reached out and tried to take her hand, but she moved away.

"You let me when you were ill," he commented.

"I don't think I was in much of a position to say no," she replied.

"It's not so bad, you'll see." He grabbed at her hand, but she again eluded him and moved further away on the porch. "I need to make the estate productive, or I will have to sell it to McAlpine."

She looked unhappily at him, as he said the name, and he forced himself to continue speaking.

"I will not be able to come tomorrow, or the next day, as I am going to Exeter to meet other French émigrés who want to join an attack on the Revolutionary army."

"Oh," she said, disappointment evident in her face.

"So you do care, milady," he remarked. "You have not a heart of stone, after all."

"You are going to France, to fight?" she questioned.

"Yes. I need to avenge my parents and also support a cause for which I feel strongly."

"You might be killed," she murmured.

"Well, I hope not, although I suppose it is a possibility," he replied honestly, but very aware it was the wrong answer to give.

She shivered, and at that moment, the sun went behind a cloud. She absentmindedly pulled the grass sharply away from Tabitha and the cat pounced on her hand, scratching it. Drops of blood oozed from the graze.

"It's a bad omen," she said.

"No, no it is not," he replied fervently and restrained himself from making the sign of the cross. Instead, he took her hand and raised it to his lips, kissing away the blood.

She looked at him in shocked silence and involuntarily glanced at the cottage to see if Esther had noticed.

126

"She has power over you," he remarked bitterly. "And she wishes to prevent me from courting you."

"She does not have power in the way you are suggesting," she replied. "She loves me and wants me to behave correctly, so that I will be free. It has been awful at Dunscombe Manor, and without her I would not have survived."

"I don't think an arranged marriage to a stranger is freedom," he said.

"It does not seem real to me. This seems real." And she looked about her at the garden and the trees and, finally, at him.

"When I return from Exeter I want to show you my house," he told her.

"That is not possible. Everyone will see me, and, in any case, I must make you understand that there is no future for us. You will die, like the others, and I will be ruined."

"No, they won't see you. I've thought about it. There is a September fair in Barnstaple. I will hire carts to take all the servants, and so no one will be there. Don't tell Esther," he muttered, and held her hand again. "Don't tell Esther," he repeated, tightening his grip and leaning so close that his mouth was brushing against her hair. "McAlpine will not kill me, and I have no intention of ruining your reputation. I must return to Wildercombe House now, but I will see you soon."

"I have two favours to ask," she said.

"Yes. You can demand of me what you want."

"I would like to make a sketch of you."

"No," he said crossly. "No, you want it as a keepsake for when you are no longer with me. You do not intend to see me again. So I forbid you that, madam. And what is your other request?"

"Harriet, who used to be at Dunscombe Manor with me, lives in Exeter. I have never heard from her since her marriage. Would it be possible to give her a letter? I know her address, and Mrs Gubb, the cook, said it is near the Cathedral Close."

"Well, I can certainly agree to the second. I will call here for it tomorrow morning at dawn."

He stood up. He leant down and kissed her cheek. Then he strode out of the garden, whistling the Marseillaise.

25

Isabella stood waiting in the dawn chill at the gate with her letter. It had taken her a long time to compose, as there had been so much to tell Harriet and so many questions to ask. She had written her name, Mrs Alexander McPherson, and the address, Ten Southernhay West, on the paper, and she gave it to Armand, when he arrived with his Alsatian soldiers, amidst a clatter of hooves, in clouds of dust.

He placed it in his pocket. "Ma belle," he whispered in her ear, his lips brushing against her cheek. She glanced at him and then at his men, who were not wearing Alsatian hats or clothes, but were dressed in a blue livery. They were, however, very well armed and managed to exude a military air, rather than that of household servants.

"We don't want to resemble an invasion force," he joked.

"No," she said dubiously, and watched as the horses thundered off down the narrow lane.

The road from Barnstaple initially followed the river Taw. It wound along the valley bottom, weaving through deciduous woodland interspersed with enclosed fields, grazed by cows and sheep. Elm predominated in the high-banked hedgerows, but there was also beech, hazel, ash and the fruit-laden rowan, whilst crimson poppies speckled the wheat stubble in the surrounding countryside. Many pack horses, carrying lime in panniers, were on the road, and huge mounds of it could be seen everywhere. By Crediton the brown soil had metamorphosed into a startling red, its dust staining clothes and discolouring boots and shoes. Even the cottages changed colour, their cob walls built with the red earth, their thatched roofs tinged with it.

As they neared Exeter, men on foot, wearing labouring clothes and carrying billhooks, scythes and staves, swelled the ranks of horses, carts and sledges already on the road. The horses slowed to a trot, as it was becoming difficult to advance in such a melée.

"What's happening?" asked Dietrich to Armand.

"I don't know," he replied. "Farm workers round here seem to have abandoned their employment."

The trickle of people became a flood, and by the time they reached New Cut, the widened postern gate in Exeter's ancient wall, they were riding in single file at the edge of an angry mob.

"Bread," came the shouts. "Bring down the price of wheat! Stop farmers hoarding!"

"It's like France at the beginning of the Revolution," remarked Hans. "It was the cost of bread which made the women march on Versailles."

They reined in their horses at the bottom of the street leading up the hill to the Cathedral, and waited until everyone had passed. Townsfolk were now joining, and even some militia, and they all disappeared along the main highway towards the east of the city, the noise gradually fading into the distance.

Medieval houses lined the road, which was intersected by narrow, dirty streets. Stalls crowded each side, selling a multitude of goods; leather, fabrics, trinkets, wooden tools and even animals. The smell of hot bread and coffee mingled with the odour of manure, which liberally covered the ground, and chickens, dogs and pigs roamed freely, impeding horses and vehicles from proceeding at more than a crawl.

They finally reached the Close, dominated by the massive stone structure of the Cathedral, its stained glass sparkling against its pale walls. Armand turned away from the potent symbol of Protestant worship, as did Dietrich, who regarded it with hostility. They made their way across the square, to Mol's Coffee House, the venue for the meeting, where a large group had gathered on the pavement, watching with gasps of horror, a man calling himself Black Jack, who swallowed a live mouse and 'mumbled' a sparrow. Hans was left in charge of the horses, his blue eyes and fair hair quickly making him a target of propositions from two ladies of the street, whom he ignored, as he watched the antics of Black Jack.

The aroma of coffee pursued them as they climbed the stairs to the first floor, where the sun was shining through oriel windows running the length of the façade overlooking the Close and the Cathedral. The chamber was crammed with men and a few women, and, at the front, stood a black-gowned priest with a large man, whose dark hair was tied back in a queue, and who was wearing a shabby brown greatcoat.

"Welcome, friends," he said. "I am Gabriel Soullans, and I come with news from the Vendée."

At the mention of the new revolutionary name of the region formerly called Bas Poitou, people booed and hissed and he appeared startled.

"I am from Bas Poitou," he corrected himself. "But although some people amongst you evidently still call it that, in France we have become used to calling it the Vendée, which covers a greater area. It is wonderful to see so many of you today, although it also gives me a great sadness, as I know you are in England, not from choice, but because you have had to flee the horrors taking place in our beautiful country. Abbé Pierre will now address you. He refused to swear allegiance to the Civil Constitution, like many of his fellow priests, and has only recently escaped from torture and prison in Nantes."

He looked at the assembled refugees and there was a moment of quiet in the chamber. A cockerel crowed from one of the stalls in the square outside, and an indistinct hum of noise rose and fell from the direction of the River Exe. Musket shots crackled and Dietrich and Armand exchanged glances.

"Are they firing on the rioters?" Dietrich muttered. "I don't think it's wise to be here too long. There are angry men in Exeter today and they might decide to stop complaining about bread and attack a roomful of French people."

"Yes," agreed Armand. "I want to join an invasion to save France, not be killed in Devon." He touched the letter in his pocket and for the first time noticed that Dietrich had a red ribbon attached to his coat.

"Thank you," said Abbé Pierre to Gabriel Soullans, in a low voice, and then addressed the gathering. He was extremely thin, a scarecrow of a man, the hem of his black cassock in tatters, his bony hands flapping the air to emphasise his words as he spoke.

"We need your help. The Republic is trying to destroy the life-blood of our region. We have fought, and are still fighting, in battle. Our Lieutenant-General, Jacques Alexis de Verteuil, was executed last December, and from January to May this year about fifty thousand people have been massacred by General Louis Marie Turreau. Our crops and forests have been burned and our farms and villages destroyed. In Anjou, seven thousand have been shot or guillotined. Help us, I beg you."

He stopped, overcome by emotion and fatigue.

"We are with you," shouted a man.

"We are with you," the cry went up from most of the people in the room.

The usually war-like Dietrich, however, said nothing, his face impassive, and Armand glanced at him curiously.

"I will repeat the words of General Westermann to the Convention," continued the Abbé, his voice trembling. "The Vendée is no more. According to your orders, I have trampled their children beneath our horses' feet. I have massacred their women, so they will no longer give birth to brigands. I do not have a single prisoner to reproach me. I have exterminated them all." He stopped again, and sat down on a chair, pain contorting his face.

The room exploded in tumult. A roar went up. People shouted in fury and it was some time before order was restored.

A man in a blue coat turned to face the assembly.

"I do not believe the situation is as bad as General Westermann described. He is probably trying to save his own skin by making his cruelty seem even worse than it really is, as he is afraid that the sans-culottes generals want to execute him. I know, for a fact, that there are still many prisoners in the Vendée, because my brother and uncle are among them. Our revolt is far from destroyed and I do not wish anyone here to think that it is not. The Republican army has behaved barbarously, but it can still be defeated."

"I agree with you," said Armand. "I am from Alsace and as I am sure you all know, it has been atrocious there. The Austrian forces managed to reach the gates of Strasbourg, but the Army of the Rhine drove them back. The Republicans denounced the Alsatian people as traitors and said they had helped the Austrians and were enemies of France. Most of their property has been confiscated. There are entire villages which are empty of both inhabitants and belongings, and at least forty thousand have been forced to flee to the other side of the Rhine. Four thousand victims have been flung into the dungeons at Strasbourg, among them many old men and women, and six hundred children. We must help the Vendée, and the Chouans north of the Loire. It is our only hope of exterminating the evil which is choking the life from our fair France."

"These are all fine words," muttered a short, black-haired man, who announced himself as Luca Fessi, from Ajaccio, in Corsica. "We must decide the detail of how we can help. There are a large number of émigrés in England and we can send both money and men to fight."

The room was now very hot, both from the sun and the many agitated people in it, and Gabriel Soullans spoke again, his face sweating profusely, whilst down in the Close the cockerel crowed once more.

"We have commandeered two ships. One will sail from Southampton and the other from Bristol, and they will land on the coast near La Rochelle. Volunteers from the west of England are asked to join the ship at either Bristol, or Ilfracombe. The actual date will be given to you later and we must be careful not to let spies know of our plans."

"Let's hope the cockerel does not crow a third time, or it bodes ill for having a traitor amongst us," commented Dietrich.

"I live at Wildercombe House in Ilfracombe," called out Armand. "I can billet some people, if needed."

"Thank you, sir," replied Gabriel Soullans. "I will coordinate arrangements with you."

The excitable nature of the gathering had masked what has happening in the street, but now the noise of drums and shouting suggested the rioters had reached the Close.

"Militia men on horses are charging the mob," a man declared, as he looked out of the window. "I think we had all better depart." He went to Gabriel Soullans and embraced him. "I will see you on the ship at Ilfracombe."

"Let's go," said Dietrich, and waited impatiently as Armand wrote his address and gave that and money to Abbé Pierre. Then they quickly descended the stairs and came out of the Coffee House into a square engorged with people fighting, throwing cobble stones and

132

overturning stalls. Hans was still waiting with the horses, trying to calm them in the midst of the riot, and Black Jack was no longer 'mumbling' sparrows, but had fallen to the ground, bleeding from a head wound.

Armand asked directions for Southernhay West from a stall keeper hastily throwing loaves of bread into a sack.

"It would be better to leave now," said Dietrich. "It is dangerous to venture further into the city."

He hesitated, "You're right, but I cannot break a promise, and it will only take a short time."

Dietrich frowned and took out his dagger from his belt. The crowd was milling around them and several people looked in their direction as they heard French accents.

"Frenchies!" a man in a battered tricorn hat exclaimed to his neighbour, who was busily engaged prising cobbles from the ground with a stave.

"Come on," said Armand, without waiting to hear any more, and cantered off, followed closely by Dietrich and the other Alsatians. They quickly made their way through the narrow streets until they reached Southernhay West, a terrace of elegant, three-storey houses. Armand banged on the door and a servant opened it, fearfully looking at the smoke drifting overhead from the rioting, accompanied by the sound of muskets firing near the Cathedral.

"I have a letter for Mrs Alexander McPherson," Armand said.

"No one of that name lives here," the man replied.

"Are you sure?" he questioned.

"Of course I'm sure. I've worked here for thirty years," he retorted indignantly.

"Do you know if she lives at another house in the street?" he asked.

"I know the names of all the families round here. I've never heard of Alexander McPherson." And he slammed shut the door.

"I must have the wrong address," said Armand. He mounted his horse and he and his men cantered down to New Cut and then galloped steadily along the road from the city of Exeter, overtaking a straggling succession of rioters. Some were being pushed in carts, their clothing blood-soaked. Others were hobbling along, and only a few appeared to be in the same condition in which they had started the day.

"It doesn't look as though good King George will be overthrown just yet," remarked Hans.

"People haven't enough to eat," said Dietrich. "It's similar to France. Their food is often just fatty bacon, barley bread and cabbage."

"Has the wheat harvest finished at Samuel Mudge's farm?" asked Armand.

"Yes," he said, looking surprised. "How did you know?"

"I saw you the other evening," he replied.

They stopped to change horses at Umberleigh. Apple orchards by the posting station near the Rising Sun tavern were heavy with fruit, and wasps were flying crazily, drunkenly settling on people and wallowing in puddles of cider on the tables. Armand drank from a tankard of the local brew, served by a maid without any front teeth. He grimaced at the acidic taste and took out his flask of brandy instead.

A second serving maid brought more tankards to the men and, as she smiled, her open mouth again revealed a lack of front teeth.

"I think it's the cider," said Dietrich. "It's very strong. It's good though. I'm developing a liking for it."

"I think you're acquiring a liking for something else," remarked Armand.

Dietrich shrugged. "Perhaps. I need to speak with you about their farm."

Armand looked at him questioningly, and Dietrich wandered to the river to watch a man catching eels. He was using entrails threaded with worsted wool and when the eels took the bait, it was impossible for them to free their mouths from the wool.

"A useful idea," he declared to Armand, as he adjusted the saddle of his horse, on his return to the tavern.

The Taw led them back to Barnstaple. The moon had risen, and although not full, it shone brightly enough behind wisps of clouds, for the riders to continue their journey without lanterns. Faces stared out at them in the darkness, some human, some animal. Travellers eager to return to the safety of their homes, scurried along in the night; wheels creaked and owls hooted, and in a cemetery by the roadside, lights flickered between the graves and the dull thud of a spade digging in the ground could be heard.

They cantered steadily through Pilton and climbed the hill beyond, then steeply descended to the valley stream. Welcoming lanterns illuminated the front of a coaching inn at Muddiford, but they ignored the loud carousing coming from its interior and carried on up the wooded hillside and across the high, open countryside towards Ilfracombe. The Bristol Channel was a dark blur on the horizon, and the sea air was fresh in their faces. The wind was increasing from the south-west and Armand smiled to see a candle flickering in the bedchamber of Esther's cottage.

26

The next morning, he presented himself at Esther's cottage, holding the letter in his hand. She opened the door, dressed in a black robe, her expression as grim as the colour of her clothing.

"She is not here," she said, without waiting for him to speak. "It was time for her to return to Dunscombe Manor. She is much better, and I believe the McAlpines are on their way from London."

He looked at her in surprise. "I was not expecting," he started to say.

"Your understanding is very limited, as I have already explained to you. You must now forget her and find someone of your own social standing, who has money," she continued bluntly.

He looked at her in annoyance. "Do not tell me what to do."

"And are you going to join the invasion of France?" she asked.

"Yes," he said.

She threw up her hands. "I think your own future is somewhat in doubt then. The Republican army is too strong. The Vendée will be crushed even more than it has already been, and you will be injured, or taken prisoner, or more likely, killed, and you will not be offering much then to a wife, whoever you find."

He looked sourly at her and pocketed the letter.

"Is that from Isabella?" she asked. "Didn't you give it to Harriet?"

"She does not live at this address. She has never lived there," he said.

It was Esther's turn to look surprised. "I expect you just didn't find the correct house."

"I did," he replied. "No one of that name has ever lived there."

She was quiet, and for the first time, appeared indecisive.

"Give me the letter. And I will return it to Isabella."

"No," he said, and strode off down the path.

"Leave her alone," she called, a note both of desperation, and of an implied threat, in her voice.

....

A band of crows stared down impassively from the window sills, as Armand and his men rode across the cobbles.

"The master is away," he was told at the front door by Reuben.

"I have business to conduct with him. Would it be possible to come in and write a few lines, which you can give him on his return?" he asked.

"Yes, your Grace," said Reuben, showing him into the drawing room and providing him with a quill, paper and ink at an oak desk. Armand started to write, hampered somewhat by the two wolfhounds licking his legs. At one point, he glanced up to see Reuben's eyes fastened on him and noticed that they were a golden hazel colour, which strangely reminded him of the fox in Esther's garden. His skin was the wrinkled, parchment white of an extremely elderly man and he looked at Reuben with interest.

"Have you been with Raphael McAlpine long?" he asked.

"Yes," said Reuben. "I used to be a cook on board his ship, the Heather, before I came here."

"You must know him well," he remarked.

Reuben stared hard at him. "Better than some," he replied, clearly not wishing to be drawn.

Outside in the courtyard, the horses were skittishly prancing; Hans and Tomas were laughing and shouting ribald comments as two serving maids passed them with pails of milk, and they could be heard clearly, even inside the thick-walled house.

Armand smiled to hear the noise he had told them to make, to draw attention to his visit, and painstakingly wrote another sentence, before screwing up the paper and starting once more. He wrote slowly. Then he crumpled it again.

"No, I have changed my mind. I will come to see Mr McAlpine when he has returned and speak to him in person."

The two wolfhounds and Reuben escorted him to the front door and he lingered a moment, patting Cain, in front of the painting on the wall.

"Why has she more than one head?" he asked.

"She is a goddess of many different faces," Reuben said reverentially. "She is Hecate."

Armand frowned. "Why is she carrying keys?"

"To open the gates between the worlds," Reuben informed him.

"And why is she holding a torch?"

"To light the way," he replied.

Armand glanced at him sourly, put his hand into his pocket and felt the reassurance of his mother's silver cross. He stepped across the threshold, and at that moment, Isabella came down the stairs, appearing hastily dressed; the ribbons on her gown were untied, and she was wearing two shoes which did not match.

"Good day, Miss Isabella," he said, bowing low.

She looked at him apprehensively, fingering the green malachite necklace at her throat.

"Good day, your Grace," she murmured.

"I was just calling on Mr McAlpine to discuss a business matter, but he is not here."

"No, he is still in London."

"I will return another day to see him."

"That is best," she agreed.

"I am interested in his plants. I have been told he has some very exotic species which need a greenhouse to flourish. I also have a greenhouse and I would like to obtain similar flowers."

"I am sure he will oblige you, your Grace."

"Where is the greenhouse situated? Is it near to the lane?"

"Yes, it is," she replied, after a second's hesitation.

"Well, I had better go now," he said.

He bowed again and left the house and rode away, up the hill, with Hans and Tomas. When he reached the end of the lane, he told them to

138

go home without him, and immediately galloped in the opposite direction, across the fields to the back of Dunscombe Manor.

He tethered his horse to a tree and entered the herb garden. He stood with his back to the wall and waited. The minutes passed and he kicked the bark in temper.

"You fool," he muttered. "How could she have understood?"

He impatiently fidgeted with his pockets and his knife, and pulled ivy from the stonework, whilst, all around him, creatures pursued their own lives in ignorance of the greater world. Bees buzzed over the poppies and the lavender; a file of ants marched industriously, burdened by fragments of leaf, and in the sky, a buzzard was being harassed by seagulls.

Suddenly he saw her. She was hurrying past the hemp plants and coming towards him. He smiled in relief, and stepped out from behind the tree.

She ran up to him and gave a frightened glance behind her.

"This is madness," she said. "You should not have come."

"I was not expecting you to be evicted so soon," he replied bitterly.

"Esther thought it was best," she said.

"I don't agree with Esther on much," he remarked, placing his arm around her waist, and pulling her behind the apple tree, in spite of her protestations.

"I don't think we can be seen here. Are you alright? You look very pale," he asked.

"I'm fine. But I would prefer to be at Esther's cottage," she said.

"So would I," he muttered. He gently touched the soft skin of her face. "I missed you."

They stood together for a few seconds. He embraced her and turned her face to his. Very slowly, he bent his head and kissed her on the lips. He drew her closer to him. Then she broke away and retreated to the wall.

"No, you mustn't. It's not fair. You know there is no future for us."

"I don't know any such thing," he retorted.

She looked at him in despair. "You are stubborn. You are rich. You are used to getting what you want."

"I am not rich any longer," he declared ruefully, taking the opportunity to put his arm around her again.

"Esther says you need to marry someone wealthy to save your estate. She is right, isn't she?"

"I will do my best to save my land, but that does not include a marriage of convenience."

"I don't want you to be killed and your eyes cut out," she exclaimed.

"You have too fertile an imagination, my beloved. Raphael McAlpine cannot harm me and you certainly do not carry a curse."

"He will be back soon. He is always here when it's Hecate's Moon."

"Hecate's Moon?" he questioned. "Does it belong to the woman who has three heads in the painting in the hall?"

"Yes, Hecate rules over three kingdoms, the Heavens, the Earth and the Underworld, and is the goddess of the moon and the night. Hecate's Moon is the time when the moon is dark in the month, before it becomes a crescent."

"Is that right," he remarked, raising his eyebrows. "Why is that important to him?"

She hesitated. "It's when he holds his meetings," she said softly.

"His meetings to discuss politics?" he asked.

"I don't know what they talk about. I don't think it is very connected with Hecate. Reuben always locks me in my bedchamber. I believe it often takes place in the wood over there." And she indicated a copse behind the greenhouse. "Sometimes there are weird noises, like animals, or chanting, but I try not to listen."

She shivered and looked in the direction of the house. "I don't like it here. I am afraid. There is evil…" She clasped her hand to her mouth. "I have said too much. Please forgive my ramblings. You have problems of your own."

"Well, I'm certainly glad I am not going to one of his gatherings. They sound bizarre. Captain Bowen is also not attending because he is going back to his ship. However, I am visiting him next Thursday for dinner. I think he has already told me all he knows, but I will ask him again."

"You are seeing Georgiana?" she questioned.

"Well, I suppose so," he replied.

She was quiet for a moment. Then she asked, "Did you give my letter to Harriet?"

"Oh, is that the only reason you have come to see me, madam?" he said, pulling a face. "And there was I thinking you wanted to meet me and even that you were perhaps not pleased I will be seeing Miss Georgiana."

"No," she protested, blushing. "No, that's not true."

"Well, she is not at that address," he said.

"She doesn't live there?" she queried.

"No. A servant at the house knew the people in the street well, and was sure that no one of that name lived in any of the houses there."

She looked at him in amazement. "It was Mr McAlpine who gave it to me."

"Well, it is wrong," he said bluntly.

"What happened in Exeter? Are you going to France to fight?" she asked.

"Yes," he admitted. "There will be a ship for volunteers sailing from Bristol and Ilfracombe."

"I have seen men who have fought in wars. They often lack arms or legs, like the lantern-keeper from St Nicholas Chapel. And sometimes they never come back," she said bitterly.

He looked at her, desperately wanting to make her happy, not sad, but only too aware of the truth of at least some of Esther's words.

"I want to show you my house," he said, changing the subject. "I've already told you I'm going to hire wagons and send all the servants to Barnstaple Fair. There will be no one there."

"I cannot see you again. You might think I am foolish and wrong, but I am afraid for your life if you continue to court me against the wishes of Raphael McAlpine. And Esther says that if you go to France to fight, you will probably be killed or injured or taken prisoner."

"Damn Esther," he shouted, and embraced her passionately again. "I love you and I want to see you."

He kissed her on the mouth, and, for a moment, she yielded to his touch before trying to push him away.

"No," she murmured. "No."

"Promise to come to my house at midday on September the nineteenth," he said, tightening his arms around her.

"I cannot, for your sake, as well as mine."

"No," he exclaimed. "Just once. Let me see you just one more time. Please," he bargained.

She hesitated, and he saw in her eyes that she was wavering. "I will find Harriet for you," he said impulsively. "I will tell you about her

141

when I see you at my house. I will not let you go until you agree."
And he embraced her again, passionately kissing her on her hair, her
face and her lips.

"I agree," she said, catching her breath and gazing at him. "Just one
more time."

He reluctantly let her go and she walked quickly back along the path,
past the black-berried belladonna and the tall plants of hemp.

Reuben watched from an upstairs window, his tiny, hunched body
concealed behind a curtain. He waited until Armand had departed.
Then he went down to the library to make preparations for his master.

27

Dietrich stood in the library looking at Armand.

The clock in the hall struck the hour, followed a few minutes later by the ormolu clock on the mantelpiece. Armand frowned as he contemplated his fellow Alsatian.

"So you want to leave my service?"

"Yes," said Dietrich calmly. "I want to marry Alice."

"You can marry her and still be at Wildercombe House."

"I need to work the farm. Her father died yesterday," said Dietrich.

"Are you talking about the barton which reverts to my estate on the death of the third leaseholder, which is, or was, Samuel Mudge?" he queried, a glint in his eye.

"Yes, I am," replied Dietrich stoutly. "I wish to take on a new lease."

"So I lose, not only you, but also a large farm, which seems somewhat more productive than my own?" he said bitterly.

"I would not leave you completely. I would always be here if you need me."

"What about the invasion force?"

"I am not going. I have thought hard about it. I am the only one left in my family. My parents and brothers have all been killed, and I am not

143

going to risk my life on a hopeless cause. I'm going to marry Alice. I wish to survive."

"I understand," Armand said sadly. "I, too, have been tempted not to go, but I must avenge my parents and help to save France from its present misery."

Dietrich looked at him. "I am sickened by all the suffering and violence I saw in Alsace. I want no more. I know I'm a soldier, not a farmer, but I would like to try and work the land."

"You can have the farm. I give it to you as a wedding present," replied Armand, and embraced him. "You have always been like a brother to me."

"Thank you," said Dietrich, as he returned the embrace. "I have another favour to ask. I would like to be married in the chapel here at Wildercombe House. Alice has said that she will, of course, convert to Catholicism."

"Yes, certainly. Is Alice the fair-haired girl, who was standing at the door of the farm when we visited?"

"Yes. There is an older daughter, but she has disappeared."

"I had forgotten. I had not connected the names. Bess Mudge must be her sister."

"Yes. There has been no word or sighting of her since she was milking their cow, the evening she vanished."

"That's very strange. I can see why Esther Cerfbeer was accused," he remarked. "Now perhaps if we're both becoming farmers, you will be more interested to accompany me than you usually are, over my estate this afternoon, and advise me on its shortcomings."

He pulled the bell on the wall to summon Mrs Widdicombe. Half an hour later, he was still waiting, and he and Dietrich had consumed nearly a bottle of Geneva.

A servant was despatched to locate Mr Widdicombe, who eventually arrived, displeased to have had to leave his usual seat at the George and Dragon. He was not delighted with the news that Dietrich was being given the Mudge farm, and that he himself was being called on that afternoon to escort Armand to see his property.

His cheeks swelled and became puce, instead of red. His sausage fingers drummed on the table.

144

"You're giving away the farm, now that Samuel Mudge has died and it has become the property of Wildercombe House?" he spluttered apoplectically.

"Yes, and I want a contract drawn up to that effect," Armand told him. "It's no business of you what I do. It's my land."

Ezekiel Widdicombe scowled and spat into the empty hearth, then wiped his sweating face with his sleeve.

"It's madness!" he shouted, glaring at Dietrich "Sheer madness. It be a good land, a bit stickle perhaps. It needs a praper owner. Not zome vurriner who dunnt know a shovel from a yowing hook."

"How do you know?" said the quick-tempered Dietrich, not understanding the Devon words, but realising the gist of what the estate manager was saying. His hand went to the knife in his belt, and Ezekiel Widdicombe backed away, his eyes slits in the fleshy folds of his face. He spat again, this time on his sleeve, and Armand regarded him with distaste.

"May I remind you that you are my servant and have no say in what I do," he shouted.

"And your wife seems to have abandoned the house. Where is she? I have a mind to sack the pair of you."

Ezekiel went quiet, but continued to scowl in resentment.

"Now I want you to show us the estate. And this time I hope to see more than a few fields of wheat and thistles."

....

Blackberries vied with scarlet hips and haws to bring Nature's bounty to the hedgerows. The maze of irregularly shaped fields, bounded by coppiced banks, resembled barren outposts within the lushness of the countryside. Stones littered groundsel-choked land, and a team of oxen pulling a long-bodied, short-beamed plough was only scratching the surface of the soil, not furrowing it.

The chants of the ploughboy, interspersed with those of the ploughman, followed the trio of riders as they made their way through a meadow of yellow-flowering furze to the linhay and dairy on the far side of the coombe.

Gurry butts, overflowing with lime and manure, lay idle by a cob wall, and thin, mud-smeared white pigs rooted amongst a mash of boiled turnips, grass and clover, in a bare enclosure. Pools of stagnant water lay in cart-wheel ruts, and clouds of midges infested an air smelling of rancid milk and manure.

Ezekiel Widdicombe dismounted and announced that they had reached the dairy. Armand and Dietrich swung down from their horses and entered the low outhouse, where a young, mob-capped girl was stirring milk in a brass pan over the embers of a wood fire. She jumped in fright to see visitors, nearly knocking over the milk pan, which trembled on its metal stand, before settling back again.

The room smelt even more strongly of manure than the air outside; an odour which emanated from a third gurry butt, propping open the door of a stable occupied by a dark red cow. Flies swarmed, circling endlessly beneath the rafters, and alighting on earthenware pans filled with milk, whilst a second girl, in a dirty apron and mob-cap, was churning cream in a wooden bowl.

"Are you making butter?" enquired Armand.

"Yess, zur," she replied.

"What are you doing?" he asked the other dairymaid.

"I be making clotted cream, zur. For junkets."

"I've been watching Alice prepare it," said Dietrich. "It's only made here in Devon. The milk has to be boiled, then scalded. It's much thicker than ordinary cream." His face showed an interest normally reserved for his hunting activities, and a flicker of a smile crossed Armand's face.

"I can see you're really becoming a farmer," he remarked.

"I am trying," said Dietrich. "However, Alice's dairy is clean, not like this. Her sister, Bess, used to milk the cows and produce the butter and cream, but now Alice has to do it all, and sometimes I've been helping her."

Ezekiel Widdicombe was standing silently by the door, and at the mention of Bess Mudge, his body twitched, and his eyes became even more lost in the folds of his skin.

Armand looked curiously at him. "Do you know anything about Bess Mudge?"

"No, never 'eard of 'er," he growled.

146

"You must have heard of her?" exclaimed Armand, in surprise. "Practically the whole of Ilfracombe was rioting near to Wildercombe House the day I arrived, because of her disappearance. I can't believe you were in ignorance of that." He stared at his estate manager.

"Young girls do as ey please," he said belligerently. "It's nought to me."

"So you do know her," said Armand. "You know she's a young girl." Ezekiel Widdicombe spat into a pile of hay and stamped outside.

"You need to sack him," said Dietrich to Armand. "The farmland here is not very fertile, but the estate is in a worse condition than it should be. His wife is as slovenly as he is and I don't trust either of them."

"You're right. But I have no one else and I'm shortly going to France to fight."

"I know you don't like him, and think he might be a spy, but I would ask Guillaume Thibaud for advice. He seems very knowledgeable about agriculture and he's been useful for a few things to do with Alice's farm. He's not a Jacobin, like Robespierre, and he did fight alongside Lafayette, your relation."

"Perhaps you're right. It's true I am suspicious of him, but I need help, or the estate will be lost, and I must organise the farmland before I leave for France."

"It doesn't hurt to ask his advice. You don't have to take it," he said.

"Yes," agreed Armand.

"Let us go to the Mudge farm now. I would like you to meet Alice."

....

Mrs Mudge welcomed Armand into the farmhouse. She curtseyed, as did her daughter, who blushed and looked shyly at Dietrich.

"The Seigneur is giving me the farm as a wedding present. It will not be on a lease anymore," he announced.

Mrs Mudge seemed to collapse with emotion and had to be helped onto a wooden settle by the fireplace. Alice brought out a smelling bottle of hartshorn, and while she was attending to her mother, Dietrich took Armand upstairs to pay his respects to Samuel Mudge, whose body was lying in a four-poster bed and who was dressed in a white wool shroud, his head resting on a wool pillow and his face covered by a white flannel cloth.

They both made the sign of the cross and stood quietly in prayer, and then went back down to the living room, where Mrs Mudge had recovered enough to be bustling about, setting out glasses, a bottle of wine and a plate of funeral biscuits, wrapped in wax paper and sealed with black wax.

"Thank you," said Armand, sitting at the table. "I am very sorry about your husband."

"God has taken him from us, but he has sent Dietrich in his place." Her voice was calm, but her hand shook so much as she poured out the wine that Alice took over.

Dietrich watched her proudly. She was dressed in a black dress, a black lace fichu at her ample bosom, her white-blond hair loosely tied at the nape of her neck with a black ribbon. Her eyes were a brilliant blue, and even although she was in mourning for her father, they shone with an unmistakeable vivacity and happiness.

Mrs Mudge, however, was clearly in a very distraught state. In spite of the warmth of the autumn sunshine she was clutching a thick black shawl over her shoulders. Her eyes were red-rimmed and her face was as ashen as that of her husband upstairs. She trembled incessantly and several times mumbled the name, Bess.

Alice led her out of the room, and, on her return, she said to Armand, "Please excuse my mother. She has lost my sister and my father in a short space of time. I am sure she will recover, as Dr Conibear is treating her, but it has been very hard for her. Mr Widdicombe has always said that we would be evicted, and we felt that he wanted our farm for himself."

"He would not have had it," said Armand in a puzzled tone. "It would have reverted to my estate."

"We did not realise your family still owned Wildercombe House. We thought Mr McAlpine had bought it."

"Why did you think that?" he enquired.

"Because he was always there. We used to see him riding along the lane."

"You think he was at my house?" he questioned.

"Well, I can't be certain. Perhaps he was visiting Esther Cerfbeer. But we believed him to be at Wildercombe House. My sister still has not

148

been found and so we do not have a body to mourn. I am sure she must be dead, but it does not seem that we will ever know."

"What exactly happened?" he asked.

"She was milking the cow in the barn and was suddenly not there. We searched everywhere, and so did all our neighbours. There were reports of strange men, near the Torrs, who looked like sailors, but we don't know if they had anything to do with Bess."

"She wasn't eloping?"

"No," she exclaimed. "There was no question of that. She was going to be married to Thomas Venner. The banns had been read at the Church."

He finished eating a sugared funeral biscuit and stood up.

"It has been a delight to meet you, even although the circumstances are sad, and I look forward to your wedding."

Dietrich embraced him and then he returned alone along the lane to Wildercombe House. He tethered his horse by the stone birds and wandered slowly up through the wood, where variegated shades of green dappled the bushes and trees. He ran his finger over a foxglove bell and watched water droplets trickling through moss. The black fungi of deadman's fingers caught his eye and he stopped.

"Too much of death today," he muttered. "What are you doing, Isabella? I pray you are safe."

He retraced his steps, his expression sombre.

28

Armand sat eating his breakfast of beefsteak, eggs, ham and mushrooms. Rain was pattering against the windows in the dining room, but towards the wood, the sky was lightening, pale blue chasing away the grey.

Ben clumsily knocked over the toast dish, and as he retrieved the triangles of bread, his hand shook.

"Are you alright?" asked Armand.

"Yes," he muttered. "I'm just a bit worried about my brother."

"What's he done?"

"Summat he shouldn't have. But it's not important." He shrugged his shoulders, a habit he had recently acquired after spending time drinking with Hans and Tomas.

"Would you ask Mrs Widdicombe to come here?" said Armand.

He downed a glass of claret and was attacking the beef steak when his housekeeper entered the room. She was a huge woman, but carried her weight well. She strode, like a man, rather than walked; her hair was scraped back from her face into a mob cap; the dark cotton of her dress covered massive arms and chest, whilst its hem and cuffs were fringed by white lace, a strangely feminine touch on such a masculine body.

"Yes, your Grace," she enquired.

"Has Mr McAlpine ever visited Wildercombe House in the years when my family did not live here?"

"He might have come to see if they were in residence, but really I have no idea," she said.

"So he was definitely not here?" he asked.

"No," she replied flatly. "Will that be all?"

"Did you know Harriet who lived at Dunscombe Manor?" he continued.

She appeared surprised for a moment. "I saw her. I didn't know her," she muttered, her expression becoming impassive again.

"Have you any idea where she lives now?"

"No. You need to ask Mr McAlpine."

"I am not pleased with your husband's management of my estate. I am also not pleased that you were not to be found yesterday when I wanted you," he told her.

"I was in Ilfracombe buying fish at the harbour," she declared defiantly.

"What fish did you buy?" he asked.

"Nothing. It wasn't suitable. They only had toe rag," she declared.

"And what's that?"

"It's salted cod from Newfoundland."

"The house is not in a good state," he said, leaving the subject of fish. "I want it thoroughly cleaned by September the nineteenth."

"Yes, your Grace. Is that all?" she replied, her words polite, but her manner churlish.

"For now," he said, looking at her with displeasure. "I want three horses brought to the front steps. Tell Tomas and Hans we are riding to Combe Martin this morning."

She marched out of the room, without replying, and he waited until she had gone, before asking Ben. "Were all the servants hired just before my arrival, or was it just you?"

"Everyone was hired at the same time. It was only the Widdicombes who were here, except for the farm workers."

In the distance, a hunting horn blared and he jumped as though he had seen a ghost.

"You seem very nervous today," remarked Armand. "Drink this," and he gave him his glass of claret. "It will steady you."

151

An hour later, he, Tomas and Hans set off down the drive on the horses. The sun was now shining and the sky had become a radiant blue. A faint outline of the moon was visible and he crossed himself at the unusual sight of the sun and the moon together.

Esther was in her garden hanging four dead crows on a scarecrow as they passed by.

"I hope you haven't murdered McAlpine's pet birds," he called to her over the hedge.

She glanced at him, as she strung up another crow, and he saw that the body of a fox was laid out on the ground below the elder.

"Did you kill it?" he asked.

"No," she snapped, her eyes misty with tears, and he knew, even before he looked, that the animal lacked its eyes. He watched her struggle with the birds and saw that she was shaking.

"When I return I will send a servant to help you in the cottage."

"No," she said. "I might be failing, but I'm not dying just yet, and I don't need assistance."

"As you wish," he replied, and continued down the lane to Ilfracombe. He passed the Parish Church, crossed the bridge over the Wilder and made his way along the main street. People excitedly thronged the path; some knuckled their heads, but a greater number regarded him and his men sullenly.

The crowd became more numerous, but was strangely quiet. A mood of expectation was apparent; faces were turned towards Fore Street, and from near the sea came the trumpeting of a hunting horn and the howling of dogs.

"What's that?" asked Hans, as a half-naked man with stag antlers tied onto his head, suddenly came into view at the corner of the road. Men with staves were chasing him, and bystanders were throwing stones and clods of manure. Blood was pouring from cuts on his head and chest, and his breeches were torn and filthy.

"What's going on?" Armand asked a woman in a lace bonnet, holding a child up to watch the spectacle.

"It's a stag hunt," she said. "He's committed adultery."

One antler dropped onto the ground and the man fleet-footedly sprinted away up the hill, followed by his more lumbering pursuers, one of whom was blowing a hunting horn, whilst the others were baying like hounds.

The sound of the pursuit gradually faded, and he remarked to Tomas and Hans, "You had better leave the fair Widdicombe alone, or you'll end up with antlers on your head like that poor fellow."

They passed through Chambercombe and Hele and cantered along the steep and winding road, which was deserted of other travellers. Sheep grazed on windswept headlands; Red Ruby cows occupied pockets of lush pasture in deep valley bottoms and two oxen, yoked together, were ploughing a field. Beyond the cliffs, the sea was ebbing from shingle coves, and off Watermouth the herring fleet was tacking backwards and forwards.

29

As Isabella fastened the malachite necklace around her neck, her fingers snagged it, and the beads scattered in all directions. She dropped to her knees, scrabbling over the floor to retrieve the black-whorled green stones, knowing that today, of all days, she needed their luck and protection.

She found as many as she could, then went downstairs and out of the house and across the gardens, smiling as she passed the apple tree where she had stood with Armand. She walked across the gravel to the greenhouse and entered its humid heat, its glass walls already misted. She looked at the dried bodies of mandrake on a shelf and chose a small root in female form. She stepped over the large dark green leaves trailing on the ground and bent down to smell the apple-scented yellow fruit. She examined several discoloured, pineapple-shaped fruits of henbane, next to the mandrake, and picked off several mites. Then the unpleasant odour from their leaves became too pungent for her in the enclosed space, she abandoned the task and left the greenhouse with the mandrake safely in her pocket as a talisman.

She was passing the apple tree again when an odd-sounding noise erupted from the lane outside the manor. Dogs were baying, but the noise seemed a strange mixture of human and animal. She listened.

Men were shouting and there was a heavy pounding of feet. They were coming closer and she opened the door to the lane to see what was happening. A bare-chested man was sprinting down the hill, an antler held by a rope around his head and neck, banging against his shoulder.

He reached the door and pushed past her. He slammed it shut, and stood, panting, his eyes searching the garden frantically.

"Don't 'ee say nothing, please," he begged.

The bizarre howling was becoming louder. She took one look at the pitiful state of the man in front of her and ran to bolt the door. The pursuers shouted and barked as they rushed down the lane, and the din gradually receded into the distance.

"Thank 'ee," he gasped. "I know I've done wrong, but there's no need to kill me for it."

He blinked repeatedly, the blood pouring from his head into his eyes.

She stared at him aghast. "Don't let the servants see you. They might tell the stag hunt."

"I expect they'll come back when they can't find me. I'd better go," he muttered.

"Can you clean yourself?" she asked, and pointed to a horse trough by the wall.

Struggling to catch his breath, he staggered to it, pulled off the antler, and splashed himself liberally with water. His cuts, however, continued to bleed; the blood mixed with the green algae from the trough, streaking his skin and giving him the appearance of an exhibit in the Fairground Chamber of Horror.

"I've got to go. They'll be back soon. They know where they last saw me."

"Yes," she agreed. "Hurry and go up the hill. I'll stand in the lane and say that I haven't seen you if they return."

"Thank you, Miss. My name's Ned Tucker. My brother, Ben, works at Wildercombe House. I'll go there and he'll help me."

"Wildercombe House?" she said.

"Yes, Wildercombe House," he repeated. "Thank 'ee. I can't thank 'ee enough."

She unbolted the door and cautiously stepped out into the lane. There was no one in sight and she beckoned to Ned to come out.

"Go over the hill by the Cairn. You're not likely to meet anyone on that path."

"Thank 'ee," he repeated, and ran hurriedly back up the lane. She waited anxiously at the door, but her only predatory companion was a buzzard on a branch, and not the human hunting party. She stayed a few minutes and then slowly returned, with reluctant steps, through the gardens to the house and her bedchamber.

The downstairs rooms had already been thoroughly prepared for the imminent arrival of the McAlpines, and the servants were all upstairs, shaking the feather mattresses and hanging them out of the windows to air. Jenny and Hannah were bickering, Mrs Gubb was scolding, and a general air of gloom had settled on the household at the thought of the unpopular homecoming.

She contemplated her reflection in the mirror on the dresser.

"Courage," she told herself, fingering the mandrake root in the pocket of her skirt. "I must do it now, or there might not be another chance."

She took a new candle, lit it from the stub she had left burning that morning, and placed it in a rosewood holder. She quickly descended the stairs and went into the library. She pulled back the tapestry to reveal the panelling, and pushed the embossed knob. Her hand shook and the candle guttered, spilling beeswax onto her skin and making her wince in pain as she hurriedly stepped across the threshold. She rearranged the tapestry, shut the door, and stood alone in the chamber.

The flame from the candle jaggedly illuminated only the floor by her feet, but a pinprick of light gleamed faintly behind her, coming from a spyhole in that part of the library wall, which was not covered by the tapestry. She ventured further into the room, glancing at the altar with its inverted crucifix, and treading hesitantly over the black and white mosaic of Hecate's Wheel.

Her hand shook, quivering the candle light; she crept past the shelf which was now empty of the two books, and entered the corridor on the left of the chamber. It smelled dankly of mould, the candlelight flickered violently, as though the air was bad, and she forced herself to keep walking along the passage, which sinuously extended, snake-like, into the bowels of the earth. A rat scampered past, water dripped intermittently onto her head and face from wooden beams which supported the roof, and her shoes squelched in puddles on the rocky floor.

An inexplicable feeling of hopelessness and despair gripped her. Her steps slowed even more. A rat again scratched nearby and she whimpered in fear. She stopped and breathed deeply and held her hand to her mouth to avoid screaming.

She rounded one corner, then another, then another. The tunnel appeared to be heading towards the sea and she started to hurry, desperate to reach her destination.

She had known it ever since she had entered the chamber, but had tried to suppress the thought. It had been there, in her mind, but she had been afraid to confront it. She knew she had been there before and ice clutched at her heart. The rock above her head seemed to be pressing down, forcing the breath from her body, suffocating her. She cried out in pain and ran along the stone passage, fearful that she would be caught and hauled back.

Suddenly, it was there in front of her. The red door with the iron bands and the skull's head she had seen when she was delirious. The candle light grotesquely threw a shadow from the bones onto the wall, its ghostly apparition mocking her, laughing at her.

She screamed in fear and forced herself to put one hand on the door and push. But she knew it would not open. She knew it was barred, and she fell, slumped onto the damp cold ground.

She had no idea how many minutes, or hours, it was, before she very slowly stood up. It was difficult to remember who she was, or what she was doing, and she realised she had experienced some sort of hysterical crisis. She looked with hatred at the door, turned and ran back along the tunnel.

She reached the chamber and stood, for a moment, in shock. The muffled voice of Raphael McAlpine could be heard in the library. She softly tiptoed across the mosaic and looked through the peephole. He was standing, talking to Ezekiel Widdicombe.

"He's given the farm to one of his men?" he exclaimed.

"Yess, zur," replied the manager of the Wildercombe estate.

"Don't worry. I will reward you with another part of his property."

"It be a good barton that," said Ezekiel Widdicombe, in annoyance.

"The immediate problem is what to do about the run. He could cause a lot of trouble for us. I want that estate. I gather he came here when I was away and seemed to want to sell it. I'll ride over and see if that's the case. I don't trust these French aristocrats. They're always trying to bring down the Revolution. It was an improvement when they guillotined Marie Antoinette. "

His words became unintelligible as he walked towards the window. Then he came back to within a few feet of her and she hurriedly took her eye from the spyhole in terror, in case he could see her. He started speaking again, his words very audible.

"They should never have passed the Catholic Relief Act in 1791. It should still be illegal to hold Catholic services. Once you let them get a foothold, you don't know where it will end. They had to pass over fifty Catholics before they got to George of Hanover to offer him the throne. Thank God they held true to the Protestant religion."

"There be a lot of hatred of the Delacroix family in Ilfracombe, because they be Catholic," said Ezekiel Widdicombe. "Us could get a mob to attack him. There be already riots to do with the cost of bread in Exeter, Totnes and Brixham."

"No, in case the house is destroyed. It didn't work out in the way I hoped with Esther Cerfbeer. She has been useful to me in the past, but now she could cause trouble and spoil my plans."

Isabella forgot her fear and placed her ear to the peephole. Anger suffused her, reviving her body and her spirits. In the distance, she could hear the high-pitched voice of Mrs McAlpine, and Raphael McAlpine's words once more became unclear as he moved away from the wall.

"Go back....await....soon time...." There was silence and she put her eye to the hole and saw that they had gone out of the library.

She did not linger. She opened the door, pulled back the tapestry and went into the room. She quickly shut the door, adjusted the tapestry, and ran across the floor. She listened to hear if there was anyone outside. There was no sound. She took a deep breath, slipped into the hall, and ran desperately up the stairs to her bedchamber.

She collapsed in exhaustion onto the bed and, as she did so, suddenly saw with shock that she was no longer clutching the rosewood candle holder. She had left it in the secret room.

158

30

The fishing fleet had abandoned Watermouth and was now sailing up the Bristol Channel towards Lynmouth. One boat had left the flotilla and anchored in Combe Martin bay, next to a vessel loaded high with coal. Two sailors were wading ashore; a third was already on the beach, standing by a remnant of brown sail laid on the sand, piled high with silver-glinting fish. Villagers carrying baskets were flocking towards him; bare-foot children were weaving through the crowd, throwing dead crabs and fish bones at each other, and seagulls were screeching as they swooped and wheeled above the feast.

A strong breeze caught the fishing nets hanging to dry from poles above the high water mark, and the gibbet at the foot of Little Hangman creaked and groaned as the tarred body of a man swung backwards and forwards.

Armand ignored both the corpse and the throng at the water's edge. He rode past the lichen-covered cottages by the cove and cursed loudly as slops thrown out of an upstairs window narrowly missed him. Hemp was growing in plots by the road, the plants even taller than those at Dunscombe Manor, and gardens and yards were festooned with cables of rope and partly made nets.

The roses and jasmine at Rose Cottage were still blooming colourfully, their fragrance following him into the low-raftered room. Henriette, however, met him in a very different state to that in which he had last seen her. Her hair was lank, her dress was dirty, and her lively expression had been replaced by one of anxiety and suffering. Marie-Thérèse was crying in her drawer by the back door, and Edouard was coughing. The scent of the flowers failed to obscure a different smell, that of putrefaction, and he was immediately fearful for his friend.

"Charles's leg has become infected," said Henriette. "We thought it was healing and did not want to waste our money on a physician, but now it's so swollen he can't walk. Guillaume has ridden to Ilfracombe to ask Dr Conibear to come immediately."

"Can I see him," he asked.

"Yes, of course," she replied, and opened the door to an adjacent scullery, its shelves lined with pots and pans for cooking. Charles was lying in a truckle bed and Armand looked aghast at him. His sweating face was strawberry-red, and the stench of disease was sickening. He was muttering in fever, his eyes wandering erratically. He stopped, as Armand entered, and screwed up his face, as though he was trying to see him. His body began to twitch and jerk, and incomprehensible words came babbling from his mouth.

"I can't bear it," she exclaimed. "He keeps talking about the guillotine, and I remember my father and mother in the cart going to their deaths and their heads rolling over the ground, and the women sitting there shrieking with joy."

She tottered sideways and he put out his hand to steady her.

"My dear. You should have told me. I would have come earlier. Are you sure you want Dr Conibear to treat him? I will send for Esther Cerfbeer instead."

"Is she the one they call the witch?" she asked.

"Yes, but she isn't. She's extremely skilled. And I have misgivings about Dr Conibear."

"No, I would prefer the doctor," she said firmly, and he was quiet.

"You think he's going to die, don't you?" she asked.

"No, no, absolutely not," he lied. "I will send my servants with food for you and the children. I do not wish you to be worried at such a time. You must concern yourself with Charles."

"Thank you," she said. "You are a true friend to us."

Horses neighed outside in the garden and a few minutes later Guillaume Thibaud appeared at the door with Doctor Conibear. Armand greeted the medical practitioner with a perfunctory nod, as Henriette hurriedly brought him through the room and into the scullery and then he joined Guillaume Thibaud, who had remained on the porch.

"I came here to find out your address. I need advice on farming for my estate. I gather you've helped Dietrich with the Mudge farm," he said.

"Yes," Guillaume Thibaud replied, an expression of surprise on his face. "I had not expected someone who believes me to be an enemy of France to ask my advice though."

He shrugged. "I need to make my estate profitable or I will be forced to sell it. And although we have very different views, you are not a Jacobin and you fought with Lafayette in America."

"He's still being held by the Austrians," Guillaume Thibaud remarked. "His wife, Adrienne, has been moved to a different prison in Paris and has only been spared death so far because of the intervention of Thomas Jefferson and the American government."

"Yes, I know. If the Austrians give him up, Gilbert will be executed."

"I don't think they will let France have him. He is safer in an Austrian prison than his wife is in a Parisian one," he said, ruffling Edouard's hair and looking fondly at him. "At least this little one is not in danger."

"Are you staying here today?" Armand asked.

"No, I must return home to Buzzacott, just along the road, where I live, but I can visit you tomorrow to see your estate."

Armand glanced into the cottage and saw that Dr Conibear had arranged bowls and instruments on the table. The scullery door was ajar and Charles could be seen, lying quietly in bed. His face was no longer red, but white, and blood from his arm was dripping into a bowl.

Henriette came out to the porch, her gown now bloodied as well as unclean, and she wiped her hand across her face in exhaustion. "Dr Conibear has started the treatment."

"My servants will return to you later with food," he said. "And one of the maids will help you in the house."

"Thank you," she replied, tears in her eyes, and picked up Edouard and held him close to her. Dr Conibear came out of the scullery holding a jar which he was stirring with a long spoon, and Armand smelled, rather than saw, the same mixture with which he had himself been anointed. He shuddered with distaste, hastily said farewell to Henriette and left.

He mounted his horse and set off with Tomas and Hans past the second cluster of houses in Combe Martin and along the main street to the sea. The tarred corpse by the beach was still swinging in the wind and he stared straight ahead, avoiding looking at the remains of what had once been a man like himself.

The breeze blew away the malodorous smell which had lingered on his clothes, and he and his men cantered rapidly back to Ilfracombe. As he passed by Chambercombe, Ezekiel Widdicombe suddenly came into view on his horse at the bottom of the hill near Larkstone. He crossed the path directly in front of him, without giving any sign of recognition, and disappeared down through the trees to the harbour.

For the first time, it occurred to him that his estate manager had been a sailor. He walked with the rolling gait often seen in naval men, and his short jacket and wide trousers would not have looked out of place on a ship.

"You're no more a farmer than I am," he muttered. "No wonder my estate's been ruined. And you are also in the pay of McAlpine."

31

Guillaume Thibaud dismounted by the first of the harvested wheat fields. He stood at the base of the huge mound of earth coppiced by elder, beech and ash, which formed the hedge.

"I come from Rothéneuf in Brittany. There are similar hedges to this there. Celtic people thought that the souls of their ancestors lived in the trees growing at the top of the bank. I don't know if the deep Devon lanes arise from the same tradition, but whatever the original reason, I don't believe it is good farming practice."

"The whole of the county has hedges like this," protested Armand. "There would be a riot if they were torn down."

"Be that as it may, although you can obtain wood from it because it is a living fence, and not a dead one of stones, in your case you have much oak on the hillsides, so you don't need to cultivate such monstrosities."

He rummaged around in the earth and exposed tree roots. "Look. This is why nearly a third of your wheat field can't be used for crops. It is the reason why this part of the ground is bare."

"Yes," Armand agreed, as a rabbit scampered over his boots.

"And rabbits are destructive," he continued. "The warren should be destroyed."

They rode along the bottom of the coombe, following the stream, and Guillaume Thibaud reined in his horse and looked at the small fields on the hillside above the water meadow.

"You want to know what crop I'm growing," said Armand sarcastically, surveying the thistles, furze and charlock in each.

"You need to have a proper crop rotation," he replied. "Your fields are not all bad. Land has to lie fallow to give it back its goodness. But this is taking it to extremes, and where you're growing turnips, they're being suffocated by charlock, which is eaten in Ireland, but not here. I will write down a suggested crop plan for you."

He spoke in a calm, quiet voice, at odds with the scars on his hands and face, which gave the suggestion of a violent past. His brown coat was too long for him, his shabby black tricorn hat appeared moth-eaten and his shoes were scuffed and muddy, but his manner was confident. The corners of his grey eyes often crinkled into a smile and he was particularly amused by the singing of the ploughman and the ploughboy.

"It is like the chanting of Mass at church," he said.

Armand bit his lip, for the sake of his estate, to restrain himself from commenting about the present state of religion in France. He had already managed to keep his quick temper under control several times during the previous hours spent in the company of a man, whose views on the Revolution were diametrically opposed to his own, and whom he still feared was probably a spy.

"The plough is the same as the Norman one you see on signs," commented Guillaume Thibaud. "So you can immediately understand that such an old design would cut a better furrow if it was changed somewhat, although it is true it has a slight advantage on a hilly field."

"Yes, I have noticed that ploughs in Devon are not very efficient, although, to be honest, I never took an interest in farming in Alsace."

"It doesn't need much to alter it. I can tell you what has to be done. It's best to get in a whip-rein team to do the ploughing. This is quite good farm land, but it's not being properly cultivated. Once it is, you have to find a market for the produce and as Lieutenant Hargreaves told you, Devonport Dockyard is a good place to start. Both the army and the fleet need supplies because they are attacking France....." he did not finish the sentence and anger crossed his face.

164

"I'll show you the dairy," said Armand, and he rode in front of Guillaume Thibaud across the furze meadow to the manure-reeking outhouse at the far side of the coombe.

"I see Ezekiel Widdicombe's high standards have been exceeded here," remarked the Frenchman, as he entered the building.

"Yes," agreed Armand sourly. "Do you know him? I believe he is an acquaintance of Raphael McAlpine's."

"Yes, I know him, but not well."

"How long have you worked for Raphael McAlpine?"

"A few years, but I only help with his wine business in Exeter, and sometimes with the importing of silks and tobacco," he added, as an afterthought.

"I didn't realise it was in Exeter. Do you know the address," asked Armand.

"No, I don't know where it is. I deal with affairs here in North Devon," he replied.

"Did you ever meet Harriet, who used to live at Dunscombe Manor?"

"Yes, I believe I saw her once."

"Do you know where she is now?"

"No, I haven't any idea. Lucky husband though. She was beautiful."

"Did she look like Isabella?"

"No, completely the opposite. She was extremely fair."

The Red Ruby cow mooed plaintively in her stall as they approached, and Guillaume Thibaud examined her udder.

"She's got an infection. She needs to be milked to ease the pain."

One of the two milk maids stood at the door and looked sullenly at them. She had been seated on the previous visit, but now, standing next to him, Armand saw she was as tall as he was. He glanced at her broad shoulders, wide girth and grey eyes, and realised he was looking at a younger version of Mrs Widdicombe.

"I be going to do that," she said, and sat down on a stool and started milking into a dirty bucket. A blue bottle buzzed and settled on the edge and was knocked into the liquid by a wayward squirt.

"I don't think I would drink much of your milk for the moment," remarked Guillaume Thibaud.

Armand shrugged. "I only drink claret, brandy or wine."

They left the dairy and followed the track up the hillside and across the Torrs. The afternoon was partly gone, but the sun still shone warmly. A raven on a craggy outcrop of rock gave a warning cry, and, for the first time that day, it crossed his mind that he had been foolish to be riding alone in isolated countryside with a man who had helped to bring about the Revolution and who surely hated him and all he stood for.

He looked back at his companion and, in that second, failed to notice the v-marked snake basking on a dusty patch of scrub immediately in front of him. The adder hissed aggressively at his horse, which reared and bolted in terror down the slope towards the sea.

He dug in his heels, cursed, and pulled on the reins, but the horse paid no attention and careered madly over the ground. Hooves thundered behind him, Guillaume Thibaud came abreast, and with one strong hand grabbed his coat and hauled him from the saddle on the very edge of the precipice.

The horse leapt into the air, and with a sickening neigh, fell downwards, twisting and turning as it did so. It smashed into a rock and lay motionless. Seagulls rose up screeching into the sky and Guillaume Thibaud cantered a short distance up the slope and dropped Armand onto the grass.

He stood up, shaken, and slowly approached the cliff edge. He stared down at the black stallion, his back and legs brokenly splayed out at odd angles on the reef below.

"He's dead!" he exclaimed in shock. "Thank you. You saved my life."

"Come on. Ride behind me," said Guillaume Thibaud, and held out his hand. He pulled Armand up behind him and they rode together across the Torrs towards Wildercombe House. They came to the cliff top, just before the wood, and the horse turned to go in the direction of the path leading to the cove.

"No," he said sharply, and pulled on the rein, but the horse resisted again, and tried to descend the hillside.

"No," he shouted a second time, and dug his heels into the horse's flanks, this time forcing him back towards the wood.

"That's strange," remarked Armand. "What made him do that?"

"He has a mind of his own," said Guillaume Thibaud, and laughed and slapped the animal on its flank

"Would you care to dine with me?" Armand asked, as they reached Wildercombe House. "I will pay you for your services after we have eaten."

166

"Yes, I would like that," he said, and, for the first time that day, a note of warmth crept into his voice.

They dismounted and Armand led the way up the steps and into the flag-stoned hall, just as Mrs Widdicombe was coming out of the library. She stopped and stared at Guillaume Thibaud, her expression unfriendly.

"I would like dinner now," Armand told her. "I have a guest."

"The roast's been ready the last two hours," she said, scowled and marched off in the direction of the kitchen.

Guillaume Thibaud removed his tricorn hat and looked at the painting of Antoinette, hanging in the hall.

"The red colour of her hair is very unusual," he remarked. "Several of Raphael McAlpine's wards had a similar colour, which I always thought was strange, as they were not related to each other."

He walked in front of Armand into the dining room. The footmen pulled out chairs for them at the table and, as they both sat down, Armand indicated the view of the trees through the window.

"My mother called it the magic wood and I still think of it as that."

He looked questioningly at Guillaume Thibaud. "Have you been in my house before? You seem to know where the dining room is. And your horse evidently knows the path to the beach."

"No, I have never been here before," he replied.

Armand stared at him, and they waited in silence, as Ben carried in a pheasant on a silver serving dish.

They both quickly consumed the bird, as well as the chicken inside it, and Guillaume Thibaud sat back contentedly and held his glass of wine to the light, critically looking at the colour.

"It is from our vineyard in Alsace. My father managed both the vines and the wine-making. He used to sell the wine, long before most nobles had commercial interests. I suppose I could make cider here if I invested in apple trees," Armand said wryly.

Guillaume Thibaud laughed. "Well, it's not quite the same, but I must say I also enjoy a glass of cider."

"You say that Raphael McAlpine's wine business is in Exeter?" Armand enquired.

"Yes," said his guest.

"It's not all smuggled then?" he remarked.

"No, it's not smuggled, but, of course, it is difficult now with the war to obtain supplies. It is necessary to buy from Spain. I just help a little. I don't really know the extent of what he does. For me, it keeps the wolf from the door, as they very strangely say here in England, where there are no wolves," he said.

"Have you family in France?" asked Armand.

"No, I have a brother in the United States of America. He used to work for Thomas Paine in Paris, but when he was arrested last December, he fled to London and then took ship to Boston."

"So you fought with Lafayette, and your brother worked with Thomas Paine?" said Armand, staring hard at his guest.

"Yes. Thomas Paine will be remembered in history as one of the main thinkers of our century. John Adams, the Vice President of the United States, said that without Paine's pamphlet, 'Common Sense', the sword of Washington would have been raised in vain. And, of course, in France, his essay, 'The Rights of Man', was very influential in our revolution. I am very proud and privileged to have known him."

Armand stared at him in horror and was speechless.

"Now that Robespierre is dead, I have every hope that he will soon be released, and my brother, Loic, is preparing a house for him in America," he said, placing his hand on Armand's arm. "My friend," he continued, in a kindly voice. "Because of your noble blood and wealth, you find it difficult to grasp the principles of what is happening in our enlightened times. People want freedom, and although the revolution in France has led to terrible crimes and barbaric practices, it was based on the right ideas, and we must fight to ensure it follows a humane path and is not overthrown."

"I hope it will be overthrown and the Bourbons reinstated," replied Armand bitterly.

"I am aware that an invasion force is being planned," said Guillaume Thibaud. "But I don't know the details, and I don't want to know them."

"Well, I am certainly not telling you," retorted Armand.

"However, I would say this," said Guillaume Thibaud. "France has a network of spies and agents in England to report on such activities, and you can be assured that any proposed scheme is a leaking sieve of information."

Armand looked at him with interest and did not reply.

"I like you. I fear you are misguided and see everything starkly in just one shade, whereas, in reality, life is more blurred than that. I do not want you to risk your life on a cause which is hopeless. Stay here in Wildercombe House and grow your crops and sell your produce. I probably should not say this to you, but I know, for a fact, that one of the leaders of the English spy network lives here in North Devon. I do not know who he is, but rest assured that any invasion force will be known about."

Armand stared at him. "Do you know where he lives in North Devon?"

"No, I don't. Only that it is near the sea," he replied.

"There was a Corsican at the meeting I went to," said Armand. "He came from Ajaccio, the home town of the new soldier everyone is talking about, Napoleon Bonaparte, who is now, I believe, a General. Perhaps it is him."

"I do not know and I do not want to know," said Guillaume Thibaud. "I am shocked by the crimes of the present revolutionary government and have had to flee, just as you have done. But I cannot support any invasion, and I hope France defeats all the countries presently ranged against it." He stood up, and for the first time that day appeared tired. "Now I must go to see Henriette and Charles."

Armand went to the oak dresser in the corner of the room and took out several coins.

"Thank you for your advice today on farming," he said, as he gave them to him. "I would like you to come again. I do not agree with your ideas, but I respect you. You saved my life and I will be forever in your debt."

"Good day, my friend," replied Guillaume Thibaud. "Take care."

He glanced at the painting of Antoinette in the hall, and then at Armand. "If you are in trouble, send a servant to me at Buzzacott and I will come immediately."

His roan was brought to the front steps; he mounted, and the horse trotted off down the drive. Armand went back into the dining room, colliding as he did so with the enormous bosom of Mrs Widdicombe, who had appeared from nowhere. She looked unpleasantly at him, and he turned away and shut the door on her.

Ben was washing the wine glasses behind the screen and he sat down at the table and dismissed the other two footmen. When they had left

169

the room and the door had again been closed, he said, "I want you to do something for me."

"Yess, yer Grace," he replied.

"I want you to go to Exeter, to Southernhay West near the Cathedral, and see if you can discover the whereabouts of Harriet, who used to live at Dunscombe Manor, and whose married name is now Mrs Alexander McPherson. I was told she lived at number ten, but when I called, no one knew of her. I found out today that McAlpine carries on a business somewhere in Exeter. I don't want you dressed in livery as a servant, but in ordinary clothes, and I will pay for your stay, for as long as it takes you to find out where she lives. I do not want anyone to know, particularly not the Widdicombes. You can have a horse and you will be paid handsomely."

"Yes, I will do it," he said eagerly. "Can I ask summat else? My brother, Ned, needs work. Could he be a footman here? He can start immediately."

"Yes, he can. I will tell Mrs Widdicombe," replied Armand.

Half an hour later, Ben was on his way to Exeter. Armand sat in the window, smoking a pipe, and looking out at the gardens.

"What would you want me to do?" he said, addressing the imaginary forms of his parents who were walking hand in hand through the rose arbour. He received no answer, their visions faded, and he continued to smoke his pipe and gaze out of the window.

32

Bess cowered in her cramped box of a cabin, the chains chafing her ankles and wrists. She did not attempt to speak to her jailors, who often touched their prayer beads and whose language sounded very foreign to her ears.

She was careful to only pray quietly to herself, showing no outward sign of what she was doing. She lived in fear of being taken from her solitude and placed with the American prisoners and Jacob, below the hatch. The stench from it, when it was lifted, was awful, and the sounds of suffering coming from there, multiplied as the days wore on.

At times, she thought she had lost her mind. The days were ravaged by odd hallucinations. She saw her parents, and her sisters, and was often standing in a flower-filled meadow, where the River Wilder was flowing, and trout were swimming in its clear water. At other times, she was calm and lucid. She smiled when she thought of Jacob Goldstein, and imagined different ways they might escape to be together.

Finally, the ship arrived. She was taken on deck and looked across to see the flat-roofed and white-walled buildings of the town of Algiers. The sun was hot and she felt ashamed as she stood there in her stained dress, her hair hanging in rats' tails over her shoulders. The other prisoners were brought up from the hold; she caught the eye of Jacob and did not look at the rest of him, as he and the other prisoners were naked.

He gazed at her, his eyes blinking in the sunlight. He tried to smile, but could not, and she stared at him, her heart broken at his pitiful state.

The ship anchored and the captives were ferried by small boats to a bustling water front. After confinement in a dark cabin, her senses were almost overwhelmed by the colours, sounds and smells around her. The people had black hair, and wore bright, exotic clothing. Oranges and lemons were piled high on stalls, and dogs and children ran everywhere.

Jacob and the Americans were marched to an alley leading up the hill, and she was ordered to follow them. People jeered and shouted as they passed, and the women shrieked in a strange fashion, almost as though they were singing tunelessly. The path was so narrow between the buildings, that only one person was able to walk there at one time; pieces of rotten fruit were thrown down onto them and she wondered if she would live to see the end of the day.

The men were led into a square with a dais at the end. They were kicked and punched onto the stage, and people came forward to look at them. A man examined Jacob's mouth and teeth, and felt the muscles on his arms, and then she was hustled along, leaving the slave market behind.

She was taken, alone, to a house at the summit of the hill, and found herself, for the first time in many weeks, with women. They helped her undress and wash herself in the first bath that she had ever seen in her life, and she was finally able to feel clean again. A meal of lamb, rice and dates was given to her, and she sat gratefully eating it, trying to rid herself of the terrible memories of Jacob and his fellow American prisoners.

The truth slowly dawned on her.

'I have already been sold. There will be no ransom for me. Jacob and the American sailors are being sold today as slaves, and they will perhaps be ransomed in the future. For me there is no hope.'

33

The evening was long. Isabella endured the company of the McAlpines and Samuel Butler at the dining table. Mrs McAlpine had returned from London dressed in the latest fashion. Her elephantine proportions were squeezed into a high-waisted, pink silk gown, matched with pink satin shoes, whilst pink flowers encrusted with pearls threaded the bouffant edifice of her hair. Mr McAlpine had visited his tailor and sported a new Paisley waistcoat, green satin coat, and a curled grey wig, which reached to his waist. Samuel Butler was not dressed in the ostentatiously affluent style favoured by his hosts, but his clothes also appeared new, and rather too tight, as he slumped drunkenly sideways, pulling part of the table cloth and crockery with him, leaving the servants to frantically mop at both his white shirt and the damask linen, to remove the spreading stain of red wine.

The prettiness of the McAlpine outfits contrasted with the ugliness of the hatred and fear surging through her mind as she looked at her benefactors. The image of the candle left in the secret room made her shiver inwardly, and she wondered how long it would be before it betrayed her. Anger that Raphael McAlpine had been responsible for the rioting against Esther, suffused her whole body, and she would gladly have attacked him with the carving knife resting on the beef sirloin in its pool of blood on the serving dish. The menorah's seven candles flickered and burned in the middle of the table and she recited in her mind the Jewish words and ritual sayings she had learned from Esther. It calmed her and she was able to sit, expressionless, giving no indication of the violence in her thoughts.

"We must prepare your trousseau," Mrs McAlpine said to her and laughed. "You will soon see your beau for the first time."

The spite in her eyes, and her mocking tone, startled her, and, not for the first time, doubts about a husband chosen by the McAlpines, caused her spirits to sink even lower than they already were. She retired to her bedchamber at the arrival of the port and biscuits and told Mrs Gubb she was going to sleep and did not want to be disturbed.

She quietly prised up the floor board and took out her box. She removed the drawing of Harriet, then replaced her treasures in their hiding place, before venturing on to the landing and listening to the sound of the conversation coming from the dining room. The McAlpines' usual drunken state after the meal had, very evidently, been quickly reached, and she was relieved to hear the slurred, high-pitched tones of Mrs McAlpine, and the slightly lower and more nasal, but equally inebriated, voice of her husband. Samuel Butler could not be heard at all, and she did not bother to try and discover his condition, having just watched him consume four bottles of wine.

She went back to her room and fashioned the shape of a body under the counterpane on her bed, by using the bolster and some clothes. Then she dressed in a dark green cloak and put on sturdy, walking shoes.

It was not yet dark, but Venus, the evening star, was already shining brightly in the sky, as she left the house by the back door. From the kitchen came the clattering of plates and the chatter of the servants. They were all eating, now that the McAlpines' meal had ended, so she knew no one would see her leave.

She ran past the forest of hemp to the belladonna plants and picked several black berries and placed them in a bag. She then went into the greenhouse and gathered thornapples to add to her collection, before hurrying to the lane outside the manor wall to begin the long trek over the hills to Esther's cottage.

Weakness from her injury slowed her steps, but she still managed to walk at a reasonable pace; the only person she encountered was Isaiah, the beggar, climbing into the warmth of the lime kiln in the field at the top of the hill.

She wearily reached the sanctuary of Esther's garden, just as the sun was beginning to set in the western sky. The scarecrow, with its burden of dead birds, was stiff against the breeze and a haze of blue wood smoke was drifting in spirals above the cottage chimney as Esther peered out at her from the window, then ran to open the door.

What's happened? Why are you here?" she asked, in surprise.

She embraced Isabella and brought her into the downstairs room, where the table had been prepared for the Sabbath meal, and was laid with its white cloth, a plaited loaf on a plate and one candle in a candlestick.

"It is just before dusk. I am about to eat," she said.

"The McAlpines have returned, but are incapable with drink, as usual, after dinner, and have no idea I have left the house. I've brought you these. I know you have not enough, now that the rioters destroyed your plants." And Isabella emptied her bag onto the table, spilling out the black berries and the yellow fruits.

"You should not have taken them," reproached Esther. "However, I am very grateful. But why have you come?"

"I explored the secret chamber today, and part of the tunnel, and I found the red door, where I think I've been to before. I took a candle with me this time, so that I could see."

"I told you not to," Esther exclaimed. "You are nearly at an end with the McAlpines. It is foolish to risk anything now. I know nothing about this secret room, or a red door, or a tunnel, but I imagine they are connected with his ceremonies and his smuggling. You must not annoy him, or put yourself in danger."

"They came back when I was still in there, so I had to stay hidden. I looked through a peephole in the wall and overheard his conversation with Ezekiel Widdicombe, and that's why I have come here tonight. I wanted to warn you. He was saying that they had caused the riot to happen at your cottage, and that you had been useful to him in the past, but you are no longer so. They also seemed to be angry with Armand, but I didn't understand their words. They talked about a 'run' and Raphael McAlpine said he intended the estate for himself

175

and did not want another riot organised for Wildercombe House, in case it was destroyed."

Esther's face whitened. She trembled, and Isabella helped her to sit down.

"Raphael McAlpine is evil. I have always known it was dangerous to give him a small amount of knowledge. But I did it for you," she said in a weak voice

Isabella embraced her. "Do not worry. I had to come and warn you. I don't trust what he might do, either to you or to Armand."

"I think the Seigneur is safe for the moment," said Esther. "And, in any case, he will soon be in France."

"Yes," she replied unhappily.

"Raphael McAlpine has agreed for me to accompany you to America," Esther said. "Perhaps that is all he means, that he will soon be rid of me."

"I don't know," Isabella said doubtfully. "Why do you want so much for both of us to go to America?"

"It is a country where Jewish people can be free, although I must say, in fairness, that I have mainly found England to be very tolerant. Sometimes problems have arisen, but there is a system of law here which treats everyone equally. America is, however, a very enlightened country with its Bill of Rights, and I think it is very suitable for both you and I to start a new life there. If Captain Petrie proves to be unworthy of you, I am sure that there will be a way to leave him, and, in any case, you will be a long way from the clutches of McAlpine."

"Armand is trying to court me," she replied bitterly.

"Armand de Delacroix will probably soon be dead or rotting in a French prison," declared Esther harshly. "And Raphael McAlpine does not want him as a suitor. He is determined that you will marry Captain Petrie, and so I imagine that he is being well rewarded financially. The Seigneur might be a Duke, but he is not in a position to pay money for you. He will be lucky to save his estate, and I fear for his life if he stands in the way of McAlpine."

Isabella looked sadly at her and took out of her pocket the drawing she had made of Harriet. "Would you please give this to him tomorrow. He is looking for her and I thought it might be useful."

"Yes, I will," said Esther, placing a second candle on the table. "Now share the Sabbath meal with me. Then Mordecai and I will walk back with you to Dunscombe Manor, and I pray that your absence will not have been noticed."

They sat at the table together, and Isabella softly chanted the ritual words. They observed the ceremony of the meal and chatted and laughed and drank the wine.

"Tell me again the story of Lilith, the witch, in the tree," she asked.

And Esther recounted the old folk tale, as she had, so many times before.

Outside, the night had fallen and an owl was hooting. The glow from the two candles was not sufficient to light the room, and Esther stood up and lit the mullein tapers from the embers in the hearth. They smoked, making her cough, and Isabella looked at her in concern.

Esther's face was very pale. The black jet necklace at her throat glittered against the wrinkled whiteness of her skin, and a silver ring, with a gem of agate, hung loosely on her bony finger.

"I am getting old. I must live long enough to get to America with you and see you happy and safe," she said.

"You are not going to die," replied Isabella, a tremor in her voice. "Have you a pain in your chest? Do you need to take digitalis? Let me prepare it for you."

"Yes, I would like that," she said.

Isabella crushed the downy, veined leaves of the foxglove and measured out a very small portion. Esther swallowed it quickly, her breathing became more regular and her face less pale.

"You have learned my secrets well," she said, smiling. The few scraps of information I have let Raphael McAlpine scavenge are nothing. The Book of Shadows he has managed to obtain, pales by comparison with what my mother taught me, and her mother, and her mother before that, going back generations through the centuries. Use your skills wisely, and when you have a daughter, pass the knowledge on to her. I feel my time on this Earth is almost over. Ever since I searched for you and found you at Dunscombe Manor, I have tried to protect you and keep you alive, and now my task is nearly done."

"What do you mean, you searched for me?" asked Isabella. "I thought it was just by chance we met."

"No, it was not," she replied. "When we are on the ship to America, I will tell you."

Her eyes closed, her frail body slumped against the back of the fireside seat, her chest rose and fell as she breathed heavily.

Isabella snuffed out the candles and the mullein tapers and cleared away the dishes. She gently kissed the sleeping Esther on her cheek and left the cottage. She trudged through the darkness of the night, holding the dagger she had brought with her, and keeping close to the hedges. She skirted the edge of the rough pastureland of the Cairn, hearing the lamenting cries whispering through the trees, of the Jewish pedlar, who had been murdered there, and it was with a sigh of relief, she finally arrived back at Dunscombe Manor. She crept in through the back door and up the stairs to her bedchamber, and clambered gratefully into her bed, falling asleep as soon as her head touched the bolster.

34

The footman showed Esther into the library, where Guillaume Thibaud was seated at the oak desk in the window, papers spread out in front of him, and Armand was standing, listening to what he was saying.

"Good day, gentlemen," she said.

Armand regarded her in surprise. "Good day. Monsieur Thibaud is explaining the crop rotation I should follow for the estate and the improvements I need to make. When I go to France he will oversee Ezekiel Widdicombe."

"Really?" she said, a note of scepticism in her voice. "And are you continuing to work in the wine trade, Monsieur Thibaud?"

"Yes, for now," he replied.

"Are you expecting to have deliveries soon?" she asked. "It must be difficult in this time of war and the present circumstances."

"Raphael McAlpine manages," he said enigmatically. "I will take my leave now. I am going back to Combe Martin, to see how Charles is. I believe Dr Conibear is visiting again today."

The footman escorted him to the front door and Armand looked questioningly at Esther, who was, for the first time, very plainly dressed, without any jewellery of jet, amber or malachite, her hair straggling untidily over her shoulders. She was breathing quickly, and there was a slight tremor in her body.

"Please sit down," he said hastily.

"Don't worry," she said. "It is not yet time for me to die."

"I was not thinking that," he denied.

"Isabella came to see me last night and gave me this drawing of Harriet to give to you. She thought it might be useful in your search for her address."

"Thank you," he said, taking the picture from her. "And how did she visit you?"

"The McAlpines have returned from London. She waited until they were drunk after dinner before leaving the house, then came to my cottage. I fell asleep at the end of the evening, and when I awoke she had gone."

"It is very dangerous for her to walk alone in the countryside at night, and it is a long way," he said sharply.

"She was worried. She was exploring the secret chamber she had found, when the McAlpines came back from London. She heard a conversation between Ezekiel Widdicombe and Raphael McAlpine through a peephole in the wall."

"She did what!" he shouted angrily.

"She overheard them saying that they had caused the riot at my cottage, and that Raphael McAlpine wanted your estate."

"I know he wants my land," he said, shrugging his shoulders. "That is not a secret. However, I wonder if she misheard about the riot. It seems unlikely to me."

"Yes, that is what I thought. The rioters stopped when the crow flew over and when they believed McAlpine was coming."

"Yes, but he would probably have arrived too late to be of any use," he said thoughtfully. "My men and I were there, which might have delayed events."

"It is not important," she replied. "It is only Isabella I am worried about."

"I don't want her roaming in secret passages and chambers. She's putting herself in danger," he exclaimed, pacing up and down the room.

"Yes, I agree. I just want her to survive until we can both go to America."

He scowled at her in temper.

She looked back at him impassively, but her chest rose and fell, and she caught her breath.

He glanced at her for a moment and then turned his attention to the drawing of Harriet. "She is beautiful," he remarked. "She is very fair."

"Yes, she is beautiful," Esther replied. "All of his wards were beautiful. I should imagine that is how he found husbands for girls who were poor."

"He obviously has a kindness in him that is not immediately apparent," he muttered. "He does not seem the sort of man to bring up so many orphans with his own money."

"That is true," she said.

"I gather several had hair the same red colour as that of my mother."

"Yes, four of them. They were all either fair-haired or red-haired."

"Not like Isabella then. She is dark."

"Yes. Isabella is also different because she has been at Dunscombe Manor since she was a very young child. The other girls came when they were quite old. They only lived there a short time."

"Do you know the addresses of any of them?" he enquired.

"No, and nor does Isabella. They were all married elsewhere. Their husbands did not live here."

"That's odd," he exclaimed.

"Well, not really," she said. "They had no relations. It seems reasonable for them to be married near the family of their future husbands."

"Did Isabella attend any of the weddings?" he asked.

"No, she didn't."

He looked out of the window towards his mother's magic wood, and he and Esther were both quiet.

"Did you or Isabella meet any of the husbands?" he finally asked.

"No," she said, very softly.

"So you don't know that these husbands actually existed?"

"Why shouldn't they be real?" she queried, breathing with difficulty again.

"I don't know. It just seems strange to me. Everything. Raphael McAlpine spending his money on these orphans. No sign of any husbands. Harriet never having lived at the address he gave, which, by the way, is in Exeter, where he also has his wine business."

"I didn't know that. However, Isabella has a picture of her fiancé, Captain Petrie," she replied.

"Has she? I would be interested to see it," he commented.

"I will try and obtain it for you," she replied.

He looked at her in surprise. "So you do think there is something odd?"

"No, I don't," she declared. "Why should there be? And he has said that I can go with Isabella to America."

"So you would trust his word?" he asked flatly.

She looked long and hard at him, her eyes very dark in the pallor of her face.

"I hate him," she said, and he almost flinched at the intensity of her gaze and the emotion in her voice. He recognised the same hatred he felt towards the murderers of his parents and, for a moment, he and Esther were united in the rawness of their feelings.

"Why do you hate him?" he asked.

Her expression changed. A veil was drawn over her face. The look in her eyes became guarded. She bit her lips and said nothing.

"Why do you hate him?" he demanded, and gripped the black fabric of her sleeve.

She shuddered. "Leave me. I have done my best. Perhaps I am wrong in trying to prevent you from having Isabella. I feel old and that time is not with me. Events are moving quickly."

He gripped her arm more tightly. "What are you saying? You always speak in riddles. Trust me, for once."

"How can I trust you? You are the son of a noble family. Your parents helped me and I am very grateful to them, but they were part of a society which oppressed and harmed, not just my people, Jewish people, but also the peasants, their tenants."

"My parents never hurt anyone," he said in annoyance. "They always helped others. They distributed free grain when the harvests failed. They were kind, good Catholics."

"It was not their fault," said Esther. "But they kept the system alive. It is men like your cousin, Lafayette, who saw the wrong and tried to change it."

"Well, I never thought I would agree with Guillaume Thibaud. But I would like to repeat his words. Life is not one colour. There are many varieties, many shades. You are seeing me, not for who I am, and my love for Isabella. You are only seeing me as an aristocrat, someone who has inherited his position and wealth. You are not seeing beyond that."

"Fine words. But it is you who is going to fight to try and preserve the old order of injustice and suffering. You want Isabella, but you are not prepared to sacrifice the vested interests of your rank to obtain her. You would leave her here alone in the power of Raphael McAlpine, even if he had not managed to murder you beforehand." Her expression and her words were harsh.

"So you think that he did kill her previous suitors?" he said.

She withdrew inside herself and stood up. "I must go now. Good day, Seigneur." And she walked out of the library, leaving him staring after her.

35

Wildercombe House echoed to the noise of scrubbing, polishing and tidying. The oak furniture gleamed and smelled of beeswax. Windows were wide-open to relieve the mustiness permeating the thick-walled rooms, and curtains, coverings and drapes had been rigorously cleaned. Armand wandered over the house inspecting every aspect of his home.

"It must be done by September the nineteenth," he told Mrs Widdicombe. "Then you will all be treated to a day at Barum Fair."

Even his father's laboratory was not exempt. The bulbous glass flasks and tubes had been carefully dusted and shone in the sunlight radiating through the windows. He looked at the extensive scientific apparatus, neatly arranged on long tables.

"It is not just Lavoisier's work which has been lost to France," he said to himself. "My father's studies on animals and plants and the constituents of the air were also important."

The eyes of a stuffed raccoon, on a shelf, seemed to watch him, and as he scrutinised it more closely, he noticed that below it, on the floor, were two cages with unusually ornate clasps, in the shape of a horse's head.

"Now where have I seen those before?" he muttered.

A bird suddenly flew past the window. "Crow House!" he exclaimed. "They were in the work room."

He unlatched the door of the first cage and looked inside. It was bare. He unlocked the second, which again was bare, except for a black feather in the corner. He stared at it and then slowly examined the rest of the room.

The old thick glass of some of the equipment appeared to have been partly renewed with a thinner, less blemished substance, and he glanced curiously at it, running his hand over its smoothness. In a cupboard, at the end of the laboratory, he found four earthenware pots with lids. Two were empty, but the third held the remains of a powder, which had an acrid smell, whilst the fourth contained two purple and yellow petals, similar to those he had taken from the thornapple in Dunscombe Manor's greenhouse. They crumbled to dust in his fingers and gave off the same unpleasant odour, which had tainted the pocket of his coat for days.

The large bulk of Mrs Widdicombe passed by the door and he called her in. Her eyes shifted uneasily from him to the room, and back again, but she stood her ground, her height and massive upper body making her as tall as he was, and her girth twice as wide.

"Someone has been using the laboratory," he said.

"No, yer Grace. That not be so."

"It's Raphael McAlpine, isn't it?" he said.

"No," she replied crossly. "I told 'ee before. Just Ezekiel and me were y'ere."

He looked at her with displeasure.

"Please have my men assemble on horseback. I will be making a visit in Ilfracombe, and afterwards I will be dining with Captain Bowen at the Castle, so I will not want dinner."

"Very good, yer Grace," she said, and swept out of the room towards the kitchen, her keys clanking at her waist.

He smiled at his mother as he passed her portrait in the hall, and went upstairs to his bedchamber. A short time later, dressed in his finest purple satin coat and waistcoat, liberally splashed with perfume, his unruly dark hair tamed with pomade and tied firmly in a queue, he left Wildercombe House at the head of a large retinue of servants.

The cavalcade passed through Ilfracombe and by the harbour, then along the leafy lanes in Chambercombe, before entering the courtyard of Dunscombe Manor, just as Isabella was opening the window of her bedchamber.

She stared at him in surprise, and he looked solemnly up at her, and bowed his head in acknowledgement. He swung down from his horse and Reuben escorted him into the drawing room.

Raphael McAlpine greeted him, the expression on his face one of sly contentment.

"Your Grace. I heard that you visited when I was away, and you said you want to sell your estate."

"Yes, I did visit. But since then I have changed my mind. The wheat harvest has been better than I expected and I have other plans now."

Raphael McAlpine's expression immediately changed from that resembling a cat which had found the cream, to that of one which had discovered the cream was rancid."

"I am willing to make a decent offer. We both know the poverty of the soil, and its failure to bring in any revenue."

"It's basically good land," retorted Armand, "but it has been mismanaged in the absence of my father."

"Mr Widdicombe has done his best," said Raphael McAlpine.

"Yes, but his best for whom?" remarked Armand. "By the way, I believe I might have two of your cages in my laboratory. They have the same distinctive clasps as yours here."

"No, certainly not," he replied. "Why would they be in your house?" Armand shrugged his shoulders.

"I have come here on another matter," he said. "It regards the wedding of your ward."

"The date has not yet been finally decided on," replied Raphael McAlpine. "It will be taking place in Virginia."

"Does Captain Petrie come from a wealthy family?" he questioned.

"Why do you ask, sir?" said Raphael McAlpine, in a belligerent tone, his eyes almost disappearing into the white-powdered folds of his face, his thin, red-painted lips pursing sourly together.

"I would like to ask you for the hand of your ward, Isabella. I wish to marry her. I am a Duke, so she would become a Duchess, and, as you know, I have land here, and a plantation in America. She would be taken care of financially, and I would be prepared to offer you a small part of my estate in North Devon."

Raphael McAlpine bristled and took a few steps back. His face seemed to redden under the powder, and his pale eyebrows arched upwards.

"She is not for sale to you, sir. She has been promised, and financial considerations have already been taken care of." He raised his voice, his manner now openly hostile. "If I were you, I would forget any inclination to marry my ward. The consequences for you might not be pleasant."

"What do you mean, sir? Are you threatening me?" Armand approached so closely to Raphael McAlpine, that his coat was brushing against the other man's coat, and he was looking down on the top of his grey wig.

"What has Captain Petrie got to offer that I haven't?" he asked.

Raphael McAlpine laughed unpleasantly. "You will never find out. She will soon have left these shores."

"Isabella has no knowledge of my intention, or my purpose, in coming to see you today. If you harm her in any way, I will kill you," he threatened, staring long and hard at Raphael McAlpine. "I bid you good day."

He strode from the room and left the house. He mounted his horse and looked up to Isabella's window, where she was still standing, watching him, a worried expression on her face. Two crows cawed on the window sill, and he wheeled his horse around and galloped out of the courtyard, followed by his men.

Just as he disappeared into the lane, Raphael McAlpine's boots could be heard pounding up the wooden stairs. She ran to the door to bolt it, but was too late, and he rushed in, his face contorted in anger. He grabbed her by the hair and pulled her to him.

"What have you been doing behind my back while I've been in London? He wants to marry you, and dares to threaten me. I'll give him 'harm you'." And he punched her once on her head.

She screamed and fell to the floor, and Mrs McAlpine ran in, moving quickly in spite of her size.

"Stop it, my darling," she cried at him. "I've told you before. You're damaging the goods. That's what you're doing." She held on to his arm and he wheeled around, panting in fury.

Isabella lay prostrate on the floor, blood pouring from her head on to her clothes and skin. It had also splattered her attacker; his face and wig were flecked with red, his new coat stained.

"Ibn Ben Said has paid a fortune. For God's sake, control yourself. We're nearly there," Mrs McAlpine cried.

"You're right," said her husband. "You're always right, my dear." He looked down at Isabella lying semi-conscious, her eyes shut.

"Is she dead? I don't think so. She's just knocked out," he muttered, poking her with the toe of his boot.

"She'll recover," said his wife. "Send a servant for Esther Cerfbeer."

"That wretched Frenchman. He refuses to sell the estate and he's been trouble ever since he came. If he and his men hadn't arrived, I would have got rid of that woman."

"Just as well you have not, my beloved. She will be useful now," she replied.

She led him out of the room and Mrs Gubb and Jenny ran in. Mrs Gubb knelt down and cradled Isabella in her arms and she opened her eyes and moaned softly.

"There, my dear," she said. "Let us help you on to the bed."

One of the crows on the sill hopped inside the open window. It flew straight to Isabella, covering her face and chest with its outstretched black wings. Mrs Gubb shrieked and Jenny knocked it with the broom she was still holding, whereupon it flapped away back through the window opening and into the trees opposite, and perched there, cawing unpleasantly.

36

The crows noticed Esther Cerfbeer as she rode on Mordecai along the lane to Dunscombe Manor. They were already gathering in flocks in the trees and their raucous cawing drowned the sweeter notes of the other birds. Several flew down from the branches, then more, and by the time she had reached the house, they were swooping around her in a black cloud; one was even perched on Mordecai, who brayed nervously.

She scattered a mixture of seeds and herbs around her, and the birds ate greedily, hopping over the cobbles. Cain and Abel retreated to the porch, slinking backwards and forwards, their tails between their legs, whimpering, afraid to attack the massed ranks in front of them.

She stiffly dismounted from the donkey and stooped and caressed the feathers of the nearest bird. Raphael McAlpine appeared at the entrance and she looked at him with a cold hostility.

He regarded her and the crows with displeasure, and when he spoke there was envy in his voice.

"I can see they still remember you. You have not lost your touch with them."

"Animals and birds remain loyal," she said. "Unlike humans, who can be treacherous."

189

"Have you the potion for tonight?" he asked.

"Yes," she replied. "But I will see Isabella first, before I give it to you. You have hurt her, I believe." She stared at him, her expression and her voice ice-cold with fury and disdain.

He flinched, a fear of her momentarily evident in his face.

"You are afraid of my powers. And rightly so," she said.

"No, I am not," he retorted. "You are a foolish old woman, who is sometimes of use to me."

"You are a sham, Raphael McAlpine," she said. "You know almost nothing. You are arrogant. You claim to be a follower of Hecate, but you use her for your own purposes and you will suffer for it."

"That is not true. I know more than you think," he declared. "I have obtained the Book of Shadows."

"You lack the skills and the wit to use it," she replied dismissively.

He glared at her, but stood aside impotently as she brushed past him into the hall and climbed the stairs to Isabella's bedchamber.

Isabella was sitting in bed, a shawl round her shoulders. Her face had a washed-clean look, as though it had been scrubbed excessively, and a bruise was beginning to show on her temple. On one side of her head, her hair was matted thick with congealed blood, and Esther did not bother with the niceties of conversation, or any sort of greeting, but immediately took out medicinal herbs from her bag and arranged them next to a porcelain bowl containing water. She carefully cleaned the wound, which had reopened, and applied a poultice tightly to Isabella's head.

When she had finished, she stalked crossly around the small room.

"How dare he," she muttered. "How dare he."

"I'm alright," said Isabella. "Don't worry. Mrs McAlpine stopped him and he only hit me once. I pretended to be worse than I was and I think he was worried I was dead."

"I despise him," said Esther scornfully.

"Not so loud," entreated Isabella.

"And why did he suddenly attack you? Was there a reason?" she asked.

"Yes," Isabella replied, blushing slightly. "Armand de Delacroix came here and made a proposal of marriage. Raphael McAlpine was furious, because he suspected that we had met while he was away."

Esther stared at her. "He did what?" she said angrily.

"Don't be annoyed. He wants to marry me, and it seemed straightforward to him to ask if he could, before I go off to America to be married to someone else," she replied.

"McAlpine will now fear you will elope with him. Armand de Delacroix has put himself really in danger," murmured Esther softly.

"Yes," replied Isabella. "I don't want him to be harmed. I would prefer to travel to America and marry an unknown man, than that he should be killed."

"I know you love him," said Esther. "I know how difficult it is for you not to marry him, but there is no other way."

Isabella blushed even more and was quiet, her eyes welling up with tears.

"There is something else," she said. "When I was lying on the floor and Mrs McAlpine came in, I heard her say that I would be damaged goods if he left a mark on me. That is the second time I have heard her say that. She also said that someone had paid a lot of money for me. The name sounded foreign and was not Petrie."

"Can you remember it?" asked Esther.

"It was a name I had never heard. It might have been Ivan Ben."

"Ivan Ben?" questioned Esther.

"Yes, I think that is it. Have you heard it before?" she asked.

"No, I have not," she said.

"It was not Petrie, which is strange," remarked Isabella. "Perhaps I have it wrong. My ear was hurting and I was on the ground. It was difficult to hear the words clearly and I could not make out the rest of the conversation."

"Sleep now. You need rest. He has not hurt you much, fortunately. If it was not for the original wound re-opening, it would not have looked so terrible."

Isabella lay down underneath the counterpane and Esther bent to kiss her on her hair. "Sleep, my dear one. Do not worry about anything. You are nearly free from here."

Isabella's eyes gradually closed, and when she had fallen asleep, Esther walked to the dresser and placed the framed picture of Captain Petrie in her bag. Then she went downstairs where Raphael McAlpine was waiting for her in the library.

"She will live?" he asked.

"Yes, she will live, but no thanks to you," retorted Esther. "I have done my best and I will return tomorrow."

"Have you the nepenthe for tonight?" he demanded.

"Yes," she said, and took out a small jar from her bag. "The elixir of forgetfulness, as Helen of Troy called it. You have not managed to make it yourself yet then? What are you going to do when I go to America?"

"I almost had it right last time," he declared.

"You nearly killed that man you tried it on. It took me all my skill to revive him. The quantities of opium, henbane and mandrake need to be absolutely exact."

"I will manage. In any case, I might not have more ceremonies here. I might put an end to it."

"Oh?" said Esther, interest in her eyes.

"Yes, I intend to have an estate and be a landowner, not a merchant. And so I will not need to have the ceremonies."

"Are you? And what estate are you intending to possess?"

He flapped his white hands. "I do not think it long before the Duke de Delacroix sells his land. The man has no money. He lives beyond his means."

"That estate has been ruined by Ezekiel Widdicombe," she said. "It can be improved and made profitable."

"Well I do not think Armand de Delacroix is the man to do that," he replied. "He is young and has no idea about farming, and is, in any case, going off to France, from where he will probably not return."

"You might be right," she said. "And, in the meantime, never lay a finger on Isabella again. I am not saying this lightly. I know what you are like. Isabella and I will soon be gone. You will be free of us."

He looked at her, a triumphant expression in his face.

"Yes. You have both been useful to me, in different ways."

"Good day, sir," said Esther, cutting short the conversation.

She left the house and mounted Mordecai. Then she and the donkey slowly made the steep ascent of the narrow lane leading from the manor. The crows watched from the trees and were quiet as she stooped forward in pain and clutched her chest. She rummaged in her bag and hastily swallowed a portion of the digitalis. She gasped for breath and sat upright again.

"I have to stay alive," she muttered. "It is not long now."

37

Dinner at the Castle was a naval affair. The food was piped discordantly in to the dining room as though on a ship. A maritime flavour was reflected in the dishes; exotic spices from the East fragranced haunches of lamb, beef and a stuffed udder, and Captain Bowen narrated exploits from his travels to distant shores.

Armand remained unmoved by the accounts and by the delights of the table. Anger coursed through him at the unsatisfactory outcome to his proposal. He clenched his hands on his knife and fork and pushed away the large portion of apple tart, doused with rum, in front of him. His gloom contrasted with the lively manner of Lieutenant Hargreaves who recounted tales of smugglers he had caught, and who had enthusiastically demanded an encore when Georgiana played the spinet before the meal.

"I understand you French have plans to send ships and men to join the rebels in France. Will you be going with the invasion force?" Captain Bowen asked Armand.

"Yes, I intend to," he replied.

"It was unfortunate that the British ships arrived off Granville too late to help," said the Captain. "We would have made a difference."

"Yes," he agreed bitterly.

"Britain wants to see this Republican Revolution overthrown and a monarchy re-established, but the government is divided on how to approach it," continued Captain Bowen. "I know the Secretary at War, William Windham, and he thinks the Bourbons are the only legitimate rulers. Lord Grenville, the Foreign Minister, thinks somewhat differently, and Pitt is different again. He thinks there should be a constitutional monarchy, but believes the Bourbons not to be capable of ruling France. What is your position?"

"I want to see the Revolution overthrown and the Bourbons reinstated," said Armand curtly.

"Everyone is afraid these radical ideas will spread here," remarked Lieutenant Hargreaves. "And, of course, we want to keep Ireland and stop it from rebelling. Any revolt has to be quickly suppressed and the French not allowed to assist."

"All countries want to protect their own self-interest," said Armand. "I can well understand that you don't want the revolution to spread to Britain, or to lose Ireland."

"And there is, of course, the problem of an invasion," declared the Lieutenant. "We have the local militia, and there are cannons here at the castle, but we have to be on our guard."

"Mr McAlpine has offered his services and those of his servants, to help patrol the North Devon coast. His studies with crows might be a bit odd, but he would be a useful man for that. We could do with more volunteers," said Captain Bowen.

"I am going to one of his meetings tomorrow night," remarked Lieutenant Hargreaves. "I gather a lot of serious drinking goes on."

"Yes, I had heard that," said Captain Bowen. "I was invited, but I'm returning to my ship in the morning, so I can't attend."

Through the windows of the dining room a carriage could be seen slowly approaching the castle. It trundled upwards, over the track across the fields, its wheels grating to a halt in the gravel at the front entrance.

"Mrs McAlpine," a servant announced a few minutes later as she entered in a cloud of sandalwood perfume, rubies glittering at her neck, and pendants dangling from her ears.

"You must dine with us," said Mrs Bowen.

"It is very kind of you, but my beloved husband awaits me at home," Mrs McAlpine answered in her shrill voice.

194

"I insist," said Captain Bowen. "You must just try a few dishes."

"Well, I do not wish to be rude, and the smell from the beef is certainly enticing," she replied.

Her gaze travelled around the guests and rested on Armand, who regarded her with hostility. Her expression became cold, her eyes narrowed in her white mask of a face.

"I will stay just a short time," she declared, and sat down gracelessly on a chair pulled out for her by a servant. The last of the stuffed udder was placed on her plate; she plunged her fork into it and consumed it greedily.

"I am intending to go on an excursion with my husband's ward on October the first," she said, as she paused between mouthfuls. "And Isabella suggested that Miss Georgiana might like to accompany us." She glanced briefly at Armand, then looked at Captain Bowen.

"Well, that is very kind," said Mrs Bowen. "Thank you. I am sure Georgiana would like to come."

"Yes, I would," agreed Georgiana. "Where are you going?"

"We are having dinner at a farm house at Heddon," she replied. "We know John Berriman, the farmer, and often visit there. It is a beautiful place."

"It's on Exmoor," said Lieutenant Hargreaves with displeasure. "The moor's filled with vagabonds and ruffians. I wouldn't have thought it suitable for ladies. Certainly not for a lady of a delicate constitution, such as Miss Georgiana." And he gazed across the table at her.

Mrs McAlpine looked disdainfully at him. "I can assure you, sir, we will be there with our servants and it is perfectly safe. I would not be going there myself, if it were not."

"Heddon is a haunt of smugglers," said the Lieutenant.

"I thought you did not find any," remarked Captain Bowen

"They had gone by the time we arrived," he replied.

"Probably never there," snorted Captain Bowen.

"Georgiana would be delighted to accept your invitation," said Mrs Bowen. "Are there any others in your party?"

"No, there will just be the three of us, and the servants, of course, who will have weapons."

"Very wise," said the Captain.

"Are you visiting Barum fair?" asked Mrs Bowen. "It is always very entertaining."

"Yes, Mr McAlpine and I generally attend," replied Mrs McAlpine.

"I will be going with Georgiana and the girls," said Mrs Bowen. "Shall we all go together?"

"I have never been," said Lieutenant Hargreaves. "Perhaps I may be allowed to accompany you?"

"Why certainly, sir," his hostess replied.

"Well, I think I can be persuaded to join your party," said Mrs McAlpine. "I believe the fair starts on September the nineteenth."

"It's always best to go on the first day," suggested Mrs Bowen.

Armand felt his appetite return somewhat at that point, and devoured a second portion of the apple tart in rum."

"I can see the ladies will be enjoying themselves while I am on navy rations," said Captain Bowen, as he turned to Armand. "By the way, I've got that information you wanted on the Santa Rosa."

Mrs McAlpine jerked as though she was a marionette and someone had tweaked the string. She dropped her knife. It clattered on to her plate, and everyone looked at her.

"It was a Portuguese ship, out from Cadiz, and was wrecked off the Torrs, about sixteen years ago. There were no survivors," said the Captain. "It was thought to be carrying families who were going to make a new life, here in Devon, and was reputed to have gold and other valuables on board."

"Thank you. I was just interested. I found a piece of wood from it on my beach." Armand avoided glancing at Mrs McAlpine, and slowly drank his claret.

"Well, I must return to Dunscombe Manor now," she announced, standing up very abruptly. As she did so, her elaborately coiffured hair fell forward, revealing an odd decoration of blood-red spots; a streak of the same colour was also visible on her sleeve, matching the rubies at her neck. He stared at her in horror, gripping his glass so tightly it broke in his hand, cutting it, and spilling wine on the cloth.

He sat silently until she had departed. Then he rose to his feet, gave his apologies for leaving the dinner so early, and rode back with his servants to the lane leading to Wildercombe House. He dismissed his men at the gate to Esther's garden, dismounted and strode grimly to the cottage.

He knocked, but there was no reply. He knocked again and Tabitha miaowed. He opened the door and she shot past his feet into the garden and ran up the trunk of the elder tree.

He went inside and glanced round the room, which was somewhat disordered, and not in its usual state of tidiness, as though Esther had left hastily. Stems and leaves had been left partially chopped on the table; parts of a mandrake root were infusing in wine in a porcelain bowl, and her cloak had fallen off its hook and was lying on the floor.

"She's left in a hurry," he muttered. He sat down on the fireside seat and looked thoughtfully at the small, seven-branched menorah on the ledge above the hearth.

"Why would you not tell me why he also owns a Jewish artefact?" he muttered.

Then he left the cottage and rode slowly, in the chill of the autumn evening, to Wildercombe House. He looked up at the vivid-red of the sunset sky, streaked with lemon wisps of clouds, and watched a skein of geese flying south in a v-formation.

"Storks," he exclaimed. A few seconds later he realised his mistake. Disappointment seared through him, and a longing welled up in him for the warmth of Alsace, the sweet smell of grapes in the vineyard and the untidy nests of the storks on the chimneys; he choked back his tears and walked alone into the cavernous hall of Wildercombe House.

38

Dusk was slowly concealing the garden and the wood. The colours were fading, blurring into a landscape where the outline of trees and bushes was no longer distinct. The creatures of the night were stirring; a russet fox sniffed the air in the middle of the lawn, and bats criss-crossed the evening sky.

In the library, the candles were already burning in their holders, a draught of air catching their flames, making shadows dance over the walls. Armand drank a glass of Geneva and suddenly jumped to see the slight body of Esther appear in front of him.

She stared at him, without speaking, her expression cold and hard.

"Where did you come from?" he asked.

"Well, I did not arrive on a broomstick. I walked in through the front entrance, as there was no one there."

"I went to your cottage. It looked as though you had left in a hurry," he said.

"Yes," she replied. "I had to go to Isabella."

"What has happened?" he asked, almost afraid to say the words.

"He attacked her after your visit."

"Is she hurt?" he cried in anguish.

"Yes. He hit her and opened the injury which had nearly healed. It bled very badly, as head wounds always do, and she must have seemed more injured than she really was. She pretended to collapse and lay still on the floor, and Mrs McAlpine took him away before he could harm her again."

"So she will recover," he said.

"Yes," she answered.

"Thank God," he muttered. "I am sorry. It was the wrong way to go about it. I should have listened to you. But I thought there was a chance he would accept me, and I did not want to discover, one day, that she had departed to America without my knowledge, and without my having made my position clear."

"Now he fears she will elope with you, so she will not be allowed out until she sets sail for America," she said.

"I don't think that is the case," he contradicted her. "She is going on an excursion to Heddon, with Mrs McAlpine and Georgiana."

"That does not seem very likely," she replied.

"I heard it today from Mrs McAlpine, when I had dinner at the Castle," he said.

She was silent for a moment. Then she asked, "Has Ben discovered the whereabouts of Harriet yet?"

"No. He is still in Exeter."

"What did Isabella say?" he finally said. "What did Isabella say about my marriage proposal?"

She looked at him, her expression inscrutable.

"You must forget her. You must find someone more suitable for you."

"What did she say?" he repeated, almost pleading.

She was silent, and he glared at her.

"There's something else," he admitted. "Mrs McAlpine was at the table when Captain Bowen told me about what happened to the Santa Rosa. Personally, I don't see why that is a problem, but from your reaction before, it seems best to tell you."

Esther's face paled and she trembled.

"Sit down," he said, and went to ring the bell to summon a servant, but thought better of it and gave her his unfinished glass.

"Drink this. It always revives me!"

She took the glass from him and sipped the Geneva and the colour returned to her cheeks.

199

"So I was right," he said. "There was a shipwreck off my beach, and the date is suitable for Isabella to have been on it as a young child. Her appearance and her name are foreign. You knew, didn't you? Why didn't you want me to know?"

"There is no proof that she was shipwrecked," said Esther, "or that the Santa Rosa was the boat she was on."

"But why have you not wanted to tell me?" he asked again, struggling to hold his temper in check. "Why are you so afraid of Raphael McAlpine finding out I am asking questions about it?"

"Shipwrecks are a sensitive subject in Devon. Sometimes ships just founder in a storm, particularly round here because the coast is so rocky and dangerous. But sometimes they are deliberately lured onto the rocks by men with lanterns."

He was quiet for a moment.

"I have never heard that before. But what does it matter? If a ship sinks, it sinks."

"Yes, but if everyone is killed, then any valuables which can be retrieved, either from the victims, or from the ship, are kept by the people on the shore. Therefore, no one can be left alive. Everyone on the ship has to die."

"Are you saying that is what happened to the Portuguese ship? Are you saying that the only person left alive was Isabella?" he asked. "Do you think McAlpine murdered her parents?"

She stood up, her face very solemn.

"I am not saying any more. I have already revealed too much. I believe it places Isabella in great danger to mention the Santa Rosa to the McAlpines, or to anyone else here in Ilfracombe, and I beg you to leave the subject alone. I wish her to marry Captain Petrie and leave North Devon. I feel she will then be safe. I also feel you are creating an unnecessary risk for yourself, as I have told you before. People die who cross McAlpine and his gang."

"I beg you, tell me what you know," demanded Armand in annoyance.

"No," said Esther sharply.

She took out a small object from her pocket. "Isabella does not know that I have removed this from her bedchamber."

"What is it?" he enquired.

"It is a picture of Captain Petrie. I thought it might be useful to you."
She did not elaborate, and he took the framed drawing and looked at
the portly and unremarkable features of Isabella's intended husband.

"You stole it," he said, and almost laughed.

"Yes," she admitted.

He looked at her closely, suddenly realising the truth of what she was
saying, and the certainty that she had not told him everything.

She left and he watched her from the window as she walked down the
drive. Her black-robed figure was quickly swallowed by the darkness
of the evening and he looked up at the sky, where there was no moon.

"Hecate's Moon," he said to himself. "That is when the ceremonies
take place. And he is having one tomorrow."

39

Dietrich agreed without hesitation to accompany Armand. He had been ploughing a field at the Mudge barton, was wearing a peasant's smock, and, for once, did not appear to have any weapon on him. Armand looked at the plough which had been modified to give it a short beam.

"Guillaume Thibaud has been advising you, I can see," he said.

"Yes, and I think you and I will be following a similar field rotation," Dietrich replied, wiping his sleeve across his sweating face, which had been burnt red by the sun and the wind. His blue eyes looked curiously at Armand.

"You want to see the ward of Raphael McAlpine? It seems an odd way of going about it."

"She's marrying someone else," he said.

Dietrich grimaced. "I knew there would be trouble when I first saw the witch."

He had arrived later at Wildercombe House, dressed in dark clothing, his black felt hat pulled down on his newly short-cropped blonde hair. Two pistols were in his belt, a sword at his side, and a knife in its scabbard. Armand had dressed in a similar fashion, with the exception of the hat, and was also well armed.

Their horses were both black stallions, and they cantered away from Wildercombe House, two lanterns swinging from the saddles, their light, however, barely illuminating any part of the drive. They went across the fields towards the Cairn, then down to the valley bottom, before following the path to the summit of the hill and across the fields leading to Dunscombe Manor. They extinguished the lanterns, and the horses picked their way over the uneven stone track, in a night which was so dark, the air itself seemed thick.

They reached the wall of the manor, dismounted, and tethered the horses to a tree. Armand opened the oak door, which creaked as it jarred against the gravel. Candles glimmered in the rooms of the house, but in the herb garden, it was almost impossible for them to see each other, or even to distinguish the nearest plants. A distinctive scent of thornapples, lavender and mint, drifted towards them, and a wind was gently soughing in the branches. However, beyond the greenhouse, the small copse Isabella had mentioned was not so oppressed by the uniform blackness. Lights were flickering and a low moaning and chanting was vibrating through the night.

"What on earth is that?" exclaimed Dietrich, crossing himself.

"It's some sort of ceremony. Where they discuss politics," replied Armand sarcastically.

A long drawn-out shriek sounded, followed by the piercing death cry of an animal.

"Is this how they discuss politics in England?" commented Dietrich.

"I want to see what's happening," said Armand. "You wait here."

"No," he replied. "I will come with you."

They walked rapidly, hugging the manor wall until they came to the wood. An owl hooted, as though in warning, but its cry was nearly lost in the eerie screaming and wailing, which kept rising to a crescendo, then subsiding, before rising up again.

They stepped from the shelter of one tree to another, penetrating further into the wood. A large oak shielded them; they looked out from behind its enormous girth and saw that in a clearing, just a short distance away, naked and semi-naked people were dancing and staggering. Bodies sprawled on the ground, writhing and twisting, seemingly oblivious to the revelry. Mullein tapers burned smokily by a black-clothed altar on which was an inverted crucifix. A black sheep was slumped across a boulder, dripping blood from its neck, and on a long table, at the far end of the glade, a naked figure was spread-eagled.

"Is that Isabella?" cried Armand in shock. "I will kill McAlpine!"

He forgot any attempt to hide himself and rampaged through the crowd, followed loyally by Dietrich. He pushed Lieutenant Hargreaves out of his way, who was wearing his tricorn hat, but nothing else. Revellers took no notice of them; they danced and chanted, their eyes glazed, as smoke and incense swirled and wreathed over their heads.

"Hecate, goddess of the night, let us worship you," they cried, the mantra swelling and falling in volume in a methodical rhythm.

Armand abruptly halted as he came near to the naked body sprawled on the table and gasped both in horror and in relief. The mound of blubber-like fat with a chalice wobbling on its abdomen and a black candle held in each enormous hand, was very evidently not Isabella.

The lady lying comatose, like a dead pig bloated in the heat of summer, was Mrs McAlpine. Her eyes were shut and she was mumbling a parody of the Mass. "In nomine magni dei nostril Satanas, introibo ad altare Domini."

Dietrich grabbed Armand. "Let's get out of here," he shouted. "It's the work of the Devil. We must save our souls."

They escaped into the trees and crashed through the undergrowth, stumbling in the darkness; branches and twigs catching at them, tearing their clothes. They emerged from the copse and trampled across the lavender and belladonna, until finally stopping, out of breath, at the manor wall. They looked back at the trees, where lights were flickering as before, and the weird cacophony of shrieking and moaning was still disturbing the night, and saw that they were alone.

"No one followed us," exclaimed Dietrich, in surprise.

"It was as though we were invisible," said Armand. "They were not just drunk. It was more than that. It was as though they were possessed."

"It is blasphemy," declared Dietrich. "They are Satan worshippers."

"Hecate worshippers, I think. Perhaps Satan as well," said Armand. "It seemed an odd mixture of witchcraft and religion."

"I recognised two of the Customs and Excise men, and there was Captain Jeffries from the Royal, and Daniel Venner, the blacksmith," remarked Dietrich.

Armand looked at Dunscombe Manor which was quiet in the darkness, and where candlelight was now apparent in only one room.

"I did not notice McAlpine," he said slowly, "or Samuel Butler, the slaver. I wonder where they are."

"It is possible they were in the crowd and we just did not recognise them. It is a black night, even with the burning tapers," replied Dietrich.

"I want to see Isabella," said Armand. "I have to."

"Is that wise?" queried Dietrich.

"Thank God she was not in the wood. She told me Reuben always locks her bedchamber door when the ceremonies take place. You can stay here. I will go to the house."

"No, I will come with you, and keep watch," replied Dietrich. "You are meddling in dangerous practices. There's wickedness going on. It is against the will of God and must be destroyed."

They walked over the plants to avoid making a noise on the gravel path, and quickly came to the courtyard. Inside the house the wolf hounds howled, and a woman's voice shouted.

"I had forgotten the dogs," muttered Armand, and he looked at Isabella's window, where candlelight was glowing yellow. "I will climb the ash. It's near the sill. And the house is not tall."

Dietrich stayed at the foot of the tree, his sword unsheathed, his dagger in his hand, and Armand shinned up the trunk. He crawled along a branch, swung himself onto the sill and clung to the ivy on the wall to stop from falling.

The unearthly shrieking and chanting was still continuing from the wood, and Cain and Abel were howling again downstairs in the house. Armand knocked on the window, the sound hardly audible in all the noise going on. He peered through the glass and saw Isabella, standing by her bed, in a white nightgown, her dark hair falling over her shoulders, her hand clutched to her mouth as she looked towards him in terror.

"It's me," he called out softly. "Armand."

She ran and opened the window and stood looking at him in amazement. "I thought you were a ghost," she gasped. "What are you doing? You will fall."

He clung on to the side of the casement and quickly lowered himself into the room. He pulled her towards him, embraced her and ran his fingers gently over her hair, which was slightly caked with blood. Anger flooded through him; he held her close to him, and caressed her, his hands passionately feeling her body through the thin clothing.

"My darling," he said. "I was such a fool. I did not expect him to attack you. I just wanted to make a proposal of marriage, in case he accepted me. I was afraid you would suddenly go off to be married, before I was able to make my wishes known."

"I am fine," she replied. "He did not hurt me much. I am used to his violence, and I pretended to be more injured than I really was."

"Yes, Esther told me," he said.

He kissed her on her hair and then on her lips, and for a moment, she yielded to him and they clung to each other, lost in their own world, far from the reality of Dunscombe Manor.

She gently pushed at his chest with both her hands, but he continued to embrace her.

"Please, you must go. This is madness. If he finds you here, he will kill you," she murmured.

"Where is McAlpine?" he asked.

"I don't know. I presume he's in the wood," she replied.

"No, I don't think so. I've just been there and I couldn't see him or Samuel Butler. I saw Mrs McAlpine, though."

"You've been in the wood, and his wife saw you," she exclaimed.

"No, she did not see me. She was ……," and he hesitated.

"She was what?" asked Isabella.

"She was busy," he said, searching for the words.

She looked questioningly at him.

"There is debauchery and depravity going on there," he said. "I am afraid for you. He is evil."

"I know he is," she replied. "I am always trying to tell you. I think he killed Daniel and Thomas."

"There was no sign of killing. Only a slaughtered sheep. There were other activities being pursued. I don't want you to stay here. Come with me now. We will be married and you will be safe." He tightened his arms around her and held her close.

"Please, stop this. You must leave immediately," she said.

"Marry me," he implored her.

"No, I cannot," she said, tears in her eyes. "He will kill you and Esther as well."

"Don't be foolish. I am not as easy to kill as that and I will protect Esther." And he kissed her again.

"He will. You do not know him. He is wicked. And are you still going to France to fight?"

"Yes, I have to," he said unhappily. "It is my duty as a son to my murdered parents, and to France. I have no choice."

"Then you would leave me unprotected," she replied.

"No, I have armed men and servants. They will look after you," he declared.

"This is some sort of fantasy. What happens if you die in France or are taken prisoner? What happens to me then? And Esther says you need to marry a rich woman in order to save your estate. I will bring you nothing, except trouble."

He was silent, and through the open window came a single scream from the direction of the wood.

"Is that Mrs McAlpine?" she asked, in horror.

"Quite possibly," he replied. "But I don't think you need to worry about her."

"Please go," she begged, as Cain and Abel suddenly began to whine and snuffle outside the door.

"I don't think he intends you to set sail for America yet. I was at dinner at the Castle and Mrs McAlpine said that you would be with her on an excursion to Heddon on the first of October."

"I did not know that. She has not told me."

"She said you had asked if Georgiana could come."

"No. That is not true. I have never gone on any trip with Mrs McAlpine. She hates me. It does not seem very likely."

"That is what I thought," he replied.

"Sometimes I feel as though I am caught in a web. I am trapped in its stickiness and cannot get free, and all around me is evil," she murmured.

"There is not evil here. I love you and I want to protect you. Please come with me now," he begged.

"I cannot. You must go," she said.

"I will only leave if you promise to come on the nineteenth to my house. I know that the McAlpines will be at Barnstaple Fair on that day with the Bowens."

She looked at him. "Really? Are you sure?"

"Yes," he said, kissing her hand.

"I will try," she murmured. "I can only promise that I will try. We will see each other one last time."

"It will certainly not be the last time," he declared, and embraced her once more. Then he reluctantly clambered back over the narrow window sill, just as Mrs Gubb's voice came through the keyhole.

"What's going on in there? Do you need me, Isabella?"

"No," she called back. "There's not a problem. I just fell out of bed. I am not hurt."

He reached out his hand to her and she held it for a second. "September the nineteenth," he said.

He tumbled, rather than climbed, from the window, and managed to break his fall by clutching at the branches of the ash tree on his way down. He fell onto the ground, and Dietrich rushed to help him up. Together they ran over the cobbles and fled through the gardens and out into the lane to the waiting horses.

They galloped furiously homewards and Armand left Dietrich at the Mudge barton.

"Thank you, my friend," he said, embracing him, and then he continued on his way to Wildercombe House.

He passed by the stone birds at the bottom of the drive and his horse started to limp. He dismounted and walked in front of it, holding the reins. The horse stumbled badly and he paused. Familiar noises of the night surrounded him in the tarry blackness; the stream gurgled, an animal scampered in the hedgerow and an owl hooted. A donkey brayed, and then a second. He stood still, in surprise.

He listened, for a few seconds, and heard nothing. He was about to carry on, when he caught the muffled tread of animals on the stones of the path through the wood. He stared into the darkness, trying to make out what was happening. A lantern shone and a man's voice cursed softly.

He slapped his horse on the rump and it trotted off lamely along the drive. He unsheathed his sword and cautiously advanced through the bracken and ferns. He crossed the stream, and crept slowly forwards. He stopped near the rowan tree and suddenly bumped into the greased coat of a donkey which was coming down the path. Behind it was another donkey, and following it, a whole file of donkeys, with large wooden tubs strapped on their backs.

A man surged out of the darkness. He was holding a lantern in one hand, its light half-hidden by a cloth, and in the other was a pistol.

"Hey!" he shouted, and swung the lantern towards him. Armand thrust his sword at the man, who jumped aside, and then sprang at him, his fist smashing into his face. He sank to the ground, unconsciousness blotting out his surroundings.

He awoke underneath a bush. He was alone. His face was in the dirt; a mouse was nuzzling his cheek and running squeaking over his hair, and he hit out at it in disgust. A long drawn-out groan escaped his lips, and he clutched his head as he very slowly sat up. He retched violently, and it was several minutes before he was able to stagger to his feet.

He very shakily retraced his steps and walked along the drive. Wildercombe House was in darkness. He slowly went up the steps and opened the front door, which was unlocked. He closed it behind him and shot the metal bolt. He made his way over the flagstones and wearily climbed the stairs to his bedchamber, where he sank on to his bed and fell asleep just as the clock in the hall struck three o'clock.

40

The following morning his face resembled a pudding too long boiled in a cloth. One eye was nearly closed, his cheek was swollen to twice its usual size and his nose appeared flattened.

"Luckily, I've still got my teeth," he muttered, as he looked in the mirror.

Breakfast was a miserable affair, consisting mainly of toast dipped in claret, and soft eggs, which he had barely finished when Guillaume Thibaud arrived.

"There was smuggling on my land last night, and I was attacked," Armand said. "I am sending a servant to the Lord Lieutenant to inform him. It was not just a few donkeys carrying tubs. There was a whole column of them."

His fellow Frenchman looked at him grimly. "Do you have any idea who it was?"

"I didn't see the faces of anyone. But I know who I suspect," he retorted. "And you were involved as well, weren't you? You help him with his wine imports?"

Guillaume Thibaud said nothing and just shrugged his shoulders.

"Quite frankly, I don't give a damn if people smuggle or not," declared Armand. "At least it's one way to get good French brandy and wine into the country. What concerns me is that they're using my estate to do so. That is why he wants to buy Wildercombe House, isn't it? It is very important to the smuggling. From my beach the countryside is practically deserted if you go over to the Cairn and then up the hill and across to Chambercombe."

"I think it is more than that," Guillaume Thibaud replied. "McAlpine really likes the house and the estate. He wants to move from Dunscombe Manor, which is much smaller, and which he feels does not do justice to his wealth and social status."

"I am not even sure it is just smuggling," said Armand. "When I first arrived I found slave manacles in the greenhouse. Has he been bringing slaves in here as well?"

"I told you. I only concern myself with the wine. I do not agree with slavery. You know my principles. You know I would never participate in any such trafficking."

"How is Charles?" asked Armand, ignoring his words.

"His leg has improved slightly. It is less swollen and he is no longer delirious."

"Thank goodness," he replied. "Young children need a father and Henriette needs a husband."

"Have you already sent a servant to the Lord Lieutenant, or to Lieutenant Hargreaves?" asked Guillaume Thibaud.

"No, not yet. But I think we both know where Lieutenant Hargreaves was last night, and probably the rest of the customs and excise men as well."

Guillaume Thibaud raised his eyebrows and shrugged again. "Have you spoken to Mrs Widdicombe about smuggling on your land last night?"

"No, I haven't. I was knocked unconscious and when I came to, there was no one there. The donkeys had all disappeared. I walked back to Wildercombe House and went to bed."

"Did you see anyone?" he asked.

"No."

He was quiet for a few minutes, and Armand glared at him with his one good eye, struggling to hold his temper in check.

"Am I right that you asked Raphael McAlpine if you could marry his ward, Isabella?" Guillaume Thibaud asked. "And he turned you down."

"Yes," he snapped.

"She is beautiful," Guillaume Thibaud said.

"Yes," he agreed.

"Do you think it would be better not to mention either the smuggling, or your suspicions, to anyone at the moment? Do you wish to annoy Raphael McAlpine further, with Isabella living as a prisoner in his house?"

"Are you threatening her, or me?" asked Armand in annoyance.

"No, far from that. I am trying to help you," said his visitor calmly, rubbing the knuckles of one hand, which were grazed and red.

Armand stared at him and suddenly leaped from his chair and grabbed Guillaume Thibaud by the lapels of his coat.

"It was you!" he shouted. "It was you who hit me!"

Guillaume Thibaud roughly pushed him away. "Calm yourself. You are right. I hit you. No one else saw you. It was a very large consignment of wine and I was at the head of the donkeys."

Armand swung his fist at him and he parried the blow.

"I would be careful," he warned. "Your face already looks like some sort of turnip to be fed to the animals."

"You took me by surprise," shouted Armand angrily.

"No, I didn't," he replied. "It was you who took me by surprise. Don't you realise that if any of the others had seen you, your dead body would now be lying in your chapel, and McAlpine would probably be back here in your estate."

"What do you mean?" asked Armand.

"You were alone. Do you think that you and your sword stood any chance against forty men armed with pistols and cutlasses? What on earth were you thinking of? You have a whole house of servants. Why don't you use them? What are you doing, skulking around in the dark by yourself? Luckily, I knocked you out with the first blow and no one else saw. I pulled you into the bushes and left you there. I came back later in the night, to see if you were alright, but you had gone."

Armand stared at him speechless. "So you knock me unconscious, and I owe you my life again. And you think I should keep quiet about what I saw."

"I think you should say nothing until you have resolved your marriage plans and Isabella is not locked up in his house, and is either married to you, or to this Captain Petrie, whoever he is. Raphael McAlpine is a very dangerous man to cross."

"Do you know anything about the murders of Daniel Stribling and Thomas Kemp?" asked Armand.

Guillaume Thibaud shrugged his shoulders again. "Their eyes were pecked out. What more can I say?"

"You mean McAlpine's crows?" he asked.

"I don't know for sure. Crows are scavengers, not killers. They flock in the air over battle fields, just as vultures do in the United States. They are not likely to attack a man. I think that the eyes pecked out of the corpses was a warning to others. A warning not to cause trouble to McAlpine. I only help with the wine business, which often brings violence in its wake. However, lucrative although it undoubtedly is, McAlpine seems to obtain his money from another source and I had wondered if their deaths were connected with that. I have no idea what it is, but I do know that he is expecting a large amount in the near future. He is very secretive about it, but I think that Samuel Butler is involved. People in Ilfracombe are very afraid of McAlpine and his men and his crows."

He walked across the room and looked unhappily out of the window towards the wood.

"Why do you work for him?" asked Armand.

"It is not easy to be a refugee in a foreign country," he said. "I need the money."

He picked up the framed portrait of Captain Petrie that had been left on the desk.

"You are a follower of the Prince of Wales?" he enquired.

"No," said Armand.

"You have his picture," he remarked.

"No, that's not the Prince of Wales," said Armand.

"Yes, it is," he replied. "I have seen him, and this is a very good likeness. Look, you can see the royal sash on his shoulder."

Armand glanced at the picture. Then he quickly placed it in a drawer of the desk.

"What are you going to do about the smuggling on your land?" Guillaume Thibaud asked. "I need to know before I leave, as you are putting me at risk, not just Raphael McAlpine, if you are making allegations to the Lord Lieutenant. A spell in Exeter prison would not please me, quite frankly. Do not forget there is no proof that smuggling happened on your estate last night. It will only be your word that you saw the donkeys and the contraband. McAlpine has many powerful friends round here. He has built up a network of contacts and has a hold on people."

"Do you mean his ceremonies?" enquired Armand.

"Yes. They are extremely popular amongst many local people, and at the same time, there is, perhaps, an element of blackmail involved, once they participate. I gather the charms of Mrs McAlpine are legendary."

Armand went pale, an expression of revulsion on his face. "It is difficult to imagine. Have you ever attended the events?"

"No," he said, in a horrified tone. "In any case, I am generally occupied elsewhere, on those nights."

Armand looked soberly at him. "I will say nothing. You are correct. I do not wish to put Isabella in any more danger, and I also do not wish you to be accused. Thank you for what you did for me last night. I realise you were putting your own position in jeopardy."

"Go and see Esther Cerfbeer," Guillaume Thibaud told him. "She will give you something for your face. She is a very clever woman."

"Yes, I know," he said.

Guillaume Thibaud departed and as he rode off on his horse away from the house, Armand opened the drawer and took out the picture.

"He was right," he muttered. "It does look like a royal sash on his shoulder." He stared at it in puzzlement for a few minutes, and then replaced it in the desk.

41

White dust from the road streaked Ben's clothes, hair and face. He stood in the library, disappointment evident in his voice.

"I couldn't find her. She does not live at ten Southernhay West, and none of the servants had ever seen her, or her husband. I tried the other houses in the road, as well as nearby streets, but people did not know of her. I went to the Cathedral and asked there, but it was all the same."

"Well, never mind. I was only hoping," said Armand, struggling to speak through his swollen mouth.

"A Scottish man from Dundee, James Davey, owns the house, and one of the rooms is used for his shipping business, but he rarely visits," said Ben.

"Thank you," replied Armand. "You did your best. Go to the kitchen and have some food."

"There was one odd thing," said Ben, lowering his voice slightly. "I shouldn't think it interests you though."

He hesitated and looked towards the open library door. Armand glanced at him, then walked over and closed it.

"What is that?" he asked. "You can speak freely now."

"Whenever James Davey comes to the house, he is always accompanied by a Mr Widdicombe, or a Mr Butler."

"Really?" he said.

"It's probably not Ezekiel Widdicombe or Samuel Butler," replied Ben, "but I was surprised, so I asked Sarah, the maid, to describe Mr Davey." His face reddened. "I had to use some of your money to treat her to some cider first in the tavern though. She said he was not tall, and always had a lot of white powder on his face, and generally wore a Paisley waistcoat."

Armand stared at him. "You did well. Go and ask the cook to give you a good piece of beef and plenty of cider. You deserve it."

Ben smiled happily. "There's one more thing. Ezekiel Widdicombe told me never to mention it or I would be a dead man. I saw it when I came with you to look at your estate."

"What's that?" asked Armand.

"He's got a mark on his arm. I don't know exactly what it is, but it's a sign of a secret organisation in North Devon. If you talk about it, you are killed."

"Can you describe the sign?" he asked.

"It is like a circle, with a second circle which has a maze inside it," said Ben.

"I won't tell anyone. Your secret is safe with me," replied Armand. "Do not be afraid of Ezekiel Widdicombe. I intend to dismiss him and his wife soon, but I cannot do it at the moment. I have to wait."

"They are murdering cut-throats," exclaimed Ben. "The whole of Ilfracombe is terrified of them. My cousin was murdered and his eyes pecked out. Everyone knows they did it, but no one will talk."

"Do you mean Daniel Stribling or Thomas Kemp?" he asked.

"Daniel was my cousin, but I also knew Thomas Kemp," Ben replied.

"Thank you," Armand said, going to the drawer in his desk, and taking out a coin. "Do not say anything about this. Here is your payment for what you have done. If you see or hear of anything connected with McAlpine, or Widdicombe, please tell me. Eat quickly and then wait for me outside the house."

"Yes, I will," said Ben, and went off, grinning broadly, to the kitchen.

Armand rang the bell and when Ned, the new footman, entered, told him to instruct six of his men to be ready at the front steps and to be armed.

"I will take my chances in France," he muttered. "But no one's going to kill me here in North Devon."

An hour later, he mounted his horse which was waiting for him at the entrance and then, accompanied by his men, rode the short distance to Esther's cottage.

He found her standing on the path outside her gate. She was bending down, speaking to something in the brook, which flowed through the rushes at one side of the lane.

"There, my beloved. See how you like it here," she was saying.

He dismounted and looked at her. Her jet necklace and hair comb gleamed blackly, but the wrinkled skin on her face had a greyish hue. Even when she straightened up, her back was bent, and she seemed tiny, as he stood next to her. Her expression, however, was fierce, and her determined spirit was clearly over-riding the increasing frailty of her body.

"Have you been kicked by a cow?" she enquired.

"No, it was human, rather than animal," he replied. "What are you doing?"

"I am letting David enjoy the stream," she said, her voice breaking with sadness. "He will soon be on his own. I cannot take him with me. He must learn to be independent."

He glanced into the slow-flowing water and saw David sitting on a flat stone.

"It is difficult to tell with a frog," he remarked. "But he looks rather miserable."

"Yes," she admitted. "It breaks my heart to leave him."

"Well, perhaps you won't be going, if I have anything to do with it. That would be a pleasant surprise for him," he said.

She looked coldly at him, and at his men.

"I am pleased to see you are better protected than usual."

"Yes, it seems best, in the circumstances. Can I speak to you in the cottage?"

She picked up David from his stone and carried him in her hand, walking slowly, her breathing fast and shallow.

He followed her and opened the door, letting her step inside first. The room was again disordered, as it had been on his previous visit, and a bright green stew of nettles was bubbling in the cauldron over a low fire. Tabitha ran to greet him this time, and he sat down on the fireside seat and stroked her.

"Let me put juniper oil on your face," Esther said.

"No, it's not important," he replied. "It will heal."

"You do not trust me," she declared.

"You have already told me you do not trust me, so I think the English saying is, 'the pot calling the kettle black'," he retorted.

She laughed and sat on the opposite fireside seat and regarded him curiously.

"So, my fine gentleman, what do you want with me?"

"I am returning the picture," he replied, taking it out of his pocket. "It is best to put it back, before anyone knows it is missing."

"Yes, thank you. You have not any use for it then," she said, with a shade of disappointment.

"It is evidently the Prince of Wales," he told her.

She literally jumped. "What!" she exclaimed. "What makes you think that?"

"Guillaume Thibaud recognised him. I did not say where the picture had come from, obviously."

"That is very strange," she remarked.

"Yes, isn't it?" I hardly think Isabella is about to marry the Prince of Wales."

"No," she said, a worried expression on her face. "Perhaps it is just a likeness?"

"He has the royal sash on his shoulder," he pointed out, and saw her breathing become more rapid and her hands tremble in agitation.

"Do you know of a group in Ilfracombe which has a mark on their arms which resembles a circle with a labyrinth of black lines within a second circle?" he asked.

"Yes, I have heard of such an organisation," she said. "I believe McAlpine and his cronies run it. He has taken the sacred symbol of Hecate's Wheel and has corrupted it. He thinks of himself as a grand master of magic, but he is a sham. In medicine he would be called a quack. He uses a hotch potch of different ideas for his own violent and illegal purposes. In Ilfracombe, people know it is not wise to cross anyone who wears such a design."

"I will bear that in mind," he replied.

"Have you heard from Ben?" she enquired.

"Yes, he returned today, and that is partly why I have come to see you. He could not find any trace of Harriet, or her husband, but the address is of a house which is owned by a James Davey, who has a shipping business. He is Scottish, wears a Paisley waistcoat, and is always accompanied by either someone called Widdicombe, or someone called Butler."

"So the address is that of McAlpine," she said thoughtfully.

"It looks like it," he replied. "But Harriet was never there, not even for a short time."

She stood up and wandered across to the window, as David splashed in his bowl of water and gave a low croak.

"He's happy now," remarked Armand.

"Be quiet," she snapped. "Let me think."

He sat silently and watched the nettles bubble and stroked Tabitha.

"There is a synagogue in Exeter," she finally said. "I sometimes visit it, as we have only a house for worship here in North Devon, in Barnstaple."

She stopped speaking for several minutes and he waited again for her to continue.

"Zachariah Zimmermann was there last Sabbath and when he returned, he said that the talk was of a Jewish man, Jacob Goldstein, sent from London by his employer, a diamond merchant. He has been kidnapped and nothing has since been heard of him. He has disappeared."

"So?" he questioned. "It's not surprising, surely. He probably had money and jewels on him and was robbed."

"Yes, probably," she agreed. "It is just that there seem a lot of people vanishing into thin air in Devon. Harriet now appears to have gone, and the addresses were never known for McAlpine's other wards, just the towns."

"And women have actually been snatched," he remarked, staring at her. "Jacob Goldstein did not have fair or red hair, did he?"

"Do not joke," she said. "The fact that all of McAlpine's girls also had red or fair hair has always niggled at me. They were so beautiful and it was very strange that they should all have either very fair or very red hair."

"And Bess Mudge also had similar hair, I presume," he said. "I have seen her sister. What about the other women taken? What did they look like?"

"I have no idea," she replied.

"Where did these women live? I will go and investigate," he said. "It seems very likely that McAlpine and his gang are involved. This marriage with Petrie is also beginning to seem extremely dubious, and although I have no intention of her marrying him anyway, I would like to know what exactly McAlpine has in mind. Really it would be best to try and find out about the marriages of the rest of his wards. I am sure that a crime has been committed and McAlpine needs to be brought to justice."

"I don't think it possible. Harriet is the only one we could have traced," Esther said as she sank down onto the fireside settle, breathing quickly. "Give me that jar on the dresser."

He walked across the room and picked it up and handed it to her. She took out a pinch of the powder it contained, and in a few minutes her breathing had returned to normal, and her face appeared less ashen.

"I have waited so long for Isabella to be free of him. I realise I am foolish to believe McAlpine. I am aware he is wicked, but, even now, I find it difficult to think that she might not be marrying this man in America. I am getting old, I suppose. My mind does not work like it used to. The crystal is always hazy now when I look at it."

He reached out and touched her hand. "I don't blame you. I know you have tried to keep her safe."

She looked into his eyes. "I was wrong, Armand de Delacroix. I do trust you. You are decent and kind, although misguided about the nature of the revolution. You need to renounce your principles about fighting," her voice faltered and she stopped for a few seconds before continuing. "But even then you would not have Isabella. Sooner or later he would kill you both, as one thing is very obvious in all this. He is going to obtain a lot of money when Isabella marries, and that is probably why he murdered Daniel and Thomas, as they would have ruined his plans."

"If he, or his men, killed them, he needs to be brought to trial," he said. "He could not harm Isabella if he was hanged."

"No one would ever testify against him," she replied. "You do not realise how impossible it is."

"Isabella has black hair. She does not resemble the other wards," he said.

"Yes, I have always been grateful for that. I always knew she was different. That is one of the reasons I hoped she would escape him. When she was lying on the floor after he hit her, she said that she had heard him say the name of the person who was paying money for her. The name was not Petrie. She did not hear it clearly, but thought it sounded like Ivan Ben."

"Ivan Ben. That is strange. Perhaps they are Petrie's names." he remarked.

"Yes," she said very anxiously, her breathing becoming more laboured.

"I wondered if it was…" her voice tailed away.

"You wondered if it was what?" he asked.

"Oh, nothing," she replied. "I am just being foolish."

He gave her the jar of digitalis again. "Stay quietly here. I will go and ask questions about the women who have disappeared. Do you know where they lived?"

"Yes, one came from Combe Martin, one from Lynmouth, and a second from Ilfracombe. I do not know the names of the first two, but the last was Jane Venn, from down by the harbour. Her father is a fisherman and spends much of the year at Newfoundland."

"I will go now. I will do my best." He rummaged in his pocket and extracted sugared plums, wrapped in a twist of muslin, the remains of a thornapple petal stuck onto the material.

"Here. This is for Isabella, if you visit her."

Esther reached into a bowl on the shelf next to her and took out some dried leaves.

"Take this. It is mugwort. It protects travellers from thieves and spirits."

"Thank you," he replied politely, and placed them in his pocket. He left her and strode down the garden path, past the scarecrow with its burden of crows. As soon as he reached the lane, he crossed himself and removed the mugwort from his pocket. Just as he was about to throw it into the stream, he hesitated.

"No," he muttered. "I need all the help I can get," and he joined his men.

42

The Venn family lived in a cottage by the Strand, and all the paraphernalia of fishing was laid out over its white walls and small front garden. Nets hung from the window sill, and lobster and crab pots were stacked high on either side of the path. Fish bones littered the ground and festooned two hollyhocks, and seagulls were squabbling over the remains of a mackerel.

The smell of fish was even stronger in the living room than out in the air, and Armand resisted the invitation of a chair to sit on. Naked children with grimy blonde hair played round his feet, and their large, red-faced mother looked with surprise at her visitor.

"You want to know about my Jane?"

"Yes," he replied. "I don't wish to distress you, but I would be interested to know what happened to her."

"She went," she said. "One minute she was here, the next, she had gone."

"Have you any idea why?" he asked.

Her blue eyes looked sad. "No," she said slowly. "No. But I hope she's happy. She was a good girl, my Jane."

"Did you see anyone strange that day?" he asked.

"Not really. People thought that some sailors were here, but I never saw anyone."

"Was it in the evening? Was there a moon?"

"It was a night with a bit of a storm. It was dark and raining."

"She was fair-haired?"

"Yes, she was always very fair," Mrs Venn replied. "She had the skin of a lady, it was so white."

He gave her a coin, as he took his leave. "Thank you. You've been very helpful."

He and his men rode past the harbour, where a large merchant ship was anchored by the quay. Hens were clucking on its poop deck and sailors with broad Scottish accents were standing at the rail, passing comments on the women dock workers. He glanced to see the flag, but it had been hauled down, and he continued on the path past Chambercombe, towards Hele and the Combe Martin road.

The sea and sky merged into a brilliant blue in the distance, the track meandering up and down the steep hills. They cantered along, the dust flying from the horses' hooves, farmyard dogs howling as they passed near Watermouth Cove, where the sea was shimmering in the sunlight. Buzzards spied on them from posts and trees, as they laboured up to the summit of Newberry Hill, and then they descended the high-hedged lane to Combe Martin bay, and were welcomed by the sharp sound of tools breaking and cutting rock from the limestone quarries scarring the valley. Clouds of black smoke were rising from the lime kilns, obscuring the sun, and an unpleasant odour tainted the sea air.

"What's that smell?" Armand asked Ben.

"They're retting the hemp," he replied. "It has to be soaked to make rope and the laces for shoes. You can see it has been harvested." And he indicated the hemp fields at the foot of Little Hangman, and behind the cottages, which were now bare of their previously very tall, dark green plants.

The gibbet was also denuded of its former tarred corpse, and Ben, with satisfaction, remarked to Armand, "His family came and took Tom Challacombe in the night. He has had a decent Christian burial."

"What had he done?" asked Armand.

"He poached rabbit," said Ben bitterly. "It is a harsh punishment for a man trying to feed his children."

"Yes," he agreed.

A small group was gathering beyond the high water mark on the shingle beach. A woman with long grey hair and wearing a shabby brown cloak, was standing on a rock, shrieking in a voice which rose and fell, almost as though she was singing.

He stopped his horse and listened to her words.

"I am the woman in the Book of Revelation, chapter twelve. My calling is from God. I fight with the Devil and I always win," she proclaimed.

He looked with distaste at her, as she continued to invoke her supernatural powers, and crossed himself for the third time that day.

"Do you want to buy a pamphlet of prophecy?" asked a man in a tall, black, shiny hat, coming up to him. "Or I can sell you a passport to heaven. It costs twelve shillings, or a guinea to you, sir."

"No thank you," he said. "I will do without and take my chance."

Men were, on the whole, remaining upright, but a gaggle of women at the back, were falling onto the sand and seaweed, groaning so loudly and hysterically, that the speaker's words were drowned out. One woman in a blue dress covered with a bib apron, was foaming at the mouth, and people moved away, circling her warily.

"I think it's a Methodist Revivalist meeting," said Ben. "My mother has joined."

"Really," muttered Armand. "It looks like one of McAlpine's ceremonies to me." And he dug his heels into his horse and cantered rapidly off up the main street of Combe Martin to Rose Cottage.

Charles was sitting on a wooden seat in the garden, his bandaged leg stretched out in front of him. Armand greeted him, coughing as the smoke from the lime kilns and the smell from the hemp combined to drift over the house. "Guillaume said you were much better."

"Yes, Dr Conibear has done well," said Charles, his face very pale. "I think I would be dead if it were not for him. The wound is still somewhat infected, but it seems to be healing, with the aid of his poultices."

"That's good," he remarked.

Henriette came out of the cottage, holding Marie Thérèse, and he smiled to see her. Her cheeks were pink, her hair was neatly arranged, her dress was covered by an apron, and she looked the antithesis of the woman he had seen a short time before.

"Have you had an accident?" she enquired, glancing at his face.

"Just a problem with a donkey. I met it in the dark and it did not like me."

"Thank you for all the food you sent," she said, "And Sarah, the maid, was very helpful."

"I am pleased to have been of use," he replied.

He was prevailed on to have a glass of wine, and sat with Charles, watching Edouard play, chasing bees with a toy sword.

"I am looking for the family of a girl who disappeared from Combe Martin. Have you any idea of her name?" he asked.

"Do you mean Ann Irwin? She went missing just when we first came to the village," said Henriette. "It was difficult for us, because we were suspected of having a hand in it, as we were foreigners."

"Do you know anything about her?" he asked.

"No, nothing," she said. "Only her name. I believe her family lived by the very small fields at the end of the village. Why do you want to know?"

"Oh, it is just something I am looking into," he said.

"You are investigating her disappearance?" queried Charles, in surprise.

"Yes," he admitted. "I can't really talk about it at the moment though."

"Is there any news of the invasion ships?" asked Charles.

"No, not yet," he replied. "Are you thinking of coming with us?"

"No," said Charles. "I should not imagine my leg would be good enough to let me fight."

"He is not going," declared Henriette, in annoyance. "He has a family to support."

"I understand," said Armand.

"They have opened up two mines here in Combe Martin. Charles knows about mining as there were mines on his estate. He has been asked to give advice and I am hopeful it might lead to something more."

"The mines of Combe Martin financed the English win at the Battle of Agincourt," remarked Charles. "It is only in recent years that they have fallen into disuse."

Armand shivered in the gloom engendered by the burning lime kilns. He put his hand in his pocket and discovered a sugared plum which had escaped from the muslin. He gave it to Edouard and then took his leave of the family

He and his men rode past the house resembling a pack of cards, and the church, and continued along the valley until they reached the medieval strips of land at its head. Several had recently been harvested of hemp and the now-familiar, rotting smell was very strong. He stopped to enquire about Ann Irwin from an elderly man smoking a clay pipe, who jabbed his finger at a tumbledown cottage in a copse of oak at one side of the path.

"They all be gone now," he said. "No one lives there now, just rats and vairies."

"He means squirrels," interjected Ben.

"John Irwin was pressganged into the fleet and his brother, Samuel, died at Fleurus," the old man continued.

"What happened to Ann Irwin," asked Armand.

"She disappeared one night. The piskies took 'er. She just vanished."

"Was it a dark night?" he questioned.

"Yes, I believe it were," he replied. "Although it be a long time ago now."

"What was the colour of her hair?" he asked.

"It were urdd," said the man. "They all 'ad urdd 'air."

"Red hair," translated Ben.

"Thank you," said Armand, and gave the man a coin.

"There is one more to see," he told Ben. "She lives at Lynmouth. Do you know the road?"

"Yes," he replied. "It goes across Exmoor." He looked curiously at Armand. "Do you think it is all connected, all these women and Harriet?"

"It seems very likely," he said. "Say nothing to anyone at the moment. If they are linked, then it is an evil and dangerous business going on, and I don't yet understand what is happening."

They followed the track up the hill, the high hedges of beech, ash and elder closing around them. The smell of the rotting hemp gradually receded, replaced by the damp freshness of grass and leaves, and the fruity aroma of blackberries.

The hedges metamorphosed into dry stone walls as they reached the higher ground, and the lush countryside became moorland. A curlew called and wisps of smoke rose from blackened heather and bracken.

They rode across the summits of hogs back cliffs which were high above the sea, the path at times careering across their heights, then plunging steeply into densely wooded ravines.

They cantered at a good pace and finally came to the track winding down the almost precipitous, densely wooded hillside above Lynmouth. They passed by Watersmeet, at the confluence of the two Lyns, and halted at the foot of the hill, where the river was cascading over huge boulders littering its bed, before channelling onto the pebble beach and out to sea.

They tethered their horses to a rail, and gratefully entered the dark, low-raftered room of a tavern, where his men quenched their thirst with cider, and Armand enjoyed brandy. Fortified, he asked the innkeeper about the disappearance of the local girl.

"Why do you want to know?" asked the man in a surly tone. He was bearded, an unusual sight, except among seafarers, and was wearing baggy trousers, also common to mariners. He stared belligerently at the Alsatians, who were dressed in English blue livery, but who were joking and talking loudly in their own language, abetted by Ben, who had learned several words, and was trying them out, much to everyone's amusement.

"Vurriners?" questioned the innkeeper.

"Alsatians," said Armand, thinking it wise not to say French, and unlikely that he would have the slightest idea where they were from.

The innkeeper did not look impressed. "You sound French," he said.

"I am the Duke de Delacroix, and I own an estate near Ilfracombe," declared Armand.

"And I'm the Duke of Wellington," the man replied, glancing distastefully at Armand's velvet coat and frilled silk shirt.

His men had now fallen silent and were holding their pistols and daggers in both hands, except for Hans who was quickly finishing his cider, the tankard in one hand, his pistol in the other.

"We'll go," said Armand, shrugging. "I will ask elsewhere."

"If you make it worth my while, I can tell you," said a young man, dressed in the uniform of the Devonshires. "Take no notice of Samuel. His wife's been cuckolding him, and he's like a fox pricked by a fuzzypig."

Samuel spluttered in annoyance, but retreated to the corner of the room, and sat down, cursing at a table.

"What do you want to know about Molly?" he said. "She was my sweetheart and we were going to be married. Then, suddenly, she just disappeared."

"Was it at night?" asked Armand.

"Yes, it was. It was dark moon night. Her mother came to get me when she couldn't find her. We searched everywhere. We thought perhaps she had fallen in the river, because it had been raining, and it was like a torrent. But her body was never found." He rubbed his face with his hands, to stop his tears. "I became a soldier."

"Did she have fair or red hair?" asked Armand.

"She was very fair," he said.

"Thank you. I am sorry for your loss," replied Armand, giving him a coin.

"Why are you asking?" the young man enquired.

"I am searching for someone who has also disappeared, and I am wondering why there are so many girls missing in North Devon," Armand replied.

"There are others?" he asked.

"Yes, several," said Armand.

"If I hear of anything more, I will come and tell you. I think about Molly every day. I just want to have her back." He blinked his eyes to stop the tears.

"I am Armand de Delacroix. I own the Wildercombe estate just outside Ilfracombe. If you hear anything I will pay you for it. Good day, sir. Thank you for your time."

He and his men left the inn and rode in single file up the track clinging to the steep hillside above Lynmouth. They cantered as quickly as they could, back across the barren moor to the smoke-laden skies of Combe Martin and the smell of rotting hemp, before retracing the last part of the journey and arriving, exhausted and saddle-sore, at Wildercombe House.

43

Isabella ate a sugared plum, and then two more. The crows peered at her through the window which was firmly closed.

"It tried to attack me," she told Esther.

"I will give you some of the seed mixture that they like, and you can give it to them if they are aggressive. Always have some with you if you go into the garden. I think McAlpine is causing them to behave in this way for his own purposes."

"Did they kill Thomas and Daniel?" she asked.

"No, I don't think so," Esther replied. She glanced at the picture of Captain Petrie, which she had put back onto the dresser, and then she looked at Isabella.

"The wound has healed over again. But it is better to remain in your bedchamber for the time being, and stay away from the McAlpines."

"I know you don't agree, but I am going to see Armand one more time," said Isabella defensively. "I have no idea what the rest of my life will bring, but it will be a memory I will treasure for ever."

Esther frowned. "He sent a servant to Exeter to try and find Harriet. He found out that neither she, nor her husband, had ever lived at that address. However, it does appear to be where McAlpine has his shipping business, and he gives a false name, that of James Davey."

She looked thoughtfully at the crow for a moment, and opened the window and caressed its black feathers.

"You mean no harm," she whispered softly to it. "You are just a wild creature."

"Don't do that," called out Isabella. "You don't realise. There's something wrong with them." And she jumped out of bed, banged shut the window and glared at the bird through the glass.

"I took the picture of Captain Petrie to show the Seigneur," admitted Esther.

"Did you? I didn't notice it had gone," said Isabella, in surprise. "Why did you do that?"

"He said it's a picture of the Prince of Wales," remarked Esther.

"No!" she exclaimed. "Are you saying that it's not a picture of my husband-to-be?"

"It would seem to be the case, if he is correct," replied Esther.

Isabella was lost for words. "What is happening?" she finally managed to say. "First of all, it did not appear to be Petrie, or his family, paying money for me. And now he does not seem to exist at all."

"The Seigneur has gone to investigate the disappearances of the young women in North Devon," said Esther bluntly.

"He has what?" she exclaimed. "Does he think there is a link?"

"It is possible," said Esther, her face very pale. "However, I expect there is a perfectly good explanation for Harriet. And we do not know the addresses of the other wards, so it's not possible to check. I will go now before McAlpine returns."

She placed a twist of muslin containing the seed mixture next to a piece of mandrake on the window sill, embraced Isabella, then walked slowly down the stairs and out into the blustery autumn day. Isabella stood by the window and watched until her black-robed figure on Mordecai was swallowed up by the trees hiding the lane. She quickly dressed, and stepped onto the landing. The servants could be heard chattering loudly in the kitchen, and she tiptoed from her wing of the house to the main building, where the McAlpines had their bedchambers. She had not been there since the arrival of Mrs McAlpine many years before, and she cautiously opened the first door.

She involuntarily gasped at the silver, gold and black room revealed in front of her, and hurriedly stepped inside. It was both opulent and unexpectedly strange. Gold embroidered curtains hung round a large, four-poster bed, and gold also threaded a tapestry, hanging on the far wall, which depicted a crescent moon in a dark sky, and the curvaceous, semi-naked body of a woman in a diaphanous robe.

"Hecate," she murmured, and gazed, spell-bound, at her beauty.

Silver motifs of the sun, moon and stars sparkled on the wall paper, and a bedside table was made of the same precious metal. The ceiling was black, a single star at its centre, and the delicate scent of jasmine pervaded the room.

A row of mouse-skin eyebrows, like marauding slugs, marched in solitary file across a gilt dressing table, and two wigs suspended on wooden frames, suggested that Mrs McAlpine's hair was not her own.

She stared in fascination, for several minutes, then ran back into the corridor and quietly closed the door. The servants' voices were still rising loudly from the kitchen, and she recognised, from their tipsy belligerence, that Mrs Gubb and Jenny were enjoying the gin bottle. She turned the door knob on the next bedchamber, and crept into Raphael McAlpine's room, her heart pounding.

It was almost like a mirror image of his wife's. It enjoyed the same wallpaper and gold-embroidered curtains on a four-poster bed, whilst a tapestry of Hecate this time showed the goddess completely naked, and without a moon in the starry heavens above her.

The wigs perched on wooden frames were also different. They were masculine, full-bottomed, stiffly curled, and there was an absence of mouse-skin eyebrows on the dressing table. She opened several drawers and quickly rummaged through the contents, but only discovered silk shirts and stockings and undergarments she had never set eyes on before.

She glanced once more at the tapestry of Hecate, then crept out of the room and descended the stairs to the hall.

The kitchen door was firmly shut and Reuben's voice had now joined that of Mrs Gubb and Jenny. She slipped into the library and resisted the temptation to go into the secret chamber to retrieve the candlestick she had left there. Instead, she hurriedly turned her attention to the desk.

She opened the drawers and rifled through the contents, but could only find odd bits of string and wax, and a small, silver picture frame, which resembled that which held Captain Petrie's portrait. She glanced at it briefly, then went over to the black-lacquered cabinet standing by the wall. She pulled out the top drawer and found a thick bundle of papers. She quickly cast her eye over them and saw that they were mainly bills of sale from slave auctions at Blackmoor Gate, on Exmoor. She put them back and opened the large drawer at the bottom.

Horses' hooves clattered across the cobbles outside and the McAlpine carriage swept past the window. Flustered, she tried to remain calm, and rapidly thumbed through the sheets of documents the cabinet held. A paper caught her eye and she read it quickly. It was a contract giving Raphael McAlpine a part of the Wildercombe estate, and had no date. The next sheet was also a contract. This time it was for the sale of the whole of the Wildercombe estate to Raphael McAlpine. Again, there was no date. She hastily replaced them in the cabinet. She ran frantically to the door and came out into the hall, just as Raphael McAlpine was entering the house.

She saw his close-set eyes look at her suspiciously, and with a beating heart, her head spinning dizzily, she slowly went up the stairs, as though she had not a care in the world.

44

September the nineteenth was blessed with autumnal sunshine. A messenger brought a letter for Armand from his sister, Antoinette, in Virginia, and he placed it in his pocket to read later.

There was not a hint of a cloud in the sky, as the servants, led by Mrs Widdicombe, clambered into the hay wains which were taking them to Barum Fair. Giant Clydesdale horses stood waiting in the shafts to pull the wagons, and everyone was dressed in their Sunday best. Hampers of food and flagons of cider were loaded on to the back, and the cavalcade set off merrily.

He was alone in the house for the first time since his arrival. He went from room to room, inspecting everything, and even visited the unfamiliar realm of the kitchens. The quiet enabled the ghosts of his parents to walk with him and he talked to his mother's portrait in the hall

"You will like her. She is beautiful and has a nature to match. I have prepared the house and it is looking its best. I will soon be back in France and I will avenge your death and that of my father, and join in the fight against the Revolution. I want you to be proud of me."

He sat on the steps by the front door, in the warmth of the sun, and read the letter from Antoinette.

My dear brother,

I think of you often and long to see you. I miss Alsace and our parents and not a day goes by, but which I do not remember them and you.

The plantation is struggling to be profitable, but I am doing my best, with the help of Heinrich, to improve matters. The tobacco crop has been badly damaged as a result of the most atrocious storm I have ever seen. We lost half the roof of the house and many of the slave cabins were completely destroyed. New ones have been quickly erected as they are built of wood.

I have been surprised to find we have so many slaves, and that our father never spoke of them. I do not agree with the practice of keeping other human beings as chattels, but I am in a quandary as to what to do. Our neighbour is Thomas Jefferson, at Monticello, who was, until recently, the first United States Secretary of State, and although he has declared that every man should be free, this does not extend to his own slaves on his plantation. The fact is that these plantations rely on free labour, in order to produce the cotton and tobacco. Heinrich has become interested in politics and is standing for election to Congress and he says the slaves must be given their liberty.

The servants in the house are very friendly and kind, but when I walk in the fields, I can feel the resentment and hatred of the men and women. There are nearly as many black people here in Virginia as white. The slaves are constantly feared and people are terrified there will be an uprising against us. However, I feel that if I freed our slaves I would be an outcast in society, as well as not being able to adequately grow the tobacco.

There is violence all the time. The slave masters and owners are often very cruel and every town in Virginia has a whipping post which is used for indentured servants, as well as slaves.

I am intending to break off my engagement to Mr James Harris. I find him very disagreeable and, on occasions, his aggressive behaviour has frightened me. Our father was mistaken to betroth me to such a man. He has already many children by his slaves, a common feature of the gentry here. Even Thomas Jefferson, is said to be enjoying a relationship with Sally Hemmings, one of his slaves, who is, in fact, the half-sister of his dead wife. Virginian society is very complicated, and I feel I have to tread very carefully in order to fit in and not be ostracised.

I am awaiting the winter, as it has been so hot and humid. I find the countryside very attractive and the hills remind me of the Vosges. There is a town called Strasburg, but it is small and bears absolutely no resemblance to our Strasbourg.

I cannot write of all my problems with the plantation and with Mr Harris, in a letter. I do not wish to distress you. I expect you are busy with Wildercombe House and the estate. However, I need your help here, otherwise I fear we will lose our land.

I hope this letter has not been too dispiriting, my dearest brother.

Your sister,   Antoinette.

He read and reread the letter, then placed it back in his pocket and waited impatiently as the hours passed. Midday came, then one o'clock. He sipped from his flask of brandy and kept his eyes on the drive.

At ten past one Tabitha arrived. She stalked over the flagstones, her tail twitching in the air with annoyance, as though he was the intruder, not her. She sat next to him, and he resisted the thought that she was Esther's familiar, and not an actual cat.

He teased her with a leaf. "Do you know your name is slang in English for an awkward old woman?" She purred in reply, and he laughed. "Yes, that's what I thought. You've been sent here to spy on me."

At two o'clock, he glimpsed a white dress and dark hair through the beech trees. He sprang to his feet and ran to meet Isabella, throwing his arms around her and kissing her.

"You are intent on ruining my reputation," she said, mock-chidingly.

"And I am colluding with you."

"You have bewitched me. You have only yourself to blame," he replied and kissed her again. He took her with pride into Wildercombe House, into the dark mustiness of the hall, and stopped in front of the portrait of his mother.

"She was beautiful," remarked Isabella.

"Yes," he replied. "She was." A coldness clutched his heart as he realised that, for the first time, he had said 'was' not 'is,' and he suddenly knew he would not see any more visions of his parents. He looked at Isabella, recognising she had helped him cross a bridge from the terrible events of the past to the present, and that it was a journey he would never make again.

He took her by the hand, and felt its soft warmth and smelled the delicate scent of her perfume, as he walked with her to the dining room. He pulled out a chair for her at the table and she gracefully sat down. He took the chair opposite, and said the prayer, and then he acted as a footman, serving her dishes of cold meat and cheese, slicing the pheasant pie, and pouring out the wine. He sat back and enjoyed the sensuous sensation of watching her eat, as the sun streamed in through the windows, emphasising the lustre of her hair and the deep brown of her eyes.

"You are already mistress of my heart," he said, looking tenderly at her. "You will soon be mistress of Wildercombe House."

"Don't say such things," she admonished him. "Let us just celebrate today. Whatever the future brings, let us be grateful for now."

"I want to arrange our marriage before I leave for France," he said defiantly. "I have been questioning people about the disappearance of young women from North Devon and I think they are connected. There's also a link with Harriet, and the other wards, as they all have very fair or red hair, which is unusual. It therefore suggests that McAlpine might well be responsible, or, at least, have played a part in whatever has happened to them."

"It is strange about their hair," she agreed. "I have never thought about it before. However, you don't need to worry about me then. My hair is black."

"Yes, very true. And I think that is one of the reasons Esther has not been too suspicious of him. However, I am not sure that Captain Petrie exists, which makes me fear for your safety as well, as it means that McAlpine is lying. And if he is deceiving you, why would that be? The answer must surely be that you and Esther would not agree with whatever it is he is going to do to you."

"What do you think has happened to them," she asked. "It seems very unlikely that they could all have vanished."

"I don't know, and, in any case, I have no way of tracking down any of them. I have only tried to find Harriet. It might be that they are all married and perfectly happy. What is this name that you think you heard? Ivan Ben? Are they perhaps Petrie's names? "

236

She looked at him. "I didn't really hear it properly. There might have been another word at the end. I think perhaps you are judging Raphael McAlpine too harshly. Don't forget that he has raised me, and the other wards, at his own expense, and I feel that I owe him a debt."

"Perhaps," he said. "Personally, I find it surprising, given the nature of the man, that he has helped so many young women."

"There is something else. It is possible he does not intend the marriage with Captain Petrie to go ahead." She stopped speaking and blushed. "I know it was wrong, but I searched his desk and cabinet yesterday, when he was out of the house. I found two contracts. One was for my marriage to you and entailed the giving up of a piece of your estate to him, and the other was for the sale of Wildercombe House and the whole of the estate to him. Neither was dated."

"What!" he exclaimed, reaching across and gripping her hand tightly. "He is going to let me marry you. My darling, we can be together, without any problem."

"That is what it seems, although I do not understand the other contract," she said.

"It is possible he just had it drawn up because he hoped I would sell," he replied.

They looked at each other, doubt on both their faces.

"You are sure that this is what the contract consisted of?" he questioned. "I am extremely surprised."

"Yes, that is what I found. But not only has he not told me, but just this very morning, Mrs McAlpine made a spiteful comment that I would soon be in the arms of Captain Petrie."

She looked at him anxiously. "I cannot believe that it could be true. I have not yet told Esther, so I do not know what she thinks. However, I am worried. McAlpine is such a violent and cruel man and I am sure that he was involved with the deaths of Daniel and Thomas. He has been so adamant I should marry Petrie. Why should he change?"

"I don't trust him," said Armand. "The local girls, at least, appear to have all been abducted, and McAlpine and his accomplices are perhaps responsible."

"I only know about the contracts because I searched his papers, which was wicked of me. So you must not say anything to him. It is best to wait," she replied.

"Perhaps," he agreed. "In any case, you are going on a trip with Mrs McAlpine and Georgiana on October the first, so I am sure that you will not suddenly be sent to America before that date." He shrugged his shoulders and repeated his words. "I just don't trust McAlpine. Perhaps you are mistaken with what you saw. I don't understand why he has said nothing to me."

"Do you know yet when you will be going to France?" she asked.

"No, I have not been sent word. But I trust in God that I will come back safely to you. That is all I can promise. And that is why I wish to be married to you before I go, or, at least, to have you pledged in marriage to me, and for you to be living here."

He embraced her and she kissed him as passionately as he kissed her. They wandered, hand in hand, through Wildercombe House and he showed her the portraits of his family. Then he took her to the attics and revealed the hidden priest hole.

"It goes all the way down to the garden. It was necessary, because it was against the law to hold a Catholic service, but that has changed now, since 1791. Are you happy to become a Catholic when you marry me?"

"It is not yet certain that we will be married, as you well know," she said, in a mock-reproving tone. She smiled at him. "However, if we can be together, I would be content to jump a broomstick for you."

"I am sure the priest would be delighted to hear that," he remarked. "By the way, where is the secret room in Dunstone Manor? Does it resemble the priest hole here?"

"No. It is much bigger, and has a tunnel at one side, which I suspect goes down to Rapparee Beach and was probably once used by smugglers. I have explored it twice, and the last time, I left a rosewood candle holder in there by mistake and it has now been placed back in my room. I found it this morning. It gave me a shock and I have no idea who has returned it."

"So someone knew you had been in the secret chamber? Someone was watching you," he said.

"Yes," she replied nervously. "It would seem so."

"Don't explore the room again," he told her in horror. "You are putting yourself in danger."

"Yes," she agreed. "I have never been allowed to know of its existence, and it's only by chance that I discovered it. I should imagine they use it in the winter, when it becomes too cold for the ceremonies in the wood."

"Yes, I should think so. Mrs McAlpine and the others were not exactly dressed for the rigours of the North Devon climate."

"Let me show you my father's laboratory now," he said, as he escorted her back down the stairs to the hall and the large room adjacent to it. "However, I do not expect you will find this very interesting," he remarked, as he opened the door.

"On the contrary, I find it extremely so," she replied, walking to the jars on the shelf and opening the lid of one.

"Thornapple," she said, noticing the petal.

"There is a strange powder in that," he commented, pointing to the last jar. "It has an acrid smell."

"Do not touch it," she told him. "It is henbane. Any substance with the word 'bane' in it is poisonous and can often kill. It comes from 'bano' in old German, and means death."

"How do you know what it is, if you have not seen it?" he asked, staring at her.

She looked at him, smiling slightly, her black hair framing her oval face. And he instantly knew that it was not McAlpine who had used the laboratory. The cages with the horse head clasps had been Esther's, and Isabella had helped her.

"I don't think this is the first time you have been in Wildercombe House. I have been showing you rooms you already know."

She looked at him. "Yes, my beloved. It is true. McAlpine was often here, pretending he owned the estate, but he is an amateur in the field of science and herbal medicine. It is Esther who has worked in this laboratory, and I was her assistant."

"My little witch!" he exclaimed.

"Esther is a scientist," she said firmly, "like your father, and Cavendish, and Lavoisier and Davey, as well as being a 'wise woman' and practised in the ancient, healing arts."

The clock in the hall chimed four o'clock, as she spoke, and they looked at each other.

"I must go," she said. "I don't want to risk the McAlpines returning before me. I haven't the time to go and see Esther. Would you please visit and tell her about the contracts."

"Yes," he agreed. "Wait here and I will get you a cloak, and we can ride back together."

He ran to his mother's old dressing room and quickly found a velvet cloak. He brought it back to her and draped it round her shoulders and then they went to the stables, where he saddled two horses. He struggled with the straps, unused to the task, and was finally rewarded with the sight of Isabella sitting side saddle on the grey mare.

He mounted his stallion and the two horses trotted off along the drive. They passed by the rough pasture of the Cairn, then down into the coombe and up the other side of the hill. A ploughing team of oxen and horses was contouring a field by the high-hedged lane, as they climbed the hill near to Chambercombe, and the chanting duet of the ploughman and ploughboy followed them as they ascended the dusty track. They halted at the summit and gazed together at the panorama of sea and hills.

"I will remember this day," she said, her expression and voice sombre.

"I think you are as fearful as I am, my beloved, that we will not be together," he replied grimly. "Come back with me now. I have men to defend you and it is what I intended originally. I had no intention of you returning to Dunscombe Manor today, but I have been swayed by news of this contract, as it would be so much easier, and there would be no risk to you when I am in France."

"With all my heart I would prefer to stay with you, but I can't. He would kill us both and, as I have said before, there is also Esther to consider. She has been like a mother to me and searched for me when I was a child. I do not want her harmed. I want her to be able to live in peace."

"What do you mean she searched for you? So she knew you were on the Santa Rosa?" he questioned.

"The Santa Rosa?" she exclaimed. "Is that the name of the ship that was wrecked?"

"Yes," he muttered guiltily. "I believe so."

"How do you know?" she asked, in surprise.

"I questioned Captain Bowen about shipwrecked vessels whose name began with san," he admitted.

"Why did you not tell me?" she demanded.

"Esther seems determined that no one should talk about it," he replied honestly. "And I did what she told me."

"She was intending to tell me about my parents when we are on the ship to America," she said.

"Well, that is not going to happen," he replied sharply.

They rode down the lane towards Dunscombe Manor, and as they approached the door, he noticed an even greater flock of crows than usual, huddled along the ivy-covered wall.

A sudden premonition of doom and danger enveloped him and he cried out, "No, I am not letting you go back in there. I have already lost my parents. This is madness. What am I thinking of?" He grabbed her by the hand. "Come back with me. Do not be afraid. I will protect you and Esther as well."

"No, I will not," she said firmly. "Have faith in our future. We will fight whatever McAlpine has planned for me together and, as you say, there is no immediate cause for concern, because there is very clearly an intended trip to Heddon. We can, at least, wait until then."

"No, I don't agree," he exclaimed. "It's obviously very dangerous for you to stay here with that man."

"Please," she begged. "I am sure I will be fine. I have lived here nearly all my life, and I am still very much alive."

He frowned in displeasure. "I cannot force you, but I don't agree. However, I will ride by every day and if you are in danger, place a ribbon on your window sill and I will come in to see McAlpine with my men."

He swung down from his horse and helped her to dismount, embracing and kissing her, before finally letting her go. He stood once more in the arch of the doorway, and watched her walk purposefully towards Dunscombe Manor, where the whole of the back of the house was now visible, as the hemp plants had been cut down. For a moment, a face appeared at an upstairs window, and he stepped back into the lane to avoid being seen.

He waited impatiently for a few minutes, then returned to the garden, but she had gone. He punched the stonework next to him in frustration, grazing his knuckles.

"You fool," he muttered to himself. "What have you done? She is alone and at the mercy of McAlpine."

45

Esther's cauldron was bubbling again, but not with nettles. Rowan berries were floating in an intoxicating brew of apples, hops, red hips and haws, and Armand settled down on the fireside seat and sniffed at it appreciatively.

Esther ladled out a bowl of the mixture and gave it to him, along with a plate of honey cakes.

He said nothing, just sat quietly, eating and drinking.

"So, you have spent the day placing yourself and Isabella in danger," she remarked, as he finished.

He looked at her. "Perhaps you are too afraid of McAlpine and do not see the reality in front of you."

"You would not be saying that if you end up in the Wilder with your eyes pecked out," she retorted.

"I don't think I would be saying much of anything, if that is the case," he replied, eating another honey cake.

"Have you seen Tabitha?" she asked. "I can't find her."

"I saw her earlier at the front of my house," he said, noticing that Esther's breathing was again slightly irregular, and that although her pale brown eyes had a lively gleam in them, her skin resembled the dry fragility of old parchment.

"Isabella told me to tell you that she was searching the desk and cabinet in McAlpine's library and she found two contracts. One was for the sale of Wildercombe House and the estate to McAlpine, and the other was for a piece of my land, in exchange for Isabella's marriage to me. Neither were dated, or signed, obviously."

"I was not expecting that," she remarked.

"Nor was I," he replied.

"I can understand the contract for your estate. It is what he has always wanted. But not that for the marriage."

"If you want to use my father's laboratory," he continued, a flicker of a smile on his face, "you have only to ask."

"Oh, so I have been found out," she replied smiling.

"I can see Wildercombe House was not so disused in my family's absence, as I thought," he said.

"Your father would have been pleased with what I was doing," she replied.

"Yes, I think so," he agreed.

"Isabella should not be searching his property," she said. "She is putting herself in danger."

"Yes," he replied. "And I do not want her in the secret room or tunnel, either."

"Unfortunately, she has a very strong character and does what she wants," said Esther.

"Evidently she left a candlestick in there when she explored it last time and it has been placed back in her room," he told her.

"What!" she exclaimed.

"Yes. Could it be one of the servants? How would they have known she had been inside the chamber?"

"I have no idea. She has lived there for so many years, and yet was not aware of its existence. That suggests McAlpine does not want her, or other people, to know about it."

She reached down a jar from the shelf above her, and took out a mixture of seeds and herbs, which she wrapped in a piece of cloth.

"Take this. I have given some to Isabella. The crows are addicted to it and they will not attack you then."

"Thank you," he said politely, placed the mixture in his pocket and stood up. "So, do you think he is going to let her marry me?"

She looked thoughtfully at him and did not reply for several seconds.

"No," she said. "No, I do not believe he will do that. I think that he wants her to marry Captain Petrie."

"But he does not seem to exist," he remarked.

"That is certainly a slight problem, although it is possible Ivan Ben is part of Captain Petrie's name," she replied. "However, I intend to be with her."

He grimaced. "You will protect her?" he said scornfully.

"I will do my best," she replied. "As I have always done."

"Isabella said that you searched for her when she was a young child. How did you know of her existence?"

She looked at him and said nothing, and this time he knew he would not receive an answer.

"Goodbye, Seigneur. And if you see Tabitha, tell her to come home."

He left the cottage and returned to the familiar mustiness of Wildercombe House. The ancient building was strangely silent, and he talked, for the second time that day, to his mother's portrait.

"What do you think I should do? Have I made the wrong decision to let her return to Crow House?"

He gazed at her blue eyes and brilliantly red hair and longed to hear her speak to him again. He choked back a sob, and went to his bedchamber, where he discovered Tabitha, asleep on his bed. He lay down next to her, grimly reflecting on the disappearances in North Devon and the possibility of harm coming to Isabella.

"At least the trip to Heddon does not coincide with Hecate's Moon," he said to the cat.

46

Esther had snuffed out the candle by the hearth, and was quietly singing a Jewish song, when she heard the tread of booted feet on the path outside. She glanced out of the window, and saw the bulk of a man.

She picked up a sharp knife from the dresser, and waited quietly in the moonlit room. The man knocked on the door and called out softly, "Esther. Are you there?"

"What do you want at this time of night, McAlpine?" she replied.

"I want to see you," he said.

"What are you doing, skulking around, like a rat in a hay barn?" she asked.

"Unbolt the door," he demanded.

"No, come in the day. When I can see your face and your eyes and know what mischief you are intending."

"Do not annoy me," he replied. "Do not forget Isabella still lives with me."

She hesitated for just a second, then pulled back the bolt, and stood away from the door, knife in hand.

"This is not a very friendly welcome," he said, as he came in, reeking of whisky and tobacco.

"You do not fool me," she retorted. "Even if you manage to dupe others."

"Such ingratitude," he shouted. "And here I am, about to pay your passage across the ocean, with Isabella, to marry her beau."

"Have you decided when?" she asked, still fingering the knife, and keeping her distance from him.

"Yes, I know the date," he said, the moonlight striking his white face, making his eyes glitter strangely. "And I will tell you in good time."

"Will it be before Hecate's main ceremony on November the sixteenth?" she asked.

"Yes," he replied. "It will be before then."

He staggered drunkenly and trod on Tabitha, who gave a startled cry, and sprang up and bit his hand. He jumped back and kicked her with his boot, whereupon she yelped and jumped into Esther's arms.

"What are you doing?" Esther shrieked at him.

"She needs to be drowned, that one," he sneered. "And when you go, I will be the one to do it, and then I will feed her body to the crows."

She glared angrily, holding the knife towards him, and he retreated towards the hearth, nearly falling over the cauldron.

"You are drunk," she said. "Leave my house and we will speak another time."

"We will speak now," he shouted. "I have brought you a contract to sell your cottage and land to me. You can only accompany Isabella if you sign it and give me everything on your departure."

"Is it dated?" she asked.

"Not yet," he said. "It will be dated when you sign."

"I will only sign when I am about to go on the ship with Isabella. I am certainly not signing it now," she retorted.

"As you wish," he said. "However, I have a favour to ask. That is why I am here."

"Well, ask it," she replied coldly.

"I need some belladonna powder."

"What do you want that for?" she said suspiciously.

"None of your business," he sneered. "But may I remind you again, that I have Isabella, not you."

She slowly went to the cupboard and took out a jar. She emptied some of the mixture into a small pot and gave it to him.

"Here you are. Use it wisely, not for harm."

He laughed mockingly and snatched it from her.

"Captain Petrie very much resembles the Prince of Wales," she remarked, watching him closely.

He looked blankly at her for a moment, the alcohol fogging his usual sharpness. Then he recovered himself.

"Yes, I believe that is often spoken of," he replied.

"Has Captain Petrie much land in Virginia?" she asked.

"Yes," he snapped.

He pulled down a bunch of thyme and rosemary hanging from the rafter and flung it towards her. He aimed a kick at David, which missed, but made him lose his balance, and he fell onto the ground.

Esther grabbed her besom broom and hit him with it.

"Out of my house," she shouted angrily.

He lumbered to his feet and lurched off through the doorway and down the garden path. She watched him mount his horse and ride away. Then she sat down, trembling, breathing rapidly and clutching her chest.

47

Gabriel Soullans gave Armand a paper on which was written the date and place of embarkation for the ship going to the Vendée.

"October the sixteenth," he said, reading the document. "And it will be anchored just off my beach."

"Yes," replied the Frenchman, gulping down the brandy which had been offered to him. He appeared travel-weary; his clothes were stained with mud, his boots were filthy. His face was dirty with sweat and dust, and he stood impatiently, his manner hurried.

"I have to be in Bristol by tomorrow evening. And I wish to cross Exmoor in daylight. It is not just the highwaymen, although they are bad enough, there are also bogs which suck in a horse, as well as a man."

He looked around him, at the book-lined walls of the library and the oak furniture, and gazed through the windows at the gardens, and the wood in the distance.

"You are lucky. Most French people in England are as poor as church mice and living in atrocious conditions. They are unused to poverty and have no trade to fall back on. You are very blessed."

"Yes, I know," said Armand gravely.

"The spy network has been strengthened recently here, because so many émigrés are trying to sell information to the French government, in order to obtain money. Therefore, I am only giving the details of the invasion force to a few people. You must keep it secret. Luca Fessi, who was at the meeting in Mol's Coffee House, has already been exposed as a spy. He came from Ajaccio, the same place as this new brigadier general, Napoleon Bonaparte, who made a name for himself at Toulon. He was recently accused of treason, but managed to defend himself well in the court and has been cleared, and is now, I believe, in Paris. Fessi's sister is married to his aide de camp, and he had been smuggling information to her."

"What has happened to him?" asked Armand.

"He has been killed," he replied. "He knew too much about our plans."

"I have been told there is a spy in Devon, who lives somewhere near the coast," said Armand.

"Yes, that is what we think. But, so far, we have not been able to trace him."

"It is possible I will not be able to join the ship and will have to make my own way to France later. I have a problem here which I must resolve before I leave England. Some of my men wish to fight, others do not. However, everyone who joins will be well-equipped."

"We are grateful for the use of your house and beach," said Gabriel Soullans. "And hope to see you with us."

Armand walked with him to the front door, where he mounted his horse and cantered rapidly off along the drive. Just as he was lost to sight amongst the trees, Esther appeared. The sky had become black and rain suddenly fell heavily. A thunder clap boomed, and a fork of lightning flashed, silhouetting her figure.

Alsace was suddenly vivid in his mind. The muskets were crackling around him, as he fled towards the Rhine. The rain was beating down on him and lightning was searing the heavens.

"What are you doing standing in this storm?" Esther's voice broke into his reverie.

He lifted his face to the sky, letting the deluge drench his hair, his face, and his clothes, and remained caught in the memory of that fateful day for a few seconds longer. The images faded and he became aware of Esther standing in the shelter of the doorway, regarding him severely.

"It is not the time to die from catching a chill. You still have a long path to travel. You will have children, and they will have children, and your line will be continued."

"Your crystal has told you this?" he asked sourly. "And did it tell you if Isabella will be the mother of these, as yet, unconceived offspring?"

She looked at him, as he stood in the downpour. "Sometimes events are not always clear. My strength and my powers are failing. I will speak to you further in the house. For a disbeliever in the dark arts, you seem to be surprisingly needy of its prophecies."

She turned her back on him and went into the hall, where she glanced affectionately at the painting of Antoinette, before entering the library and settling herself on a chair by the desk.

He retreated from the rain into the hall, strode wetly into the library and seated himself opposite her.

"You look like a drowned rat, Seigneur," she remarked.

"And does your vision for me include Isabella?" he asked again.

She hesitated. "The reason I am here is that I want to tell you McAlpine visited me last night, in a drunken state. From his words, there did not seem to be any doubt that Captain Petrie exists, and that he intends Isabella to marry him, and for me to accompany her to America. He also has a contract to buy my cottage and land, and if he does not receive it, I will not be allowed to go with her."

He looked at her angrily. "Your land is really part of mine. It was given to you by my parents. He obviously wants to put it back together. That suggests he still thinks he will obtain the Wildercombe estate."

"Yes, that is what I thought." She looked down at the document which had been left on the desk.

"Is this the date for the invasion ship? I thought I recognised that man. It was Gabriel Soullans, wasn't it? I saw him once at Exeter."

"Yes, but it is meant to be a secret."

"Well, in that case, perhaps it would be better if you placed it somewhere more private. You are still determined to go and fight?"

He shrugged. "I intend to go, but, at the same time, I don't want to leave Isabella undefended, and without being married to me."

She threw up her hands. "You are living in a fantasy land. Be careful how you tread on McAlpine's feet. You know that your mother would not have wanted you to join in this doomed revolt."

"And my father?" he questioned.

"I am not sure. He was more of a scientist than a soldier, although he did fight in the New World. Have you any idea what is happening in the Vendée?"

"I know what has occurred in Alsace. And I have heard of the events in the Vendée."

"They have deliberately massacred women and children, as well as men. They have killed thousands by putting them in ships and sinking them. It will always be remembered as one of the darkest hours of the Revolution," she said.

"And yet you still support their revolutionary ideas," he retorted.

"Yes, I do. Just as I support the founding of the United States of America, and their ideals. Don't go to fight. There is no hope of success. You will not return, or, if you do, your body will be maimed and broken. There are ships organised to take you there, but there are no ships to bring you home. You will be abandoned in a countryside already destroyed by war. The Royalist cause is lost in France. As I have already told you, stay here and farm your estate, and marry a lady with money."

"Thank you for your advice," he said sincerely. "I know you mean well by me."

"Good day, Seigneur. I will go and see Isabella now. I have told Tabitha to come and live at Wildercombe House, when I go to America, so I hope she will be welcomed."

"Yes, I think she is already preparing for your departure, and that of my beloved, and is making herself at home here. Perhaps you would like me to care for David as well? Have you any other animals I could look after?"

She frowned, and he smiled at her. "Also, I would like to point out that I have already come to your assistance when I first arrived at the riot at your cottage. You are placing yourself at risk, as I have told you before, with prophecies and herbal potions. It is, I believe, against the law in England to pretend to be a witch, although, very strangely, it is not illegal to actually be one."

Esther stood up, her expression enigmatic, and walked quickly out of the house and across the garden, followed by Tabitha, who suddenly shot out of the rose arbour, and caught her up.

48

It was late in the evening and Isabella had finished preparing her clothes for the excursion to Heddon the next day. She had snuffed out the candle and was lying sleepily in bed, when she became aware of shouting coming from the library. She listened, but found it difficult to catch the words, so she crept to the door and onto the landing.

Raphael McAlpine was clearly in a drunken rage.

"Ye hae ideas above your station," he bellowed, and there came the sound of glass breaking, as though he had smashed a bottle.

"I beg you, not her! The others were different. But not her!" Reuben was pleading.

Raphael McAlpine bellowed again, his words unintelligible to her, and then there was silence. A complete and sudden silence, as though they had left the room. She wondered if they had gone into the secret chamber and she remained standing on the landing for some time, trying to hear more, but there was nothing. She returned to her bed, very fearful for Reuben, whom she had known for as long as she could remember; and she flinched as she recalled the venom in her guardian's voice.

She drifted into a disturbed sleep and was suddenly woken by the sharp noise of hooves on the cobbles. She jumped out of bed and peered from the window. It was difficult to see in the darkness, but one horse appeared to have a rider, whilst the other did not. She stared at it, and made out a large object wrapped in cloth, lying across the saddle. They quickly left the courtyard and she shivered in fright in her nightgown, as the sound of the horses faded away.

"Reuben," she muttered. "Reuben. What has happened? I pray it was not you."

She sat on the edge of the bed and listened, but there was only the rustling of the trees and the hooting of an owl. She returned to her bed, trembling uncontrollably, and pulled the covers over her head to try and distance herself from Dunscombe Manor and what she had perhaps seen.

The morning had not brought her relief. Reuben was not in his usual seat in the kitchen, and Mrs Gubb told her he had gone to Exeter to help with the wine business. She found herself unable to eat and fled back to her bedchamber, where she dressed, with a feeling of dread, for the visit to Exmoor.

....

She sat with Georgiana and Mrs McAlpine in the farm kitchen at Heddon. They dined on trout and a haunch of venison, and John Berriman, the farmer, supervised the maid bringing in the dishes. The lattice window was grime-encrusted; only a few rays of sun filtering weakly across the table, catching the dead eyes of the trout, and revealing cracks in the crockery. Antlered stags gazed down, sightless, from the walls, and two lanterns hanging from the low rafters, creaked as they were caught in a rising draught of air. A bluebottle buzzed on the venison, three flies circled endlessly above a model of a ship on an oak chest, and the air smelled strongly of mildew and tobacco.

Georgiana sat very upright on a stout wooden chair, her red riding habit embroidered with yellow silk roses, tightly fitting her arms and bosom, but flaring out in ample folds towards her booted feet. Mrs McAlpine was also dressed in red, and the farmer had made a joke about leprechauns, which had left the three women staring at him in puzzlement.

254

She nervously touched the pocket of her riding jacket, where she had concealed her silver-handled dagger, and tried not to think of Reuben. She looked through the window at the densely wooded coombe, and noticed a large raven, with its distinctive, diamond-shaped tail, the harbinger of death, fly upwards and perch on the branch of an ash.

The stark wildness of the moor had been in contrast to the countryside by Ilfracombe. The barren uplands of bracken, purple-pink heather bells, and yellow-flowering gorse, were bare of all other bushes and trees, except a few lichen-covered stunted elms, and spindly hawthorns, wind-sculpted in bizarre shapes. It was the first time she had come to Exmoor, although it was a frequent haunt of the McAlpines for stag-hunting. Mrs McAlpine had confidently ridden her horse, her large frame swaying to the movement of the animal, and the coldness habitually seen in her expression had been replaced by the same look of excitement she had when about to go to the hunt. She had ridden fearlessly across the bracken heights of the hogs back cliffs; she had been the first to plunge into a deep gorge fissuring a hill, and had frenziedly hit her horse with her riding crop to make it race up the almost perpendicular slope on the other side.

Georgiana, by contrast, had an air of terror about her, as did her horse. She clung to the side saddle and reins, and both she and the animal had to be coaxed to venture across the unfamiliar and frightening terrain. The vaunted retinue of armed servants consisted only of Tom and James, the two gardeners. They had pistols in their belts, but no other weapon and Isabella had glanced uneasily about her for the whole of the road so far.

Mrs McAlpine was enjoying herself. She laughed at the vulgar jokes of John Berriman, and her speech coarsened, both in her choice of vocabulary, and in her accent. Georgiana looked at her in disdain, and daintily ate small mouthfuls of the trout.

"Are we going back soon?" she asked plaintively.

"Oh, I have a real treat for you, my dear," replied Mrs McAlpine, her pudgy fingers poking at a violet on a pastry cake. "We are going along the valley to see the beach."

"Is that where the smuggling was meant to be taking place, when Lieutenant Hargreaves had to leave the dinner?" Isabella enquired.

"Possibly," Mrs McAlpine replied sourly. "There are many coves around here."

The farmer left the room as they neared the end of the meal, and spoke to someone outside the window. His words were indistinct, but the voice of his companion was more audible.

"Aye, I ken it's the first lassie. Dinna fash yersel."

Mrs McAlpine's eyes rested on Isabella for a moment. She looked back at her with hatred, and was surprised when the other woman was the first to glance away, one eyebrow arched higher than the other in her unnaturally white face. She drank heartily from a cup of brandy, then rose to her feet.

"It is time to go," she announced, and Isabella and Georgiana followed in her wake and out into the verdant lushness of the coombe. They mounted their horses and set off seawards, along a narrow path through the deciduous trees.

"Come and ride behind me," she called to Georgiana. "I wish to show you the view."

Isabella fell back; Georgiana took her place and they slowly progressed in single file. The horses' hooves clattered against the stones, frightening a jay, which flew to the uppermost branches of a tall oak. They advanced along a slight incline, and entered the ravine of Heddon, whose hillsides fell precipitously to the valley bottom, where the stream, swollen by the recent rainfall, was tumbling over a boulder-strewn bed.

Isabella looked anxiously about her, whilst Georgiana's face had beads of sweat on her forehead. The two gardeners fell further behind, the gap between them and the women steadily growing, as Mrs McAlpine increased, rather than lessened, her pace.

They reached a lime kiln at the edge of a pebbled beach, and the stream, now unrestrained by its banks, flooded out between the stones. The pinnacle of a mast was visible, just past the headland, but the ship itself was hidden by the cliff, and the cove was deserted.

Stones and gravel, from a grey expanse of scree-covered slope, just before the kiln, suddenly rattled on to the path in front of them. Isabella looked upwards and gasped in horror to see two burly men in tarry jackets and wide trousers, wielding cutlasses, sliding down the hillside. They landed next to Mrs McAlpine, who gave a weak scream. "We have no valuables," she cried. "Spare us."

The two servants were nowhere to be seen, and Isabella took out her dagger and held it towards the men.

"Don't be silly," shouted Mrs McAlpine to her angrily. "They are stronger than we are."

The nearest man grabbed Georgiana, and pulled her off the horse, as she shrieked in panic. Isabella threw her dagger at him, and it caught his arm, sticking into his sleeve, and causing blood to drip onto his hand. He pulled it out, cursing, and dropped it into a bush. He bundled Georgiana over his shoulder, and ran laboriously to the beach and across the pebbles, followed by his companion. A longboat, manned by sailors all pulling strongly at the oars, emerged from the far headland, quickly cutting through the choppy sea and gaining the shallows. The two men splashed through the water; Georgiana was thrown into the stern, her riding dress falling over her head, indecently exposing her white-stockinged legs.

Isabella momentarily sat in shock on her horse, before jumping down and retrieving her dagger from the bush. Then she rushed to the beach, where she nimbly made her way over the uneven stones to the sea.

"Come back," called Mrs McAlpine. "Don't interfere. They don't want you."

The longboat set off through the breaking waves and veered towards the headland. In minutes, it had disappeared, and Isabella was left alone, staring after it. The mast beyond the headland moved slowly out of sight and the only sounds were those of the waves crashing onto the shore, and the lament of a curlew. She glanced at the scree slope where Mrs McAlpine was calmly standing, now joined by Tom and James, and waded into the water to try and see round the headland. The beach shelved steeply; she shuddered in fear at being in the sea, and hastily floundered back to the land, where she stood, her skirt wet, tears impotently coursing down her cheeks.

The thundering beat of horses galloping down the ravine made her look in terror, and she prepared to flee towards the cliff. Mrs McAlpine turned, and she saw that, for the first time that day, there was an expression of fear on her face, whilst Tom and James backed their horses closer against the scree, holding their pistols awkwardly.

49

Armand, at the head of a large group of his men, halted next to Mrs McAlpine. He looked at the slight figure of Isabella standing near the sea and relief flooded through him.

What are you doing here?" Mrs McAlpine spat out the words angrily.

"Good day, madam," he replied coldly. "Are you enjoying your excursion?"

"Georgiana has been taken," she replied. "She has been kidnapped."

"Who has taken her? Where have they gone?" he demanded, glancing quickly at the cliffs and beach and then at Isabella, who was now running over the pebbles towards him.

"Two men. They came down the hillside and have left in a boat. We were not able to do anything. We were overpowered," she muttered.

"They did not take you then?" he queried.

"Well, no," she spluttered. "Why would they do that?"

"Why would they take Georgiana?" he replied, looking at her closely.

"I have no idea. Out of my way, sir, so that I can return home and tell her parents the awful news," she cried.

"Keep her here," he told Tomas. "Don't let her go."

He rode to the edge of the beach, dismounted and strode rapidly over the boulders to greet Isabella.

"Sailors have kidnapped Georgiana and gone by boat past the headland, where there was a ship, although I cannot see the mast now," she called out to him.

He stopped and looked at the empty sea, then shouted to his men. "Tomas and Hans, ride along the cliff. See if you can discover a ship, and find out its flag. The wind's from the west, so it will probably be sailing along the coast. Joseph and Jacques, go to Ilfracombe and raise the alarm that Georgiana Bowen has been kidnapped and is in a ship going up the Bristol Channel."

The four men immediately galloped away along the gorge and he turned to greet Isabella, as she breathlessly reached him, trembling, her eyes red with tears. He restrained himself from embracing her and kept his back to Mrs McAlpine so it was difficult for her to see or hear them.

"Calm, my beloved," he said softly. "It is possible she will be found."

He looked down at her skirt and shoes. "Why are you wet?"

"I went into the water to try and see the ship, but it became too deep," she said.

"Thank God you have not been snatched like Georgiana. I would have arrived too late to have saved you. I meant to be here much earlier, because it seemed likely that some sort of unpleasantness would occur, although I did not expect this. However, I was delayed in Combe Martin, because a friend of mine, whose leg was injured, has suddenly died."

"It was very apparent she was the one they wanted. They made no attempt to take me, or to steal any jewellery from Mrs McAlpine," said Isabella. She lowered her voice. "I think Mrs McAlpine and the farmer knew. I believe it was planned. It was the way they looked at each other, and spoke. I heard him talking to someone who sounded Scottish, which is not a very common accent here in Devon. And there is also something else which is very distressing. I heard Reuben and McAlpine arguing yesterday evening and in the night I saw a horse leave, carrying something large. Reuben was not there this morning, and Mrs Gubb said he has been sent to Exeter to work. "

He stared at her for a minute. "That sounds very strange, especially with this happening here. Do you think it might have been Reuben who put the candleholder back in your room?"

"I don't know," she replied. "It is possible. He has always been very kind to me."

He glanced across the beach at Mrs McAlpine. "It's very brazen for Georgiana to have been kidnapped in daylight. The other girls all disappeared at the night of the dark moon, Hecate's moon, but this has been done differently. Why? It is also the first time, as far as we know, that one of the McAlpines has been at the abduction."

He looked round at the cliffs and the cove. "We had better leave. The ravine and this isolated beach are very suitable for an ambush."

He glanced anxiously at her. "I also have news. I know the date for France now. It's October the sixteenth. I will wait to see if McAlpine brings me the contract to sign to give him a part of my land for our marriage, but if he does not, I will not join the ship, and I want you to come and marry me, regardless of McAlpine's plans."

"I am sure Esther is right. He will kill us both if we thwart him," she answered.

"I will protect you," he said.

"I don't want you to die. I would prefer to marry Petrie, than for that to happen. And I am also fearful of what he might do to Esther. You can't protect her."

He touched her face tenderly. "You are too fearful of him. He cannot harm me, and if you are in Wildercombe House, he cannot harm you either. I will have armed men at Esther's cottage to guard her. Don't go back to Dunscombe Manor now. We will return to Ilfracombe and go on together to my estate. I will buy any clothes that you need. You can just leave everything behind."

"No," she said. "You know that Esther would not allow you to protect her. It is best to see if McAlpine produces the contract and allows me to marry you without any problem." She looked at him for a moment. "Did you say you will not be fighting in France?"

"I will not go if our marriage has not been resolved," he replied.

"But you will go if it has?" she asked, with a frown.

"Yes. I owe it to my parents and to France, to join the Catholic army in the Vendée."

She regarded him sadly. "I will return to Dunscombe Manor and we will see what happens."

"But you will marry me?" he said.

"Yes, I will marry you, and not Captain Petrie, but I am not sure how we will manage it," she replied solemnly.

Happiness surged up in him. For a moment, he forgot the grimness of the day; the sadness of Charles's death and the abduction of Georgiana. He longed to hold Isabella in his arms and make love to her. Instead, he gazed joyfully at her and managed to refrain from moving closer, as they stood together on the pebbles, the waves lapping near to their feet.

"I don't want you to return to Dunscombe Manor, my beloved," he repeated his words softly.

"Don't worry," she said, smiling tremulously. "I think we only have a short time to wait and then we will see what McAlpine is intending for us."

They walked slowly back together over the beach to the lime kiln, and Mrs McAlpine looked at them, a strange glint both of triumph and anxiety in her eyes. When they reached her, she bent down to Isabella from her horse, and whispered in her ear.

Isabella paled, but looked steadfastly at her with scorn.

"You seem to have brought very few servants to defend yourself," he commented sarcastically to Mrs McAlpine, anger rising in him as he guessed the threat she had just made to Isabella. "I will escort you home to Ilfracombe now."

"No, I do not need your assistance," she said.

"It is obvious that you do from what has happened," he replied curtly, and indicated to her that she should ride on, whereupon she laughed, hit her horse with her riding crop, and galloped off down the path through the ravine.

He looked at Isabella. "What did she say?" he asked.

"It is not important," she replied, and smiled at him.

"I suspect she was trying to frighten you about the deaths of Daniel and Thomas and bend you to her will, by threats against Esther, or me, if you do not return to Dunscombe Manor," he said angrily. "We will ride with her, but keep close to me, although it is unlikely we will be attacked by highwaymen on the moor as there are too many of us, and, as far as the kidnappers are concerned, I think they have achieved what they wanted."

They set off and caught up with Mrs McAlpine at the farm house at Heddon, where she had stopped and was talking to John Berriman.

"They got away, did they?" the farmer remarked, with interest in his voice, as Armand reached him.

"Yes," he said curtly.

"The blackguards," John Berriman commented, his voice and expression, however, now appearing flat and disinterested. He did not ask any questions and waved his hands dismissively.

Armand glanced at him angrily. "We are not talking about thieving. A young girl has been kidnapped. I will get the Lord Lieutenant to investigate you and your farm. It all sounds very suspicious to me."

"Be off with you," the farmer shouted, retreating into the house and slamming the door.

They crossed the moor at a steady pace, by a different route to the one Mrs McAlpine had chosen, and which did not hug the coast so closely. They passed no other travellers, but the blue expanse of the Bristol Channel, often seen beyond the cliffs, was busy with a variety of ships, whilst Georgiana's rider-less horse was a constant reminder of her abduction.

He turned round frequently to look at Isabella, and every so often regarded Mrs McAlpine with an expression of contempt and anger. High-hedged lanes finally replaced the moorland, and they once more travelled along the road from Combe Martin to Ilfracombe, reaching Chambercombe in the evening twilight. Venus was shining brightly in the evening sky, near a shadowy outline of a pale moon, and wood smoke was rising in blue wisps over the cob-walled cottages, as he escorted Mrs McAlpine and Isabella down the steeply winding lane to the entrance of the manor house.

"I will go and see Mrs Bowen now," he said coldly to Mrs McAlpine, as he reined in his horse. "I will tell her what has happened. And perhaps you can visit in the morning to give her the details."

He looked sadly towards Isabella. He said nothing, but bowed his head slightly in acknowledgement. Then he abandoned her, with a heavy heart, to Dunscombe Manor and the McAlpines.

50

He sat down on the fireside seat, next to Tabitha, as the early morning sunshine warmed the room, and he recounted what had happened.

"And Isabella is safe?" Esther said. "They only took Georgiana."

"Yes," he replied.

"Thank God," she remarked in a trembling voice. "It is all very strange. I wonder where the poor girl is today."

"It is not strange at all. Georgiana has red hair. It is powdered white, but I have noticed its true colour and all the women taken have had either fair or red hair. Isabella also thought that Mrs McAlpine and the farmer knew what was going to happen."

"That does not surprise me," Esther said. "I have always wondered if McAlpine had a hand in the disappearances, even before it seemed possible that his wards were also involved. There will be no way anything can be proved, of course."

"It is also odd that it did not happen at the nights of the dark moon, like the others," he replied.

"Yes," she said thoughtfully. "Perhaps there would have been no other opportunity to abduct Georgiana Bowen. The McAlpines enabled it to happen, by taking her to such an isolated place, with such a lack of armed men."

He glanced round the room, which was bare of any hanging mandrake root and lacked bunches of herbs.

"It is very tidy here. I can't see David. Is he in the stream? Have you been given a date? Are you preparing to go?" he asked.

She did not reply.

"You think it will be soon," he questioned. "If so, why is it very close to the abduction of Georgiana?"

"I do not think there is any connection," she replied.

He stood up. "Charles de Landenberg died yesterday. I think you knew him."

"Yes. I was at Marie-Thérèse's birth. I thought he was getting better, in spite of Dr Conibear."

"So did I. It will be very hard for Henriette alone."

"Guillaume Thibaud will help her. He is a kind and decent man," she replied.

"Yes," he agreed.

He took his leave and walked back along the garden path, noticing that the fly agaric toadstools had vanished, and that most of the herbal plants had been uprooted and placed in a compost heap. The garden was as empty as the house.

"She is about to go," he muttered, and quickened his step back along the lane and the drive to Wildercombe House, where he gave instructions to Mrs Widdicombe to prepare the house for the billeting of men for the invasion force. He then went to the stables, where his horse was brought out for him, and he set off with Hans and Tomas towards Chambercombe.

He stopped at the harbour and surveyed the multitude of ships and fishing boats at anchor and saw that over by the jetty was the same vessel he had noticed a short time before. It still did not have a flag, and he watched a stocky man with a bandage wrapped round his upper arm, who was smoking a pipe on a wooden chest in the prow.

He rode along the Strand, past the cottages overlooking the harbour, and reined in his horse on the quay, next to a pile of lobster pots. He looked down at the vessel, which had the name 'Dundee Lass' painted in gold on the hull, and which had a large number of cannons protruding from portholes. He scrutinised the ship, ignoring the hostile glare of the man with the injured arm, and looked with interest at a longboat, tied at the stern, which was being vigorously scrubbed by a sailor.

He went up to a fisherman by the lobster pots who was sorting mackerel into baskets. "Whose ship is that?" he asked.

"Raphael McAlpine's," the man replied.

He regarded the ship again for a few minutes and then spoke to the fisherman again. "Do you know where Lieutenant Hargreaves and the Customs and Excise men might be?"

"In the tavern," he said, pointing to the nearest alehouse. "They're always in there."

He left Tomas and Hans outside with his horse, and entered a low-raftered room which was thick with smoke and smelled of fish, where Lieutenant Hargreaves was seated at a table, poring over a map with two fellow officers. He approached him and the Lieutenant glanced up, his face haggard, his eyes bleary with redness.

"Are you looking for Miss Georgiana?" he enquired.

"Yes," Lieutenant Hargreaves replied. "We've been doing it, with the militia, since you raised the alarm yesterday from Heddon. It was too dark for much of the night, but we have been patrolling along the coast since dawn. Can you tell me what happened?"

"I arrived too late. She was already gone," he said.

"They did not take any valuables?" the Lieutenant enquired. "They just kidnapped her? Why would they do that?"

"She is not the first, as you know. There have been several other women snatched from Devon, and I fear that they are being used for some vile purpose. What about that ship in the harbour, the Dundee Lass? Have you searched it?"

"For what reason?" he asked. "It belongs to Raphael McAlpine. What's he got to do with any of this?"

"Isabella thought she heard the innkeeper at Heddon speaking to a man with a Scottish accent. She injured one of the men with her dagger, and I noticed that a sailor on board the ship has a wound to his arm," he replied.

Lieutenant Hargreaves stared at him. "No. I cannot search McAlpine's ship," he said bluntly.

"Why not?" said Armand. "Is it because you have been to too many of his orgies in the woods?"

"How do you know about that?" the Customs and Excise man stuttered, his face reddening.

"I saw you. And you, and you," he declared, looking at the other two Customs and Excise officers.

"You attended as well?" questioned Lieutenant Hargreaves in surprise.

"Not exactly. I was passing through," he replied.

"Well, I cannot search his ship," the Lieutenant said flatly.

"Have some courage, man," shouted Armand in temper. "Georgiana's life is at stake. Are you afraid you will be killed by his Hecate's Wheel gang?"

There was a sudden silence in the tavern. The fishermen and sailors stopped drinking and talking. He reached for his sword, but no one threatened him. Instead, everyone was staring at Lieutenant Hargreaves.

"Search his ship," growled a man, his face scarred from forehead to chin.

A second man called out, "Don't forget poor Bess Mudge."

"No, don't be a fool," shouted another. "McAlpine brings in a lot of revenue to Ilfracombe."

"Yes, and you are paid to stop all this smuggling," said Armand angrily.

"There is no proof that McAlpine is involved in smuggling, or in anything connected with Georgiana's disappearance," shouted the Lieutenant, his face flushing even more. "You are causing trouble. Be off with you back to France. Join the invasion ship. Go and get yourself killed and Ilfracombe will be well rid of you and your Catholic family. Raphael McAlpine is a fine, upstanding member of the town and it does you a disservice to suggest otherwise."

"If you are not prepared to search for Georgiana properly, you are not worthy of her," Armand retorted.

"You are right," said a serving maid by the stairs. "We are all living in fear here."

Armand retreated out of the alehouse, walking backwards towards the door, his sword in his hand. No one attacked him, and as he reached the safety of the street, shouting and swearing erupted from inside the tavern, and a bitter argument appeared to be raging.

He looked towards the ship, peacefully riding the incoming tide, seagulls perched on its masts.

"Ride as fast as you can to Filleigh, to the estate of the Lord Lieutenant, and ask him to come with militia, and search the Dundee Lass for Georgiana Bowen," he told Tomas.

He quickly mounted his horse, and he and Hans cantered across to the Strand, and up the hill towards Chambercombe. He descended the lane towards Dunscombe Manor, reached the entrance, and glanced through the gate at Isabella's window. Nothing stirred. No ribbons fluttered from the casement. For once, there was not even a crow in sight, and he turned and retraced his route back to Wildercombe House.

51

The ship lay at anchor in the lee of the headland. The crescent-shaped cove was calm, only a weak south westerly breeze rippling its surface. The silver sand was scuffed by the prints of men's boots, and indented by long grooves where gigs had been drawn up. Casks were being filled with water from the spring on the hillside, and, above the high water mark, a fire was burning, which was crackling and sending up plumes of black smoke. The flag on the mast was the Red Ensign and Armand looked at it with surprise.

"I was expecting the fleur de lys," he remarked to Gabriel Soullans.

He laughed, "No, we do not want the English to think we are invading them. It is lucky we can embark from this isolated beach. It is rare to have so many Frenchmen in one place in England."

"Some are just boys," said Armand, looking at a lad wearing an overcoat which was too large for him, who was throwing pebbles into the sea.

"Yes, some have been brought by their fathers, and some have not any fathers and have come alone."

"I did not realise so many émigrés lived here."

"They are not all from Devon. Some are from Cornwall and Somerset. But they are all French, and they want to fight for the Royalist cause in the Vendée."

"Two of my men from Alsace have volunteered. But the rest want to stay in Ilfracombe for the moment. Many of their families are living beyond the Rhine and they hope to rejoin them there."

"Are you coming with us?" asked Gabriel Soullans.

"Yes, I intend to. I am expecting a contract to be brought to me later today to sign, and then I will be in a position to fight in France."

He left his fellow Frenchman on the beach, and walked slowly up the cliff path, and down through the wood. Autumnal colours of red and orange brightened the gloom, and leaves lay in drifts, muffling his footsteps. Sadness seared him, and he tried not to think of leaving Isabella. He smiled as he saw the rowan tree, where she had sat the day he rescued her from the waves, and when he reached the stone birds on the pillars, he turned away from Wildercombe House, and strode to Esther's cottage.

He knocked, and she called out weakly, "Is that you, Seigneur? Come in."

He entered and found her sitting on the fireside settle. Her face was white and her grey hair straggled over her shoulders.

"Are you ill?" he enquired.

"Age is overtaking me," she replied ruefully. "But the digitalis powder serves me well. The ship has arrived, I believe. I heard French voices in the lane."

"Yes, it will sail tonight," he said.

"And will you be on it?" she asked.

"I hope to be. Yesterday a servant came from McAlpine to say that he will visit me this evening, and will bring something which will benefit me greatly. So I presume he means the contract giving him a part of my land in return for Isabella in marriage. I will leave her at Wildercombe House, while I am in France, so she will be safe from him, and she will be near you."

Esther said nothing, but regarded him in annoyance.

He looked at her. "Well. You were wrong. He is going to forget about Petrie, or whoever he is."

"What about the other contract? The one for the whole of your estate," she asked.

269

"As I said before, he is probably just still hoping to buy it from me," he replied.

"And what about the contract he wants me to sign to give him my cottage, when Isabella marries Petrie?" she asked. "That does not make sense."

He looked at her grimly.

"He is like a spider. He is sitting on his web and is waiting for you to stumble into it. And not just you. I am still afraid that Isabella will be caught as well. She will only be safe if she does what he wants. He is obviously going to receive a lot of money from Petrie and this is not the case with you. So, I repeat. I do not believe it and I think you are rushing headlong into some sort of trap."

She stopped, breathless, and it was some minutes before she was able to continue.

"I do not think that I will be able to go with Isabella to the United States. I will try, but I believe that my cottage, which has been my sanctuary, will be my last refuge on Earth. Take Tabitha with you now and feed her and she will start to feel at home." She clutched her chest, gasping for breath again, then began to breathe more easily, her eyes searching his face.

"Do not join the ship, I beg you. Everyone knows of its existence. It will be lucky to get as far as Land's End in Cornwall. The French will be waiting for it."

"I don't want to go," he said bitterly. "I want to marry Isabella and live here at Wildercombe House, but I feel it is my duty to fight."

"It is not what your mother would have wanted. I knew her well. Even if you cannot have Isabella, at least you can stay here on your estate and survive. They will all die, these fighters for the Vendée. There is no hope for them."

"You are not in good health," he said, sitting down opposite her on the fireside seat. "If you die, the knowledge about the Santa Rosa will die with you. Tell me what you know, or what you suspect."

She regarded him for several minutes, her expression one of reluctance.

"McAlpine has an ornament similar to the one you have. The seven-branched candleholder. But his is silver and is obviously extremely valuable. What is a man like that doing with a Jewish artefact, which, I believe, you called a menorah?" he asked.

270

"Yes, you have remembered correctly," she said. "A long time ago, in Spain in 1492, an Edict was proclaimed which said that Jewish people had to convert to Christianity or leave the country. Those who converted were called conversos, as well as other names. Some of them continued to practise the Jewish religion secretly and the Inquisition tortured and killed any it could discover. Mass burnings took place called autos da fé. The Inquisition is weak now and concerns itself mainly with trying to stop the flow of revolutionary literature from France into Spain and, in my opinion, will soon be abolished. Not in my lifetime, but sometime quite soon. There are, however, a few pockets of conversos still remaining, particularly in Portugal, in a town called Belmonte, and they continue to practise their original religion."

She breathed with difficulty, and stopped talking.

"Do you want the digitalis?" he asked.

"No," she said, and shook her head.

"Sixteen years ago, some of the conversos in Belmonte told the Jewish community in North Devon that they were chartering a ship, and would be emigrating here. We were ready to receive them into our homes, but they were shipwrecked, just as they reached the shore."

"The Santa Rosa," he muttered.

"Yes, the Santa Rosa," she replied. "It seemed strange at the time, because there was not a storm and the weather was very good. I know that the reefs off the Torrs can be treacherous, but, even so, it was a shock. We came and found all the bodies on the beach the next day. They were going to be buried in a mass grave, but we took the ones we knew were Jewish. Their clothes were different to those of the sailors. The ship was very close to the shore and it had been completely plundered of everything valuable, and the corpses had also been stripped of all jewellery. They had died horribly. They did not look as though they had drowned. They appeared to have been bludgeoned to death or stabbed."

"So the ship was deliberately wrecked," he said.

"Yes, that is what we thought," she replied.

"And what about Isabella? How do you think she survived?"

"We could not find the bodies of either her, or her mother, and we wondered if they had somehow escaped. We believed McAlpine to be one of the wreckers, and so I visited him and noticed the painting in his dining room of the Portuguese earthquake in the middle of the century. I did not ask him directly, but offered my services to him as a herbalist. I soon discovered that a little girl had suddenly appeared and was living in his house. She was not his ward then. She just roamed free in the kitchen and the garden. He took no notice of her, and was often away. She was very dark and did not look English."

"Isabella," he said. "But what about her mother?"

"There was no sign of her," she replied.

"But why would he have kept a child?" he asked.

"I don't know. Perhaps that man, evil as he is, has some sort of conscience. Perhaps he could not kill her. Perhaps he just brought her back and did not bother about her as she was so young. We will never know. But I am sure that Isabella is the only survivor of the Santa Rosa, and I have looked after her as though she was my own daughter. I have taught her all my skills, just as my mother taught me."

"But why are you so afraid he might kill her?" he asked.

"Because the conversos were bringing all their money and valuables to England. McAlpine has enriched himself on the proceeds of his violence. He owned Dunscombe Manor at the time, but was poor and struggling. Now he has a fleet of ships and is a very wealthy man. If Isabella is the true survivor of the Santa Rosa, then she has been deprived of what is rightfully hers and it was a mistake on his part not to have killed her. He has also married Mrs McAlpine and she has a jealous hatred of her. And that is why I did not want you to meddle."

"He will hang for it," he declared in anger.

"You see, I cannot trust you," she said. "You are too young and impulsive. Isabella has to be protected both from your hot-headedness and McAlpine's cruelty. I believe she is nearly free of him because he is intending to receive money from her marriage, and I don't want any obstacles put in the way."

He looked at her. "Thank you for telling me. However, I intend to marry Isabella and I will wait until tonight to see what McAlpine has to say."

"Be careful," she said. "Do not trust him."

"Yes. I will be on my guard," he replied.

"It will be more difficult to bring African slaves to the United States, now that Congress has banned their transport to and from its shores. This will really hurt McAlpine's trade, as it is mainly what he uses his ships for. It is clear, however, that he is hoping to receive much money in the near future, and that is why I am still very concerned for Isabella. It seems unlikely that the Petrie family would pay a lot of money for a poor, unknown woman they have never seen."

"Perhaps I will find out tonight," he said, standing up. "I had better go now."

He left Esther sitting by the hearth, tiny and frail, her eyes closed. Tabitha followed him to Wildercombe House and he took her to the kitchen and instructed the cook to feed her from now on. Then he spent the day setting his affairs in order and preparing the weapons he would need for France. He passed by the portrait of his mother in the hall and avoided her eyes.

"Esther's right," he muttered. "You don't want me to go."

He watched the clock, as well as the drive, and at eight o'clock was finally rewarded with the sight of Raphael McAlpine, accompanied by several servants, riding purposefully towards the house.

Mrs Widdicombe herself, showed him into the library, where he stood waiting, the house now very quiet as the émigrés had all embarked on the ship, which was due to sail at midnight.

"So the Vendée will sacrifice more blood," Raphael McAlpine remarked, as he entered the room.

"How did you know of the date for the embarkation?" asked Armand.

"A little French bird told me," he said.

"Who?" demanded Armand.

"I cannot reveal my sources. I could put lives at risk," he replied, his manner polite, but with a rawness to his speech. He strode arrogantly round the room, looking out of the window, and touching the polished wood of the furniture, as though he was the owner, and Armand eyed him with contempt and dislike, which he attempted to conceal.

"I have decided to let Isabella marry you. If you give me the land we have spoken about, she will be yours. A signature is all that is necessary, as I have noticed before that you do not have a signet ring."

He produced a document from a bag he was carrying, and gave it to Armand. He quickly read it and saw that it was, indeed, the contract. He signed it without hesitation, and handed it back to McAlpine.

"And now my dear sir, let us celebrate your future marriage to my ward, as well as your success in battle in France. I have brought a special bottle of wine for the occasion, which is one hundred years old," he declared, as Mrs Widdicombe came into the library with two glasses on a tray, which she placed on the desk.

"You were expecting me to sign," said Armand.

"Yes, I had little doubt. My ward is very beautiful," McAlpine replied.

"I would like Isabella to come here tonight and stay at Wildercombe House while I am away. Would that be acceptable to you and to her?" Armand asked.

"Of course, my dear sir. I can understand you would like to see her before you leave."

Armand pulled the bell on the wall to summon a footman.

"I will take care of any arrangements," said Raphael McAlpine, as Mrs Widdecombe poured out the wine. "I will send her to you straight away."

"No," insisted Armand. "I will go myself and accompany her here."

"Well, let us first drink to the successful outcome of our meeting," he said, giving Armand a glass and taking the other himself.

"A toast to your marriage with Isabella."

Armand hurriedly drank the wine, grimacing at its unexpected tartness, whilst McAlpine also put his glass to his lips. He placed the contract, which had a second sheet attached to it, into his bag, bowed, and was shown to the front door by the housekeeper. Horses could be heard galloping off down the drive, and he went in search of Dietrich, who had come to say farewell, and was waiting in the dining room.

"I am going to marry Isabella," he told him. "I have just signed the contract with McAlpine to give him a part of my estate and I will ride to Dunscombe Manor now and bring her here."

He embraced Dietrich, and as he did so, a wave of nausea overcame him. He swayed, his knees buckled, and Dietrich helped him to a chair.

"I need a drink," he said, shaking.

Ben poured him a glass of brandy and he drank it hastily. He pulled at his cravat and the neck of his shirt, which were suffocating him. Sweat was trickling down his face and he could hardly see. He felt Dietrich lift him up and clung on to his arm. Ben supported him on his other side, and together they helped him stumble to his bedchamber. He fell onto his bed, his whole body shuddering.

"Did McAlpine do this?" he mumbled through swollen lips. "Was it the wine?"

"He was only with you for a short time," said Dietrich.

"He brought a bottle and I celebrated with him," he muttered, not sure if the words which were in his head were the words he was actually speaking. "Call Mrs Widdicombe."

His housekeeper loomed at him, her face enlarged into grotesque proportions. "I am sure it has nothing to do with Mr McAlpine. Perhaps the meat was off at dinner. I will have a word with the cook."

"Go and tell Gabriel Soullans, the man in charge of the embarkation, that the Seigneur will not be joining the ship. He has fallen ill," said Dietrich to Ned.

He heard the words, but did not understand them. Nausea made him retch. He was in a cauldron, being boiled alive and leaves, spiders and frogs were pouring down, choking him. Ivan Ben, Ivan Ben, the name kept repeating endlessly in his mind, and in a moment of logic, which cut through his delirium, he suddenly understood. "Ibn ben!" he shouted. "A Moorish name! She's going to be sold as a slave!"

He choked and gasped and sank into darkness.

52

The outside sky was darkening as Esther sat at her fireside seat. Horses had galloped down the lane towards Wildercombe House, and now their returning hoof beats stopped at her gate.

Steps sounded in the garden and she opened the door, to be confronted by Raphael McAlpine.

He stood, blocking the last rays from the sunset, and she trembled as she saw him.

"It is time to go, old woman. You can accompany Isabella to the United States if you sign the contract giving me your cottage and land."

He held out a document to her and she took it and held it to the fading light from the window. She slowly read, then, even more slowly, signed her name at the bottom of the page, and gave it to him. Her eyes filled with tears, which she wiped away, and she picked up the small bag she had packed with her possessions.

"Have you visited Armand de Delacroix?" she asked.

"Yes, and the outcome has been satisfactory," he replied.

"What do you mean?" she asked.

"I will tell you in good time," he said enigmatically.

"Where are we going?" she asked.

"The Dundee Lass," he replied. "She is moored off Rapparee tonight and will sail tomorrow."

Esther rode on Mordecai, Raphael McAlpine and his men surrounding her on their horses. They encountered few people, but those they did, hastily looked the other way. They went right to the end of the harbour wall; the men dismounted and Esther wearily climbed down from the donkey.

"What will happen to him?" she asked.

"I will have him in my stable," he replied.

She looked nervously at the ship anchored by Rapparee beach; the skeletal outline of its masts black in the moonlight, and lanterns on its prow and stern gleaming a feeble yellow.

Raphael McAlpine whistled to the vessel and a gig was lowered and splashed into the water. Two sailors rowed it across to the steps of the harbour wall; he and Esther were helped to clamber on board, and it returned to the Dundee Lass.

The hull of the ship was dark above her; she stood up unsteadily in the small boat and was picked up by one of the men, as though she was a rag doll. He flung her unceremoniously over his shoulder, climbed the ladder fixed to the side, and deposited her on the wooden planks.

Raphael McAlpine mockingly bowed. "Your cabin awaits, milady."

She looked sourly at him, then followed him into the rancid-smelling quarters below decks. He opened a door in a narrow corridor and stepped back to allow her to enter.

She went inside and glanced around her apprehensively. There was no window. It was more of a cupboard than a cabin, and had a shelf as a bed, covered with dirty rags. There was no lantern or candle, and the only light penetrated weakly into it from the gangway.

"What sort of hell hole is this?" she asked. "I cannot spend a whole voyage cooped up in here. And where is Isabella going to be?"

"You do not need to concern yourself about your accommodation. You will soon be residing in the sea with the fish," said Raphael McAlpine. "I will be rid of you. You know too much about my affairs and how I originally came by my money. Not only will I gain your cottage and your land, I will no longer have to worry about any accusations you might make."

Esther gasped in horror and clutched at her chest.

"What about Isabella?" she exclaimed.

"She will be in a harem. I will receive a lot of money for her, just as I have for the rest of the girls."

"But she is not fair- or red-haired," she muttered.

"She will be enslaved to a different man. It is only Ibn Rahman who has a taste for women with white skins and very blond, or red, hair."

She flailed her arms at him, but he laughed and pushed her onto the bed.

"You think so much of your healing skills and your knowledge. And now I have you completely in my power, and will do with you what I wish. It is useless to shout out. No one will hear you. Your life is finished, old woman, and for Isabella a new one will begin as the possession of a Moor."

"And Georgiana? Where is she? Is she on the ship?" she asked.

"Perhaps," he said. "Or perhaps not."

"Why did you save Isabella from the Santa Rosa?" she muttered.

"I saved her mother. She was beautiful, even more so than Isabella. She pleaded with me on the beach, just as I was about to kill her. I was young and foolish, and took her back to Dunscombe Manor with me. I hardly saw her child. She was holding onto her skirt and half-hidden."

"What happened to her?" she asked.

"I killed her in the end, of course. I realised my mistake. Everyone has to die if you wreck a boat. But I did not bother about Isabella, because she was too young, so did not understand. I hardly noticed her until she became older, and then I could see the potential for another sale to the Barbary Coast, and, at the same time, rid myself of the only survivor of the Santa Rosa."

He started to go out of the door and turned to look at her.

"By the way, I am sure you will be pleased to know that I am about to own Wildercombe House and the estate. That fool, Delacroix, signed to give me a part of his land, but the paper underneath is well imprinted with his signature and I only have to trace it to produce a replica on a contract giving me everything."

"But he will know what you have done," she protested weakly.

"I do not think so. He will be dead. In fact, I should think he is already dead," he remarked.

"How?" she cried.

"How do you think? It was you who gave it to me," he said.

"The belladonna," she gasped. "You have poisoned him."

"Yes, I would imagine it has done its task well. I could not risk him going off to France, as I would never have obtained his land. If he had died in battle there, someone else would have inherited, and I would have had to start again. It was just luck that he wanted Isabella and was prepared to give away a part of his estate, and so signed for me. But that is enough conversation. Goodbye. You have been useful to me, but now you are too much of a liability, and would have prevented me from enslaving Isabella."

Esther glared venomously at him. Her body stiffened and she stood up. Her eyes were dark with hatred, her voice shrieked in a howl of fury, "I curse you, Raphael McAlpine. You will die a miserable death, and the crows will do to you what they have done to others."

His eyes twitched nervously and he stepped backwards, fear on his face. He banged shut and bolted the door and she was left in the dark. She sobbed in despair and fell onto the bed, struggling for breath. A rat scratched in the corner and scurried away; the rising tide caught the ship, causing the wooden timbers to creak as it strained against its anchor towards the beach at Rapparee.

53

Armand writhed in agony on his bed. "I can't reach her. The crows are drowning. Killing," he mumbled.

"He is delirious," said Dietrich to Ben. "I will go and ask Esther Cerfbeer to come, as he has taken a dislike to Dr Conibear. Do not let him leave his bedchamber, and do not give him any weapon."

He quickly left Wildercombe House and galloped on his horse to the cottage in the lane. He strode up the path and pushed open the door, which was ajar.

"Esther Cerfbeer," he called. "Are you there?"

The room was empty, and there was no answering sound from upstairs. He stood for just a moment, before running back to his horse and galloping off on the same route to Chambercombe that he had taken with Armand on Hecate's night; the moonlight illuminating the track, revealing a black and white countryside, robbed of colour by the night.

He arrived at the door in the boundary wall, flung himself down from his horse, and tethered it to a tree. He entered the gardens and ran towards Dunscombe Manor. He stopped by the yew tree and glanced at the windows, where candlelight flickered in Isabella's bedchamber and the dining room, but where the rest of the house was in darkness.

He strode to the ash and climbed it, as Armand had done, disregarding the branches creaking ominously under his weight. He inched along until he reached the window and rapped sharply on the glass.

Isabella immediately opened it and looked at him in surprise.

"Dietrich!" she exclaimed. "What are you doing?"

"The Seigneur is very ill. I think McAlpine has poisoned him. I went to Esther Cerfbeer's cottage, but she is not there, so I came to see if you know where she is."

"I will meet you down at the front door. McAlpine is not here. There is only his wife, who is drunk, in the dining room," she replied. "Esther has taught me her skills. Let me see what I can do."

She did not wait for an answer, but hurriedly shut the window, snuffed out the candle, and pulled on her cloak. She tiptoed down the stairs to the hall and very quietly opened the main door. As she did so, she noticed a scrap of yellow on the floor and picked it up, immediately recognising it as the silk rose which had decorated Georgiana's dress at Heddon. "She was here," she muttered in surprise. "She was here in this house after her abduction."

She placed it in her pocket and stepped outside into the courtyard, just as Dietrich came running over the cobbles to meet her.

They rushed across the garden to the wall; Dietrich mounted his horse, pulled her up behind him, and they galloped up the lane and across the fields to the Wildercombe estate.

They stopped briefly at Esther's cottage to see if she had returned, and she looked round her, in disquiet, at the abandoned home.

"Her bag has gone that she has packed to take to America," she said. She felt the embers in the hearth, which were still warm, and took down the jar from the shelf where Esther kept her money.

"It is empty. She would only leave to sail to the United States. She must be with McAlpine, although he has not told me that it is time to go. I wonder where she is."

"We can find her another time. We must go to the Seigneur now," Dietrich said impatiently. She glanced anxiously once more at the cottage, then hurriedly ran back with him to his waiting horse and they galloped the short distance to Wildercombe House.

Armand's bedchamber was crammed with servants. The whole household had gathered; the babble of voices and the presence of so many bodies had terrified Tabitha, who had retreated to a corner, and was spitting and hissing at anyone who came near her. She flew out as Isabella entered and rubbed against her ankles, miaowing piteously, but she ignored her, and pushed through the throng to the bed, where Armand was sprawled, his shirt open.

His face was flushed and he was mumbling incoherently. His gaze was wild, and he threw out his arms to her as she came near.

"Four," he shouted. "Four Isabellas."

"Everyone must leave," she said to Ben. "I need quiet to treat him. Would you also bring wine, hot water, bowls and spoons."

The footman shepherded everyone from the room and she sat down on the bed next to Armand. She felt his forehead and touched his dry lips.

"Has he drunk much?" she asked Ben.

"Yes," he said.

"Has he vomited?" she asked.

"Twice," he replied.

"Look at me," she ordered Armand, holding his head in her hands. "Look straight at me."

He screwed up his face, as though he was attempting to focus on her, and she carefully scrutinised his eyes, before placing him back onto the bolster.

"His pupils are dilated," she said to Dietrich. "He is extremely thirsty and delirious and has nausea. He has all the symptoms of belladonna poisoning."

"Belladonna?" he queried.

"Yes. It is also called deadly nightshade. Has he eaten any black berries?"

"I don't know," he replied. "He drank wine with McAlpine to celebrate the signing of a document for your marriage."

"He signed the contract?" she said. "McAlpine was here?"

"Yes. It was after that he fell ill," Dietrich replied.

"It is nothing to do with Mr McAlpine," declared Mrs Widdicombe scornfully, who had been standing, watching the scene. "I myself poured the drinks. It is probably something he has eaten, which has disagreed with him."

Isabella stared at her in anger.

"Take that woman out of the house immediately," she told Dietrich. "She is an ally of McAlpine's. I don't know exactly what has happened here, but I do not trust her to remain."

282

The housekeeper glared at her.

"You cannot command anyone in this house. You and that witch will soon be gone," she sneered.

"Get out," said Dietrich, drawing his sword, and advancing towards her. "I believe you have helped to harm the Seigneur. Give me your keys and get out."

The housekeeper did not stay to discover his intentions. She unfastened the keys from the chain at her belt, threw them contemptuously onto the floor, and scurried hastily from the room, in spite of her bulk, her mob cap falling from her head.

"I must go back to Esther's cottage," said Isabella. "Let me ride your horse. It will be quicker. I need to fetch an antidote to the poison, otherwise he will go into a deep sleep and die."

"I will take you," replied Dietrich. He turned to Ben. "Do not let anyone go near him."

He and Isabella quickly returned on his horse to Esther's cottage. She hurriedly chose what she needed from the various jars of herbal potions, then clung again to Dietrich's coat, seated precariously on the rump of the horse, as he rode recklessly back to Wildercombe House

She ran into Armand's bedchamber, and saw, with horror, that he was now breathing heavily and his eyes were closed. She shook him, but he did not respond, and lay motionless on the bed, as though unconscious. She took out the powdered fly agaric from the jar, moistened it with water in a bowl and spooned it into his mouth. He groaned and tried to push her away, but she persisted, and slowly managed to give him the exact quantity necessary as an antidote.

She worked for several hours. At one point he cried out in a terrible, agonising shriek; his body went into a spasm, his features contorted, but she gave him more of the medication, and he gradually calmed.

At midnight, she finally sat exhausted in a chair by the window. He was sleeping quietly, his breathing was steady, and his skin was no longer flushed. He had stopped crying out for drink, and his muscle spasms had ceased.

"You have cured him," said Dietrich, looking at her respectfully.

"I think so," she replied. "I don't believe this is the prelude to death. He would have worsened if it had been so."

"Where did you get your knowledge?" he asked.

"From Esther. She has taught me. We owe his life to her," she said.

She stood up wearily. "I must go home. I want to know what has happened to her, and only McAlpine can tell me that."

She took out the yellow silk rose from her pocket and showed it to Dietrich.

"I found this on the hall floor as I was leaving. It comes from the dress Georgiana was wearing the day she was snatched at Heddon."

"Are you saying McAlpine was involved?" he asked.

"It seems certain," she replied.

"You should not return to Crow House. I cannot ask the Seigneur, but I think that would be what he would say. He will be angry with me tomorrow if he finds out I let you go back there."

"It is my own decision," she said. "I must find Esther, and I am beginning to suspect where Georgiana is."

"It is too dangerous. I refuse to let you go. You must wait here until he awakes."

At that moment, the muffled boom of cannons came from beyond the wood, in the direction of Lundy Island. A dull explosion jarred the air. A red-orange flash momentarily lit up the night sky, followed by a yellow glow.

"What is that?" she exclaimed and ran to the window, joined by Dietrich, Ben and Ned.

"Is it the ship?" cried Ben. "Has it been attacked? Have the French come up the Channel? We have to give the alarm."

"We will be able to see from the headland," said Dietrich. "Come with me, Ben, and you stay here, Ned. I will send the Alsatians to guard the house." He glanced at Isabella. "Do not attempt to go to Dunscombe Manor. The men will prevent you if you try to do so. The Seigneur will help you find Esther when he is better."

He hurriedly left the chamber, as the bells of the Parish Church pealed out from Ilfracombe. A cannon boomed again, and bats flew in front of the window, black shapes against the fire-brightened sky.

A faint whiff of gunpowder and smoke invaded the air, and Isabella waited, watching from the window, until she glimpsed Dietrich and Ben in a group of people hurrying towards the wood.

"Would you go and get me some wine," she asked Ned.

He looked at her. "You are going back to Crow House."

"Yes," she answered firmly.

"You helped me when I was chased by the hunt," he said. "I would not be alive if it were not for you. Go quickly before the Alsatians arrive. Dietrich said he would tell them to keep you here."

"Thank you," she replied.

"Take care, Miss. I know you grew up there, but McAlpine is a very dangerous man."

"Yes," she agreed. "But I cannot wait until morning. It might be too late. I have to find Esther and Georgiana."

"Good luck. I will go down to the kitchen, so that I don't see what you do. Dietrich will be angry, but my shoulders are broad enough to bear it."

He left the room without a backward glance, and she went over to Armand on the bed.

"Goodbye, my dear one," she said, kissing his forehead. He stirred slightly, but his eyes remained closed. She softly touched his hair, and, emboldened, kissed him again, this time on his lips.

"You will not wake till morning, my beloved. The herbal potions are powerful. I have to go now as Esther needs me. I pray that we will be together once more, and, if not in this life, then in the next."

She kissed him passionately again before running down the stairs and out of the house to the stables. She found Dietrich's horse already saddled, and scrambled onto it, sitting astride the animal like a man. Then she cantered, at a steady pace, past the house and along the drive.

No one saw her go, except an owl sitting on the branch of a beech tree. The wind was rising and the trees were swaying and creaking in the moonlight. Droplets of rain pattered onto her face as she went first to Esther's cottage, to see if she had returned, before riding across the countryside to Dunscombe Manor. She tied the horse to a tree and slipped in through the doorway.

The moon had now disappeared, the rain was falling more heavily and she quickly approached the house, using the apple trees as shelter. Lightning flashed once and she gasped with fear as she was suddenly revealed in the bright garden. A thunder clap sounded as she reached the courtyard, but the rain and the night obscured her again and she looked at the windows where candlelight glimmered only in the bedchamber of McAlpine. She tried to open the front door, but it was bolted, and she returned to the back of the house and pushed up the scullery window, which had a broken catch.

A torrential downpour of rain suddenly beat against her as she hastily climbed over the sill. The storm lashed at the glass, the wind howled and she gratefully scurried over the flagstones to the hall, where she turned aside from the stairs, and entered the library.

She hurried to the tapestry, the linnet quiet in its covered cage, the white brilliance of lightning briefly lighting the room. She froze, then pulled aside the tapestry and fumbled desperately for the embossed knob. Her fingers found it; she pushed, the door opened to reveal the hidden chamber and she stepped into the claustrophobic blackness. She glanced around her, as the chamber was momentarily lit up by the glare of a fork of lightning and saw the same altar table and upside-down crucifix as before. The bookshelf was again bare, but the black candles in the metal stands were now just stubs. There was no sign of Georgiana.

She took a deep breath, and pulled the tapestry back into place, so that the doorway was concealed. The room was now as black as pitch. She whimpered in terror, and very slowly made her way along the wall, feeling its flaking plaster with her hands. The smell of mould and decay enveloped her, and she gradually moved towards the side of the chamber. The unpleasant odour intensified and the ground under her feet was no longer hard mosaic flooring, but a yielding softness of earth.

"I'm in the tunnel," she muttered. "I have to reach the red door. I am sure Georgiana is either in there, or has been there."

A moment of hysteria made her laugh out loud. "No, it will be the black door in this darkness. I won't be able to see its colour."

Upstairs in the bedchamber of her husband, the scantily gauze-clad Mrs McAlpine had been dancing sensuously to Hecate's picture in the moonlight, and now stood looking out of the window. Sandalwood incense exotically perfumed the room, as Raphael McAlpine quickly pulled on his breeches and shirt.

"I am sure it is nothing, my dear. Cain and Abel would have barked. No thief would dare to break into my house."

"Well, someone was definitely trying the front door," she retorted. "It was not my imagination. And I also heard footsteps."

"Our plans have nearly borne fruit," he said. "I now possess the Wildercombe estate as Delacroix must surely be dead. Esther Cerfbeer is the only person to know about the belladonna, the only person with the skill to have saved him, and she will shortly be on her way to Davy Jones's Locker. And the sale of Georgiana Bowen and Isabella to our friends on the Barbary Coast, will substantially increase my wealth."

He took his pistol from the dresser, and picked up a candle burning in its holder, then went out to the landing and cautiously descended the stairs. He entered the library and cast his eye quickly round it. There was clearly no intruder, and as he stood in the doorway, about to return to his wife, he looked again towards the tapestry, which was not hanging completely straight. It had caught on a chair and was untidily arranged. He walked over to the wall and pulled it back. He turned the embossed knob, the door opened, and he very slowly advanced, holding his pistol in one hand, and the candle in the other.

....

Isabella continued to feel her way along the wall. At times, fresh air wafted across her face, diluting the stale dankness, and she realised there must be shafts above her, leading to the garden. Thick wooden posts, at regular intervals, supported the tunnel, which was winding towards the sea. Time, in the overpowering darkness, had become meaningless. She had no idea if she had only been entombed a few minutes, or whether much longer had elapsed.

Her exploring fingers abruptly touched the hardness of metal bands on wood and she knew she had found the red door again. She ran her hands over it, shuddering as she encountered the skull. She stood tensely, an inexplicable happiness surging through her.

She struggled to remember, but could not. Unlike her memories of the shipwreck, there was just a blank in her mind. Only emotions gripped her. She knew she had wanted to return here. She knew she had been prevented and dragged away. She knew she had lost a part of her. She had lost love and kindness, and been abandoned to cruelty. But there were no faces she could recall. She could not explain what she felt, or what had happened.

She touched the door and found the handle. She pulled; it creaked alarmingly and opened. A faint light and a smell of whale oil, greeted her. She peered into the room and first saw a lantern on a table, her eyes attracted to its flickering gleam, like a bird caught in a cat's hypnotic gaze.

She gazed around, her eyes slowly growing accustomed to the gloom, and suddenly cried out involuntarily in shock.

A figure was tied to the far wall. Chains manacled her ankles and wrists, a gag encircled her mouth and head, and eyes stared at her desperately. It was Georgiana. Isabella sprang towards her. She pulled the gag from her mouth and Georgiana gasped for breath.

"Help me," she pleaded.

Isabella looked at the chains, which were locked.

"Do you know where the key is?"

"No. That terrible man has it. He has imprisoned me," she sobbed.

"I will see if I can find a stone to smash it. If I can't, I will get help," Isabella cried.

She ran frantically around the chamber, overturning a chair in her haste to locate a heavy instrument. A chest was at the side of the long room, and she ran to it and opened the lid. She screamed in shock and dust fell from the ceiling.

A body lay huddled inside. A wizened, mummified body, whose hair was long and black, even after sixteen years. A red velvet dress shrouded her, and she clung to the cask, trying not to faint. She knew she was looking at her mother.

"What is happening?" asked Georgiana in a piteous voice.

She gently shut the casket, tears trickling down her face.

"Nothing," she said, in a shaking voice. I can't find anything to free you. I will go for help."

"Will you?" said Raphael McAlpine, in the doorway, holding a pistol. "And how do you propose to do that?"

Georgiana shrieked repeatedly, in despairing cries of anguish.

Isabella picked up the chair and rushed at him with hatred. It caught him a glancing blow on his cheek, and blood trickled down his chin and onto his shirt. She backed away, but he lunged at her, and caught her wrists. She kicked him, but he hit her with the butt of the pistol, and as she fell, he dragged her across the ground and threw her against the wall. He quickly chained her wrists and ankles with manacles, as she continued to struggle against him, her shrieks joining those of Georgiana. Then he gagged her with a filthy rag from the bed.

"My little chickens," he said, standing back to examine his handiwork. "My little chickens, all cooped up and ready for a sailing trip to exotic climes."

He quickly tied the gag around Georgiana's mouth again, cutting off her screams in mid-flow. He extinguished the lantern, laughed mockingly, and left the room, slamming the door shut behind him.

Isabella lay chained on the ground next to Georgiana. The cloth from the gag was suffocating her. She tried to spit it out, but could not. The foul taste made her retch and she endeavoured to suppress her nausea. The horror of the knowledge that she had found her mother and that McAlpine had killed her, mingled with the foul-smelling darkness, and she spiralled down into a ghastly nightmare of semi-consciousness.

54

Armand woke late. Autumn sunshine was pale in the room, and Tabitha purred next to him on the bed.

Dietrich was standing by the window, a pistol in his belt, his sword on the table in front of him.

He blinked in the light, and sat up, holding his head in his hands.

"What are you doing here?"

"Don't you remember?" asked Dietrich. "You were poisoned."

"Not really. Everything is a blur, but I need a drink. I am very thirsty."

Ben poured him a glass of wine and he swallowed it in one gulp.

"It was belladonna that made you ill," said Dietrich. "Isabella treated you with herbal potions."

"Isabella. I think she talked to me. She kissed me. And the name 'Ivan Ben'. There was something I wanted to remember about it." He frowned and shook his head.

"I don't know about that," replied Dietrich. "She saved your life. She also told me to get rid of Mrs Widdicombe from your service, so I dismissed her."

"You both thought she was guilty?" enquired Armand.

"Yes. McAlpine brought the wine, which was probably drugged, and she poured it."

"I don't recall much of the evening. It is as though I was very drunk and having visions. However, I do remember signing a contract to marry Isabella." He suddenly stopped and looked sharply at Dietrich. "Where is she? You said she was here. Is she asleep?"

"I don't know where she is," he admitted. "When you fell ill, I went to Esther Cerfbeer to see if she could help, but she has disappeared. So I rode to Dunscombe Manor, and climbed the tree to her window, and she came back with me. The ship with the émigrés was attacked off Lundy, and when I went to the beach to see what had happened, she left, although I had told her not to. "

"The ship has sunk," repeated Armand, in shock.

"Yes, it is thought that two French frigates were lying in wait off the island. We heard the cannons firing. Fishing boats and merchant ships sailed from Ilfracombe to look for survivors, but no one has been found," Dietrich said angrily. "Gabriel Soullans came here this morning."

"He was not on the ship then?"

"No, he was intending to go on one of the other boats. He said he had found out who the traitor is, the person who is spying for the Revolutionaries, and that he was going to kill her."

"Her?" queried Armand. "It's a woman?"

"Evidently," said Dietrich. "He said she lives in Combe Martin."

"Combe Martin? I should not think there are many French women in Combe Martin."

"No, only Henriette de Lansberg," replied Dietrich.

"No, it can't be her," he declared. "No, she would never betray us."

"He left many hours ago, just before sunrise," said Dietrich. "We would be too late to stop him, if it is her."

"Esther is right. She said I am in a spider's web and do not understand what is happening," said Armand bitterly. "I am stumbling around, like an ignorant fool."

"And where is Esther?" asked Dietrich. "Where has she gone? She is hardly young and beautiful like the girls who have disappeared."

"I don't know about Esther," said Armand. "However, I do know that I must bring Isabella back here, before anything happens to her. We will be married. It was foolish and reckless of her if she has returned to Dunscombe Manor. Get the men ready. I want everyone armed. I will take her from McAlpine by force, if necessary."

Hoofbeats sounded on the gravel coming towards the house and Guillaume Thibaud could be seen through the window, carrying a small bundle in one arm, and with a child sitting in front of him on the horse.

Armand shakily left his bed and ran quickly downstairs to meet him outside the front door. Guillaume Thibaud did not dismount, or acknowledge him, but handed him the baby he was holding, who was wrapped in a shawl and crying bitterly. Armand stood awkwardly, with the infant in his arms, looking first at her, and then at the tearful little boy still on the horse.

"I have to go back to Combe Martin. Henriette has been killed, and I did not know where to bring the children. Can you take them in?" Guillaume Thibaud asked.

"Of course," he said, in a shocked voice, lifting down Edouard with his free hand. "Did Gabriel Soullans kill her? Was she the spy?"

"Yes," Guillaume Thibaud replied. "I think she was desperate for money, after the death of her husband, and she acted against her principles."

Armand stared at him in horror, tears welling in his eyes.

"Poor Henriette. I should have helped more."

"She was responsible for the attack on the ship and all those men killed," said Dietrich sharply. "Including Tomas and Mathieu."

Guillaume Thibaud frowned, and without saying anything further, rode off down the drive.

Armand gave the two children to Sarah, the housemaid.

"Care for them. Their home will be here at Wildercombe House with me."

He looked sombrely at Dietrich. "This revolution has set brother against brother, and friend against friend. When will it end? I must go to Isabella now. Have you any idea where she went last night?"

"She wanted to find Esther. She suspects McAlpine tried to poison you, and that he has abducted Georgiana. She showed me a rose from Georgiana's dress she was wearing that day at Heddon and said she found it in the hall at Dunscombe Manor."

"But why would McAlpine want to kill me? I had just signed a contract to marry his ward. I think it's probably just a coincidence I fell ill after his visit."

"I have no idea. But that is not what Isabella thinks," replied Dietrich. "And we both know there is evil going on in North Devon. We saw it at that ceremony to Hecate. There are killings of men and abductions of young girls, like Bess, and it poisons life in Ilfracombe. People live in fear of McAlpine and his gang. It is not just smuggling. I don't see much wrong with that."

"Yes," said Armand. "I must go immediately to Chambercombe."

55

He rode at the head of his men through the narrow streets of the town, which were awash with water, and strewn with debris of branches and leaves, from the storm. He halted on the hillside overlooking Rapparee beach and glanced down at the Dundee Lass, moored just off the cove. The October day was blustery, white-crested waves were rolling in from the Bristol Channel, crashing against the harbour wall, and the rocks by Hillsborough. The high tide had created an island of Lantern Hill, and the sea was flooding over the Strand and into the flat marshland beyond.

On the jetty stood a tall man, and even from the hillside opposite, Armand could see the ornate decorations on his coat, and hear his shouted commands.

"It's the Lord Lieutenant," he exclaimed to Dietrich. "The man we met on the road to Bideford."

"Yes, so it is. It looks as though he must have received your message and is about to search the ship for Georgiana."

Red-coated militia men were swarming along the quay, and embarking into small boats, two of which had already reached the stern of the Dundee Lass. Sailors were running frantically over the decks of the ship and the sails were being slowly hoisted. Muskets fired, and wind caught the partly erected canvas, making it billow out; the ship jerked, but was held fast by its anchor.

"Well, if Georgiana is on board, she will be found," remarked Armand. "And if I am wrong in my suspicions, I will be very unpopular with the Lord Lieutenant. We had better hurry to Dunscombe Manor. McAlpine will be furious with this, when he finds out."

They cantered up the steep hillside of Chambercombe, which was furrowed by numerous small streams which had appeared overnight. They followed the lane down through the wood and came to a bend in the road where earth had subsided on to the track; trees and bushes had been uprooted and fallen untidily, their roots spread-eagled in the air. Water streamed in torrents, draining from the land above, and the horses splashed through it, until they reached the courtyard of the manor.

He glanced at Isabella's window, but there was no sign of movement, except that of crows, which were flocking in greater numbers than before, perching on the window sills and on branches. Dietrich glared aggressively at them.

"They have been pecking the eyes out of my sheep. I have strung them up on a fence as a warning, and Alice has baked some in a pie."

McAlpine himself opened the door, just as Armand was dismounting. He jumped back and looked at him in bewilderment, as though he was a ghost; his pale eyes in his white-powdered face darting furiously from Armand to Dietrich and then to the Alsatians, before staring at Armand again.

"You have no need to bring such an army of men to my door," he declared, in a blustering manner. "This is England, not revolutionary France, although I hear that French frigates have put in an appearance off Lundy. I expect our fleet will soon catch them."

Armand ignored his words. "Apart from your poisoning me, the only thing I remember from last night is that I signed a contract with you for my marriage to Isabella. I have come to claim my bride and am not leaving without her."

Raphael McAlpine stood in the doorway, the muscle twitching in his eye, as though he was winking at a joke. He regarded Armand in cold fury.

"If you have been ill it is nothing to do with me. However, I will send a servant to ask her to come down. I will, of course, honour my word. Would you care to enter?"

"No, I will wait here," replied Armand curtly.

Raphael McAlpine spoke to a servant in the hall; steps could be heard on the stairs and after a few minutes, Jenny, the maid, returned.

"She is not in her room. Her bed has not been slept in," she said.

"She is wild and reckless," declared Raphael McAlpine. "I have done my best with her, but she does what she wants, and has caused endless trouble to my fair wife. I am afraid, your Grace, I have no idea where she is. She is probably, at this moment, in some young lad's bed."

"How dare you!" shouted Armand, drawing his sword.

"If you want to have a duel with me, then arrange the time and place," said Raphael McAlpine contemptuously. "In the meantime, would you please get off my land. I have other affairs to take care of, rather than pandering to the needs of you and your floosy."

"I am not leaving until I have Isabella, or you tell me where she is," shouted Armand, grabbing him by his coat. McAlpine immediately gave a low whistle, and the crows swooped aggressively off the branches and sills into the air.

Armand reached into his pocket and retrieved the mixture Esther had given him. He scattered it around, and the birds alighted on the seeds, cawing and fighting. More crows flew down from the trees; several of the horses panicked and reared up, and Dietrich fell from his stallion, which careered in circles over the cobbles.

One crow flew directly at McAlpine's eyes, and he flapped his hands at it in disgust. He blindly took a step forward and tumbled off the front porch into the path of the horse. The animal trampled him, and he crumpled, lifeless, to the ground, his head and clothes red with blood.

"He's dead," exclaimed Armand, and watched in horror as the man's body was immediately covered by a seething mass of birds.

"Let the crows have him," said Dietrich. "We must search the house."

He and the Alsatians ran through the building, quickly exploring each room, whilst Armand questioned Mrs Gubb and Jenny, who not only knew nothing, but had not even realised Isabella had left the previous evening.

"We must trace her route from Wildercombe House to here," said Dietrich. "Perhaps she was attacked on the road, or was caught by the storm and sheltered somewhere. It is possible McAlpine has nothing to do with her disappearance."

"He was alone here without any of his men," said Armand to Mrs Gubb. "That seems strange. Where have they gone?"

"Two of them were in the house this morning," volunteered Jenny. "I think they went with Mrs McAlpine when you arrived."

"I did not see them go," said Armand. "Did they leave through the back of the gardens, by the lane?"

"I don't think so," she replied. "I was collecting apples over there and they did not pass me."

"Isabella once mentioned she had found a secret room in the house. Do you know where it is?" he asked.

Mrs Gubb had no idea, but Jenny thought she had once heard it referred to by Mrs McAlpine, when she was talking about Hecate and the ceremonies."

"What do you know about Hecate?" he questioned.

"When it is the night of the dark moon, we have to prepare food, and leave it in the library," said Mrs Gubb. "After that we are locked in our rooms, and have to stay there all night. We can hear shrieking and laughing, but try not to listen to it, and McAlpine always pays us extra."

"Look again," said Armand to his men. "Pull down all the curtains and lift the rugs. There might be a hidden trapdoor."

Mrs Gubb and Jenny joined in the search, which once again proved fruitless, and Armand sent Hans to search the route from the back of Dunscombe Manor to Wildercombe House.

He almost immediately returned to say he had found the horse often ridden by Dietrich, tied to a tree, on the other side of the boundary wall.

"She did come here," exclaimed Armand. "I think she is still nearby."

He wandered outside into the courtyard, where McAlpine's body had been removed by the gardeners to the greenhouse, and he looked with distaste at the crows which were again congregating on the sills and branches.

"How did she find the room?" he muttered. He stood by the ash tree underneath her bedchamber, and looked across to the wall facing him.

He saw the decaying foliage and the outline of an old window, and rushed back into the house, calling everyone into the library.

The tapestry had already been taken down, and he examined the wall. There was no obvious door, and he ran his hands over the wood, feeling for some sort of mechanism. He touched the embossed knob, and the panel sprang back, revealing the dark chamber beyond.

"Get a lantern," he shouted, peering into the blackness, and waiting impatiently until Mrs Gubb brought one, smelling strongly of the rancid odour of whale oil. He entered the chamber, frowning in horror, as he saw the upside-down crucifix on the altar, and the black candles. He crossed himself, and Dietrich muttered a prayer. He swung the lantern and saw a tunnel from which a trickle of water was emerging, slowly creeping towards the mosaic of Hecate's Wheel on the floor.

"I will go with Dietrich and Jacques, in case it collapses," he said, as he held up the lantern to see more clearly. "It looks as though the storm is causing water to seep in."

He led the way and they splashed hurriedly along in the narrow, confined space, their heads brushing against the roof. They turned a corner, and saw the dull red of a painted door. Metal bands barred it, a skull hung on a rusted nail, and Dietrich swore loudly as he saw it.

"Isabella once talked about this and, at the time, I thought it was just her imagination," he said.

It was already partly ajar, and he kicked it open, to reveal a dark chamber, pungent with mould and decay. The water was the same depth as in the tunnel, and the lantern light caught the glint of metal chains attached to spikes on the far wall, with islands of furniture; a bed covered in dusty rags, a table, a chair, and a long oak seafaring chest. A pewter plate, on which were the remains of a crust of bread, was floating over the floor, a mouse swimming away from it.

"There were prisoners chained in here," he exclaimed. "They have gone."

"Two people," said Dietrich. "Two people were manacled to the wall. That is why there are two stakes."

He pulled up the lid of the chest and shouted in disgust. Armand joined him and gazed down at the mummified corpse.

"I think it is Isabella's ….," he said. He was unable to finish his words, and quietly closed the chest.

"It is evil. Complete evil," uttered Dietrich. "He deserved to have the crows attack him. He should have been hung, drawn and quartered."

"The water is rising," said Armand. "I think the storm has caused the tunnel to give way and a stream is coming in."

"Yes, we need to get out of here," replied Dietrich. "It is slowly flooding. We do not want to be trapped."

"I will go on alone," said Armand.

"No, we will stay with you," replied Dietrich firmly. "What's that?" he suddenly said, as a faint sound of splashing sounded in the distance.

"I think people are coming towards us, from the coast," muttered Armand, peering into the darkness of the tunnel. "Someone is talking."

They waited and listened, and after a few minutes, a high-pitched voice, speaking angrily, could be heard.

"Hurry up, you slut, or I will leave you behind, to rot, like your mother."

"It's McAlpine's wife. Is she with Isabella? We will hide and take them by surprise," said Armand, retreating into the chamber.

A man could be heard speaking gruffly, and a second man cursed. They reached the red door, and Armand and his men sprang out, their swords in their hands. In front of them were two sailors with cutlasses who were herding along Isabella and Georgiana, their mouths gagged. Mrs McAlpine was behind them, holding a lantern, and she shrieked in fury.

Armand grabbed Isabella and pulled her behind him, but the man next to Georgiana held his cutlass to her throat, shielding himself with her body.

"Let us go, or she dies," he shouted as Georgiana slumped against him in her dirty red silk dress with its yellow roses, tears running down her cheeks.

"We won't follow you," said Armand. "I give you my word. Let us have the girl."

The first man ran off down the tunnel towards the house, and Mrs McAlpine screamed after him. "Don't you dare abandon me. My husband will kill you."

"I don't think he will be of much use to you in this life," commented Armand.

The second sailor glanced in fear at the drawn swords just an arm's length away. He threw Georgiana roughly towards Dietrich and also took to his heels, splashing through the water.

"The men will get both of them when they reach the house," said Dietrich.

Armand quickly pulled the gag from Isabella's mouth, whilst Dietrich did the same for Georgiana, who swayed on her feet, shaking violently.

"We must go quickly," cried Isabella. "There's been a land slip further down. That's why we have returned, as we were not able to get out at Rapparee. I think the tunnel is about to collapse."

Jacques picked up Georgiana and carried her rapidly along, whilst Dietrich pushed Mrs McAlpine in front of him, prodding her with his sword, to make her hurry. Armand held Isabella's hand and they splashed desperately through the water as the roof cracked, and debris crumbled onto the path behind them. There was a dull roar and part of the roof slowly caved in, exposing tree roots.

They ran frantically, the lantern light flickering, and reached the secret chamber, just as earth and stones again collapsed, blocking the entrance to the tunnel and stopping the water from flowing.

"I don't think that route will ever be used again," Armand remarked.

They stepped out into the brightness of the library, where the two sailors were standing in surly silence, guarded by the Alsatians. Armand stopped and embraced Isabella, holding her tightly against him and kissing her face and her hair.

"We have to find Esther," she said, as he held her in his arms. "We were going to McAlpine's ship at Rapparee and I believe that is where she is held."

"The Lord Lieutenant is already searching the Dundee Lass, as I thought Georgiana was on board. So Esther will be found, if she is there," he told her.

"I must go to her," she cried tearfully.

"Yes, my beloved. We will ride there now. Hans will take Georgiana back to the Castle, and Dietrich will guard Mrs McAlpine, until she can be arrested."

Isabella went to Georgiana and embraced her. "I will visit you, when you have recovered. I must go to the harbour now to look for Esther."

She and Armand quickly left the manor house, and she stood, for a moment, in the cool air of the courtyard, looking up gratefully at the grey clouds and the bright, autumnal leaves of the trees.

"My mother was there," she murmured. "The collapse of the tunnel means she has finally a grave."

"Yes, I saw the casket," he replied, placing his arm gently around her again.

"And now I must find Esther. She has also been my mother," she said.

He mounted his horse, and pulled her up behind him. She placed her hands round his waist, burying her face in his coat, and they galloped off up the hill towards the harbour.

....

Strands of seaweed littered the quayside and gulls screeched as they swooped and dived in the air, whilst others were silent on lobster pots. The Dundee Lass was still at anchor, but her decks were deserted, and her sails had been taken down. A column of militia men was marching by the harbour wall, and people were clustered by the Lord Lieutenant at the end of the quay, where a body lay on the ground.

A coat had been placed over Esther, and she was not moving. Her face was white and her pale brown eyes looked up at the sky, as she murmured softly in her own tongue.

Isabella jumped off the horse and ran to her. She pushed through the crowd, and threw herself down and held her hand.

"You are free," murmured Esther, smiling. "You are free now."

"She has refused to be taken into a cottage," said the Lord Lieutenant to Armand. "We discovered her imprisoned below deck. I do not think she has long to live in this world."

"I will die here in freedom, in the open air," muttered Esther, clutching at her chest, and grimacing in pain. She gasped for breath, clinging to Isabella's hand.

"My beloved child," she murmured. She closed her eyes, and gave a long, last sigh, as life ebbed from her.

Isabella knelt beside her, sobbing, and Armand cradled her in his arms, tears also streaming down his face.

56

The sky appeared on fire; a huge, blood-red sun hung over the mountains. The air was hot and still, and cicadas chirruped. A camel grunted bad-temperedly outside the walls, and within the mosaic-tiled courtyard a fountain was cascading into a pool, suffused with the colours of the sunset.

Bess was dressed in silk pantaloons and a loose silk tunic, similar to the other women around her. A sapphire necklace was round her neck and sapphire earrings gleamed in her ears. Children played, laughing and running over the patterned floor.

She prayed silently. For a moment, she saw again Ilfracombe harbour and the little chapel on Lantern Hill, and her sister, Alice, before erasing the image from her mind.

"I will survive, as Jacob said," she told herself. "This is my life now. My only link with my past will be my religion, which I will keep secret. It will be in my head, a place no one can reach, or take from me."

She watched the sun finally sink below the horizon and shivered at the sudden darkness of the night.

57

The sun was setting as the wind filled the sails of the ship. It ponderously left its berth by the quayside and sailed past the harbour wall, past Rapparee, past the rugged cliffs of Hillsborough, and out into the choppy waters of the Bristol Channel. It turned westwards, its prow facing towards the United States of America and Virginia.

The diminutive figures of Georgiana and her sisters had waved goodbye from the grounds of the Castle. Guillaume Thibaud, the new manager of the Wildercombe estate, and Dietrich, had waved from the jetty, and now Edouard was racing round the deck on his toy horse. Tabitha prowled along the quarter deck, then sat, disdainfully sniffing the salt sea air.

Isabella held Marie-Thérèse, who was clutching a mandrake root, its human form decently dressed for the occasion with a red and blue ribbon, and Armand placed his arm around his new wife.

"She is already learning the skills of Esther, I see," he said.

"Perhaps," she replied.

They stood together as the sun quickly sank below the horizon. The sky suddenly became black and Armand and Isabella took their small family down into the warmth and light of the cabin.

Tabitha continued to sit on the quarter deck, purring softly, her eyes staring up into the darkness of Hecate's Moon.

www.ingramcontent.com/pod-product-compliance
Lightning Source LLC
Chambersburg PA
CBHW062118170626
46813CB00002B/497